FAT GIRL on a PLANE

FAT GIRL on a PLANE

A NOVEL BY
KELLY DEVOS

HARLEQUIN® TEEN

ISBN-13: 978-0-373-21253-8

Fat Girl on a Plane

This edition published by arrangement with Harlequin Books S.A.

For questions and comments about the quality of this book, please contact us at CustomerService@Harlequin.com.

Printed in U.S.A.

Fat Girl on a Plane

is Kelly deVos's first title

with Harlequin TEEN!

FAT GIRL on a PLANE

AUTHOR'S NOTE

This is not a Cinderella weight loss story.

I can remember the exact moment I knew I wanted to write this book. Like my character Cookie Vonn, I was declared too fat to fly on a trip from Phoenix to Salt Lake City. As I sat there clutching my copy of *Vogue* magazine, terrified that I might not be allowed to board the plane and that I might never see my luggage again, I was struck by certain aspects of my situation. First, that airplanes, by nature of the cramped spaces they create, can become places where some reveal their intense dislike of plus-size people. But also that so many industries, like fashion and beauty, thrive and profit not by elevating the girls and women they are supposed to service but by making them feel bad about themselves.

So I wrote the first chapter, where Cookie boards her first plane. I decided to tell this story using dual timelines that show her before and after a major weight loss to demonstrate, by direct comparison, how differently society treats those considered thin and those it views as "overweight."

I have a long history of dieting, sometimes successfully, sometimes not. Often, I was motivated by a desire to fit into that "perfect dress" for a special event or to make myself more attractive to someone else. I was convinced that being fat was holding me back. But I've realized *I* was holding myself back. I kept myself from meeting new people, going places I wanted to go and doing the things I wanted to do.

I had to let go of that.

And here I am living my dream of becoming a published author.

I don't know if I will decide to lose weight in the future, but if I do, my efforts will be wellness focused and will not be the result of pressure or shaming. If you decide to diet, that's okay. If you don't, that's okay too. Your body is no one's business but your own. We are more than just our bodies.

We are the sum of our abilities and accomplishments and hopes and dreams and friendships and relationships. It's what we are inside that matters.

Kelly

SKINNY: Day 738 of NutriNation

No. You can't just buy two seats in advance. That would be easy.

Let's say you weigh five hundred pounds and know for a fact you can't fit into a single seat on the plane. It doesn't matter. One person equals one seat reservation. You can thank global terrorism for that one.

I'm waiting for my flight to New York to start boarding.

I watch the fat girl at the airline counter. She's about the same age as me, with a cute pink duffel bag that's covered with patches.

The girl's talking to the flight attendant, trying not to cry. "What am I supposed to do? How am I supposed to get home?"

Maybe I should tell her how it works. Two years ago, I was her. Two years ago, I weighed three hundred and thirty pounds. They said I was too fat to fly.

I would tell her one thing.

There's nothing wrong with being the fat girl on the plane.

soScottsdale <New Post>

Title: We're SoReady for an Early Look at GM

Creator: Cookie Vonn [contributor]

Okay, Scottsdale, time to retire those bling jeans once and for all because new Fall fashions are on the way and it's shaping up to be a great season. This weekend *SoScottsdale* will attend a Gareth Miller preview meeting held at G Studios in NYC. What is a preview, you ask? Well, if you're Vogue editor Anna Wintour, top designers invite you over early in their preseason planning process to kiss your ring and show you their fabric and production samples. If you're *SoScottsdale*, you get ten minutes with the biggest name in fashion and a behind-the-scenes look at his plans for New York Fashion Week. What does Miller have in mind? Expect more knitwear that transitions perfectly from runway to store shelves, dressy denim and a color story that combines neutrals with gem-tone bursts. Next week, we'll update you on everything you need to know to plan your Fall and Winter wardrobe.

Notes: Marlene [editor]: *Nice work, Cookie. Rework that opening sentence. Our advertisers sell lots of bling jeans!*

FAT: Two days before NutriNation

Here's what happens. You have to show up at the airport and hope for the best. Flight attendants get to decide if you're too fat to fly.

I'm on my way to New York. Tomorrow, I get to see my first fashion preview. I'm the *SoScottsdale* blog's nod to the brave new world in which 48 percent of Americans are classified as overweight.

I don't know if I'm going to make it there.

This is how it starts. There's a plane change at O'Hare. I get the feeling the airline employees are watching me from behind the counter. I tell myself how paranoid that sounds. But I find myself pulling my arms close to my body, trying to look as small as possible in my seat in the waiting area.

The smallest of the three of them, a petite gray-haired woman, approaches me as I sit in a long row of passengers waiting to board. She gestures for me to join her near a window that overlooks the runway. In the distance, the lights of Chicago's massive buildings twinkle through the terminal's windows. There are people in those buildings, coming and going, moving through their homes and offices, sending signs of life into the darkness.

"I think you'll need a second seat, dear." The flight attendant has a bright, cheery demeanor. Like she's Mary Poppins when not on duty in her faded cotton-wool-blend uniform. "This is awkward, I know."

"I'm on a layover. I haven't gotten any bigger since I got off the other plane forty-five minutes ago," I say.

She smiles at me. Fake sympathy. "We have to go by what we see, dear. You know, depending on how full the flight is. We have to make a judgment call. I realize it's awkward."

Yep. Awkward.

I follow her back to the ticket counter.

These are my options:

a) Pay for a second seat. That'll be $650. Plus tax. But oh, there's a problem. The flight is sold out.
b) Wait for a flight with extra empty seats. That'll still be $650. Plus tax. When I get home, I can call the hotline for a refund. But oh, the next flight with empty seats is, um, tomorrow.

You'd think Ms. Spoonful of Sugar would have thought this through a bit before she dragged me up to the counter.

"I don't have six hundred bucks," I say.

"Maybe you could call your parents, sweetie," she suggests.

I scowl and adjust the sleeves of my hand-knit cashmere sweater. "My parents aren't sitting by the phone with a credit card."

"A young girl like you—" People always tell me I look like I'm twelve years old.

"I'm seventeen," I say. "And if it weren't for the plane change, I'd still be on the flight."

"We have to make a judgment call," she repeats.

"I just want to get to New York."

"I'll put you on standby," she says with another insincere smile. "If everyone checks in, you'll have to wait for the next flight. If not, I can sell you another seat."

"How am I supposed to pay for it?" I glance behind me at a bald man who shifts his weight and rolls his eyes, checking his watch every few seconds.

"You've got about an hour to figure that out, dear," she says.

It's an agonizing hour. I've got less than twenty bucks in my bank account. I can't get ahold of my mom. I'm pretty sure the last time she paid child support, Grandma spent the money on Pampers.

I consider calling the blog office and decide I'd rather walk back to Phoenix than tell my boss, Marlene, I'm too fat to fly. She's throwing a massive bash for her grandparents' fiftieth anniversary this weekend and her assistant, Terri, has four kids with the stomach flu. The situation is a perfect storm that won't happen again. I won't get another chance to cover an editorial preview as a student intern. A Gareth Miller preview. Real designers at work.

I run my fingertips over the Parsons application tucked in my bag. Fred LaChapelle will be there. He's the dean of Admissions, and Miller is his favorite alum. I've been dreaming of Parsons since I was five, when my grandma handed me a biography of fashion designer Claire McCardell and I couldn't read the book's words but I saw the clothes and I *felt* them. McCardell invented American sportswear in the World War II years and was the first woman with her own label. McCardell's women roamed sandy beaches, rode their cruiser bicycles to small-town markets and used cocktail dresses like weapons. They were free and fabulous and powerful.

I hoped, and wished and believed, that this was who I was meant to be. McCardell studied at Parsons and I know, more than I know anything else, that I need to start there too.

My portfolio will get me in. On paper, I'm the perfect applicant. The daughter of a supermodel who can stitch in a zipper in my sleep. In real life, I'm not Barbie; I spent my summer frosting doughnuts for eight bucks an hour instead of hanging out at Michael Kors, and it's tough explaining why my mom made $1.2 million last year but the ATM makes a *boing!* sound when I stick in my card.

Still, I make magic when I make clothes. If I can get Miller and LaChapelle to see that, then it won't matter that my grandma's rainy-day fund is barely enough to cover the application fee to the school. They'll make sure I get a scholarship and, come next year, I'll be packing for Parsons.

You have to make this work. In my head, I repeat this mantra over and over.

But what happens if I can't get on the plane? I can't afford a hotel. My luggage is already checked. It's going to JFK with or without me.

The whole thing is all my fault, I know that's what everyone is thinking. Saying behind my back. If I would just stop stuffing my face with candy bars and fettuccine Alfredo, everything would be perfect.

I have to do it. I have to call Tommy. He's been mowing lawns since the fifth grade and stashing the money in a savings account. He's my best friend, and I'm pretty sure there's something in the Friendship Rule Book that says he has to come through in times like these.

"I didn't know who else to call," I say into my cell phone. They're reading unfamiliar names over the intercom system. The waiting area is filling up, and the pilot passes me on his way to the plane.

"It's okay," Tommy says. It's noisy on his end too. He's busy being nerdy at a FIRST Lego League competition.

"The flight attendant said I'll probably be able to get a refund. If not, I'll pay you back. I promise."

"Cookie. It's okay." He doesn't even ask why I need the ticket or seem to care when I'll pay him back. He's that nice.

"I'm really sorry, Tommy."

"Don't worry about it."

I luck out, I guess, and there's a cancellation. The gray-haired woman types in the number of the credit card that Tommy's dad gave him for emergencies. She gives me another boarding pass and a large red sign that reads THIS SEAT RESERVED in bold, black letters. That's when the fun begins.

When I say she helps me board the flight, believe me, I mean it. She opens up the door to the ramp even before pre-boarding begins. She takes me and another man right onto the plane. He's probably eighty. He's got a jumbo oxygen tank connected to his nose. It's on wheels, and the flight attendant pulls it behind her as we walk.

She helps him into an aisle seat in the first row. "You can sit anywhere you like," she calls out to me. Since AirWest is one of the few airlines where you can still choose your own seat, I make my way to the middle of the plane. "Just place the reserved sign on the seat next to you." She finishes with the ancient man and brings me a seat-belt extender.

"You know, you look very familiar. Miss Vonn, is it?" she asks.

"I get that a lot," I say. "I guess all fat people look alike."

She puts her hands on her hips and glares at me. Like she's just finished being extraordinarily kind and I'm a jackass for not appreciating it.

"Enjoy your flight." This is her last burst of insincerity before she leaves.

For, like, twenty minutes, it's me and the geezer, alone on the plane. He keeps turning his head around, as much as he can, maybe trying to figure out why I'm there.

The plane fills up. Everyone that passes stops to read the red sign. I make up a few stories in case anyone asks.

A woman with a slobbery toddler does, in fact, point to the sign. "That's reserved?" she asks. I see she has several other kids in tow and the remaining seats are spread out.

"I'm traveling with the Federal Air Marshall," I say.

Her mouth drops open, but she keeps on walking.

I start to organize myself. Make sure my magazines are within easy reach. A couple more people filter by as I'm untangling my headphone cord.

A girl in a Marc Jacobs striped maxi dress, reeking of Kenzo

Flower perfume that barely masks the cigarette stink, approaches my aisle. From her dangly earrings to her cheek bronzer, there's something so impersonal about her look. Like someone else dressed her. Maybe she went to net-a-porter.com and clicked the "shop the issue" link. This is what happens when you have more money than style.

The girl eyes me with disdain, like she'd rather sit next to a monkey wearing a diaper than a fat person. I expect her to move on. Instead she reaches for the RESERVED sign.

I put my hand on it, making sure the sign stays put. "That seat is reserved."

"Yeah, for me, I guess," she says. As she taps her foot impatiently, her head wobbles oddly on her neck, making it look like her chin-length bob is some kind of weird wig. "This is the only seat left on the plane."

The way she says it—*Like, duh, stupid, do you think I'd be sitting by you if I didn't have to?*

"It's mine," I growl. "They made me buy it."

"It's. The. Only. Seat. Left." She jerks her head from side to side as she spits out the words. People are turning around. A flight attendant is making her way up the aisle.

"What's the problem, girls?" the flight attendant asks.

"I need to sit here. Obviously," Miss Money Bags says, smoothing down her thick black hair.

"This is my seat," I say. "They made me buy it."

The flight attendant glances around. "It's the only seat left on the plane."

"They told me at the gate that I'm too fat to fit into one seat and they made me buy a second ticket," I say. I can't get hysterical.

"But you can fit into one seat," the flight attendant says.

"Mostly," the girl adds.

"That's what I told them. But they made me buy another seat anyway." I want to cry but I don't; I can't. You cry, and people know they've got you. I've had years of practicing waiting until I'm alone. In the shower or in bed late at night.

"Well, if this young lady here sits next to you, you'll automatically qualify for a refund. I'll make sure your credit gets issued as soon as we land at JFK." She smiles kindly at me. "It's win-win for everybody."

"I don't want a refund," I tell the woman in a dull, low voice. Everything is quiet on the plane. No one else is talking. "I've been humiliated at the airport. Had to wait on standby. Had to call my best friend and beg for money. Gotten escorted onto the plane with a man so old he could be my grandma's grandpa. I had to carry this—" I shake the red sign "—like it's my Scarlet. Fucking. Letter."

Pointing at the seat next to me, I keep going. "I don't care about refunds or win-wins. Or if this plane crashes into the fucking ocean. I want *this* goddamn seat."

The flight attendant drops all pretense of friendliness. "We make the call on whether or not you need two seats."

"I know. The nice lady in the terminal explained all this when she took my six hundred bucks."

She sighs and turns to the other passenger. "I'm sorry, but you'll have to go back to the gate and work this out."

"Are you fucking kidding me?" the girl demands. "Tell Cankles to move her red sign and the plane can take off." She again tries to slide into the seat next to me.

The flight attendant places her arm across my row to block

the girl and then backs her to the door as their conversation continues. "Since she has two tickets, I have to treat this like an overbooking situation. In these cases, the passenger with the last boarding pass issued gets booked on the next flight."

"The next flight? Tomorrow?" the girl asks. Her voice is becoming higher pitched and semi-hysterical. "But I'll miss..."

I don't get to hear what she will miss. The instant she's back on the entry ramp, another attendant closes the plane door with a thud. The guy on the other side of the aisle gives me a dirty look.

At the front of the plane, I spot a blur of curly, beachy hair. *Tommy.* The feeling of relief passes as my rational mind connects the dots. Tommy's back in Mesa, and the guy up front is stowing his girlfriend's purse in the overhead compartment.

I close my eyes as the pilot reads a bunch of announcements and the flight attendants give instructions. A few minutes later everything is quiet and still.

The plane charges down the long runway, the cabin lights dim and I try to picture myself up there in first class, holding hands with Tommy. That reality feels reserved for the posh and perfect. It's a members-only club I don't know how to join.

What I do know is that, after this trip, I'm not doing this again.

I'm done being the fat girl on the plane.

SKINNY: Later on Day 738

"Thank God," he says as he smiles at me.

It's him. After all this time, I'm meeting Gareth Miller.

And he's smiling at me.

The plane has stopped in Dallas, and it would figure that my fashion idol would get on and plop down next to me. I'm filled with dread. Or panic. The kind of panic that makes me consider heading for the emergency exit and taking the evacuation slide onto the runway.

He takes the aisle seat. "There's some whale of a woman raising all kinds of hell in the airport because they want her to buy more than one ticket."

And he's a douchelord.

Never mind. I'll push *him* down the evacuation slide.

Gareth Miller leans in toward me, like we're now in a conspiracy together and says, "I hate to be rude." It's a hushed whisper. "But she needs two. At least two. Back before I had my own plane when I had to fly commercial, I always got stuck next to them. Them and the crying babies. Or sometimes fat gals *with* crying babies."

I scoot back and glare at him. "Sounds like you'd be a lot happier on Air Force Asshat," I blurt out. I sort of wish I hadn't said it. I'm on my way to New York to interview the guy and it's probably not the best idea to pick a fight with him. I turn to the window and try to seem busy stuffing my iPad in the pocket on the seat in front of me.

"Oh, now, shoot, I've gone and offended you." He pushes his hand in my line of sight. "Gareth Miller. And no, I don't think I'd be happier. Asshat One is having mechanical issues."

Forcing myself to stay calm, I shake his hand lightly and say, "I'm Cookie."

I've been thinking about this meeting for two years. Fantasizing about it since I caught a glimpse of his profile through a slit in his maple-paneled studio door. In my imaginary version of our first meeting, he flips through my sketchbook, loudly announcing that my designs are the best he's ever seen. Then he insists on making sure I get a scholarship to Parsons and an investment to start my own line. But I guess we'll be sitting next to each other in beige airline seats instead.

"Cookie," he repeats with a laugh. "That a really sweet name."

It takes all my self-control not to give him an epic eye roll. People always think they're so original. Like this is the very first time someone's ever thought of making a joke like that.

"My mom ate chocolate chip cookies in the hospital after I was born," I tell him, trying not to stare at his chiseled features. "I guess I should be happy the nurse didn't give her a candy bar. Or I'd now be known as KitKat or something."

"Gimme a break," he says with an appealing grin.

It's kind of funny but I force myself not to laugh. Gareth Miller might be skating through life, saying whatever he wants and relying on his appeal to make it all okay. But that whale of a woman used to be me. Still feels like me. I put my hands into the empty inch of space at the edge of my seat. This is what two years of NutriNation has gotten me.

I *really* hope he doesn't notice I'm wearing a Gareth Miller sweater.

The flight attendant is making long, smooth waving motions with her arms and gesturing toward the exit rows. I pull out the airline safety card and read along, looking up for the oxygen mask.

"I think this may be a first for me. Someone is actually checking the crash instructions," he says in his drawling accent. He's from Montana and has a sort of cowboy couture charm.

"I like to be prepared in the event of an emergency."

"I hate to break it to you, but if the plane crashes, we'll all be dead," he says with another smile. He's able to make this line sound like the best news I've had all day.

"Not true." My stomach flip-flops but I give him a fake smile of my own. "Most crashes occur on takeoff or landing, and the rate of survival is about 56 percent. We're at a disadvantage here in first class since the safest seats are in the back of the plane. But since you don't mind dying, I'll just crawl over you if there's an emergency. And you can be part of the 44 percent who don't make it."

"Well, I'd die a happy man," he says, his eyes drifting over me. "And do me a favor, Cookie, at my funeral, you give the eulogy. Make sure everyone knows I made that sweater and gave my life so you could keep looking so fine while wearing it." He points at the smooth cashmere top. It's covered in whimsical, eight bit cherry clusters. A combination of quality and caprice. Gareth Miller's signature style.

Of course he noticed the sweater. Sigh.

"I said I designed that sweater. That doesn't impress you?"

I nod and hope he finds something else to do with his time besides stare at me. He's either staring because:

a) I look like my mom and he's trying to figure out why I seem familiar,
b) I have mascara smeared on my face or maybe a leaf stuck in my hair or
c) some other kind of reason that's giving me hot flashes.

Two out of the three of those things are nothing to get excited about. I remind myself that I don't *want* to want someone like Gareth Miller to like me. And anyway, I've spent hours writing hard-hitting interview questions. I don't need my momentum spoiled by four hours of good-natured chitchat. I try to get my headphones in before he can say anything else.

"You know, you look awfully familiar," he says. He cocks his head and adds, "I mean, I know that sounds like a line. A truly bad one. But I can't shake the feeling that I've seen you somewhere before."

The first-class attendant approaches us. "Something to

drink before takeoff?" she asks. Her glance dances from Gareth to me and a grin spreads across her face. "I get a lot of good-looking people sitting in my section, but you two are just fabulous."

I'm not used to this. To compliments and attention. My stomach's producing acid in overdrive. I'm pretty sure I'll have an ulcer by thirty.

"I'll have a glass of white wine," Gareth says.

"I'll just have a Diet Coke," I tell the woman.

Across the aisle, I make eye contact with a man in a Men's Wearhouse navy suit. He smiles at me.

All I can think is that a man shouldn't wear a striped tie with a striped shirt.

I turn back to my window, watching a crew load luggage into another plane a couple of gates away. The last time I was on a plane, that guy wouldn't have even made eye contact. He'd have been praying that he didn't have to sit next to me.

The plane's air conditioner kicks on and I catch a whiff of Gareth Miller's cologne. It's not fair that he should look and smell so good.

Trapped next to his appeal and his "charm," which oozes out like an unwanted infection, I scrunch myself into my seat and pray I make it to New York without killing him.

FAT: Two days before NutriNation (two seats take me to New York)

Here's why people are fat. Losing weight is hard. Really fucking hard.

Two peanut butter cups equal forty-five minutes on the treadmill. So enjoy. And start running your ass off.

Let's say you smoke two packs a day. You get sick of being winded when you climb up a flight of stairs and those commercials that show the guy cleaning the hole in his throat really start to get to you. So, what happens next?

Take your pick from any one of about a thousand free hotlines you can call. There's lozenges, inhalers and patches to help you quit. If you have decent health insurance, your doctor might hook you up with some Chantix.

Need to lose weight?

You're on your own. And most of the world is working against you.

They play food commercials on TV 24/7. They make you watch spinning golden french fries while you're trying to run off that candy bar. The stereotypical date consists of dinner and a movie. All holidays and parties end with cake or pie.

I finally land in New York a little before 10:00 p.m. I've gotten one step closer to meeting Gareth Miller and seeing LaChapelle. While I wait for the airport shuttle, I call Tommy. His Lego events go on forever and there's a ton of downtime. He picks up on the first ring. We talk about the plane.

"I really think you're oversimplifying things," he says. "People aren't fat because of peanut butter cups."

"Yeah," I agree. "Because if they were, we could load all the peanut butter cups on a rocket and blast it to the moon."

He continues as if he hasn't heard me. "Some people have medical problems. Some people have tried diets and they haven't worked. And some people are happy the way they are."

I know he's right. But what about *right* now?

"You think juice cleanses work?" I ask.

"I don't know. I guess," he says. "But that's not a great long-term plan. I mean, how long could you possibly survive on juice?" There's a pause. "My mom's doing Nutri-Nation. You could try that."

"You think I should? You want me to be your supermodel?"

He sighs. In the background I can hear Korean pop music and the whir of the high-pitched engines Tommy and his geek friends attach to the Lego cars they build. "I don't *want* you to be anything. I *want* you to be happy." There's another pause. "You remember Fairy Falls?"

I snort. Of course I do. That's where we became friends.

The fat camp with an idiotic name where we both spent two Christmas breaks.

"Doesn't it bother you at all that your parents dumped you like a sack of old clothes in Duck Lake, Wyoming?" I ask.

"No," he says. "And that's my point. I know your mom—"

"My mom treats me like I'm a pair of designer jeans that are too baggy," I say.

"I know. I know." He's getting impatient and talking faster so that I can't interrupt. "That's the whole point. You keep letting your mom tell you how you're gonna feel about yourself. Fat camp wasn't all that bad. If it weren't for Fairy Falls, we probably wouldn't be friends. We can thank our parents for that."

"Thanks for the analysis, Dr. Phil, but I'm not letting my mom tell me how to feel. I just don't want to be like her. That's all," I say.

"Eating a banana or cracking a smile now and again won't make you vapid and self-centered," he says. "But you keep punching yourself in the face and hoping your mom will get a black eye."

"It just seems so unfair," I say.

"Cookie, some snotty girl on a plane isn't a reason to come down on yourself." His goofy, boyish grin transmits even through the phone. "I like you the way you are."

I smile in spite of myself, even though I secretly think he'd like me more if I looked more like my mom.

As the shuttle pulls up to the curb, I hang up and shimmy my way into the back of the van. It's not easy getting back there, but I know it's the best way to avoid dirty looks from other passengers.

I think of Tommy as I watch the yellow streetlights pass. I try to remember the exact moment that I knew I wanted to be more than friends and the exact moment when it occurred to me how impossible that is.

It's my first time in New York.

Even the buildings are tall and thin.

"You going to the Continental Hotel?" the driver calls from the front.

"Yeah," I say.

"Sorry. That place is a dump." He chuckles as a man slides into the front seat.

I close my eyes and imagine that I'll open them to a whole new world.

We drive.

SKINNY: Day 738...details

Gareth Miller continues to stare. I consider throwing something in the aisle so he'll have to turn in that direction.

"You know an awful lot about airline safety for someone so young," he says.

Yuck. What a cheesy way to ask someone's age. "I can use Wikipedia, and I'm nineteen." This is a mistake.

I don't know why I give him that detail.

He smiles again. "Ah, I remember nineteen. Where'd your boyfriend take you for your birthday?"

I've never had a boyfriend, and I don't want to tell the King of Fashion I spent the evening crying into a diet soda while Tommy was probably somewhere making out with my nemesis.

"What did you do on *your* nineteenth birthday?" I hedge.

He laughs, revealing a smile that would shame a toothpaste ad. "Ever been to Flathead County, Montana?"

I shake my head.

"Well, you can have dinner at the Sizzler. Or a kegger down at the lake. My pop settled on the latter."

"Weren't you already at Parsons by then?" I ask.

He pauses, regards me a bit differently. "We *have* met before. I knew it. Do a fella a favor and give me a hint where it was." He turns a bit red. "We haven't ever..."

At the front of the plane, the flight attendant is buckling herself into her seat. A few seconds later, the 757 races down the runway.

I glare at Gareth Miller. "You have that much trouble keeping track of the women you sleep with?" I let him squirm in his seat, facing the real possibility that he'll have to spend four hours next to a stranger with whom he'd shared forgettable sex. He's making a big show of watching the plane lift off the runway.

"We've never met," I say. "But I get the ParDonna.com newsletter."

He leans away from the window, breathing more comfortably. "Well, yeah, I had already moved to New York by then. But my dad always insists I come home for my birthday. It's during the summer, so the timing isn't too bad. The weather is nice."

"It's freezing in Montana in the winter." I tuck my fingers into the ends of my sweater.

"You've been there? In the winter?"

I sigh. He's still got that pensive expression on his face. Like he won't quit until he figures out who I am. And it's possible, given enough time, he might be able to guess. I decide to get out in front of it and tell him.

"Yeah. I went with my mother. She did a photoshoot there

a few years ago. Leslie Vonn Tate. That's probably why I seem familiar. People say we look alike."

He's impressed. His eyes widen. "Leslie Vonn Tate. Sure, I remember. The Atelier Fur thing. Bruce Richardson shot it in Whitefish, right?"

The Atelier Fur thing.

A totally avoidable clusterfuck. If only Grandma's hairdresser had used one more roller.

FAT: Two years before NutriNation

Mom's in the living room of Grandma's tiny yellow house, striking a slumped pose on the 1980s brown plaid sofa. In her off-white Valentino shift dress, she's more the picture of a model on an ironic *Nylon* magazine photoshoot than a mom hanging with her daughter. She's got Lois Veering on speakerphone.

"The day of the supermodel is dead. Truly dead," Lois Veering moans. She's the editor of *Par Donna*. Nobody likes Veering. I'd bet fifty bucks that she won't last, that it's just a matter of time before her assistant edges her out.

She's calling Mom. Because anybody who's anybody hates fur. "And they're strutting around naked in the trades. On my shoots demanding vegan pizzas and goji berry smoothies," she says. "I need you, Leslie. I really need you."

In spite of the best efforts of sexy celebrities and inked-up athletes, fur companies keep raking in cash—around $15 billion a year. Their sales are up worldwide. The Eastern

European nouveaux riches and the wives of Chinese millionaires, they want their mink.

"The biggest threat to fur is global warming," Veering sneers.

And the biggest threat to fashion magazines is sluggish ad sales. Atelier Fur has big bucks. They want a cover. A supermodel. They want photographer Bruce Richardson.

Mom's there to pick me up from the tiny yellow house for a spa weekend in La Jolla. It's my bad luck that Grandma gets home early from her hair appointment.

"We can just do it another time, Mom," I say. "It's no big deal."

Grandma comes in. Takes one look at Mom, phone in hand.

"Cookie, go wait in your room," Grandma says.

"It's fine, Grandma. Everything is fine," I say.

"Go," she orders.

Of course, I can hear them through the paper-thin walls.

"You got one daughter, Leslie. One," Grandma says. "It's her sweet sixteen. And I didn't plan nothin' 'cause you said you were coming to get her."

"I'll clear my schedule in a week or two," Mom says. "Cookie's fine with it."

"Yeah," Grandma answers. "She's just about jumpin' for joy."

"Well, I guess she's carrying on the grand family tradition of being disappointed in her mother," Mom snaps.

"Oh, I see," Grandma replies. "I was a shitty mother to you. And you get special permission to be shitty to *your* girl? Well, you say what you want about me, Leslie. But I made dresses for all seven of Nina Udall's bridesmaids so you could have a cake with sixteen candles and a fancy party dress to celebrate in."

"I have to work. Lois Veering is asking me to do a job. Do you have any clue what happens to models who say no to Lois Veering?"

I imagine Grandma's disgusted face. The beads of sweat forming at her gray-blue hairline. "Shoot, Leslie. You got plenty of money. Plenty of fancy things. If you're paradin' around half-naked in a magazine, it ain't cause you *have* to, it's cause you *want* to. And I ain't never asked you for money. All I ask is you try to be decent to your child. If you say you're gonna do something, you keep your damn word."

If only the hairdresser had used one more roller, Mom might have been gone by the time Grandma got home. Instead, I spend the next half hour wondering what I can wear to Whitefish. The high temperature there is thirty-seven degrees. I've got one light sweater and a windbreaker.

"We'll pick something up on the way," Mom says.

And *on the way* means at the airport gift shop. I have to go to a men's store. Nothing fits anywhere else. Because Grandma came home from her hair appointment early, I'm going to spend my sixteenth birthday in a fire-engine red sweatshirt. It's covered with hideous suns wearing sunglasses and the horrible, synthetic fabric barely stretches over my stomach.

Veering must really have something on Mom. Montana is cold as all fuck. I'm not talking about "tongue stuck to a pole" kind of cold. I mean so cold you wish your toes would fall off so you won't have to feel them anymore.

I'm surprised a few hours later when the car service pulls up in front of the Travelodge. Mom thinks hotels with fewer than five stars belong in third world countries.

"Don't worry," she says. "I have the whole thing all worked out. Tomorrow Lois says we'll wrap the shoot by two. And they have a wonderful spa up at the lodge. I've got us booked for hot rock pedicures."

She looks at me expectantly, waiting for me to get out of the car.

"We're staying here?" I ask, trying to make some kind of sense of what's happening.

She pats my arm. "Don't worry. I had Cassidy make the reservation. It's all paid for. They should have my credit card."

"You're leaving me here? By myself?" I ask.

She turns to the window. "Well…I got the magazine to pay for your airfare but…um…they wouldn't give me another room at the lodge," she says. "Budget cuts."

Of course Mom wouldn't dip into her own bank account so I can get a nice room too. "Why can't I just stay with you?" The taste of the burrito I ate for lunch is rising in my throat.

She pauses.

"Chad's coming and…"

"Fine." I get out of the Lincoln Town Car and slam the door behind me. The driver scurries out of the front. He drops my suitcase on the ground in front of the sparse gray motel office.

Mom rolls down the window. "The lodge is about fifteen minutes from here. I'll call you when I'm on my way in the morning."

They don't have a reservation for me in the office. I spend the next two hours waiting for Mom's frazzled assistant, Cassidy, to show up with a credit card.

"So sorry, Cookie… I was supposed to call…but Bruce asked me to pull all these comps from your mom's old books…and…" She gives the Norman Bates clone at the counter Mom's credit card as she rattles off a long list of random jobs she's been assigned.

She frowns at me. "I feel terrible leaving you here," she says. "I'd invite you to crash with me but I've already got the makeup girls." Then she's gone in a flash of print leggings and Uggs.

"Is there anything to eat around here?" I ask Norman.

He shrugs. "Cattleman's is up the road. Maybe half a mile. Vending machine near the laundry room."

I rifle through the content of my purse. I've got my tips from Donutville. Seven bucks.

Because Grandma came home from her hair appointment early, I feast on Doritos, Twinkies and Diet Coke. The room's TV gets four channels.

The next morning, Mom doesn't call. I check out and walk to town. There's a gas station, a casino and a cute little car wash. Cassidy picks me up in front of the Travelodge around two.

It's snowing in Whitefish. The town is somehow wholesome, with evergreen garland strung through the streets and silver bells hanging from lampposts. White powder dusts the

1930s storefronts. It's the kind of place that should be on a postcard with the words *Wish You Were Here.*

Mom's tucked away in the corner of the Ace Hardware. "They let us use this place for hair and makeup. We couldn't get trailers," Cassidy explains. "Bruce was going bananas at the thought they'd be in the shot."

A hairstylist hovers over Mom, twisting her blond hair onto large Velcro rollers. "Oh, Cookie," Mom says without glancing up from her phone. "We're behind schedule. There are problems. With the snow and the light and people walking up the street. But don't worry, Cassidy changed our appointments to..."

I spot Chad Tate surrounded by cowboys in jeans and Tony Lamas. He mimics throwing an invisible football. As he completes his imaginary pass, the crowd breaks out into cheers and hoots of laughter.

Oh sure. Having a washed-up, all-star quarterback as a stepdad is great. If you don't mind the fact that's he's dumber than a bag of hammers and wishes I'd crawl off and die in a hole.

"I'm going home," I say.

"Back to the hotel?" Mom corrects.

"Checkout at the *motel* was at ten. I'm going home."

For the first time she takes a look at me. "Would you mind getting me a bottle of water?" she asks the hairstylist.

"Cookie," Mom says the instant the hairstylist is out of earshot. "I can't control the weather or the position of the sun. But I promise..."

My empty stomach grumbles. I spot the craft service table in one corner, but it has already been ravaged by the breakfast and lunch crowds. It now holds one lonely bagel and a half-empty jar of Snapple.

"I'm tired and I want to go home," I say.

"I'm sure you're dying to turn this into a referendum on how horrible your life is," she begins, "but..."

"You're busy and this was a mistake."

"I'm working," Mom says. "Someone has to. What do you think your dad's mercy missions pay? I'm supporting five people."

I push the thought of Dad out of my mind and focus my anger on what's in front of me. "Well, maybe the child support checks are getting lost in the mail. Grandma thinks you're dumping all your money into Chad's sports bar. This week she's making two holiday formal dresses to pay the water bill," I say.

"It's normal for restaurants to lose money during the first five years," Mom says, pressing her lips into a thin, white line. "And whether you like it or not, I'm still the parent here. I'm sorry to inform you that you can't just announce your plan to leave the state."

"Let's go and ask Chad," I suggest. "I'm sure he's thrilled I'm here."

"You know, it hurts that my husband and my daughter are enemies," Mom says.

"Right back atcha," I say and walk away.

"Cookie, don't you dare think you can—"

A tiny bell rings as the shop door slams behind me.

Cassidy runs out to catch me. Bluish black circles have formed under her eyes.

"There's a coffee shop right around the corner. Your mom says to wait until—" She breaks off with a huff.

Behind her the wiry photographic genius Bruce Richardson leans over the top step of a tall ladder. "Cammie! We've got light for *maybe* another thirty minutes. Get Leslie out here stat. And clear this street. The last thing I need is that fat ass in my shot!"

Cassidy eyes Richardson with the crazed expression of someone on the verge of totally losing it. "It's Cassidy," she mutters under her breath.

But we exchange glances and she chews her lower lip. We both know I'm the fat ass Richardson means.

"Please. Wait here, Cookie," she tells me, and she disappears into the hardware store. I know she feels bad. For me.

But I don't want her sympathy.

And I don't want to be in fucking Whitefish, Montana.

"Cookie. Perfect name for that girl. The jokes almost write themselves," Richardson says as I walk toward the coffee shop.

SKINNY: Day 738 and strange benefactors

"Sure," Gareth says, "I remember that issue of *Par Donna*. Richardson's nothing if not memorable. And weird. The corsets and furs, I get. But what was with those rodeo clowns?"

I shrug. "Sorry. I don't have much insight into his process. From what I could see, he spends most of his time on a ladder screaming at people."

The flight attendant serves him his white wine with a dazzling smile. Gareth takes my soda and places it on my tray. I'm praying for a break in the conversation long enough that I can finally slip in my headphones. I'm pretty sure a woman across the aisle from me is considering tossing me from the plane and taking my seat.

"You been on a lot of shoots?" he asks.

"Nah," I say.

"Not into the world of fashion?" he asks, arching his eyebrows.

I couldn't help but smile. "My grandma taught me to sew when I was five. She'd put on *Breakfast at Tiffany's* or

Casablanca and we'd hand-bead wedding dresses. Claire McCardell said that fashion isn't about finding clothes, it's about finding yourself. That the girl who knows what to wear knows who she is."

Gareth smiles a bit wistfully. "That's kind of how I got started too." I already know this.

"You work in fashion?" he asks.

I hesitate.

"I'm a blogger," I say.

"You blog about fashion? Professionally?"

I nod and take my iPad out of the seat pocket. He puts his hand lightly on mine to stop me from turning it on. My stomach flip-flops at the touch of his slightly calloused fingertips.

"And I guess you're not very good at it?" he asks with a smirk.

I drop my headphones and they land against the iPad screen with a click. "I'm guessing you've never read my blog. So how would you know?"

Gareth Miller chuckles. My face heats up. I hate his rogue appeal. I want to throw cranberry juice on his crisp linen shirt.

He ignores my death stare and continues to smile. "I'm *Vogue*'s Designer of the Year. I'm on my way to New York Fashion Week, where tickets to my show are nearly impossible to get. There're a million fashion blogs. And, not to be immodest, but sitting next to me is a once-in-a-lifetime opportunity. Shouldn't you be trying to interview me? Working me over for samples or show tickets? Cookie, darling, I think you're showing a real lack of initiative."

He's teasing. But still, the comment stings. I pride myself on my fashion expertise.

"Well, you'd be wrong. I already have an appointment to interview you."

"Really?" he challenges. "Once we get to New York?"

"Yes."

He pulls his phone out of his pocket and reads from the screen. "Huh," he says in surprise. "On Sunday afternoon. This is your blog, *Roundish*?"

"Yes."

Gareth shifts around in his seat. "It's...uh...it's a plus-size fashion thing?"

Ha! It's my turn to smile. I finally feel like I've got him on the run. "Yeah. The title's from that Karl Lagerfeld quote. You know, how nobody wants to see round women? Well, I do want to see them. And make sure they look and feel great."

"Any particular reason you want to do plus-size when you're not plus-size yourself?" he asks.

Yes. For every time I stepped into a store and they didn't have anything in my size. For every time I found a designer I loved and then found that their stuff only went up to a size eight. For the fact that I had to lose weight in order to be taken seriously as a designer or blogger. That's what I should say. Instead, I shrug. "Everyone wants to dress the super tall and super thin."

He doesn't look at me but continues to read. "You're a finalist for the CFDA media award. My publicist seems to think you plan to demonize me. Create sort of a Karl Lagerfeld/Adele–type controversy."

"My subscribers have questions."

"What kind of questions?" he says, his eyes narrowing.

"I plan to have them ready for you on Sunday at 2:00 p.m."

"Maybe you need background info? Maybe you want to ask how I got started?"

I shake my head. "You're Gareth John Miller. You're thirty-one years old. You were born in Santa Fe but moved to Kalispell at the age of two. Your dad's a rancher. Your mom's an artist living at Arcosanti. Your contact with her has been minimal. Your grandmother taught you to sew doll clothes at a young age. When you were a junior in high school, you made prom dresses for the entire cheerleading squad. The dresses became the portfolio you submitted with your application to Parsons. It's still regarded as their best incoming student submission. You're the youngest graduate in the school's history. When you were twenty-four, Louis Vuitton Moët Hennessy offered to finance your label. But you turned Bernard Arnault down. Instead, your father mortgaged the family ranch and gave you $150,000 in working capital. Your three lines, Gareth Miller, GM by Gareth Miller and Gareth Miller Kids, earned over $90 million last year. And your brand is one of the few of its size without some offering of plus-size fashion."

He watches me in a new way, sizing me up. "I stand corrected. You clearly do your homework. And you were planning to sit on this flight for four hours and not say anything to me?" He checks his phone again. "I think I paid for that seat."

"It's too late to take it back," I say, remembering Gareth's helpful publicist.

"I certainly wish I had read this email before I…so I

would have known I'd be sitting next to…but I had to rush over here from…" he mutters. For the first time, he's nervous. "That thing I said before…about the woman in the airport…"

I should *so* let him sweat this out. He's chewing his lower lip in this annoyingly endearing way and I enjoy watching him way too much.

"I only plan to blog about what you say during our official interview." Where I'm supposed to convince him to launch a plus-size capsule collection. My sponsors want tweets that trend.

He relaxes and smiles, again reading from his phone screen. "Ah, but it says here you'll be blogging and tweeting live from my show. And I'll be dressing you." His brown eyes darken. "I think I'll enjoy that very much, Cookie."

"I'll be wearing something you designed." I correct him even as my insides wobble like one of Grandma's Jell-O Bundt cakes. "I've been dressing myself since I was five."

He folds his hands and rests them on the tray in front of him. He's back in his element. "Right. Well. What would you like to wear?"

FAT: Three years before NutriNation and fat camp sucks

"I'm not wearing that, you fucking fascist."

I scowl at the Jack LaLanne look-alike. He's holding out a green T-shirt. It's got the words *Fairy Falls* printed on it in thick block letters. Along with an illustration of a pixie that could have been drawn by Andy Warhol on crystal meth.

Even better. There's a pair of sweatpants in the same pukey hue.

"Then I hope you like hiking naked, Miss Vonn. We're heading out at nine o'clock. Participation is not optional." The crusty camp owner has dull gray hair. When he was young he probably had dull brown hair. His mouth extends into a dull, thin line. His bulging muscles want to bust out of the weathered camp tee he wears.

I glance around the small cabin. Some upbeat person would probably describe it as rustic, but I'd call it a wooden shack. There are two narrow, steel-framed bunks on opposite sides of the room, and a whiteboard hangs on one wall. Someone has written "Juniper Cabin. Bunk 1: Cookie Vonn.

Bunk 2: Piper Saunders." There's no sign of my roomie. She arrived before I did and was apparently happy to join the Fairy Fucking Falls group activities.

"Walking around naked is actually illegal, Mr. Getty," I say. "And I want the clothes I packed." The ones I made. The ones that fit me perfectly. "Do you have any idea how hard it is to precisely tailor a pair of chinos? Or coordinate three different floral print separates? And I have a Moschino bag I almost lost an eye for during a fight at a sample sale."

"If we're going to have a problem here, Miss Vonn, I can always call your mother." Menace laces Getty's voice. He thinks he's delivered the ultimate threat.

"You could," I agree with a sweet smile. "And if, by some miracle, she comes to the phone, please tell her I would very much like to speak with her."

Getty presses his lips into an even thinner, whiter line. "It's simple, Miss Vonn. No uniform, no hike. No hike, no lunch."

He comes back at nine to find me sitting on my bunk. Still wearing the chevron sweater I knitted and the midi skirt Grandma made from a hand-dyed jersey.

I'm reading a fantasy novel. Wishing I could jump into the pages and become a princess with a unicorn. Getty stands in front of me. He casts a gloomy shadow over me and onto the wooden wall of the cabin.

"Why did your parents send you here?" he asks. He flips through papers attached to the clipboard he carries.

"Chad Tate sent me here," I say, "because he likes to fuck my mother. And fuck her over. So this is perfect. I'm here. And he's spending Christmas getting laid on an all-expense-paid trip to a five-star resort."

Getty ignores me. "They chose this camp because I get results. Ten pounds in three weeks. No exceptions."

"There is no *they*," I say. "My dad's a doctor. He's in Ghana as part of a Catholic medical mission. He would never have agreed to send me here." I wrap my arms around myself. Truthfully, I have no idea what my dad would agree to. He's been nothing more than a voice on the phone or bland messages in my email inbox for almost ten years now.

I stopped replying last summer.

Again the old man ignores me. "And the way I get results is simple. Calories out exceed calories in. That's it. I don't get involved in this Freudian, psychobabble, 'food is your friend' bullshit. I don't care if Mommy didn't hug you or if Daddy's too busy to pay attention." Deep folds emerge in Getty's leathery forehead as he squints at his paperwork.

"I want my own clothes," I say. I have to stay angry. It's my only defense against Getty's words, which hit a little too close to home.

He grunts. "And I hope that thought provides adequate consolation when everyone else is eating chocolate pudding at lunch."

He slams the door behind him, creating a shower of dust that falls from the cabin's roof. I keep reading.

It's afternoon when I hear the hikers trudge through the camp. The cabin door opens, and it's the first time I get to meet my gung ho bunkmate. She and I are about the same size, so it's pretty easy to imagine what I'd look like in that horrid green uniform Getty is trying to force on me. Piper

Saunders's brownish red hair is tied in a bun on the top of her head.

She tiptoes into the cabin and sees me. Piper opens her mouth, on the verge of saying something, closes it again and spends a couple of minutes rifling through a trunk near her bed. The door smacks behind her when she leaves the cabin. She comes back a little while later, sits on the bunk across from mine in silence and chews a granola bar with deliberation. We've done nothing but stare at each other by the time she leaves for dinner.

By then, I'm a celebrity. A crowd gathers outside my cabin. I can hear them through the thin wood walls as they start to argue. Half of them think I'm the leader of a new resistance and they want to join my fat-ass army. Piper speaks for the other half. "She's a stuck-up bitch. Her mom's some big-time model in New York, so she thinks she's too good to wear the uniform. I hope they let her starve." She has a thick Australian accent.

I kick the door open. Everyone outside jumps back and then they exchange embarrassed glances. "Say that to my face. Say it. To. My. Face."

My teeth are clenched and my fists are balled up. Piper's shrinking back from me and I'm sure I can take her. Despite what she thinks, I didn't grow up in a Fifth Avenue penthouse. In my neighborhood, you watch your back.

The crowd circles around us. I'm seconds away from starting a fight.

Getty pushes his way through the ring and grabs my elbow. He marches me to the camp office. I want to laugh as he tries to contact my mother. I know it's Cassidy on the other end of the line. "I'm calling about her daughter." Pause. "Thailand? Did she leave any contact information?" Pause. "Her grandmother?"

Getty turns to me, but I shake my head. "My grandma's on a trip to the Holy Land. My mom was supposed to…" I trail off. It's weird to admit that my grandma had to plead with Mom to babysit me. "My grandma had to go. The congregation paid for her trip." It sounds defensive. Even to me.

Getty's attention is focused on his call with Cassidy while I'm trying to make sense of how I ended up here. How Mom sent Chad Tate to pick me up. How he dumped me at this camp like a bag of dry cleaning. The tears well up.

But I beat them back as Getty hangs up the wall phone. "Well, well, Miss Vonn. It seems you weren't exaggerating."

"Sorry to disappoint you," I say. "But my mother won't be shocked if I refuse to shimmy into those sweatpants you provided." *My mother* wouldn't notice if I ran away and joined the merchant marines.

"No," he agrees with a humorless smile. "But she also is unlikely to object if you don't get dinner tonight." He outright laughs as my stomach grumbles. "See you in the morning, Miss Vonn."

Piper avoids me. It's dark when she comes back to the cabin. Until lights out, she lies in her bunk, huddling against the wall. Even from across the room, I can feel her nervous energy. My sweater's collar scratches my neck. The skirt leaves my legs cold and bare.

At ten, there's shouts of "lights out." Piper flips the switch near her bunk.

"Relax," I call out into the night. "I don't plan to attack you while you sleep."

There's silence.

Sort of silence. Crickets chirp. Outside a dying fire pops and crackles.

Then, "What's your problem, anyway?"

Piper is asking this. Her voice is soft, girlish.

And I don't know the answer. "You want me to limit myself to just one?"

She laughs. "I would kill to be you," she says.

"Yeah, right," I mutter.

The girlish tone in her voice disappears. "You look like a plus-size model. And if you'd just—"

"—lose weight I'd look just like my mother," I snap. "I know."

"You don't want to look like her? You don't *want* to look like Leslie Vonn Tate?" Piper sounds surprised.

"I don't want to be *anything* like her," I say.

"So," she says slowly. "Why won't you wear the uniform? It's not that bad."

"It's okay, I guess," I say. "It's just that I make my own clothes. And what I wear is the one thing that I can…"

"Control?" Piper finishes.

Another silence.

"How'd you get stuck here?" I ask her, eager to change the subject.

She doesn't answer right away. I start to think she's fallen asleep when she almost whispers, "Online contest."

"Wait. You *wanted* to come here?" I demand.

"Yeah, Cookie Vonn," she says. "I *wanted* to come here.

My family. My mum keeps saying we're all big-boned. My brothers have such big bones, they get tossed from the cinema for taking too many seats. There are five of us. No one's been asked to a dance."

I say nothing.

"Coming to this camp is twelve thousand Oz dollars. So you can think I'm pathetic if you want. Maybe I am pathetic. I had to write this whole big thing. 'How would Fairy Falls change your life?'"

"I don't think you're pathetic," I whisper.

"I want to get married. To hang glide. To surf," she says. "I want to go to the senior dance. My mum thinks the five food groups are meat pie, lamb leg, fish-and-chips, chocolate biscuits and lamingtons. This is my only chance."

I should say something. I know it. About how life has to be about more than just one chance. How there has to be more to life than how we look on the outside. How happy endings can't be reserved for the thin.

But there's a knock at the door. A soft knock.

"Cookie? Cookie Vonn?"

I open the door a crack. That dickhead Getty called lights out a while ago, but the guy outside the cabin holds a small, battery-powered camping lantern.

"I thought you might want some dinner," the guy says. Piper leans forward on her bunk, trying to catch a glimpse of what's happening.

"Who're you? And why do you care if I get dinner?" I ask.

He shakes the lantern next to his head of blond, curly hair. "It's me. Tommy." He says this like I should recognize him. Like we've been bosom buddies all our lives.

"Tommy who?"

He lowers the lamp and his shoulders slump. His camp tee is a couple sizes too big. It'd be a stretch to say the guy has twenty pounds of extra weight on him. Whoever shipped him off to fat camp is more evil than Chad Tate.

"Tommy Weston."

The name doesn't ring a bell.

"My mom works for the Cards. We met at the Cards versus Giants game."

I think about that game. The only thing I remember is Chad Tate spilling beer on my new pair of oxford loafers.

"I see you at Donutville every Sunday when I pick up a dozen for church."

Yeah, you and every other Catholic within a five-mile radius.

"Oh, come on! I sit behind you in Trig."

That sort of rings a bell. Like maybe I've seen his poofy mop as I pass back quiz copies or something.

"Yeah, okay. Hi. What do you want?"

Out of the corner of my eye, I see Piper recoiling in horror. I'm pretty sure I'm losing whatever ground we gained during our heart-to-heart.

"I heard about the thing with Mr. Getty. And, well…my mom knows your dad… I thought you might be hungry… I thought maybe I should—"

I put my hands on my hips. "Chad Tate's not my dad."

"Yeah, sure. Sorry." He holds up the lantern again. He's like the blond boy from the cover of *The Little Prince*. Hopeful. And a bit lost. "So you don't want to go on a picnic? See Fairy Falls?"

I bite my lower lip. "Fairy Falls is a real thing? Not just

some bizarre-o marketing gimmick from the mind of Herbert Getty?"

"It's real. We went up there this morning. It's more of a walk. Took about forty-five minutes. Come see it." He smiles and his teeth glow green.

I know I can't hike in my skirt and wedges. "Did he put you up to this? Did Getty send you over here to trick me into wearing that Hulk costume?"

His mouth clamps shut and he shrugs. "Wear whatever you want. I'm just offering you a sandwich."

Sandwich. I have no idea when Getty will let me eat, and that's enough to motivate me. "Okay. Hang on." I shut the door and tug on the oversize green sweats. Piper gives me a smile and a wave as I lace up my Converse and leave the cabin.

"Hey! Don't hurt me, Hulk," Tommy whispers as I join him outside.

"Ha ha. I'm wearing the sweats. Now, where's my sandwich, Pavlov?" I experiment with the placement of the sweatshirt's ribbed edge, trying to figure out which option makes me look less fat. No one option seems better than any other. And the green color is such a crime against humanity that it probably doesn't matter anyway.

He dims the light and motions for me to follow him up the path. "You know, it doesn't look that bad. Why did you make such a big deal out of it?"

I have to stay close to keep from tripping in the darkness. And I don't say anything. Partially because the land has started to rise in an incline and I'm having trouble breathing. Partially because I no longer know the answer. Something about Piper got to me. Made me think that camp wouldn't be all bad.

"Wouldn't it be easier to just go with the flow once in a while?" he asks.

"That's what Churchill…said when the Nazis…invaded Poland." I hope the panting isn't too obvious.

"Ah, so you're comparing me to Hitler now?"

The moon rises higher and higher in the sky and it feels like we've been walking all night. We finally come to a stop and Tommy turns the lantern to full brightness. He holds it up, illuminating the rocky edge of a water hole. White steam rises off the surface and sends a rotten-egg smell in our direction.

"The Grand Prismatic Spring," he says in a booming voice. In a quieter tone, he goes on, "You should see it during the day. It looks like something from another planet. The colors change. Sometimes you see a deep blue, sometimes gold and then red."

"It's the algae," I say. "And bacteria. This place is basically one big infection. And it smells like one too."

He laughs, and we start walking again. *Typical.* I just caught my breath. I can hear rushing water ahead in the distance. Tree branches poke into the pathway and with another wave of the lantern, Tommy is saying something about fires and forest thinning. He's not huffing and puffing like me.

He stops and spreads a camp blanket over a patch of moss, yellowish green in the moonlight. I stand near the edge of a rocky ledge facing into the darkness. Behind me, I hear a thud as Tommy drops his backpack, and in front of me, the patter of water rolling off the cliff. He joins me with his lantern and holds it up over a skinny stream of water.

"Fairy Falls," he says.

"It's not too bad." I smile. In spite of my hatred for the camp, for Getty, for Chad Tate, there's something interesting about the gray granite rock formations and the tree trunks that litter the hillside. It's like the opening sequence of a bad teen horror movie. Or the site of a giant game of pick-up sticks.

"Come on," Tommy says, grabbing my hand.

We sit on the cold blanket. From inside his backpack Tommy unpacks ham sandwiches, sea salt quinoa chips and apples. And chocolate pudding. It's pretty gross camp food. But after the day I've had, it's a gourmet feast.

"Look, I know you're not happy to be here," he says.

"Um, yeah," I say in between bites, "is there a reason you find the prospect of eating lettuce wraps and getting up at four in the morning to jog so thrilling?"

Tommy shrugs and opens his pudding cup. "Jogging's okay. I guess I don't *love* salads. And we don't have to get up at four."

I put down my sandwich. "Okay. But why are you here? You're…not fat."

He smiles. "My mom had a weight problem growing up. She keeps going on and on about genetics and history repeating itself. So here I am."

"That totally sucks."

He thinks about this for a minute. "Well. It was either this or visit my grandma and spend the whole break trying to cross-stitch Walt Whitman quotes. And this is fun, right?"

I sigh. I knew he was playing the odds. It happens a lot. Guys will be nice to me in the hopes that I'll go on the cabbage diet and end up strutting around a catwalk in a bra like my mother. People say we look alike. I'm the image of supermodel Lindsay Vonn Tate as seen in a funhouse mirror.

Before I can tell Tommy Weston to go screw off, he points at a small reddish blob on the horizon. "You ever watch Arcturus?"

I followed his gaze up to the night sky. "What's that?"

"A star. Fourth brightest, actually. The Bear Watcher."

I snorted. "Great. Now you're Bill Nye the Science Guy."

He ignores me. "My dad used to tell me this story. About how they used the light from Arcturus to open the 1933 Chicago World's Fair."

I sit cross-legged and stare at the star too. "How did they do that?"

Tommy turns to face me. "Well, they set up photocells and used several large refracting telescopes to—"

"Okay. Forget I asked," I say, and we both laugh.

"The point is that there's Arcturus. It can be this impersonal ball of gas floating around thirty-seven light-years away, having nothing to do with anybody or anything. Or we can take a telescope, focus its light and shoot it over a crowd of ten thousand people. And it's up to us what we do." He's watching the dark sky. Wishing on a star.

There's something sweet about him and this world he's imagining. "So this is your dad's version of a motivational speech?" I giggle. It sounds kind of weird.

"My dad's a physics teacher. He likes to go with what he knows."

We pack up the garbage and walk back to camp. The walk back is way more pleasant than hiking up, since it's mostly downhill.

When we arrive at *Juniper*, he extends his hand. "Friends?" he asks.

"Friends," I agree.

I watch him go over to the boys' side of camp. Low, snow-covered mountains billow across the landscape behind him.

Inside my cabin, Piper's still awake. "Some counselor brought your bag. Don't worry. I said you were in the toilet. I guess Mr. Getty's lawyer says, strictly speaking, he can't refuse to give you food."

I shrug and pull the bag into the corner near my bunk. "I think I'll just wear the uniform. I mean, what's the big deal, right?"

Piper grins at me. "Got anything else in there besides fancy clothes?"

Unzipping the bag, I hold up several magazines. "Can I interest you in a copy of *Seventeen*? I never leave home without one."

Fairy Falls sucks.

Not being alone completely rules.

SKINNY: Day 738 of NutriNation and there's nothing to eat

Miller's people have pulled out all the stops. I guess they must really be worried I'll make him out to be the anti-Christ.

I ride in a fancy limo to the Refinery Hotel. The driver makes a point of telling me to have anything I want from the minibar. He tells me three times.

Finally he shakes his head. "You pretty girls never eat."

My right eye starts to twitch. "When Gareth Miller rides in a limo do you think *he* eats?" The rest of the drive is pretty quiet.

The Refinery is an opulent palace of white marble and maple paneling. It looks like only cool Swedish people should be allowed to stay in the rooms. Piper hangs around in front, standing underneath a glass overhang, trying to fold a black umbrella. One awesome thing about this trip is that it's also an opportunity to hang with my BFF.

"You made it!" she calls.

"You look great." I point to her hair. "You've gone a bit darker."

Piper nods. "Yeah. I'm trying to pull off Dannii Minogue. And, of course, I'm wearing a Cookie Vonn original." She gestures toward her outfit like a game show model. She's paired her platform heels and jeans with a sweatshirt I made. It's my own pattern of distressed retro rockets inspired by the TWA Moonliner rocket I saw that one time Grandma took me to Disneyland.

Piper is my muse.

Hubert de Givenchy had his Audrey Hepburn. Calvin Klein got a decade of inspiration from Kate Moss.

I have Piper, who's bold and beautiful and brainy. Someday, when I have my own brand, I hope girls like Piper will be standing at department store cash registers buying armfuls of my stuff.

The first year or so after Fairy Falls, Piper was pretty much the camp's poster child. It was like she lived to eat lettuce wraps and read *Runner's World* magazine. I'm sure somewhere in Wyoming, Mr. Getty was probably shitting himself with excitement at the thought of getting a new testimonial for the camp brochure.

She lost fifty pounds.

And then.

Her weight loss totally stalled. She got down to twelve hundred calories and exercised so much that she was even doing calf raises on the school bus. We Skyped twice a week, and I don't think she cracked a smile in six months.

One day during a video chat, she leaned in close to her screen and said, "I'm a size twenty and I'm going to stay that way. I have become a Giver of Zero Fucks. I'm going to do what I want to do and be happy."

And then she did.

My attention snaps back to a guy standing on the sidewalk. He starts to say something. "Hey! Are you from—"

Piper pulls me through the hotel's sliding glass doors before the guy can finish saying *Australia.* We both roll our eyes. Piper gets this routine a hundred times a day.

"I'm *so* glad you're here," I say. "Can the guys at Columbia get any studying done with you around?"

She laughs, revealing rows of teeth set straight by her orthodontist dad. "I wish you were there. Remind me why you're at ASU again."

"Because it's free. And I'm broke," I say. But Piper knows all this. At ASU, I've got a full ride. I know she's giving me the opportunity to vent about my mom, but I already spent enough time thinking about Mom on the plane. So I tease her. "Remind *me* why you're pre-law again?"

She pushes her dark, chunky bangs out of her face. "The way you say *pre-law.* Like it's a naughty word or something. Someday when you're a powerful designer, you'll need someone to sue all those jerks who make knockoffs of your handbags. And you need to hurry up and get famous so I can sell this jumper on eBay. Pay off my student loans."

I check us in. The whole process makes me feel like such a, well, grown-up. They ask if I want the bellman to bring up our suitcases. My mind races with questions about tipping and conversation etiquette. I mumble something and leave the counter.

Piper and I drag our own bags to the black elevator doors. "You ready for a wild night on the town, girl?" she asks. We make our way down a long hall. Our room is enormous, with more maple panels on the walls and oversize white pillows on the beds.

Trouble is, neither of us is really all that wild. Piper spends most of her free time watching *Law & Order* reruns and reading biographies of Ruth Bader Ginsburg. I'm usually home on Saturday nights prewashing my fabrics or learning to program my new embroidery machine.

Piper flips open the hotel information binder. "There's a restaurant here. Parker & Quinn. Gourmet burgers. I guess you can watch the chef make them."

I flop back onto the thick white comforter of my queen bed. "Great. I get to watch someone cook food I can't eat."

She rolls her eyes at me and flips to another page. "Okay. What about this? The Refinery Rooftop."

I lean over her shoulder. "It's a bar."

"I have my fake ID," she says. "And look. You can see the Empire State Building."

We decide to go. I mean, we're nineteen, we're alone in New York and our room's secured to Gareth Miller's credit card.

Piper's right about one thing. The view is amazing. Light from the Empire State Building beams through the terrace's glass roof. It's a whole building, a complete structure that seems to be saying, *You can do it. You can get where you need to go.*

And for somebody, sometime, this rooftop probably is romantic. Round lights are strung from iron posts and candles flicker on the long, wooden tables. But it's Saturday night and the place is littered with middle-aged sales people discussing deals. And off in one corner is Roberta's fiftieth birthday.

We take a couple of seats at the bar. Piper orders a lemon drop martini and I have a Diet Coke. She starts to argue but I hold my hand up. "You know I never waste calories on alcohol."

"I wouldn't call it a waste, Cookie," she says with a wan smile.

I snort. "I would. I mean, I haven't had a Dorito in two years. If I'm going off the wagon, send in the Cool Ranch, please."

Piper stares at me. In the orange candlelight, her eyelashes cast long shadows down her cheeks. "So this is it, right? You're finally going to meet Gareth Miller? Meet the man behind the door?"

I pause, struggling to come up with a way to explain the total weirdness on the flight. "Actually, I already met him. I guess his private plane broke down. He sat next to me. Got on when we stopped at DFW."

She leans forward and slaps my arm lightly. "And you're just now mentioning it! Tell me everything."

I shrug. "There's not that much to tell. I mentioned the blog. The interview. He asked about my mom."

Piper bites down on her lower lip. "So, awkward?"

"A little."

She replaces her worried expression with a leer. "Was he totally hot?" I break into hoots of laughter as she wiggles her eyebrows up and down.

Two guys sit near us at the bar, having a loud conversation that carries over ours. "—like it's my fault she's stuck in the back office. The senior analyst job involves travel," the one nearest Piper says. "You think I can send that gal to Wuhan? The last time I sent a fat lady to China, the client's daughter asked for tips on how to get her pet rabbit to gain weight."

"Oh. Ouch. Cold," the second man says, taking a long sip of a tall beer.

I realize Piper and I have both stopped talking and are watching the men in horror. I try to get a conversation going again. "So did you go to that seminar on the different kinds of law? Any thoughts on what kind of lawyer you want to be?"

Piper smiles. It's actually more like a Cheshire Cat grin. "Yeah. There are a lot of cool branches of law. In fact—"

"—and I told her. Get rid of that candy dish on your desk. Hit the StairMaster once in a while. *Then* come back and talk to me about a promotion," the man goes on.

We stop talking again. I check out the guy's suit. I don't understand people, but I totally get clothes. It's an Ermenegildo Zegna. Navy. Two button. Wool. Easily $3K. This guy. The way his graying hair has outgrown its haircut but his shirt's been recently pressed. Careless wealth. Easy power. A dangerous combination.

"Yeah," Piper says, loud enough that it catches the attention of the douchelords. "We learned about this thing called employment law where I can sue rich assholes who won't give promotions to fat women."

Mr. Navy Suit turns to Piper. "That's not illegal," he says, glaring at her.

"Yet," she replies, pronouncing each letter sharply and returning his glare with equal force.

The man drops a hundred-dollar bill on the counter and leaves the bar.

The bartender approaches us with another round and we order some food. Piper gets a burger and I ask for a chicken Caesar salad with the dressing on the side.

I grin at her. "I think you just chased a multimillionaire executive out of a swanky restaurant. You really are my hero."

She snorts with laughter as a waitress arrives with our plates. I watch in envy as a bacon cheeseburger is slid in front of Piper. The corners of the cheddar cheese melt and drip. I force myself to get busy removing all but the five croutons I'm allowed to eat from my salad.

Piper doesn't bother to pretend her burger is anything other than completely delicious. "You know, you could have a cheeseburger too, Cookie."

"Not on the plan," I say, poking at my bland chicken, unable to keep the bitterness out of my voice.

"If your plan is causing you to make that face, I think it's time for a new plan," she says.

"We can't all be Givers of Zero Fucks," I say.

"Yes, we can." Piper scoops up a few seasoned fries.

I glance at the Empire State Building. "If it weren't for NutriNation, I wouldn't even be here. Let's face it. There's no way NutriMin Water would've sponsored my blog if I didn't use their product to lose weight."

She grabs my bag from the back of my chair and rifles through it.

"What are you doing?" I ask. "What are you looking for?"

"Your crystal ball? Or maybe the multiverse goggles you

use to see alternate dimensions. They must be in here, right? I mean, otherwise how could you really know for sure what would happen if you made different choices?" she says.

I grab my bag. "Oh, so it's all just in my imagination? You heard those two guys. Fashion is even worse. Fashion is where they take thin people and call them plus-size models. Where they refuse to dress fat celebrities for events and say that size-six women are fat actresses."

Piper takes a sip of her drink. "Yeah. There's fat-shaming everywhere. But it's up to us what we do about it. I mean come on, Cookie. You're going to design plus-size clothes but not be plus-size? You're gonna live your life like you're terrified of a fucking cheeseburger?"

"I'm not afraid to eat a cheeseburger," I say. I'm not totally sure this is true, so I keep going. "And I hate to break it to you, but in fashion, I *am* plus-size."

She frowns at me. "Well, I'm going to be the best lawyer on this or any other continent, and I'll sue any fat-shamer who tries to stop me."

"We can't all be you," I tell her.

"We can be whatever we want."

Piper is totally wrong. In fashion, being fat is a cardinal sin. A cackling villain who kidnaps puppies and turns them into coats would be more popular in the world of fashion than a fat designer. But I hardly ever get to hang out with Piper in real life and I don't want to waste our time arguing. I change the subject to Columbia, and we spend the rest of the meal joking about Piper's awful new roommates.

We charge our meal to Gareth Miller's corporate Amex and go down to our room.

I crawl into bed and turn out the lights but can't relax. I imagine the five croutons I ate are having a fistfight in my stomach. I toss and turn. I think again and again of Gareth's dark, brooding eyes as he says, *I think I'll enjoy that very much.*

"Have you heard from Tommy?" Piper whispers from the other queen bed.

"No," I say, trying not to think too much about this.

"And that's not a problem for you?"

"No." It's pathetic, thinking about the time he kissed me. He made his choice, and there's no going back.

"He's a wanker anyway." Piper turns in her bed a few times and fluffs her pillow. "Night, Cookie Vonn."

I dream of a world full of Dorito-trimmed Christmas trees and curly-haired Ken-doll boyfriends.

soScottsdale <New Post>
Title: Summer Sportswear on Sale
Creator: Cookie Vonn [contributor]

Ladies, can we talk about American sportswear for a second? It's no accident that sportswear rose in popularity as the women's suffrage movement gained steam. Think for a second about nineteenth-century clothing, about corsets, linen bonnets and petticoats that flowed over steel hoops. Women had places to go and things to do. But how far could they get in corsets that caused fainting spells, sleeves that didn't let them extend their arms and skirts that caught fire if they turned their backs to the stove? Modern women needed separates like skirts and shorts and shirts that could be washed and worn, mixed and matched. Sportswear is where fashion meets feminism.

What does this have to do with anything? Well, niblets, with fall fashions hitting the racks, most stores are in full-on fire sale mode, putting summer styles on clearance. Meaning you can save big on a sportswear splurge. From a simple swimsuit by Tory Burch, to classic Wayfarer sunnies, to the Tommy Hilfiger striped nautical tee, after the jump, we'll have sportswear essentials every girl ought to have in her closet.

Notes: Marlene [editor]: *Love the historical primer but not sure if readers will care. Kill the intro and get on with the list. And do we really want to call our subscribers "niblets"?*

FAT: One day before NutriNation

"Sorry. Who are you with?" The hipster's looking down his nose at me, through a pair of horn-rimmed glasses I suspect are fake. He stands behind a desk that guards the entrance of Gareth Miller's narrow garment-district studio. Directly behind him is a tall, maple-paneled door.

Behind him is the studio. And I am about to go inside.

I'm dressed in my best work outfit. A fitted black tee with an off-center V-neck and a midi-length skirt from fabric I silkscreened with vintage arcade characters. Plus-size Donna Reed meets *Freaks and Geeks.*

As the guy rearranges his plaid scarf, I'm pinching the Donkey Kong on my stiff, cotton skirt. "I'm with *SoScottsdale.* It's a Phoenix-based design blog."

A second guy with knee-length shorts and a floppy cap joins Mr. Skinny Jeans behind the desk. It's not lost on me that the two of them are crowded into a space I couldn't fit in.

"*SoScottsdale?* What the hell is that?" says Mr. Skinny Jeans.

Mr. Floppy Hat reaches over Mr. Skinny Jeans' shoulder and taps a few times on the computer's keyboard. "Oh, you know. That new whack-a-doodle down at Blue PR wants us to do more regional stuff. Open up a couple of the reviews. Says we need more street-level buy-in."

"Whatever the hell that means," says Mr. Skinny Jeans. He stares at the monitor for a minute. "Yeah. I see it here. *SoScottsdale.* But someone's already checked in. Kennes Butterfield."

He gives me a dismissive nod. Like everything's all worked out now. "But *I'm* with *SoScottsdale*. I'm Cookie Vonn."

Behind Skinny Jeans, Floppy Hat snorts with laughter. He turns away, but I see his shoulder shake. "Well, you might want to tell them that, sweetheart. Kennes Butterfield's the name they put on the list. She got here an hour ago."

A chic woman with a pixie cut, clad in fitted jeans and an Elizabeth and James Dover tee, breezes in. She doesn't stop at the desk. Mr. Floppy Hat holds the door while checking his cell phone.

The door is open for maybe ten seconds. I see a slice of Miller's profile. Just his nose, really. And the edge of his dark hairline.

The door closes with a heavy thud. Closes on my opportunity to ask Miller how a kid from Montana created a fashion empire. To meet LaChapelle and personally plead with him for a scholarship. *It's over.*

This is not how it's supposed to be.

"But Gareth Miller's in there." I'm sort of stuttering. Like a stupid. Fucking. Idiot.

Skinny Jeans and Floppy Hat are both laughing. I leave

through the front door as one of them says, "Yeah. This is his studio. He's bound to be here once in a while."

I'm standing on the curb outside Miller's gray building as taxis whizz by and lights pop on in offices across the street. I'm having a meltdown. But for some people, it's business as usual.

I pull my phone out of my bag.

"I'm sorry, Cookie. I really am." This is how Terri answers the phone.

"What the hell is going on, Terri?" I say.

"Marlene had to send someone else to the preview at the last second," she says. The wail of a baby drowns out her next sentence.

My teeth are clenched. I'm pacing and waving my arms. But nobody looks. Because this is New York. I could be in a flaming Big Bird costume and no one would notice. "Who?"

"Marlene will explain when you get back to the office," Terri says.

"When I get back to the office? Terri, are you serious? Somebody should have explained before I made a total fucking ass of myself at G Studios."

Terri's voice is weak through my receiver. Taxis honk. Somebody yells something like "You can't park in the red zone."

"Cookie, you're right. I should have called. But every surface in my house is covered in projectile vomit. I could barely get out of bed this morning. It sucks. And I get why you're mad. But—"

I ignore her. I can't turn off my temper. "I got up at the crack of dawn to be here by nine. I had to walk down here since I couldn't afford to take a taxi and also eat. And by the way, the Continental is a total dump. I mean, what kind of room has four twin beds? Who's supposed to be sleeping in there? One Direction without Zayn Malik? Oh, and I'm pretty sure the gangsters on the hotel stoop have a plan going to harvest and sell my organs. Then, I get to the studio and—"

"Cookie!" Terri's using her angry-mom voice. "I know. Listen. I wanted to call. I should have called last night. While I was still feeling okay. But this girl, Kennes Butterfield, or whatever her name is, she missed her plane. And there was a chance she wouldn't make it. I know how much you wanted to go. So I was hoping she wouldn't make it."

"She missed her flight?" I ask. I have a sinking feeling. The kind you can't exactly explain. The kind that won't go away.

"Yeah. Between you and me, this girl is a piece of work. I guess she got into a fight with another passenger. Got grounded at O'Hare."

Silence. My rational brain tries to say its piece.

There are tons of flights out of O'Hare. People get in fights on planes all the time. There can't be a connection between the glossy-headed bitch on *my* flight and what's happening now.

Except that's not my luck. Not my life.

Terri's still talking. "Her rich daddy got her a seat on a private plane and she beat you to New York. Some people have all the luck, I guess."

My stomach drops further.

"And look, I know it's not ideal, but the girl's not a blogger," Terri says with a sigh. "She'll pass you her notes and pics. You'll still be the contributor of the article. You'll get hits and some exposure."

"If she's not a blogger, what's she doing there?" I ask.

There's a pause. "Oh God. Justin's gonna throw up again. Gotta go. Try and have a nice day in the city. We'll work everything out when you get back."

I stand outside where full sun now hits the studio building.

The one upside of being forced to buy the full-priced ticket is that I can change my flight. I'm going home.

SKINNY: Day 739 of NutriNation

It's nine on a Sunday morning when the limo driver drops me off at the studio. I've been told over and over by Gareth's people that *he'll give me an hour.* They say it in a hushed tone, like they're telling me he's going to be my bone marrow donor or something. It's weird.

Skinny Jeans no longer works at G Studios, but there's a guy behind the desk who was probably cloned in the same facility. Because Lumbersexual is the next iteration of the hipster evolution, this new front-desk guardian has a long beard, cuffed jeans and work boots.

"I'm—"

"Cookie Vonn," the guy says with a smile. "Gareth's inside. He's expecting you."

"Nice sweater," I say as the door swings open.

"Thanks" is his friendly response to my sarcasm. He picks a piece of lint off the chunky, red wool.

Given that I've spent two years imagining what it would be like to pass through the maple door, the reality is a bit disappointing. There's a small entryway that creates about three feet of space between a conference room and the main door. On the right, a narrow hallway lined with boxes of fabric, piles of gift bags and stacks of magazines disappears into darkness.

An elfin face pops out of the conference room door. "Wow. You are pretty."

I fight off the urge to glance over my shoulder to confirm it's me she's referring to. I guess it's nice to be complimented, but it doesn't make me feel like I'm being taken seriously.

The woman holds the door open and motions for me to take a seat at a walnut-colored table. It looks expensive. Probably from Herman Miller. "I'm Reese."

I shake her hand. Reese is my contact in Gareth's office. We've been emailing back and forth for the past few weeks. She falls into a chair opposite me.

"Okay, so I know that Mr. Miller's time is limited. I have a list of the questions I think I can cover in less than an hour. And I printed out my measurements, in case that helps us stay on schedule." I try to hand her the small card but she just smiles. "It will help Mr. Miller pull the right size dress for me to wear."

Gareth glides into the room and gives her a curt nod. Reese gets up and leaves, shutting the door behind her with a quiet click.

"My time isn't all that limited. I prefer to take my own measurements. And please don't call me Mr. Miller." He's wearing his charming smile, weathered jeans and cowboy boots. His roughly raked dark hair shoots up to create an effortless pattern. The strands hover in the air, on the verge of falling.

"Let me guess. Mr. Miller is your father?"

"That's right," he agrees. "Stand up straight and hold out your arms."

I've been through the measurements thing a thousand times with my grandma and I know my digits by heart, but it seems like doing what he wants will save time. I'm surprised that the most uncomfortable moment is when he takes the waist measurement and not the bust. His hand rests for a second, very lightly, on my belly. Someone who wasn't watching Gareth Miller's every move probably wouldn't have even noticed.

The more my face heats up, the more in his element he seems to be. I glance at his biceps and quickly look away.

He paces around me, making notes on a small sketchpad. "You're blonde. But not exactly a winter.

"It's your eyes," he decides. "They're blue."

"Wow. They're not wrong when they say how observant you are."

Gareth chuckles. "The gold flecks. They make all the difference. Let you carry off warm colors. They probably look green when you wear green."

He's right. And I hate it.

"All right," he continues, snapping the pad shut. "I know what I'm gonna do."

He sits back down at the table and picks up the list of questions I typed up on my brand-new laptop. "Hmm. Yes. No. My grandmamma. At my ranch mostly. I hate the city. It doesn't inspire me. There's no such thing as a color philosophy. Color is mood. Season. Temperament. What's the one thing a designer can't live without? The right seamstresses and that is a matter of fact. I've never really thought about it, which frankly means it probably isn't relevant at this point."

I'm scribbling frantically on my notepad. "Typically, in an interview, I get to actually ask the questions. Listen to the answers. Ask follow-up questions." He doesn't answer my question about why the largest size he manufactures is a size ten when the average American woman is between a twelve and fourteen.

"And you'd describe interviewing someone like me as a typical part of your career up until now?" It's sort of evil, the way he can insult me and still come across as charming. I know I'm in some kind of trouble because every time I breathe, I suck in icy air, feeling like I've swallowed a thousand mint Tic Tacs.

"You're very modest." I'm struggling to feel as irritated as I make myself sound.

"Modest? No. Hungry? Yes. I thought we might have a spot of late breakfast. You must be hungry since I made a point of telling them not to feed you at the hotel."

Truthfully, I didn't bother asking anyone about breakfast. It's a meal I've always done without. "It's really charming the way you're referring to me like I'm a bear in Jellystone Park. Don't you have to get ready for your show?" I ask.

He laughs again. "This isn't *Project Runway.* We don't run 'round like chickens with our heads cut off makin' the clothes today. We did a full rehearsal last week. I'm in good shape."

Now I'm mad for real. I don't know much, but I know

fashion. I know how clothes are made and what designers do to prepare for a show. "I only meant that on a show day there must be a lot of demands on your time. I can't be the only person wanting to interview you today."

"You're not." Gareth makes a token effort at appearing sheepish. But it's a look that really doesn't work for him. "And now I've offended you when I meant to do the opposite. Because there are a thousand people I could be talking to right now. And I want to talk to you."

My cheeks heat as he goes on. "Ah, Cookie Vonn, whatever we'll be to each other, let's always be honest, okay? We both know that there's only one question on this list you really want to ask. Only one you need to ask, because I get the idea you understand me pretty well. Will I make a plus-size capsule collection? Well, come convince me."

My knees are jiggling at the hint that we'll ever be anything more than a famous designer and the nerd following him around. But he's giving me the opportunity. He clearly knows why NutriMin Water sent me and what they're hoping I'll get from him.

He stands up, and there seems to be nothing else to do but tail him as he breezes out of his studio. Reese runs in circles around him the way an overenthusiastic puppy might treat its owner. Gareth doesn't stop walking as she talks loud and fast, saying things like, "Mitchie wants front row and there's no way," or, "They've gotten the feedback issue on the rear speakers addressed."

He tells her only one thing. About the dress I'll be wearing. "The Crista-Galli. In green. Size six. Send it over to the Refinery for Cookie to wear."

There's a car waiting at the curb. A dark, perfectly polished Town Car, which I'll later find out is NYC code for dedicated, private driver. Gareth Miller never stops to think I won't have breakfast with him. He holds the door open for me in a gesture so ingrained that he does it without looking up from his phone.

I scoot in all the way to the driver's side, pressing my leg against the door, feeling claustrophobic at the thought of being in another close encounter with a man who could really be called devilishly handsome, a man who belongs in a Harlequin novel. I barely made it through the plane ride.

He slides in too, making a skeptical face at the distance between us. I notice the stubble on his cheek, that the first two buttons of his black shirt are undone, that his jeans are weathered in all the right ways. But more than anything, there's a scent.

No one smells like Gareth Miller.

Like cinnamon and wild honey and cedar wood and fire.

I blurt out, "What's that smell?"

Gareth does the first gentlemanly thing he's done all day. He pretends he hasn't heard me. "I'm sorry?"

I reach into my bag for my notebook, taking the opportunity to suck in a deep breath while my head is inside the massive bag. "Your fragrance. Are you wearing it?"

"Is that a backhanded manner of saying you like the way I smell?" And just like that, the gentleman is gone again. The devil has pushed the angel off his shoulder.

With a click of my pen, I make a great show of pretending to take notes. "I'm supposed to be writing about my experience here today. So I'm giving you a chance to talk about products that you sell."

The grin widens. "Well, thanks for that. And in your official capacity as a dedicated reporter, I'd like to tell you I'm thrilled with my collaboration with the Keels Fragrance corporation who've helped me to bring my signature scent to market. I consider Gareth Miller Homme an essential for today's modern man."

We're driving up Fifth Avenue, and I'm having flashbacks of my last visit to New York. This trip seems both easier and harder at the same time. The view is a lot better from the back of a private car. But for the first time, I feel like I've got something to lose.

Miller reaches out and takes my notebook so I'm left holding my pen in midair. "Off the record, I don't wear it." He moves over, tilting his head toward me in an invitation to join his secret world. "Between you and me, there's a *perfumeria* near my ranch and the old lady there, she must be a hundred or something. In the village, they say she makes love potions. She mixes this for me."

"Why not make your signature fragrance smell like… like…how you smell?"

"Some things aren't for sale, Cookie."

The way he says this, with his smile fading and his dark eyes crinkling, suggests he's thinking hard about everything he's put on the market.

But that passes fast and he smiles again. "Besides, if I sold this stuff to everybody, how would I get you to look at me the way you are right now?"

I turn toward the window so that he can't see my mouth

hanging open. We're passing through the fashion district, where, in a few hours, he'll present his show to a worshipping crowd.

I'm both relieved and disappointed when we arrive back at the Refinery. I realize that I must have taken things too far and that Miller has decided to have breakfast with someone a bit more pleasant. At least I won't have any more opportunities to make myself look stupid.

When he gets out of the car, I'm back to internally freaking out again. I sit there like an idiot for a minute while he holds the Town Car door. I'm there so long that he leans down and waggles his eyebrows.

I'm getting out of the car, pushing my blue Goyard St. Louis in front of me. I scored it at a NutriMin event and it's pretty much my prized possession, my go-to accessory when I want to feel fabulous. Trying to make a glamorous exit from the car, I swing the bag way too wide. Only Gareth's fast reflexes keep me from whacking a woman who's the spitting image of Betty White in the gut. But the near miss is startling enough that she drops her own purse. Drinking straws, sugar packets and several rolls of toilet paper scatter all over the sidewalk.

I throw myself down to the concrete and try to scoop the contents back into the woman's bag. And I'm momentarily distracted by the fact that the woman's purse is actually much nicer than mine. A vintage Louis Vuitton Noé bucket bag. Probably 1960s, judging from the darkening of the monogram pattern. The stitching is in excellent shape, but the leather tie is frayed and won't keep the bag closed.

While I'm busy thinking about how they really don't make things like they used to anymore, and wondering why someone with a $2,000 handbag needs to go around town swiping basic necessities, I become conscious of the fact that the woman is talking to me. Getting pretty agitated, really.

"Girl! Girl! I say. What in the world are you doing?"

This is what the lady is sort of shrieking.

What I'm doing is holding on to the end sheet of one of the rolls of toilet paper and trying to use it to drag the whole roll toward me, which is having the opposite effect from what I intend. The roll is bounding up the sidewalk and is several feet away. A businessman crossing the street steps on it on his way into the hotel.

Gareth kneels down, desperately trying to get the drinking straws before they're all knocked into the gutter. The driver even helps us. He's got fistfuls of dirty sugar packets that it doesn't seem right to give back to the lady.

We're taking up a lot of space on the sidewalk and people grunt and snort in impatience as they pass. The woman makes a couple of attempts to lower herself to join in our efforts to pick up her things, but she can't make it down.

I realize that she's probably got arthritis in her knees like my grandma, and she looks like she wants to cry, which makes me want to cry.

"Oh, there, now. There," she says. "Please just give me my bag."

I get up on my knees and hold it out to her, but Gareth takes it instead.

He gives the woman his most charming smile. "I sure am sorry about all of this."

"I'm sorry too. I'm sorrier than he is," I add, scrambling off the ground.

Gareth nods at me but the woman can't take her eyes off him. He taps his driver on the arm. "I'll be very busy for the next coupla hours and my friend Joe here will be bored out of his mind. Why don't you let him drive you home? And on the way he can duck into the market and replace the items we've lost here."

"Oh no, no, I couldn't possibly…" the woman says, but she's already busy sinking into the posh interior of Gareth's car.

Before the driver slams the door, the woman bites her lower lip and stares at me. "Well, dear, I must say, I can't recall ever meeting someone quite so uncoordinated. Lucky for you, you've got your looks." She breaks into a smile at the sight of Gareth. "And you've got yourself a very nice fellow there. A real keeper."

My mouth falls open. Here's another first. Being pegged as someone's sugar baby. I bite back a retort. I mean, I did almost knock her off the sidewalk.

Gareth waves the car off. It pulls away, and his face shifts into a skeptical mug. This isn't a man who dreams of being kept by anyone.

"That was…uh…" I struggle to complete the sentence. Weird? Surprising? Older women seem like they'd rank right up there with fat gals and babies on the list of people Gareth would love to push onto an iceberg and send off to sea. "Um…um…nice?"

His devilish grin returns. "Ah, I'm offended by your shock, Cookie Vonn. I figured it was the least I could do, considering you seemed so hell-bent on tossing all that poor lady's toilet paper into the street and making sure she has no sugar for her coffee."

My face heats up. "I'm not sure how I was supposed to know that the lady was making her way through Midtown scooping paper products into her handbag."

Gareth laughs. "Well, that's New York for you. I only wonder what Georges Vuitton would say if he knew that the Noé bag could be used to hold twelve rolls of toilet paper instead of five bottles of champagne."

I brush off my navy pleated skirt and laugh. "Well, he always was practical. I think he would have approved. After all, he only put the LV logo all over everything to prevent counterfeits."

Gareth motions for me to follow him. "Funny, isn't it? They added the design to stop counterfeiting and now it's the very thing that makes counterfeits desirable. Sometimes, things don't go as planned."

Yeah. Funny.

He turns and walks about a hundred miles an hour, and I'm almost running to keep up with him as he makes his way to the hotel's main restaurant, Parker & Quinn. Although the place is packed, a greeter meets us at the door with two menus in hand and escorts us to a giant booth in the very back.

On the table in an ice bucket, there's a bottle of champagne, which the greeter uncorks before he leaves. Miller gestures for me to sit first and then moves in so close that our knees lightly brush. "Let's try sitting together this time, okay? So we can hear each other."

He pours me a glass of champagne, which I stare at because I'm nineteen, under the legal drinking age, and because I never waste calories on alcohol. "Let's get the unpleasant stuff out of the way right now," he says, also leaving his glass untouched. "Why don't I have a plus-size collection? Because I own a fashion business. A business. I've never romanticized it. Never lied to myself and said I'm in it for some reason other than the money. If I just loved to make pretty dresses, I would've stayed in Whitefish and dressed Miss Montanas and Cowboy Queens."

"But—"

He cuts me off. "But look how many overweight people walk the street. Look how many plus-size women there are. Someone has to dress them. There has to be profit there somewhere, right? Well, maybe. But the thing is you can't just dress plus-size women, you have to also pull off something of a magic act. You have to make them look thin. Otherwise, they won't be opening their pocketbooks. Especially not for clothes at a luxury price point."

I'm starting to really hate the word *overweight*. What's the ideal weight that everyone is supposed to be and why do people like Gareth get to decide who's "over" it? Anyway, these are old arguments, and so infuriating coming from him. My anger is rising. "When did you get so lazy? You of all people. You know how to fit clothes. And I don't buy for a second that it would be any harder for you to tailor plus-size. Your own grandmother couldn't fit into the clothes you sell. What does she say to you?"

He shrugs. "Thanks for paying the mortgage again, Bubee."

His cynicism catches me off guard. My imagination didn't

prepare me for a world in which Gareth Miller doesn't love making clothes. But then I say, "Wait. She calls you Bubee? Why?"

"You'd have to ask her."

He picks up the glass of sparkling gold. "Truce, okay? I promise I'll give it some thought. We can discuss it more after the show."

Now we're getting somewhere.

"Can I tweet that?" I ask, fighting back a smile.

"Yes."

I reach inside my bag for my phone, but he adds on to his statement. I wonder if he's always like this. If, for him, everything is conditional, is quid pro quo.

"On the condition that you wait until after breakfast. And we have a toast."

"Okay. What do you want to drink to?"

I learn that Gareth Miller likes to test people. "Lady's choice."

As I hold the flute by the stem like my mother does in her shoots for Movado wristwatches, I run through the options. *To your health. To your show. To New York.*

But I come up with something better. "To love potions. The kind they make in Montana."

He doesn't raise his glass, eyeing me in confusion. "What kind of love potions do they make in Montana? It doesn't take much to make sure the bull and the heifer go to the hoedown and do the do-si-do, if you know what I mean."

My face is flushing again and my palms break out in a sweat. "Didn't you just spend the entire car ride telling me this charming story about a perfume shop near your ranch?"

He really laughs this time. Not a chuckle but a real belly laugh. "My ranch is just outside Camino a Seclantas."

When I clearly have no idea what he's talking about, he adds, "Remember Mr. Miller?" he asks. "My father's ranch is in Whitefish. Mine is in Salta, Argentina."

"Okay, then. To Argentinean love potions." Whitefish is a world away from Argentina. Another reminder of the distance between Gareth's world and mine.

Our glasses clink together as he says, "I'll drink to that."

I put the flute down and switch to the water glass in front of me. "I'll have to get you to write that down so I can stop by next time I'm in the area."

A waiter approaches our table, sees the menus we haven't even opened and retreats in silence.

"Don't bother," Gareth says. "I'll take you there after the show. And that, my girl, is a promise."

"Sure. And I'll treat you to Taco Bell at the ASU Student Union the next time you come to Phoenix," I answer with a snort.

He takes the last swig of his champagne and tilts his flute in my direction.

"Welcome to the big time, Cookie Vonn."

FAT: Days 1–2 of NutriNation

"Welcome to NutriNation," says a woman behind a gray counter.

This is the start of my new life.

I arrived home on Saturday night just as Grandma was about to walk up the street to her usual bingo game. She didn't ask about the trip or why I was home early. I've always loved that about Grandma. That she knows when not to talk.

There were no messages from Terri or Marlene, no notes or emails to explain what happened in New York. I paced around my room, talking to myself and knowing I had to find something to do with my angry energy.

Someone always seemed to have the stomach flu on date night, so I was able to pick up an extra shift at Donutville. It was mostly dead, but the regulars were there at the counter and I was extra fake nice, refilling their coffee before they even asked. At the end of the night, there was a little over fifteen bucks in my tip jar.

Which worked out, because it costs twelve bucks and change to join NutriNation.

The next morning, I headed over to the meeting, which is in a new strip mall a couple of miles from Grandma's house. They have one Sunday meeting and it starts promptly at noon. So here I am.

I meet Amanda Harvey. She's pretty much Wonder Woman. During her intro, I find out she has five kids, two jobs and a weekly planner that would make Batman feel like a slacker.

There's something odd about the way she dresses. Like she Googled "business casual" and hit the clearance rack with her Kohl's Cash. She has thick chunks of coarse brown hair that she's smoothed with a flat iron. If Mattel made a suburban mom doll, they'd use Amanda to make the mold.

Because fat people must be God's inside joke, the Nutri-Nation is sandwiched in between a Starbucks and a Fosters Freeze. "You'll never see anyone from here over there," Amanda says. "All my NutriNation people go to the Starbucks around the corner. I guess they think they're invisible over there."

Joining is easy. It occurs to me, midway through the process, that these people deal with weight issues for a living. And they know what they're doing. They don't weigh you in public, ask you for your size, measurements or age.

The scale display is behind the counter, so no one can see my weight. No one except me. Amanda discreetly passes me a weight-tracking booklet. And there it is. In neat numbers written with a cheap ballpoint pen. Three hundred and thirty-seven pounds.

It's my first meeting, and I don't talk to anyone. Before it starts, I don't even look at anyone. After Amanda introduces herself, she points out a few people in the group. Kimberly is celebrating the loss of one hundred pounds. Rickelle sits next to me. She tells us how she dropped one-fifty and now runs marathons. Dave lost two hundred pounds while stubbornly refusing to stop drinking beer.

They're talking about emotional eating. I don't pay too much attention. I've spent a long time thinking that I'm fat because Grandma keeps too many cookies in the house.

But, man, it's like Amanda's got telepathy or something because she immediately says, "Now, we've talked a lot about how we can't assume that people are overweight solely because they overeat. Likewise, we can't make assumptions about *why* people overeat. Sometimes people eat because they're stressed or bored or upset."

In the seat next to me, Rickelle murmurs, "Or their mother came to visit and won't go back to Cleveland."

I can't help but think of my mother. There's no way I'd let her drive me to eat. When I was seven, she didn't show up to my birthday party and sent her assistant with a cake. I tossed it in the trash. *I'm not an emotional eater.* But there are other memories. Of Grandma taking me for ice cream every time my mom forgot to call. Of my favorite grilled cheese when Mom took off with Chad Tate. I don't want to think about these things, and I spend the rest of the meeting studying the posters on the wall that show frolicking thin people.

New people have to stay after the meeting. Amanda explains the program. Tells us how, for all of eternity, we're going to be food accountants. Reading labels. Calculating how many points we'll need to deduct from our daily food budget for our diet dinners. Entering stuff into the app or in our food logs.

There's one big rule. *You bite it, you write it.*

If you eat twelve almonds, it's two points. If you eat fifteen almonds, it's three. So only eat twelve almonds. Otherwise, you're screwed.

I'm not taking notes. I'm writing my manifesto.

"Do you have a question?" Amanda's smiling at me.

I look around, and it's just her and me in the room. My face gets hot and I gather my stuff. I have no idea how this whole thing is supposed to work.

She glances down at my notebook. "Cookie Vonn's master plan," she reads, slowly, because it's upside down to her. "May I?"

She holds out her hand. She wants to see my list. I don't immediately give it to her. But if I want to get to Parsons and get my happily-ever-after with Tommy, I need this to work. And for it to work, I may have to trust someone. I get the idea I can trust Amanda. It's just a hunch.

I fork over the list. And she reads it.

1. Weigh 120 pounds.
2. Get out of the friend zone with Tommy.
3. Get killer size 6 wardrobe.
4. Get scholarship to Parsons.
5. Rule the world of fashion.

She stares at the list that I've been making on my Kero Kero Keroppi notepad. She cocks her head and tears out the sheet of paper.

I'm horrified and terrified that maybe she wants to hang it on the wall. The way restaurants display their first dollar bill.

And then I'm mad.

She rips the list in half. My mouth falls open as the two pieces sail into the trash can. "It isn't going to work like that," she says.

With my fists balled up, I suck in a big breath. I'm ready to tell her where she can stick her opinion.

But she cuts me off. "Losing weight is hard. And honestly it sucks. It takes time and work. And you could be doing great, Cookie. Then in six months or six weeks or six days, you're tired. You pull out that list, and you won't have anything you can cross off. That's when people quit."

She hands me a different notebook from her own bag. It's labeled My Weight Loss Journey. At first, I think it's really stupid. It has headings like My Weekly Goals and Five Things I Like About Myself.

She circles a section called Non-Scale Victories with a red marker. "This is what I want you to focus on. Did you drink all your water? Write that down. Did you take the stairs instead of the elevator? That's the kind of thing. I want to see this next week. We're out to feel and be healthy. The weight loss is a side effect."

Amanda smiles and pats me on the arm. "You know, I get a lot of people in here trying to drop pounds to fit in a wedding dress or make somebody fall in love with them, and it never works. It's like trying to win the Super Bowl to show people how nice you look in a helmet. If you're not in it for the right reasons, you won't end up any happier, no matter what you see in the mirror or on the scale."

My gaze travels back to the posters of the grinning thin people. There's a complete and utter lack of pictures of healthy people getting great scores on their cholesterol tests.

"I know," Amanda says.

"Um…what?" I'm getting a bit worried that this lady is having my private thoughts beamed into her brain.

"That companies like NutriNation make a fortune selling the idea that fat is bad and thin is good. That's the company talking.

"This is me talking," she goes on, pointing to herself. "I've been doing this a long time, and I'm telling you, thin people aren't any happier."

I think Amanda is absolutely wrong. She's never worked in fashion. In that world, not only are thin people happier, they're the only people allowed to exist. Still, my lungs deflate and my self-righteous anger is gone. I take the book.

As I leave she says, "I think you *will* rule the world of fashion. I mean, look at you." She waves her hand toward my chambray dolman sleeve dress and continues, "But for the record, you don't need to be a size six to do it."

For the rest of the day, I'm curled up in my Papasan chair making notes. I make a new list. Five things I really do like about myself.

1. I make clothes like a boss.
2. My eyes. They're blue and the same shape as the drawings they always give you when they show you how to do your eye shadow.
3. My hair. I've been growing it out for three years and

have finally gotten to the point where it doesn't look like a rat's nest when I wake up.

4. My sense of color. I see it in a way many people miss.

5. My teeth. Three years in braces has to pay off somehow, right?

I get my stuff packed for school. The next day, I'll be starting my new project in my Clothing class. It's an evening-wear assignment, and I've decided to prove that plus-size bridesmaid dresses don't have to be a catastrophe. After her last batch of prom dresses, Grandma had six spare yards of radiant Chinese silk. When it moves, the fabric ripples like the teal ocean water that hits distant white-sand beaches. I've been hunting through the discount notions bin at the Sally's Fabrics store for weeks to make sure I'm not another girl in a bad pastel dress with a butt bow when I go to my cousin Tina's wedding.

It seems like everything is going to be okay.

Then all of a sudden it's just another manic Monday and I'm late for AP History. My grandma says that a good education shouldn't be only for the rich. So I've got a boundary exception that lets me go to Mountain Vista High School, which is the best in Mesa. And since the religious right loves to make their own clothes, the school has several good sewing and fashion-design classes.

But they don't put the best school in a neighborhood like mine, and getting across town is my own problem. I haul ass each day for twenty minutes to park my beat-up old Corolla alongside the shiny Priuses and BMWs. The orange low-fuel light comes on as I wiggle my tiny car in between two Suburbans.

Mr. Smith, the history teacher, knows my situation and is mostly cool if I sneak in a couple minutes late and snag a seat in the back.

And that's what happens today.

From that desk in the back of the room, I have a great view of my usual chair next to Tommy. It's occupied by the owner of a sleek, black bob. The girl from the plane, the one who can only be Kennes Butterfield, is leaning over, copying Tommy's notes. Touching his arm flirtatiously every now and then.

If there was one single moment when I realized that Kennes would try to take everything I've ever wanted, this was it.

SKINNY: Days 739–740 of NutriNation

I cruise around behind the scenes of Gareth's show, snapping pictures and making posts. But my notes about the show don't attract much attention.

Meanwhile, my lone post-breakfast tweet, @GarethMiller will consider plus-size capsule collection, is trending. For a few hours, it's at the top of the leaderboard. Later, *Harper's Bazaar* picks up the story and it trends again.

Gareth's people give me a seat in the second row. I'm a little disappointed, but I realize it was irrational to think they'd jettison the editor of *Vogue* so that my seat would be front row center. For a nineteen-year-old blogger, row two is huge.

Everything in the whole place is white. White walls. White runway. White chairs. White GM gift bags embossed in white.

From my seat, I spot Lois Veering as she makes her way in. They put her in the fourth row, which, in fashion, means you might as well be dead. I hope I don't have to talk to her. I'm not sure what I would say.

Her old first-row seat is occupied by her former assistant, new *Par Donna* editor, Celine Stanford, who I secretly suspect might be a robot. Her head whips from side to side like the Terminator scanning a crowd for Sarah Connor.

I'm struck by this sort of paranoid idea that people are looking at me, checking me out. The dress Gareth gave me to wear makes me look a bit more like my mother than I would like. Then two boring guys in off-the-rack suits take their seats on either side of me. I find out that one of them is Gareth's business manager and the other is his lawyer. They *are* staring at me. Not in the way a man might stare at a woman because he's hot for her. But the way you watch someone when you're trying to figure out if they're a threat to you. When you want to know what their weaknesses are.

Gareth walks the runway at the close of the show. I catch his eye for an instant. There's this moment when I feel like it's him and me, alone and connected in the tent. I shake that off. That idea is bizarre too.

Afterward, Celine Stanford tweets one word.

@CelineStanford: Meh. #GMSpringSummer

I'm not surprised. I can see Stanford's yawn reflected in the dress I'm wearing. I found out that a Crista-Galli is an Argentinean tree that yields waxy, suggestive flowers in an eye-popping shade of bloodred. But the polished polyester dress inspired by that exotic sight is somehow bland. And derivative. The flowing skirt of 1980s Halston. The plunging neckline of Gucci-era Tom Ford. The popsicle-colored palette of Gareth's own past collections.

On my blog, I always try to be real. Even though assholes shouldn't be allowed to be charming, maybe I *am* charmed by Gareth Miller. Maybe I can't accept that someone so talented would be the brains behind a snoozer of a Spring/Summer collection. But for the first time, I find myself *trying* to look for positive things to write about. There was a maxi dress with a unique pattern of tiny, grinning saguaro cacti twirling braided ropes. The jewelry was nice.

I don't see Gareth after the show. The GM people are busy behind the scenes, uncorking champagne, guiding editors into photo ops and distributing swag bags. It's all the right things but it feels off somehow. Reese puts me in a Town Car and sends me back to the Refinery.

At this point, I'm pretty sure I'm done. That I had my Cinderella moment with a famous fashion designer, and now it's back to real life. I've got nothing to complain about, really. I even get an email from Lucy, my contact at NutriMin Water, telling me how thrilled they are about the tweet and the increased traffic to my blog.

And honestly, I'm ready to go back. I've got a full day of classes on deck on Monday and will be spending my nights up to my armpits in indigo dye for a project for my Textiles 201 class.

The next morning, I say goodbye to Piper, hit the hotel's gym for my usual five miles on the treadmill, and finish packing for my three o'clock flight back to Phoenix. I'm planning to head to the airport early and am pulling my bags to the door when the phone rings. It's Reese. "Hey, Cookie. Sleep okay?"

"Yeah. Great. I've had such an awesome trip. Thanks for everything. And thank Gareth for me too, okay?"

There's a pause. "Why don't you tell him yourself? He's hoping you'll meet him on the rooftop in a few minutes."

I check the clock. It's a few minutes before ten, which is checkout time at the hotel. "Okay. Should I do that now? Should I take my luggage downstairs first?"

"Don't worry about that," Reese tells me. "I'll arrange for you to get a late checkout. Just get upstairs as soon as you can."

She hangs up, but I'm standing there still clutching the hotel phone. My mind is racing through a total freakout. I'm wearing a pair of heather gray sweats and a T-shirt that I planned to sleep in on the plane. I haven't done my makeup, and my hair is in a messy bun secured by the only ponytail holder I could find.

I shimmy into a midi skirt I made from an old 1980s videogame bedsheet and an atomic pink sweater I knitted that has cutouts on the shoulders. I spend about ten seconds wondering if I should add a pair of neon leg warmers to my outfit, but realize I don't have time to pull off the retro irony.,There's two minutes for foundation, mascara and blush and nothing I can do about my hair. It would take too long to fix it.

Ten minutes later I'm leaving the elevator and making my way onto the semideserted rooftop, which hasn't opened for lunch yet. A few of Gareth's people cluster in the back corner, all clad in jeans and black tees as if that's the official

GM uniform or something. They're in the middle of some kind of a debate.

"I'm saying you should think about it, Gareth. Consider the suggestion, that's all. Darcy may have a good idea here." I recognize the speaker. He's the manager who sat next to me at the show.

"The retail preorders were strong. Same as last season. And the season before that." Gareth's voice. My heart beats faster. I hate Gareth Miller. I also hate that he looks so good.

"The same means no growth," Mr. Manager says. "We have an opportunity here to do something outside the box."

"Yes," Gareth agrees in an irritated tone. "Let's give it 110 percent and hit the ground running with an idea designed to show how we push the envelope over here. Have I left anything out? I do so love these business clichés."

The manager responds with equal anger. "Well, what's your plan? Ignore the fact that this collection is not being received the way we want? The way we need it to be?"

"The preorders were the same. We have to—"

Mr. Manager must know Gareth pretty well because he cuts through him. "We have to accept that buzz for the current collection drives the reception of the next one. When we do Fall/Winter in March, we need to have people talking about something besides these clothes. Darcy's idea gives us that."

When Gareth doesn't reply, Mr. Manager says in a huff, "It's not just you here, Gareth. Not everyone has a private ranch and a ten-figure bank account to fall back on. You have two hundred employees who want to keep their jobs."

Gareth sighs. "A nineteen-year-old blogger?"

Typical.

For the first time, a woman speaks. I assume this must be Darcy. "I guess she's good enough to screw but not good enough to train?"

"I'm not screwing her," Gareth says.

"Okay, so that's still on your to-do list," Mr. Manager says.

Blargh. Not only is Mr. Manager a major asshole, somehow the idea of Gareth keeping a list of women he wants to sleep with seems right in character. I never want my name on that kind of list.

I'm coming closer to them now. I can make out that Darcy is a small, thin woman in her forties with purple hair cut in a sharp pixie. She too is wearing the standard black T-shirt. I'm not sure if I should clear my throat or say something to let them know I'm there. My pulse races as I duck behind one of the restaurant's service stations.

Gareth ignores Mr. Manager. "And my point is that there's nothing to suggest she knows how to design clothes."

"She's a sophomore in the fashion program at Arizona State." Darcy passes her phone to Gareth. "Supposedly quite good."

Gareth holds the phone close to his face. I can't imagine what he's looking at, since I haven't posted any of my own work on my blog.

"Moreno thinks she's something of a prodigy," Darcy says.

"Lydia Moreno?" Gareth asks, his face going blank.

FAT: Day 6 of NutriNation

The first time I see Dr. Lydia Moreno's name is on an interview letter. My Clothing teacher, Mrs. Vargas, sets it up. She's getting worried that I don't seem to have a plan beyond finding a fairy godmother to pay my Parsons tuition.

Mrs. Vargas holds me after class and hands me the letter. "I've set up a meeting for you," she says in a tone that leaves no room for argument. "I know. I know. Parsons. Parsons. Parsons. But you should also be aware that next year ASU is adding a brand-new fashion-design program to their college of fine arts. They've been poaching faculty from places like FIDM, Parsons and RISD and shelling out big bucks for workshop presenters like Michael Kors. The program could be a good fit for you, and because they're new, they have scholarship options that aren't based on your parents' income."

She circles the meeting time and location with a red pen. "And I know Lydia Moreno. She is absolutely the best. Your talent and her direction would be an unstoppable combination. Take your application and your five best pieces."

This is how I end up pushing my garment rack through a ridiculously large parking lot, across University Drive and up the Arizona State campus.

Because I've got no money, I have to park in the cheapest lot, which is on the opposite side of the universe from where I need to go. My rack won't fit on the free shuttle, so I have to trek through a school that's basically the size of a city. It feels like I'm walking forever past brownish structures with impossibly long names like the George M. Bateman Physical Sciences Center.

I'm having ten million feelings all at the same time. I'm nervous. Sorry for myself because I don't really want to go to ASU. And sort of relieved to have something to do after school besides think about how empty my stomach is.

It's been almost a week since I started NutriNation, and I've been hungry every single second of every single day. Sometimes, when I'm sitting at my desk in class, I have one of those moments from cartoons where the person in front of me suddenly looks like a giant, basted turkey.

My rack clicks and rattles as it rolls through the mostly quiet campus. Everybody I walk by seems to have it so together. They've got canvas knapsacks and cups of coffee and are probably going off somewhere to talk about whether the universe is real. They mostly give me the side-eye as I pass.

The meeting is in a place called Discovery Hall, and the way-not-to-scale map I printed out is pretty much no help in finding it. I have to circle around a few times before I finally work up the nerve to ask someone where to go. Another guy clutching yet another cup of coffee points to a beige structure. It's sort of ridiculous that the building itself has SCIENCES lettered along the top, along with the names of a bunch of dead guys, yet the words *Discovery Hall* appear nowhere.

Copernicus's name is on the building, but I'd like to see him try to find it.

Discovery Hall is small, and it's not too much trouble to find room B125. The office is tiny and already cramped, even though it's only me and my rack in there.

I stand and wait for Dr. Moreno.

I wait long enough that I start to worry. What if there is no scholarship? What if there is no new fashion program at ASU? What if the universe is not real? I tug down the ribbing of my sweater. Make sure the seam of my A-line skirt is positioned perfectly on my side.

Thanks to the smack of flip-flops against the tile floor, I hear someone coming.

This is the first time I see her. She's got a tight bun, a makeup-free tanned face and a Diane von Fürstenberg wrap dress made from a blue floral print.

She extends her hand. "I'm Dr. Lydia Moreno."

"Hi. Hi… I'm…I'm…" I don't exactly know why I'm so intimidated by Dr. Moreno. I'm contemplating how she's kind of fabulous and how the DVF dress is made of a printed fabric I've never seen before. Dr. Moreno must have sewn it. And also, isn't it marvelous that DVF sells patterns for her dresses so that anyone with a will to sew can have one?

"Cookie?"

"Here," I say automatically. I'm a complete idiot. It's not like she's taking attendance or something.

"Right," she says, fighting back a laugh. "You're Cookie

Vonn? Theresa Vargas has told me all about you." She's sitting at the small desk in front of me now and motioning for me to sit.

"Yep. Yes. I'm Cookie. That's me."

Dr. Moreno smiles. "Sorry about the cramped quarters. We'll be in the art building once the program starts next fall, but right now we have to settle for office space wherever they can squeeze us in."

I nod but am distracted again by a stack of messy boxes near the desk. On the very top is a diploma from Parsons in a slim, stainless-steel frame.

"You went to Parsons?" I take my seat. The narrow chair squeezes my thighs.

"Went there. Taught there." Moreno says this like it's no big deal. Like she hasn't lived my dream life.

She watches me for a second. "Okay. Who is it? Marc Jacobs? Tom Ford? Gareth Miller?"

"What?"

"You've got that look. That *I want to go to Parsons just like* fill in the blank."

"Claire McCardell," I say.

She grins. "Going way way back in the day, huh? Well, I love her too. American Sportswear at its finest."

"Yes!" I say with way too much enthusiasm. "She's probably the best American fashion designer of all time. And no one has heard of her. Well, I bet Ralph Lauren and Tommy Hilfiger have heard of her, because there's no American look without McCardell. I mean, the Popover Dress. Ballet flats. Playsuits. The book *What Shall I Wear?* And ooh, the Future Dress. Claire McCardell went to Parsons and..." I trail off, suddenly realizing that this line of discussion might cost me the only educational option I have left.

Dr. Moreno doesn't seem offended and laughs again. "And you think you need to, as well? McCardell chose Parsons in her day because there was nothing else to choose. Neither of us know what she would do if she were sitting in your chair."

No, I don't know what McCardell would do if she were sitting in my chair. Probably not be feeling stuffed into it like a hot dog in a bun the way I do.

"Okay," Dr. Moreno says with a wave at my rack. "Let's see what you got."

Clothes.

All the awkwardness evaporates.

I got this.

I unzip my first garment bag. "Okay, here's my first piece. A plus-size Bettina Blouse in sky blue, hand-dyed, raw cotton. People always say learn from the best. Hubert de Givenchy was the best of the best, and the Bettina Blouse was one of his most famous creations. My Clothing teacher told me I was wrong to make a size-twenty shirt with puffy sleeves because fat people don't need padding. But careful tailoring and trimming is the secret to making it flattering to all figures."

Dr. Moreno pops out of her chair and takes the hanger from me. "Ruffled broderie-anglaise sleeves. Good. The Point de Gaze lace is a very nice touch. Add something dainty to something voluminous. Smart."

I return the blouse to the rack and pull out my next outfit.

"Ah," Dr. Moreno says as I unzip the bag. "Your homage to McCardell."

I grin at her. “Yes. Plus-size, brick red, plaid skirt and blouse in bright white cotton faille. This look is my tribute to her classic designs. And yes, I did a big, bold plaid. Many designers say plus-size should stay away from plus prints, but they’re wrong. The right cut is everything.”

“Are all your pieces plus-size?” she asks.

My confidence wavers a bit. “Um. Yes. That’s what I do. Plus-size fashion.”

“Good,” she says simply.

I can’t help but grin. Nobody ever just says *good.*

We go through my remaining pieces. My hand-knit cashmere sweater. The jacket I made from Grandma’s old, threadbare Pendleton blanket. My own take on the Popover Dress, made from a worn and distressed denim ombré.

Dr. Moreno checks everything. The stitching. The garment structure. The placement of seams and darts. When she’s finished, we sit again.

She takes out a notepad and places it on the desk alongside my application. “Okay, Cookie. Tell me, why is fashion important?”

Oh, I got this too.

“Fashion is art, and I’m not just talking about the Chado Ralph Rucci exhibit locked up at the Met. It’s one of the few kinds of art that everybody gets to participate in. Fashion turns each of us into our own museum. We curate ourselves at the closet door each morning. And for some people, that’s the only creative decision they ever get to make. It’s a pair of khakis and a T-shirt, but to the guy who picks them, it’s an exhibition. Of style.”

Dr. Moreno smiles. "And what motivated you to focus on plus-size fashion?"

I shrug. "Claire McCardell said all women deserve great clothes. Today, some women have access to them and others don't. I want to design for the girls other designers refuse to dress."

As I pack up my stuff, Dr. Moreno says, "Of course, we'll be sending out the official notifications in the next few months. But between you and me, you're a shoo-in for the scholarship."

"Oh. Oh. Thanks. Thank you." I put all the enthusiasm I can muster into this statement.

Dr. Moreno helps me zip up my garment bags. "Give it some real thought, Cookie. You want to be a tiny fish swimming around in the Parsons shark tank? Okay. But you'll get the same education here, and you'll be a big fish with opportunities I guarantee won't come your way at Parsons. As my mama always says, *Más vale ser cabeza de ratón que cola de león.* Better to be a mouse's head than a lion's tail."

Right now, standing next to slim and trim Dr. Moreno, I feel like an oversize fish in a small room.

She smiles and shakes my hand. "Hope to see you next fall."

I make a clumsy show of trying to get my rack out of the door. "Oh. Um. Thanks. Thank you."

The last thing I see as I leave the office is Lydia Moreno's foil-stamped Parsons diploma, mocking me from its casual perch in the corner.

SKINNY: Day 740 of NutriNation... the fine print

"Yes, *that* Moreno," Darcy answers, naming my faculty sponsor at ASU. "She thinks Cookie might be even more talented than you are."

"Well—" he hedges.

I do a mental run-through of the stuff I've made for Dr. Moreno's classes over the past year or so for some kind of clue as to what he's seeing. Maybe some of my knitwear pieces? Or the series of little black dresses I made as last semester's final project?

Gareth hands the phone back to Darcy. "It's good." He says it like there's nothing he hates more than making this admission.

Darcy keeps going. "From a PR standpoint, my idea is a gold mine. The daughter of supermodel Leslie Vonn Tate."

My blood runs cold at the mention of my mother.

"I know Leslie Vonn Tate, and that girl might be even better looking. I sat next to her last night and—" Mr. Manager says.

"Nobody cares what you think of Cookie's appearance," Gareth interrupts.

"Wow. Touchy subject."

Darcy doesn't acknowledge the interruption. "Who has been through an inspirational weight loss journey and now writes a blog designed to help everyone find figure-flattering fashions."

Gareth chuckles. "I guess this is a preview of the press release."

This all makes me want to break out in hives. I'm not out to inspire people to lose weight. I want to inspire them to buy my clothes.

Still, I'm starting to really like Darcy. And to wonder how she keeps it together. "You work with her. Guide her through the process of creating a small plus-size collection."

He laughs again. "That's kind of an oxymoron."

I roll my eyes.

Gareth Miller is an ass.

"Ten pieces. Things we can put into rapid production easily. Using fabric we've already created. You make sure she designs the right things. We go for a January Microshow. Then we release the capsule collection online and in a few select locations."

Ten pieces. I could make ten pieces with Gareth Miller. Real clothes in real production. In school, it'll be a year before we even start talking about manufacturing. This is the kind of opportunity people claw each other's eyes out for.

"Neiman Marcus is interested. They're open to testing it," Mr. Manager adds.

"Saks too," Darcy says. "And her blog sponsor, NutriMin

Water, is totally on board. They'll pay her and pick up the cost of her accommodations."

"Money's not the problem, Darcy."

"Then what is?"

There's another long moment of silence, and I'm pretty sure now is the time for me to stop hiding behind the glassware. But my thoughts are all jammed up, like thread that's been sucked down into the bobbin. Am I supposed to be flattered that Gareth doesn't deny wanting to screw me? Or pissed that he clearly thinks I'm incompetent?

When Gareth says nothing, Darcy adds, "The point is, come March, people are talking about this and not what happened yesterday."

"Okay," Gareth says. "We'll do it. But not here in New York."

I force myself to approach their table as Darcy says, "Where, then?"

Gareth doesn't have time to answer before Mr. Manager stands and offers me his hand. "Cookie Vonn. Nice to see you again. I'm—"

"Leaving," Gareth says. "I'll finish up with the preorder reports and then we'll meet you in the office shortly."

Darcy gets up and leaves with Mr. Manager. She doesn't introduce herself but does give me a broad wink. Gareth gestures for me to join him at the table.

I take a seat across from him. "So…who was that?"

He's busy reading a stack of papers and is almost dismissive when he says, "My publicist, Darcy Evans. And Nathan Rish. My business manager."

I'm not sure what to do, so I just sit there, tapping my foot as he makes check marks here and there on a dense table of numbers. His black shirt is somehow more luxe than his employees' and it somehow manages to pull off the contradiction of looking worn *and* expensive. He hasn't shaved or done anything that would suggest he's spent a single minute thinking of his appearance. And he looks like a god.

The seconds tick by and Gareth doesn't acknowledge me again until I start rooting in my bag for my phone. It's like the bottom of my purse is some kind of an alternate universe where things appear and disappear without any reason.

"What you're wearing. Did you make it?" he asks.

"Yes. And good morning to you too." As good-looking as he is, he's still an ass. A presumptuous ass who thinks I'll drop everything to fix his publicity problems.

He's an ass. He's an ass. I tell myself this over and over even as my traitor brain is cranking out excited hormones. *Cookie Vonn for GM now available at Saks.*

"Even the sweater?"

"Oh. What? Yes." I know I need to get it. The fuck. Together.

"You knitted it? By hand?"

Now we're talking clothes. My language. I snort. "As opposed to what? The professional knitting machine I've got stashed underneath my bed?"

At the word *bed*, his gaze finally snaps up. He reaches out and rubs the fabric of my sweater between his fingers. My palms start to sweat and I have nothing to rub them on. The fleece of my sweater might felt.

"From?" he asks.

"What?"

"The sweater," he clarifies. "What's it knitted from?"

"Alpaca. One hundred gram."

"Darcy tells me you're an aspiring designer," he says. "That would have been a good thing to mention on the plane."

"Oh…uh…well…" I stammer.

"I hope they're not paying you by the word over at that blog of yours," he snaps.

"I *told* you before. I love making clothes," I snap right back.

"Darcy has this idea that—"

This time I interrupt him. "I heard." I try to make my voice as cold as possible. I want him to think I hate him. Even as I struggle to stop staring at his mouth.

He rubs his chin with his hand and cocks his head. Finally looks me in the eye.

The emotional iceberg is already thawing and I shrug. "You guys didn't exactly keep your voices down. I could hear you the instant I got off the elevator."

"Well, then it's settled." He returns his attention to his spreadsheets.

My face is growing hot and I'm sure it's as red as the fancy tomatoes the staff is probably slicing in the kitchen. "How is it settled? You haven't even asked me if I want to do it!"

Gareth drops the papers. "Well, don't you? I mean, you came here to convince me to create a plus-size collection. And now you have. You say you love to make clothes. If that's true, then the idea of seeing your stuff on racks should get your motor going."

"*I* haven't convinced you to do anything. Your people

think this is a move that lets *you* make the best of a bad public relations situation."

He frowns. "I see. The idea that this plan is mutually beneficial is what bothers you? You'd prefer a scenario where I'm your fairy godmother selflessly making your dreams come true?"

My simmering anger boils over. "I'd prefer a scenario where we're honest with each other. What happened to 'whatever else we'll be, let's be honest'?"

He smiles. His perfect white smile that is infused with the promise of Montana on a blue-sky sunny day. I can't stay mad.

"Okay, this is a move that's honestly good for you and me. Probably in equal measure. But it's your choice," he says.

My mind races in a million directions.

"So?" he prompts.

"I...I have school..." I say.

He squints at me, gives me a crooked smile. "Come see how fashion really happens, Cookie Vonn."

"Yeah. Okay. Yes."

After that, things happen fast. I'm in the car with Gareth and then back at G Studios. Darcy and Nathan are there along with Gareth's personal lawyer, another lawyer that represents the company and a notary. The company lawyer is wearing the black tee uniform, but it's not the GM label. This is revealing. Gareth doesn't like him enough to dress him.

There's a speakerphone where several reps from NutriMin Water chime in from time to time. I find out I'll be paid $25,000 plus expenses to work with Gareth for three months, through the end of the year. This sounds like an absurd amount of money to me. I made $9,842 the entire previous year working at Donutville. I try to picture $25K. In a suitcase. Or as a number printed on a check.

I also find out that someone, probably Darcy, has already contacted ASU. I'll be given incompletes in my classes and be able to make up the work during the spring and the summer sessions.

Gareth's plan is for us to use the studio at his ranch in Argentina. After he announces this, the lawyers start pushing paper at me. Contracts. Nondisclosure agreements. Paperwork designed to help me get an expedited passport. I find out I can write and tweet about my progress as long as I don't make any claims about G Studios. Anything like that has to be approved by them. And that process takes up to two weeks.

The final document is titled, "Personal Nondisclosure Agreement and Waiver of Future Financial Support."

"What is this?" I ask.

Gareth watches with stormy eyes as his lawyer explains. "In the event that anything personal develops between you and Mr. Miller, this agreement precludes you from making any public statements about said development or from seeking unpromised financial support."

"Personal relationship?" I repeat. "And why would I seek financial support?"

Everyone at the table stares at me like I'm the stupidest, most naive person they've ever met. And I guess I am for not realizing what could possibly happen.

It's the lawyer who's left to stammer, "Well…ah…I suppose…a personal…friendship might develop…and in that case…"

I sign the paper without asking anything else.

The notary stamps this and Gareth gets up, signaling to everyone that it's okay to leave.

"I have some conditions."

"You do?" the lawyer asks. He straightens his T-shirt and casts a sideways *aha* glance at Gareth. "And these are?"

Everyone sits back down, and there's a weird tension in the room. Like I'm behaving as they feared I would.

"Okay. Well. I didn't know we were having this meeting, so my stuff is not typed up like yours is," I tell the lawyer.

"Go ahead and say whatever you like and I'll take notes."

I'm not sure what drives me to do it. But I know that I have to do whatever I can to level the playing field. "Okay. While I work with Mr. Miller, there can be no fat jokes."

"Fat. Jokes?" the lawyer says slowly.

"Yes. No *a small plus-size collection is an oxymoron.* No *I hate sitting next to fat gals on the plane.* Fat people are people, and they deserve to be treated like it."

"What have you really got if you can't laugh at yourself?" Gareth asks.

"Dignity," I say.

"Fine. No fat jokes. What about short people jokes? Can I still make those?"

"Can I tweet them and tag you?" I fire back.

Darcy is biting her lip. I suspect she's trying not to laugh. Gareth covers his mouth with his hand, leaning on his elbow as he sits at the conference room table.

"Next, I won't talk about my mother. She doesn't get

mentioned in the press releases. Or my blog. If you want to work with her, hire her instead of me."

"Okay," Darcy says reluctantly.

"And finally, Mr. Miller must agree to answer, honestly, any questions I have about clothing design, construction or his background in fashion. This is supposed to be a learning opportunity for me."

All eyes turn toward Gareth.

"Done."

I leave with Reese to go back to the hotel.

On the way out, I can hear Darcy talking.

"Gareth, you might be biting off more than you can chew here."

The last thing I hear is him chuckling and saying, "Don't worry, Darce. My daddy always told me I have a right big mouth."

FAT: Day 9 of NutriNation

"Ouch."

"If you don't want to get pricked by the pin, you have to hold still."

It's lunch at Mountain Vista. Tommy and I are in the Clothing room and I'm fitting him for a new English-cut, gray wool suit he plans to wear to his parents' twentieth wedding anniversary. It's turning out better than I expected.

I'm relieved I have something to do. I took me all of three seconds to wolf down my NutriNation-friendly lunch. The apple slices, cheese cubes and almonds are swimming around in my stomach wishing a candy bar would come visit.

"Shouldn't you match this to my eyes or whatever?" he asks, running one hand through his curly hair.

I'm kneeling on the floor in front of him. "Stop. Moving. And your eyes are brown. You want to wear a brown suit?"

"Isn't that what women always do—match everything to their eye color or whatever?"

Snorting with laughter, I say, "Most people have one of, like, four different eye colors. Fashion is going to get *ex-*

tremely boring if fabrics only come in brown, blue, green and hazel."

He groans. "Never mind."

I crane my neck to look at him. My stomach turns over a couple of times. "This color is perfect. You look perfect."

The moment is sort of tense and his face is turning pink. I hunch back down and keep working.

Once I get over the initial awkwardness of dealing with things like inseam measurements, making menswear is fun. Unlike when I drape my flowing skirts and dresses, stuff for guys is constructed and precisely tailored. It's sort of like suddenly becoming an architect after spending years as a painter.

"I saw you talking to my nemesis today," I say. Since last week, Kennes Butterfield's been trying to beat me to class to get my seat next to Tommy.

"Hardy, har," he says, checking his phone and shaking free the pin I'm inserting.

There's something off about his response.

I stop hemming Tommy's left pant leg and glare at him. "I'm not kidding, Tommy. She took my seat in the Gareth Miller preview. I've been working at *SoScottsdale* for over a year, and that was the first real opportunity I've gotten. *And*, thanks to her, I'll never meet LaChapelle and talk to him about Parsons."

"Come on. It was a long shot in the first place. And you got her kicked off the plane. So, don't you think you two might be even now?"

Tugging the pant leg down hard, I resume pinning, paying less attention to whether or not I stick him. "Sure. Her crushing my lifelong dream is exactly the same as me making her wait two extra hours at O'Hare."

He doesn't answer, so I add, "Did she mention she called me *Cankles*?"

"Um. Yeah. That's not cool, but she's under a lot of pressure," he says with a sigh. "Her parents got divorced. Then her mom moved her out here. She really feels the need to impress her dad with all this new blog stuff."

"She told you all of this in between the segments of Mr. Smith's lecture on the Viet Cong?"

He shakes his head. "She has independent study for third hour too. In the library. You think you've got it bad. Just imagine if Jameson Butterfield was your father."

I take his advice and imagine the life of luxury that Jameson Butterfield's 500-million-dollar mobile-phone fortune must buy. "I'm picturing it. And it doesn't look so bad from where I sit."

"You of all people should know that having a famous parent isn't all it's cracked up to be."

Through clenched teeth, I say, "She. Called. Me. Cankles."

"I'll talk to her, okay?" Tommy says. "Get her to apologize."

Perfect. Just what I was going for. Tommy spending more time talking to Kennes.

I'm done pinning the cuff of the trouser and Tommy steps behind the modesty screen to put his real pants back on. "Want to hang out after school? My dad's got the pinball machine working again," he says.

My face relaxes. "Thanks. But I have to go to *SoScottsdale* after school. Then I'm pulling the swing shift at Donutville. We're on for Friday, right?"

Back in his jeans, he says, "The Star Party at the Riparian Preserve. Wouldn't miss it. Hey. What did Kraken say about the doughnuts?"

Bob Kraken owns Donutville. He's known for being pretty cheap. But he likes Tommy and approves of his attempts to get the kids from church into astronomy. There are a bunch of ten-year-olds from Christ the King meeting Tommy for the open house, and the plan is to bribe them with free sugar.

"He said I can stop by around four and pick up anything left over from the morning. And Steve said he'd make extra stuff so that there would *definitely* be leftovers." Steve is an old coot of a baker who dislikes the rules as much as I do. He's my compatriot in arms at Donutville.

"Great." Tommy and I leave the Clothing room together. The click of the door conceals a growl of my stomach.

After school, I make the twenty-minute drive to the blog office.

Technically speaking, working at *SoScottsdale* is my last class since I get independent study credit for the work I do there. I'm required to be in the office five hours a week and do whatever work they assign. Every once in a while, Marlene has to fill out a bunch of paperwork for the school.

The first thing to know about *SoScottsdale* is that it's not actually in Scottsdale. The rent is too expensive, so Marlene has the office set up on the Tempe-Scottsdale border in a small business park off Hayden. She has an ongoing war with the post office. Mail to the office takes an extra day because Marlene lists Scottsdale as the blog's official city.

When I walk in, I'm already pissed. No one has said boo to me since my shitty weekend trip to NYC. Terri's at the reception desk on the phone. I blur by Brittany's and Shelby's desks, and they aren't there. They're interns too, but they go to Mesa High.

Marlene is in her office staring into space. Waiting for me.

"You're my best contributor," she says before I can even take a seat in the chair opposite her. There's a series of bulletin boards lining the walls covered with pictures of the season's looks along with similar items from local boutiques. Other than that, this isn't a fashionable office. The walls, the carpet, everything is gray. The boring metal desk could have been rented from anywhere.

"Have you been getting my emails? My voice mail messages?" Marlene hasn't spoken to me since I was locked out of the preview.

"Things have been out of control around here," she answers. "Terri's just back today and then…"

I ignore all of this. However busy Marlene has been, it's impossible to believe she couldn't manage to send a single text or email or to pick up the phone.

"I always send glowing reports to the school."

"Some horrible hobgoblin took my seat at the G Studios preview," I say. "And even worse, she seems to want to go all *Single White Female* on me and take over my entire life."

Her gaze darts back and forth. "Close the door," she says.

My heart sinks a bit as I get up to do this. I notice Marlene looks great. She's lightened her long hair a shade, making it closer to platinum blond, and is wearing a pleated skirt that is either one of the best knockoffs I've ever seen or from the brand-new Proenza Schouler collection. You'd have to drop at least a grand to get a piece like that.

"Roger left me."

"What?" I ask. I hate to say it, but my first instinct is to wonder what the hell Marlene's husband has to do with the fucked-up situation in New York.

I'm lucky that Marlene interprets my confusion as shock, because worrying about seeing the latest designer clothes when someone is telling you they're headed for divorce court is kind of jerky. "It was sudden," she continues. "Left me. For our dental hygienist of all people."

"Oh. God. I'm sorry. How are your kids?" Marlene has two kids in college, both at expensive East Coast universities.

She shrugs. "They were less surprised than I was. I guess I didn't want to see it coming."

Marlene stares into space again and then keeps going. "I'm worried. About finances. I won't have Roger's income. Tuition payments are coming due. Starting this website was my dream. But I didn't think there was much of a choice. Last week, I sold it. I sold *SoScottsdale*."

Light bulbs are going off in my head. "To Jameson Butterfield?"

Her shoulders tense and she frowns. "Terri told you?"

I snort. "Please, Marlene. I can put two and two together. It was his 'dumber than a sack of hair' daughter who took my place in New York."

Marlene folds her hands on her desk and relaxes. "Butterfield's been buying micro sites in emerging markets. B-Mobile wants to create a friendlier image, so they're trying to advertise in different ways."

"Probably a good plan considering they're being sued by the federal government for antitrust violations," I grouse.

"Yes. Well. He thought *SoScottsdale* might be a good medium and could also give his daughter an opportunity to develop some business acumen."

Oh, you have got to be kidding me. Kennes wants my BFF and *my job?* "The only thing his daughter is going to develop is a case of varicose veins from wearing heels that are so disproportionate to her height."

Marlene cocks her head and shifts into stern boss mode. "Cookie, you're my best contributor. I hope you like working here and feel that your experience is helping to prepare you for college and for your future career. I don't want to lose you. But if you force me to choose between you and Kennes Butterfield, I have to choose her. And that's not personal. That's me doing what I have to do to take care of my family."

I truly hate it when people tell you something's not personal. All it means is that they don't want you to make them feel bad for doing something really shitty to you personally. I glower at her.

"I know you and Kennes got off on the wrong foot. But I promise, she's not so bad. Give the new situation a chance. She's going through some tough times at the moment. It's not easy having the secrets of your parents' marriage on the cover of *OK!* magazine."

This is the second time in one day that I've been asked to sympathize with someone who's had every opportunity handed to her on a silver platter. I'm one heartbeat away from telling Marlene to take this job and shove it.

But she says, "We'll have a bigger budget and I'll try to think of a way for you to get back to New York. Mr. Butterfield's PR people have much better connections than I do. I'm going to do everything I can to get you to another event."

A carrot. A bit of hope. A tiny little chance I could make it to Parsons.

Marlene gets up, opens her office door and motions for me to go into the conference room. "Hey, everybody. Cookie's here," she calls out.

When I enter, Kennes is already in the room, sitting at the head of the long black table. It's the two of us alone for a second. "Cookie, huh?" she says with a smirk. "What, was *Doughnut* already taken?"

Before I can formulate a response, Shelby and Brittany come in. From the expressions on their faces, it's clear they don't know about the sale. Terri takes a seat and Marlene stands at the front of the room to make the announcement.

When Marlene introduces Kennes as the new "associate editor" of the site, I'm pretty thrilled that my own revulsion is mirrored on the faces of everyone else at the table. Marlene makes a few more boring remarks about how this is the dawn of a new era, and then we're back at our desks.

The interns all share an area we call the bull pen. We've squeezed three computers, towers of magazines and even a small coffee maker into a U-shaped cubicle. It's cramped but kind of cool. Sort of like a fort of fashion.

I sit down and can't, for the life of me, figure out what

Shelby and Brittany are even doing. Brittany is inserting a pencil into the electric sharpener for a second, removing it and comparing it to other pencils laid out in a neat row on her desk. Shelby is on the phone. She listens to the phone, types a bunch of stuff on her computer and then listens some more.

"Um… So?" I prompt.

"So, *Kennes* is setting up her office," Brittany spits out, like she's been waiting for a while to get this off her chest. "She says neatness is next to godliness and needs all her pencils sharpened to the same length."

"No. Way."

Shelby presses three on the keypad to pause the message yet again. "I would kill to have that job. I'm transcribing her voice mail. She got all these messages from people in her family and wants me to type them so she doesn't have to listen to them herself. If I have to hear one more old lady say, 'I'm so proud of my little sweetums,' I'm going to throw up everything I've eaten in the last twenty-four hours."

"Wow," I say with fake sympathy. Inside, I'm delighted they hate Kennes as much as I do.

"How much would I have to pay you to back over me with your car?" Shelby asks. She wraps her thick brown hair into a top knot and resumes listening.

"Enough to pay for my legal defense at least," I say with a grin.

I'm logging in to my computer as something lands on the desk with enough force to make the coffeepot vibrate. There she is. Kennes in her size-two distressed jeans and halter top.

It's a bit of a stalemate since she's waiting for me to say

something to her. But I've got all my energy invested in keeping myself seated in my chair and not jumping up and head-butting her.

"Marlene says you need this for the post." She doesn't offer anything in the way of introduction, nothing to acknowledge what has happened. "And I jotted down some notes. Go ahead and work that into a couple of blurbs and quote me in the piece."

On the desk, she's dumped copies of pictures she took with her phone, a few scraps of fabric and an array of cocktail napkins from different bars with her notes on them. What strikes me right off is that everything in her notes is totally and completely wrong. The girl probably needs a personal shopper to keep track of her shoe size.

The other thing is that the clothes in the pictures are fucking phenomenal.

Kennes got to see them and I didn't.

I pick up one of her napkins, holding it by one corner using my thumb and forefinger. "Ah, so, for the record, you want me to quote you as saying these dresses have cap sleeves when they actually have kimono sleeves? And that those shoes are wedges when they're really platforms? Should I include a key to your terminology? Like, today on *SoScottsdale*, we'll be referring to dogs as cats?"

Brittany lets out a single snort of laughter. Kennes's eyes narrow and she pushes an empty cup in the intern's direction. "How 'bout some more coffee, hon?"

Brittany turns her back on Kennes and refills the cup with a dramatic eye roll.

With her mug in hand, Kennes wobbles back to her office on the Gareth Miller heels I suspect she hijacked from the preview. She calls back, "Just email the story to me by tomorrow, Cankles, so I have time to approve it before it goes live on Wednesday."

Brittany stares back down at her pencils, letting her blond hair fall in front of her face. The three of us don't talk for a while.

Later on I'm doing my homework in my room. For English class, we're studying the story of Pandora's box. In retaliation for receiving fire from Prometheus, Zeus gives Pandora a beautiful box full of all the evils in the world. She opens it, inflicting suffering and even death on mankind. In class, we're talking about how people always blame women for all the misery in the world.

But there's something else in the box. Hope.

What does it say about life that the gods considered hope a misery?

soScottsdale <New Post>

Title: Gareth Miller Gears Up for Fall

Creator: Cookie Vonn [contributor]

So, as promised last week, here is your exclusive sneak peek at what top designer Gareth Miller plans to send down the runway at New York Fashion Week!

The collection is shaping up to be this wacky and weird combination of separates that don't usually go together made from warm Fall fabrics that burst with the occasional neon pop. Here's what *SoScottsdale* saw. An emoji cashmere sweater. A pair of baby blue corduroy shorts with a navy, rubberized trench. Bodycon dresses with kimono sleeves in plaids and houndstooths. Accessories such as bright pink bangle bracelets and construction-orange trucker hats. These colors, these patterns, these clothes aren't supposed to work together.

But they do.

SoScottsdale's new associate editor, Kennes Butterfield, daughter of ultrapowerful B-Mobile tycoon Jameson Butterfield (Disclosure: Butterfield is the owner of *SoScottsdale* and is currently under investigation for antitrust violations), gushed, "There was such a combination of styles and silhouettes that everything looked like everything. The kimono sleeves looked almost like caps. Platform boots suggested the always popular wedge."

There's nothing left to do but wait for Miller to send these fresh, original, groundbreaking designs down the runway. Stay tuned for coverage of Fall Fashion Week.

Notes: Marlene [editor]: *Great job, Cookie! Remove the reference to Jameson Butterfield and have Kennes do a read-through of her quote.*

Notes: Kennes [associate editor]: *BIG thanks for getting this done so quickly. Fix my quote to what I actually said. Also, I hope you know that I do not gush.*

SKINNY: Days 741–742 of NutriNation

I hope I know what I'm doing.

I'm at JKF standing outside the Admirals Club talking to Grandma on the phone. It comes as news to me that there is such a thing as the Admirals Club, which is a special lounge where rich people can wait for their flights without having to mingle with the common folk.

Gareth goes straight to the bar and orders a Scotch, neat, while I dig in my purse for my last twenty. "It's on me," he says, tapping his fingers on the polished bar.

I locate my money at the bottom of my bag, where it's crumpled into a green ball. "Oh. I'll have…I'll have a Diet Coke. And I'll…I'll get the tip." My mind races as I say this. Do I ask for change for my twenty? Or is twenty dollars even enough of a tip for the whiskey the bartender is pouring from a bottle shaped like Aladdin's lamp?

He grabs my hand and shakes it until I release my twenty and it disappears into the darkness of my bag. "Here's a tip.

When a gentleman is tryin' to buy you a drink, say thanks and keep your money in your purse."

The bartender places a cocktail napkin on the bar and sets the soda on top of it. He's chuckling and nodding like Gareth has delivered a universal truth, like *the world is round* or *all squares are rectangles.* Maybe it *is* a universal truth. In the international airports. The private clubs. The alternate universe inhabited by the thin and beautiful.

As the bartender slides my soda down the counter toward me, he smiles and looks me in the eyes the way few strangers ever did in my pre-NutriNation days. Somehow it feels really phony to me.

Gareth has moved on. He's on the phone and is pretending to watch the stock market ticker whizzing by at the bottom of the television screen. I call Grandma, and she's the first person who doesn't respond to my news like I've just won the lottery or something. I can see her frown through the phone.

"This sounds like some kind of harebrained deal, like what your momma would cook up, girl. And I ain't too happy about any plan that involves leaving school on account of a man," she says.

"I'm not leaving school. They're going to let me make up the work. This is a once-in-a-lifetime opportunity." Even as I say this, it strikes me, down in some place I can't allow myself to acknowledge, that she's right. That I do sound like my mother. That I don't think life is ever about a single, onetime shot. Every day is filled with opportunity. Every day can be made into something special. "The stuff I design will go in real stores. Then I'm going back to school."

"Well. I guess we'll see now, won't we?" Grandma says.

Gareth doesn't talk much on the plane. He gives me a geography lesson on Argentina, then reclines his first-class seat and goes to sleep.

Salta, he said before passing out, *is in the northernmost part of the long and thin country.* Normally, he flies by private jet. It's faster and he can have the plane drop him on a landing strip a couple miles from his ranch.

Because we're in a hurry for reasons no one has explained to me, Gareth didn't have time to find a pilot. We're flying commercial, and the flight isn't nonstop. We have to land in Buenos Aires. Gareth said this several times, shaking his head in disbelief like he'd found out that the pilot was on a suicide mission to circle the sun or something.

We're on the plane for eighteen hours. Did I mention that?

We're on so long that I have no idea when day ends and night begins. So long that I wonder how the people back in coach are able to resist the temptation to oust us from our more comfortable seat beds in an airplane revolution.

Clearly Gareth has traveled way more than me and has a whole strategy for dealing with the flight. He's got noise-canceling headphones, a million books loaded on a Kindle and some kind of weird mask he probably ordered from a late-night infomercial that covers your eyes and ears.

I have one book, a romance I finish before we even hit South America, a few magazines and a sweater I'm knitting from the brand-new, lipstick-red jersey yarn I special-ordered from London. I get through a whole sleeve as Gareth snores. At this rate, I'll easily be able to wear my holey stitch design on the plane ride home.

He shows signs of life as the plane taxis down the runway at the Salta airport. Outside, the climate feels similar to Phoenix, which is always warm and dry in September. There's a limo waiting at the curb. Gareth ducks in without saying a word to the driver.

"What time is it?" I ask Gareth.

"A little after four. Did you sleep on the plane?"

I shake my head.

"Probably for the best. You'll sleep well tonight."

There's a glass panel between the limo driver and us and I can see my refection in it. I can almost see the airplane grime that covers me. The weirdest part of the whole thing, though, is that I'm traveling with someone I barely know. I don't know what the rhythms are to Gareth's life. When does he eat? Or sleep? Or exercise?

"I need a shower," I say. "How long does it take to get to your ranch?"

"About two hours," he says.

I slump in the seat, getting ready for a long ride. But he says, "I thought we'd stay in town for a few days."

"Really? Why?" I ask.

He doesn't look at me as he gives his first two reasons. He's checking his phone, reading messages that mostly appear to be from Nathan. "The ranch is in the middle of nowhere. It's easy to get lost. I don't like to drive up there at night if I can avoid it."

He turns to face me. Somehow, he's even more dark and handsome than when he stepped on the plane. The stubble on his face is forming a beard that borders on suggesting danger.

"You asked what inspires me. Well, you should see Salta, especially at night. There's an exact spot in Julio Square where Lerma stood when he founded the city in 1582. There's over four hundred years of life here. People walking in the cobbled square, working in the buildings, worshipping in churches that became more modern and more French and Italian as Argentina became a cosmopolitan country. I draw a lot of my ideas from the town. It's where I come to see color and shape."

He returns his attention to his phone and texts furiously for the rest of the drive. We arrive in Salta right before sunset. The sky could be made from cotton candy. Gareth misses the lights as they pop on and glow in the windows of little shops, the laughing old men clustered around an old-fashioned newsstand and something that smells like sizzling ribs on a grill. We travel through the historic district, which is filled with creamy, pastel colonial-era mansions with wrought-iron accents that are now an array of stores, hotels and offices.

Gareth checks us in to the Plaza Hotel. I totter along behind him, wishing I could imitate the jet-set way he marches through the lobby. The concierge has real, old-timey, metal keys that hang from green tassels and he gives Gareth only one.

I stare at the key as Gareth takes it. One key. One room.

Our bags are carried off by a bellman in a green uniform. Gareth takes me outside to a courtyard as a waiter brings out a bottle of white wine. "Salta is famous for its Torrontés wine," Gareth says. He uncorks the bottle and pours me a glass. "Why don't you take a few minutes and unwind out here while I unpack?" I nod and watch him climb the staircase that hugs the building and disappear through a set of double doors.

I call Grandma to make sure she knows I've gotten in okay. The patio walls have been painted a terra-cotta color that glows orange as the sun sets, and cobalt blue tile covers the floor. Through an iron gate I can see the brighter light of the street, where the blue doors are opening and closing, and people passing by in their bright clothing. It's clear what Gareth means about the city. It has a pulse. A cool facade with a heart of fire.

Gareth is gone about thirty minutes, long enough for me to wonder if I ought to go searching for him. I start to have panicked visions of him waiting for me to go upstairs and seduce him or something. And believe me, I'm not experienced like that. When you divide your time between sewing with your grandma and blogging alone in your room, opportunities don't tend to present themselves. I don't even think I've seen enough romantic movies to be able to give a plausible performance.

I tell myself I'm being stupid. The room must be one of those giant suites for rich people. The kind rock stars trash with massive, epic parties. I'll probably get up there and find Pete Wentz passed out on the couch. Otherwise, it's a sexual harassment lawsuit in the making.

When Gareth returns, he's already shaved and is wearing a new pair of jeans, a freshly ironed white shirt and a black blazer. I think about my rumpled skirt and gunked-up sweater. Then I imagine the poor bastard that had to run around with the iron.

"Wow. Is there a valet up there or something?" I ask.

"A valet?"

"The shirt. They ironed it so fast."

"They? Cookie, I was making clothes professionally when you were doing the Cha Cha Slide at the middle school dance. I can iron my own damn shirt."

He sounds irritated but as my mouth falls open, he grins at me. "I'm going to sort out some dinner for us. Take as much time as you like getting ready." He presses the green tassel in my hand and continues into the main hotel building.

Get ready.

For what?

I get into the room and it *is* enormous. It's got a sitting room, a dining area and a library where it looks like Sherlock Holmes should be hanging out smoking a pipe. There's wood paneling as far as the eye can see. My luggage is sitting in front of the door to the suite's smaller bedroom. I step inside. I've got my own little twin bed. From where I stand, my eyes trace the parquet floor to the larger room at the other end of the hallway. To Gareth Miller's bed.

And now there's one question.

What shall I wear?

I drag my suitcase to the bed, open it and rifle through the clothes I've packed. If Claire McCardell is right and when you know who you are, you know what to wear, then why am I standing here staring at my suitcase? Who am I? What am I trying to do?

In one hand, I hold a little black dress. It's a GM Lycra minidress so short that, in my pre-NutriNation days, I would have considered it a shirt and been sewing up a pair of leggings to match. I drop the dress on the bed.

I pick up a blue-and-white-striped dress I made myself. It's a midi-length version of McCardell's Future Dress with a high neck and a bow that sits right below the chin. This is a dress that says *I'm serious about fashion.*

This is really it. The moment of truth. I could be the intern that falls into bed with my boss or the one who tucks myself into my own twin bed at the end of the night. I clutch the blue dress. Maybe I'm not ready to go to dinner in a dress that barely covers my ass.

Except what's my big alternative plan? Stay a virgin forever? An impossibly sexy man, a man whose talent has preoccupied me for years, has brought me to an exotic land and has presented me with the perfect time and place. I think that what I want is to experience his world. To experience *him.*

I leave both dresses on the bed and hit the bathroom.

I'm in the shower so long that I begin to wish I'd packed a chair. I shave my legs twice, lather up with the hotel's own brand of lotion and wash my hair. I rinse and repeat. I'm checking every inch of myself. Every weird freckle I've ever noticed. Every random hair. The stretch marks on my stomach have faded. A little. I've spent the last year lathering myself up with Mederma and Cocoa Butter. It's working.

Slowly.

After a rough blow-dry of my hair, I twist it into a top knot and apply light makeup. Decision time.

I pull the short black dress over my head.

I guess I'm ready.

Or I could climb out the window. I'd survive the fall.

The suite has its own dining area, which I pass on my way to find Gareth. The room's lit with tall taper candles, and tea roses have been set out on the table. Something in there smells amazing. It's Provoleta, a gourmet Argentinean take on my favorite comfort food—grilled cheese. As much as it smells delicious, I'm so nervous I can barely choke down the sweet wine.

"How did you find out about this place?" I ask Gareth during dinner.

"This hotel?"

"This city. What made you think of buying property here?"

He smiles. "Ranchers talk. They're always saying the grass is greener somewhere else, if you know what I mean. I heard about this place when I was a boy. It captured my imagination. I thought I'd be happy here."

"Are you? Happy here?"

"I am right now, Cookie."

We leave the dirty dishes on the table. Gareth doesn't fuss with them. He kind of smirks while I stack my plates and refold my napkin. Rich people are like this. I guess you reach a certain income bracket and then there's always someone waiting around to clean up after you. We end up milling around awkwardly in the sitting room. A table lamp bathes the room in soft yellow light and the windows open to the moonlight.

I'm holding my arms very close to my body, squeezing myself into a thin, stiff line. When you're fat, you're very conscious of the area you occupy. Of all the people in the universe, the overweight are the most conscious of personal space. We never want *you* to have to rub up against *us*. It's possible that feeling never goes away, even if you lose weight.

I smile. A weird, fake smile where lips sort of catch on my teeth.

Gareth steps closer to me. "So..."

I'm not sure I'm ready for this.

I catch a glimpse of myself in an ornate, wood-framed mirror hanging on the wall. I'm flushed and overheated. There's nothing especially romantic about my bug-eyed expression either. I'm more like the chief suspect in an episode of *Law & Order* than anyone's love interest.

"We could, uh, watch TV or something," he suggests.

Okay. I try to relax my face. "Sure. Right after that game of backgammon," I say. I hope this sounds flirty, confident and sophisticated.

He leans down. Puts his hands on my hips. Kisses the spot right below my ear. His sharp stubble rubs against my neck. Together, we back toward his room.

The way he stares at me. With a hunger he didn't satisfy during dinner. The rational part of me is internally screaming, *He has done this a hundred times before.* Models after shows. Interns working late.

But there's power in this moment, which is the reverse of everything I have experienced until now. There's no sitting around wishing and hoping and praying he wants me. I get to decide if I want him.

And I do.

I turn the lights off and try to tug that slutty thing GM calls a dress over my head.

Things start to hit me.

I take a few hot, panicky breaths.

Will Gareth see my boobs?

Will he touch my boobs?

Who is supposed to have the condoms?

Has everyone done that thing where they practice putting a condom on a banana? I haven't done that thing. Not even one single time.

What happens after sex? Is it like in the movies where people snuggle for hours and have long conversations about important future plans?

Somehow, I can't get my left arm out of the shoulder strap of the microscopic GM dress I'm half wearing. It gets caught in my hair, and I'm kind of twisting around trying to fix the mess. The whole thing is a so-not-cool, not even slightly sexy, dumbass dance.

I'm able to free my hair. I pull the knit fabric back down over me and trip over the bench at the foot of the bed just as Gareth snaps the light back on.

He comes to tower over me where I lay sprawled on the carpeted floor, with one of my legs stuck in an odd position on the bench. Gareth holds out one of his hands. I take it and he hoists me to a more normal seated position on the bench.

The bun that was positioned on the top of my head is sliding down to one side, leaving me with a ridiculous comb-over.

Gareth rubs his stubbly chin and covers his mouth so I can't tell if he's smiling or scowling or what. All of a sudden it hits me. His face is so unfamiliar. We barely know each other.

"You know…maybe…maybe we shouldn't move…quite so fast," I stutter.

He sits on the bench, puts his arm around me and gently guides my head onto his shoulder. "Well, good things are worth the wait. Always."

Gareth kisses my forehead and I feel myself relaxing, my side molding into his.

"Besides," he says. "This room really does have a very nice backgammon set."

FAT: Day 13 of NutriNation

There's a psychology to food consumption.

Major food companies keep a team of witch doctors hidden away. They've got PhDs in fields that sound harmless, like Consumer Behavior and Cognitive Psychology. Every once in a while, their corporate overlords let them out of the lab. When they do, there's one question on the table.

How can we get people to eat more?

Ever looked at a nacho cheese corn chip and wondered why the hell it's covered with a hyperactive orange coat of Maltodextrin and artificial flavoring? The first chips had the nacho flavor mixed in with the corn, but companies told their super scientists to deliver better sales. Research shows that taste buds metabolize powdered flavor faster and send high priority *happy happy* signals to the brain. The stomach doesn't get a chance to say it's full. It's the definition of mindless eating.

Sure, some of the food scientists want to use their power for good. They'll tell you about the Delboeuf illusion. This is the idea that people serve themselves more food if given a larger plate. The brain thinks things are relative. Prefer small portions? Get a small plate.

For the most part, though, food companies want your money. And need you to loosen that belt and help yourself to a second serving.

Which brings me to Donutville.

I show up at the tiny doughnut and coffee shop a little after six.

Steve's working at the baker's table, punching a large ball of dough. He never says what his age is, but if I had to guess, I'd go with midfifties. He's sort of like a *Pete's Dragon*–era Mickey Rooney. He doesn't have any kids and maybe that's why he takes care of me. When I get to Donutville, he's got stacks and stacks of boxes of doughnuts that are "left over" from the earlier shift. But they're fresh and warm.

"Say hi to your boyfriend for me," Steve calls as I leave.

"Tommy's just a friend," I tell him. But I blush. I guess I've realized I no longer want that to be true and have no idea what to do next.

"Right," Steve says, pulling down the brim of his Donutville hat.

I load my car, pray my last gallon of gas holds out and drive over to the Riparian Preserve. It's just before dusk at the landscaped desert park that serves as a sanctuary for Arizona's birds. It's actually kind of pretty out here. A narrow stream runs into a small lake that's bordered by yellow flowering graythorn. Off in the distance, a few snowy egrets hop on their spindly legs.

The Astronomy Club members are there, setting up their

telescopes. Tommy is waiting for me with a jug of 5W-30 motor oil and an iced latte. "You know, you're not supposed to hear that ticking noise," he says as he pops the hood and empties the contents into my car.

I take a sip of caramel yumminess. "Thanks for the joe."

He nods, gets out his own telescope and a few minutes later he's being crowded by a gang of ten-year-olds jockeying for first place in line to look through the lens of the scope.

They all take turns. Tommy shows off Arcturus, which is low off the horizon. The boys are way more impressed by the moon, rising with a silver shimmer into the night sky. The craters have names. This is what Tommy tells them as he swivels the telescope in that direction.

"All of them?" one of the boys asks.

"They've named a couple of hundred at least. Some after astronauts like Neil Armstrong. Some after the ancient Greeks. Um...Aristotle has a crater. And Euclid."

"Why does it look so big?" I ask.

"The moon?" He's surprised by the question.

"It looks so much bigger when its low and then when it's overhead it's so small."

He smiles. It's his wide-eyed, goofy grin, the expression of a boy who stargazes with his dad and builds robotic cars out of Lego. "They think it's an illusion."

He explains about the Ponzo illusion. It's the idea that the brain compares objects when it judges scale. Something on the horizon looks big because the brain compares it to trees and buildings and other things it expects to find in that space.

When the moon floats alone, high in the sky, the mind

has nothing to gauge its size by. It's like the small portion of food on the giant plate.

It turns out that relativity is everywhere.

I set the doughnuts up on a picnic table and spend much of the rest of my time wiping sticky hands and chasing away random cats.

We're packing the boys back into the church van when another car pulls into the parking lot. A shiny black German car that barely makes any noise as it arrives.

There she is. Slumming around in a distressed Wildfox sweater covered with blue stars and a pair of cutoffs that fall an inch below her ass cheeks. Kennes Butterfield.

"Hurry," I tell Tommy. "If we can get everything loaded in the next thirty seconds we won't have to talk to her."

There's a pause.

"I invited her."

My heart drops into my stomach. For the first time since camp at Fairy Falls, I want to kick Tommy. After buckling the last kid in a seat belt and slamming the side door, I whirl around to face him. "What the hell—"

Kennes is coming closer and Tommy whispers, "She doesn't know anybody. If you don't want to talk to her, you can take the boys back to the church."

"How will I get back here to get my car?"

I'm making no effort to keep my voice down and Tommy has his hands up defensively, trying to calm me down. "I'll meet you there in ten minutes and give you a ride back here."

Kennes is standing a few feet from us now. She scrunches her nose and gives a cute little wave to the boys in the van. "Hi, Tommy. Hi, Cookie."

Hi, Cookie?

I'm silently willing her to call me some sort of name so that Tommy will be forced to choose where his loyalties lie. But she doesn't. She just stands there with her perfectly straightened hair and perfectly glossed lips and a pleasant but confused expression on her face. Like she's baffled by the fact that I hate her.

"Fine," I snap at Tommy.

I grab the extra boxes of doughnuts and put them in the back of the van. As Tommy tosses me the keys, I call back, "Ten minutes."

Of course he doesn't come for me.

Most of the parents are already in the Christ the King parking lot, waiting when I pull in with the white van. Only little Eddie Marshall's mom isn't there, but she shows up after about five minutes.

Then I wait.

I stand there holding on to the extra doughnuts for dear life, like they're a fucking security blanket I can't live without.

I wait as the church building empties out. As the lights go off. And until Father Tim comes out. "Tommy's supposed to come and drive me back to the park."

"You can't stand out here all night."

The gray-haired priest doesn't like to talk. He avoids doing counseling and discourages people from coming to confession. But I appreciate his silence as he drives me to the Riparian Preserve in his old minivan.

The park is empty and completely dark with only the

parking lot lit by a series of creepy yellow lights. My car is alone in one corner. Dilapidated and used. Like me.

"Can I assume that bucket of bolts has enough gas to get you home?" Father Tim asks.

"Yes." I say it so fast it sounds like a lie even to me.

Father Tim reaches into his glove compartment and presses a ten-dollar bill into my hand. "Just in case."

"I—"

"Let's not have a big scene, eh, Cookie? Just get home safe." He starts to walk away but turns back. "You know, every time your dad sends in one of his mission reports, he asks about you."

"He knows where to find me." If possible, I feel even more alone.

Father Tim waits until he sees me get in the car and then drives off in the direction of the church.

Just in case. Those words keep echoing in my head like a scene in a really cheesy movie. I never thought I'd need a backup plan to prepare me for the moment my best friend left me for dead.

Father Tim's money gets me a few gallons of gas and I get home around eleven. Grandma is already asleep. I know this isn't a slight. The lady gets up at 4:00 a.m. But it makes me feel even more abandoned.

At the kitchen table, I'm looking at the half-full boxes of glazed doughnuts and can taste the sugar dissolving on my tongue. I could eat a dozen by myself. It won't fix anything, but I'll feel good again.

For a little while.

I guess this must be what Amanda Harvey meant by emotional eating.

Scooping up the boxes, I march out the wooden door and into the darkness of the backyard. Underneath the porch light Grandma's dog, Roscoe, is eating a ham sandwich off a plastic plate. He glances up but doesn't bark as I head back to the trash can. I open the boxes and dump the doughnuts on top of the rotting banana peels, clump of aluminum foil and discarded cereal boxes. I don't want there to be any chance they can be recovered.

Inside the house, I rummage through my fabric box. I spend the rest of the night furiously sewing a midi skirt from some stretchy, caution-sign-yellow jersey that Grandma picked up on sale at Sally's Fabrics. I even add special, loopy, heirloom stitching to the hem, which is a real pain in the ass with jersey.

Kennes Butterfield has shot me forward like a rocket into some future space. She's taught me a lesson. There's a hunger stronger than the desire for food. The hunger for revenge.

SKINNY: Day 749 of NutriNation

It's our last day in the city. Tomorrow, we'll be leaving for Gareth's ranch. Since the night I fell over like a total clown, we've been more like travel buddies. We walk around the city during the day and spend the evenings dissecting Gareth's career. This manages to be both thrilling and disappointing. I'm kind of glad nothing happens between us and also sort of wish that it would.

Each night, Housekeeping leaves a mint on my twin bed.

Before dinner, Gareth says he has something special planned. We take a hired car to San Martin Park and head over to the Salta Tram, a ride that carries tourists to the top of Cerro San Bernado and offers a view of the city. It closes at sunset, a few minutes after we arrive, but of course that means nothing to Gareth. He's worked it out such that we take our seats, sitting across from each other, alone in a gondola. The only ones going up while everyone else comes down.

We rise, and a flash of warm light crosses his chiseled profile, creating a highlight over his nose. Something about it reminds me of glimpsing his face through the narrow slit in the doorway the first time I came to New York.

"You know, I saw you once before. When I was in high school I worked for a blog that gave me a trip to the city and I went to G Studios. I was hoping to meet you. Beg for a job or something, I guess." I don't know why I don't tell the truth or mention Parsons. Probably because I don't want to answer for my failures.

"But you couldn't make it past the guard dogs at the front desk? They can be a bit overzealous sometimes. My father came to the studio once and they wouldn't let *him* in because he didn't have an appointment." He moves over to sit next to me. The gondola creeps up the *cerro*, giving us plenty of time to watch the last daylight fade behind the city. Tall, modern skyscrapers form the perimeter of the city with the older districts fanning out behind until they reach the Cordillera mountains. Salta is much larger than I realized, and it goes on and on. "Ah, well, I wish we would have connected," he says, taking my hand.

I laugh. A dry laugh without any real humor. "Yeah. I know how much you love fat gals. You wouldn't have even looked in my general direction. Or if you did, it would have been to call me…um…a whale of a woman."

"You don't know what I would have done."

When I give him the side-eye, he continues. "You're talking about what I said that first day on the plane. Okay. Point taken. That was me being an ass." His hand releases mine and falls limp in his lap. "I don't know. I mean, I didn't start out this damn insensitive. I was the same as you. In the beginning. Out to make sure every person I dressed felt like a million bucks. And then it became more about making a million bucks and I couldn't figure out how to get back to where I was before."

At the top of San Bernado, there's a small waterfall. Nearby, a picnic table has been covered with a stiff, formal white cloth and stacked with fruits and cheese and wine. As we walk, we pass a man in a uniform. He gives Gareth a nod, ducks into a gondola headed back down and then we're alone.

I fall into one of the steel chairs, dab a bit of Brie onto my plate. "So, not only is it lonely at the top, but once you make it up you might not know how to get back down?"

Gareth smiles and points at the glittering water as it pools. "The best dress I ever made was for my grandmamma. For her fiftieth high school reunion. And it was nothing. A sequin shift dress. You could pattern it in half an hour. But the sparkles moved like that waterfall. I fit it perfectly, musta spent an hour pinning it exactly right. When she put it on... her face glowed like a light bulb. That's why I wanted to design clothes. For the way they can make people feel."

He reaches across the table and threads his fingers through mine. "So believe it or not, Cookie, you're not the only person with a love for the craft. You're not the only one who can spot talent. If I had seen your portfolio, you woulda been working for me and not NutriMin Water. And that, my girl, is a matter of fact."

Whether what he says is fact or a rose-colored reimagining of the world or more appealing words that flow from Gareth's deep reservoir of charm, it's what I need to hear.

What I want to hear.

Something warm fills my insides. Like in this little picnic spot, there could be an alternate world where people could be valued according to the size of their potential, not the size of their bodies. Gareth Miller and I could exist in this world.

We sit for a while in silence, listening to the water babble against the rocks. I take deeps breaths, in and out, occasionally the tablecloth rustles in the breeze. Gareth drums his fingers on the table, keeping time with the beat of my heart. When the sun is almost down and nearly everything is blue, we leave the half-finished *fromage* behind and make our way back to the tram.

He takes my hand, transferring an electric energy between us. I find, in that moment, I'm no longer awkward or insecure or worried that he'll see my stretch marks.

I know what I want.

The instant we're in the gondola, I slide the dark blazer off his shoulders. It's a cool wool, finely woven, smooth and expensive. Probably from his bespoke line, the handmade, custom clothes he produces for A-list actors and billionaires. Gareth takes it from me and tosses it on the bench next to him with the air of someone accustomed to fine things.

I move my fingers down his chest. *Slowly.* Button by button. I fumble and find patches of hair and warm skin. *Breathe.*

Gareth loses patience with my slow crawl before I finish the fourth button. He reaches for his wallet inside one of the inner pockets of his jacket. We exchange a look and I give him a small nod.

He lifts me onto his lap and hikes up my dress around my waist. With ease, assurance. Gareth Miller. Probably a charter member of the mile-high club. He puts on his own condom and pushes my thong to the side. Of course. He always knows what he's doing.

Right now, I know what I'm doing too.

I don't care that my knees bang against the plastic bench or that the gondola rocks in a way that makes my stomach turn over. There's the noise, the clangs and thuds of gears and pulleys as we go down. I have to brace myself, planting my hands on the plexiglass behind me to keep from falling back, leaving palm prints on the clear surface.

I let go of all that and focus only on the feeling of his lips on mine and his hands on my body. It's right and wrong and messy.

And perfect.

I pull my mouth off his and focus on his eyes. The last of the sunlight disappears and I can barely make out their exact shade of brown.

We don't talk or tell each other how much we're in love or that we'll be together forever. It's not romantic. Or graceful. There's only hands moving and our bodies trying to fit together in some kind of way and the sound of our breathing.

We are.

We are two people who don't have the slightest idea where they are or how they got there. Whatever we were. Whatever we will be. In that moment, we just are.

We are two lost people who've found each other.

And.

Everything.

As we near the bottom of the hill, I hear voices. I scramble off Gareth's lap and hurry to fix my clothes. The gondola stops at the station and a man opens the door. I don't look back at Gareth as the man helps me out and onto the concrete.

But Gareth's hand is on my back as we go to the parking lot.

We pass another man in a uniform. He says something in Spanish and laughs.

"Well, never a dull moment with you, eh, Cookie?" Gareth whispers in my ear.

I don't say much. I'm lost in my thoughts on the car ride back to the hotel. I always assumed that skinny people knew exactly what they wanted and were boldly going through life trying to get it. Step by step. Action and reaction. And if I could *look* like them, I could *feel* like them. I'm thinner now, but no one sent me my copy of life's instruction manual.

Even Gareth doesn't seem to know what he's doing all the time or know exactly what he wants out of life. We're trying to pattern out our relationship in the same way we design clothes. Pinning, tucking and darting parts of reality, trying to create a garment I'm not sure we have the skill to construct.

Gareth reaches for my hand and his fingers brush across my palm. I fight off a shiver.

Today, I did what I wanted to and, for an instant, I understand what I want.

Whatever this is, I want it to last.

I take his hand and hold it tight. I leave it for another time to try to figure out if our story is a fairy tale coming true or a dream that I'll inevitably wake up from.

I hope this will last.

soScottsdale <New Post>

Title: Built to Last: A Fall Wardrobe for Forever

Creator: Cookie Vonn [contributor]

Now, we've talked a lot on this blog about the need to invest in high-quality pieces. It's better to own five perfect, tailored, high-end garments than five hundred poorly constructed, ill-fitting frocks. Looking different every day ≠ looking good every day.

Let's imagine we've been pinching our pennies. What do we invest in? Two words: Japanese denim. I know, I know. Denim is American. Our pal Levi Strauss invented the stuff. What's so special about Japanese denim and why does it cost so much?

Let's be real here. Most of us live in our jeans, so a good pair is a smart investment. What's way cool about the Japanese approach to denim is that their longtime obsession with vintage Americana has led them to perfect the old-timey looming process. In short, they make it like *we* used to—on old looming machines that deliver thick, unique, unshrunk, unsanforized denim. If James Dean rose from the grave, he'd be rocking a pair of Strike Gold Standards.

One sad thing about Japanese-made jeans is the lack of availability in plus-sizes. Most brands max out at a size thirty-eight waist. Here's to hoping that someone steps in and fills that gap in the market.

In the meantime, we've got a roundup of what's what in the world of Kojima-made jeans.

Notes: Kennes [associate editor]: *Remove that boring plus-size part. What is unsanforized? And are we actually recommending that people buy jeans that will shrink?*

Notes: Cookie [contributor]: *You really don't know anything about textiles, do you?*

Notes: Marlene [editor]: *Kennes, denim enthusiasts often prefer natural fabrics like unsanforized denim that has not be prewashed or preshrunk. Cookie, post is too focused on denim for enthusiasts and may not appeal to the majority of our readers who are more casual shoppers. Add other jean types and brands, especially from our sponsors.*

FAT: Day 15 of NutriNation

It's Sunday.

I'm jogging.

Let me repeat that one more time. I'm jogging.

It's true that I almost have to trick myself into doing it. I have to imagine there's a tyrannosaur a few paces behind me, screaming and waving his arms. No, scratch the waving. He's carrying an oversize burrito from Filiberto's, trying to stuff it into his massive jaws. His arms are too short, and the contents of the burrito spill down his leathery green body.

This is what drives me. The dinosaur can't eat a burrito either.

No. Scratch that too.

What really drives me is the fact that Tommy probably spent last night making out with Kennes Butterfield, and that the Cookie Vonns of the world lurk in dark parking lots while the Kennes Butterfields are living through a nonstop game of Mystery Date.

My group from NutriNation meets in the Safeway parking lot at 4:30 a.m. It's September in Arizona, so it's relatively cool now. But in the summer, being outside after seven is borderline unbearable. We make a loop around the neighborhood and through the golf course. People go at their own pace.

Rickelle slows down to fall in step with me. I know she used to weigh three hundred pounds, but now she could be on the cover of *Runner's World*. Her blond ponytail bobs up and down.

She checks her purple Garmin watch. "You're doing it."

"What?" I ask. This takes the last of my air and I'm relieved that my Corolla is not far off in the distance. We're rounding the last part of the trip.

"You ran all the way from the golf course. At least a quarter of a mile."

I'm doing it.

I just ran a quarter mile. Without stopping.

I make it back to the parking lot, sweaty and completely out of breath.

Dave and Kimberly are ahead of us, lingering near a black pickup. Dave is showing off his water bottle. As I come to a stop near him, Dave says, "The bottle mouth is really wide. I can get ice cubes in there. Easy. Cheesy."

Kimberly reaches out to take the bottle from him.

I burst into tears.

"Okay. You don't have to put ice in your water if you'd rather not," Dave says. "I know they say room temperature is best—"

"Dave!" Kimberly interrupts. "Are you hurt, Cookie? Are you okay?"

A crowd gathers around me. Everyone is checking my feet

and ankles. I feel like an idiot. I've always been a 'go outside if you need to cry' kind of girl. It takes a minute for me to be able to say anything, to say what I mean.

"I ran all the way from the golf course. I'm running. I'm running."

Dave hits me on the back. "Hell, yeah, you are."

Then we're all laughing and exchanging sweaty hugs and I'm able to smile even though I'm still crying. The people in the parking lot understand this moment. The moment you set a goal and are able to accomplish it. To have some kind of control over your life.

"Good job, Cookie," Rickelle says. "See you tomorrow, right?"

"Yes," I say with a smile.

Back at home, I take a shower and then go back to sleep. Grandma must know I had a rough night, because she doesn't roll me out of bed for church. I hear the door slam as she leaves to walk over to Christ the King. I shut my eyes.

I usually play Monopoly with Tommy after church on Sunday while Grandma stays to socialize with the Knights of Columbus. Today, I'm sure he's not coming, and I tell myself this is okay. I can catch up on my homework before my shift at Donutville. Spending all afternoon writing an essay on *The Once and Future King* sounds, like, mega super fun, and I get dressed and pull out my books.

I hear rustling in the living room.

We live in one of the shittiest neighborhoods in Mesa. I figure either Grandma has come home early from church or the Pioneer Park Gangsters are paying us a visit. The thing is, Grandma never comes home early from church.

I go around the room, searching for options. Here's the moment that I wished I played lacrosse or softball. But my room lacks anything that could be used as a weapon. A curling iron is the best I can do. I adjust my sweats and T-shirt, grab my phone and go to investigate.

It's Tommy.

"I saw your grandma at church and she told me to come on in," he says. He's sitting at the kitchen table, setting up the Monopoly board as if nothing whatsoever has changed. He pops a Cheetos into his mouth and adds, "She hooked us up with snacks."

My mouth falls open. There are so many things I want to say. Like *Get the hell out.* And *Who do you think you are?* I'm holding the curling iron so tight that I'm losing feeling in my fingertips.

"You wanna be the thimble, right?"

"The thimble? The *thimble*? Are you fucking serious?" I say.

He looks up and pauses, his mouth full and bulging with orange snacks. "Wuh?"

"What? *What?* How did I get home Friday night?"

There's another pause as he swallows the Cheetos. I can almost hear the wheels of his mind turning slowly.

"*I'll meet you at the church in ten minutes, Cookie, I'll drive you back to your car, Cookie.* Any of that ring a bell?"

"Oh."

Tommy is staring at the Monopoly board as if it's a magic mirror and some kind of message or response will materialize there. "I…I was…I was…"

"I know what you were doing."

"It's not like that," he says, kind of pleading with me to agree with him. "She…Kennes…is having such a hard time… We were talking… I lost track of time…and I feel so stupid because you're right… I should have…"

I point at the door.

He stalls, nodding at the curling iron. "You getting ready to do your hair or something?"

"Get out."

"Cookie. Come on. I have the game all set up."

I drop the curling iron on the table, pick up the game board and carry it to the side door. Golden, fake one-hundred-dollar bills fly through the air as I walk. I open the door and throw the game hard into the carport. It lands on the windshield of the Corolla. Pieces scatter everywhere.

"Take it with you," I say, holding the door open and motioning for him to walk through it.

He comes to stand next to me at the door. We both watch as orange Chance and yellow Community Chest cards blow around the carport, catching underneath the dirty wheels of my car.

"Cookie, come on. I'm sorry."

I keep holding the door and don't look at him.

"I screwed up."

"You left me for dead in a deserted parking lot."

He frowns. "How *did* you get home?"

"Father Tim."

His soft, boyish expression returns. "So it worked out okay, then?"

"Yes. Because Father Tim treats me better than you, I didn't have to wander home like a lost puppy."

He frowns again and straightens his old T-shirt. "Father Tim does *not* treat you better than I do. I know I screwed up. But how many times have I come through?"

The truth is, if I counted all the times, I'd be standing by the door until sundown, still counting. Tommy has always been there every time my car broke down, every time I was short on money, every time Grandma and I needed something done around the house.

"That's right," he says, interpreting my silence as agreement. "If all those times don't mean anything, then I guess we're not good friends like I thought."

I stare at him, not sure what to do next.

"I'm sorry, Cookie."

"That was really lame, Tommy."

"I know. It won't happen again."

I hope it won't, but some part of me suspects that it will.

I close the door. "Okay. Well. What do you want to do? Monopoly is out."

He laughs. "Ticket to Ride maybe?"

I nod and head to the closet to get it out.

We set up the game and succeed in deluding ourselves into thinking that things are back to normal.

I want things to go back to normal.

SKINNY: Day 752 of NutriNation

“People don’t know what they want. Not really.”

Gareth holds a pincushion shaped like a tomato and stares at the muslin panels hanging from the plus-size dress form. Somehow, he manages to make this posture appealingly masculine.

We’ve been at his ranch in Camino a Seclantas for two days. I’m kind of surprised that it’s an actual ranch and not just a rich person’s house in the middle of nowhere. Gareth owns several hundred head of spotted criollo cattle, several Peruvian Paso horses and even two white llamas. On one side of the property, there are a few low, stucco buildings where the ranch’s gauchos and their families live. Gareth built himself a more modern, hacienda-style house that forms a U-shape around a large courtyard. He explains that he kept some of the elements of the older buildings, including the algarrobo blanco wood floors and the brick fireplaces. But he’s got all the amenities, like a home gym and Wi-Fi.

I make a mental note to hit the treadmill in the morning.

Since that night on the Salta Tram, we’re living like we’re

a honeymooning couple. A world where we've never gone through that *let's get to know each other* part of the relationship. I like it more than I want to like it.

One thing's for sure. I hate to snuggle. I guess I'm big on personal space. I can't help but think about every time someone gave me a dirty look when I accidently brushed them with my chubby arms. Every night I'm almost falling off the edge of the bed. Sleeping ought to be a no-contact sport. I've been going room to room searching for extra pillows, thinking Gareth might not notice if I build a fluffy wall between us in the middle of the night.

Today, for the first time, we're working. Gareth's studio is on the first floor in the very back of his house. The rear wall consists of floor-to-ceiling windows that face a cactus-laden wash and a small, rocky butte. The scene reminds me of home.

"The difference between a dressmaker and a fashion designer is that a dressmaker gives the client what she wanted last week, while the designer tells her what she wants next season."

As he circles the dress form, I'm sitting at a table near his elbow, reviewing swatch samples of materials Gareth says G Studios has "hanging around." Wherever the stuff is hanging must be enormous, because there are dozens of fabrics to choose from.

I brush my fingers over a piece of mustard-colored *peau de soie*, a textured silk. It's warm and rough to the touch.

"Too expensive," Gareth says, glancing up for a second. "A size-twenty skirt of that stuff would retail for a grand. Nobody would pay that."

We've decided to make the samples in size twenty, although the capsule collection itself will extend up to size thirty-two.

"How are these—"

Before I can add *organized* to my question, Gareth answers. "By cost. Front is for bespoke. Middle is the signature line. Go to the back. To the cottons. Poly blends."

In broad strokes, we've agreed on what we plan to do. We'll make ten pieces. A set of coordinated separates, including a skirt, a pair of pants, a blouse and a printed tee. Two dresses. A light trench coat and a patterned sweater. A scarf and a hat.

But Gareth seems to want to design it all like he's making oversize pajamas for his usual clientele. He's suggested converting the trench coat into a poncho several times.

"Nobody wants to wear a poncho," I tell him.

"Someone must want to," he argues. "They make them. Someone buys them."

"Yeah. People on boats cruising around Niagara Falls. Or those killjoys at Disneyland who can't stand to get soaked on Splash Mountain. People wear ponchos to avoid getting water or bird poop on themselves. No one fashionable wears a poncho."

"Well..."

"Okay. Okay," I say. "Go up to your closet right now and come back wearing one of the fabulous ponchos from your collection."

He stops mentioning the poncho.

Gareth drops the muslin and stands behind me. I've sort of

gotten acclimated to the way he smells, but there's something irresistible about him. He wraps his arms around my waist.

He whispers in my ear. "If you're interested in playing dress-up, we could always..."

A surge of adrenaline shoots through me. Is this how the fabulous people spend their afternoons? Rolling around in their big beige beds? I shiver nervously.

I remember the email from my sponsor asking for a status update. "NutriMin Water is expecting me to do something besides parade around in a Princess Leia bikini. We have to get some work accomplished today."

He frowns at me.

"I want to use this." I pass him two swatches. One is a polished cotton with large, wide Southwestern-style stripes in various shades of blue and teal. The other is an ultrasoft blue jersey with a repeating print of small, cartoon cowboys on bucking broncos. "Maybe do a midi skirt and an embellished tee."

"You're thinking these giant stripes for the skirt? I know we agreed no jokes. But all humor aside, my grandmamma always said, *Men don't make passes at girls with big—*"

This time I interrupt him. "It's all in how you drape and seam it. You do remember how to drape things, right?"

"Yes, Cookie Vonn," he drawls. "I believe I do."

Gareth gets to work, draping the design on the dress form. He knows things about fabric I've never seen. More than Grandma. About where to pin. About where to place darts and seams so that the silhouette feels easy, unrehearsed and artless.

"The trick," he says, "is to let people show off their best

features. People think draping is about concealing tummies. Cutting sleeves the right way so their arm fat doesn't look like bat wings. But they're wrong. The right fit shows what you want people to see and makes sure they don't notice anything else."

He comes up with the idea of creating the skirt from triangular sections to break up the oversize stripes. The whole thing takes him maybe fifteen minutes and the design is better than anything he presented at Fashion Week.

"So I have this muslin cut. I can give it to you to pattern, right, Cookie? You do remember how to make patterns, right?" He's teasing me, with an almost boyish grin.

He disappears into a connecting room and returns with two bolts of each of the fabrics, then passes me the cut pieces of muslin and a bolt of the cotton. "You get started on the skirt and I'll pattern the shirt."

"You look like you're having fun," I say.

"I am," he says with a small smile.

"That's the thing about you. About your clothes. They always have something fun about them."

He stops and watches me, but doesn't say anything.

"That day at the Refinery," I add, making a big show of searching his tool kit for the fabric shears, "you didn't look like you were having fun."

"Things haven't been fun. For a while now. I don't know why."

He's pinning the front panel of the shirt as his expression turns dark and he says, "But I know one thing. When we're finished, we're definitely playing dress-up."

"I am *not* wearing a Princess Leia costume." I'm able to sound more confident than I feel.

Gareth answers with a casual shrug. "No problem. I left that in my other suitcase anyway. But I'm sure, together, we can come up with something equally fun."

FAT: Day 28 of NutriNation...the middle of the night

To pick up some extra money, I pull a double shift at Donutville on Saturday night. Steve puts too much apple filling in the mixer with the fritter dough. The gooey gunk sloshes all over the floor, and I have to mop it up.

Steve has the nerve to try to claim that the filling package was mislabeled. But he does make me a cup of coffee exactly the way I like it as a peace offering. And he's a little less surly than usual, so it's hard to stay mad.

After work, I go home and collapse on my bed, still in my uniform that reeks of chocolate frosting.

I'm having a dream about a seriously annoying woodpecker. I gradually wake up and realize that the tapping sound is coming from my window. Peeking out, I focus on the silhouette of Tommy's poofy hair. Stumbling through the hallway, I head to the side door, trying to be quiet and not wake up Grandma.

"Come on. Let's go," he whispers as he steps inside.

"What? Go? Go where?" I take a couple of steps back and

slouch into one of the chairs at the kitchen table, resting my head on a vinyl place mat.

"Just get dressed," Tommy says. "I'll explain on the way."

I hesitate for a minute, but he's nodding and giving me an appealing smile. "'Kay. Write a note for Grandma in case she wakes up."

A couple minutes later, I'm back in a pair of leggings and a light sweater I made from an ultrafine gray wool. The best thing about my leggings is that I always sew in pockets.

"You smell good," Tommy says.

"I smell like Raised Chocolate Frosted. Two for a dollar," I grouse.

"Well, the way to the heart is through the stomach, I guess."

My hands instinctively travel to my stomach and tug on my sweater to make sure it's covered. We step into the night and I lock the door behind us. "Uh-huh. And where are we headed? Is our destination through the stomach, as well?"

"Very funny."

We get into his truck but he doesn't answer. "Well," I prompt.

"Seriously?" he asks as he starts the engine. "Haven't you been watching the news?"

I snort. "All I do is go to school, make doughnuts and write blog posts that some she-devil pretends to edit. Not a lot of downtime for CNN."

"Then lucky for you that I've got my status updates turned on. Tonight the biggest meteor in more than twenty years passes close to earth and since it's a new moon, we should get a good look." He drives quickly through the neighborhood and heads for the freeway.

We drive south for what seems like an eternity. I yawn and blink over and over to stay awake. "Okay. Seriously. Is this really a ploy to get me to go on a cruise of the Mexican Riviera with you? Because if we drive much farther we'll be in Cabo San Lucas."

Finally, he pulls onto a lonely, deserted exit and drives east. "To get away from the highway lights," he says.

Tommy hands me a red flashlight and pulls out a couple of lawn chairs and blankets from the bed of the truck. It's quiet and dark and still. We take our seats and wait to watch the sky fall.

Our arms dangle over the sides of the chairs. I consider reaching for his hand. I think about it and my heart beats a little faster. About what it would mean for our friendship. Or for my life if he had to reject me. My palm sweats. I let my fingers fall slack until they are almost touching his, until I can feel the energy radiating off his skin.

I can't do it. I pull my arm back into my own chair. My stomach sticks out of the chair farther than Tommy's does. Hugging my arms close to my sides, I wish to be something other than a roundish lump in a lawn chair.

I think of Fairy Falls and the night I met Tommy. He ended up losing around thirty pounds after camp. I wonder if this changed things for him. I wonder if losing weight would change things for me.

"Do you think you're different now? Since you lost your weight?"

Tommy shakes his head. "No. I think I'm the same. I feel

the same." There's a pause. "And anyway, there's more to life than this idea that everybody ought to be losing weight all the time. My cousin got celiac disease and lost fifty pounds. She's basically skin and bones and constantly eating protein shakes to try to gain some weight. And people keep complimenting her, telling her how great she looks. I think she might punch the next person who asks what kind of diet she's on."

We're quiet for a minute.

He hands me a can of Diet Coke. "Cookie, do you ever feel like you're hoping for something to happen and you're not sure if it ever will?"

I shrug and stop myself from looking at his face. Between the fact that I'll probably never get to Parsons and my growing realization that the world of fashion simply doesn't want a person who looks like me, Tommy's basically described my entire existence. "Yeah. I guess."

The first meteor drops toward the earth, creating a streak of white light before disappearing behind a saguaro cactus off in the distance. "Like falling stars. They seem like they can touch the earth. But, of course, they never do," Tommy says.

"Isn't that a good thing?" It's a cool night. I put down the cold soda can and tuck my hands into the sleeves of my sweater. "I mean, isn't it bad if a meteor hits the earth? Like, isn't that what killed the dinosaurs?"

He laughs. "That *was* a good thing. For us, anyway. If dinosaurs still roamed the earth, mammals would be no bigger than chickens and about as intelligent."

"You can always make a wish," I say.

He turns to face me. In his black T-shirt, he's almost a

floating head. "What do you mean?" he asks with an odd sense of urgency.

I don't know why he's being so weird. "On a falling star," I say. "Even if the meteor won't come to earth."

"Yeah, yeah. Maybe I'll try that."

We sit in silence for a few minutes as the shooting stars become more frequent. Making tracks across the dark sky. The night silent except for our breathing and the sound of a passing car echoing from the highway. I consider making a wish too.

"Do you think my wish could come true?" he asks.

I smile. "If it could happen to anyone, it would be you."

He's perfect. Completely perfect.

"Thanks for bringing me out here. It's beautiful," I say.

"Yeah. Yeah." He's still facing me.

"You're not even looking at it," I tell him.

He squares himself in his chair. "Yeah. It's beautiful."

For some reason I think of Kennes. How she's everything I'm not. How she wants to take everything I've got. The cool night air reminds me of standing on the curb that night Tommy ditched me to hang out with our town's It Girl. I hug myself to fight off the chills. "I don't want things to change," I tell him.

It's the wrong thing to say. I *do* want things to change. I put my arm back over the side of the chair, but the moment is gone. He's busy fiddling with some kind of long-exposure setting.

"Yeah," he says quietly. "I guess they won't."

The stars continue falling, hoping, in vain, to collide with the earth.

SKINNY: Days 757–772 of NutriNation

"I think it's beautiful," I tell Gareth.

It's our last day at the ranch. We're reviewing the micro-collection we've created.

The clothes are rich in color with the deep, bold blues of our starry nights, the oranges of the sunrise and the browns of the desert countryside.

He nods. "Not too bad. We make a good team."

Part of me is relieved to be going home. The other part wishes I could hide out with Gareth at his ranch for all of time, sewing clothes, watching the moon rise over the cacti, rolling around in the perfectly pressed sheets of his bed.

And I'll miss working out in his fancy home gym.

"This is it," I say, trying to create some kind of transition between my escape from and imminent return to reality.

"It?"

"I want to say thank you for everything. Thanks for—"

Gareth hasn't shaved in a few days and has a dark, almost full beard that sometimes scratches and sometimes tickles me when we kiss. It's unfair that I have a hundred products to moisturize my face and a million things to do to keep my hair from sticking to my head while he pops up each morning oozing sex appeal.

He shakes his head and interrupts me. "Why the swan song, Cookie Vonn?"

My face turns red. "Well, we're done. And based on all that paperwork I signed…I'm going home and…I'm not sure if…"

"Home?" he repeats.

"Yeah." I realize that the whole scene is super awkward. I'm wearing nothing but one of Gareth's old black T-shirts. He keeps glancing down at my bare legs. I should have gotten dressed up in a more appropriate outfit. "I mean we're done."

"With the design aspect of the project, yes," he agrees. He takes my hand. The look on his face. I've seen it before. I figure he's leading me back to our room. Soon to be only his room again. He surprises me by pushing me hard up against the wall of the studio. Behind him, through the floor-length windows, I can see the sun start its rise over the butte, creating a gorgeous orange glow.

His hands reach for the hem of my shirt, or his shirt really, drawing it up the small space between us. "All this paperwork you mention," he whispers in a dry voice, his breath on my neck. "Do you recall signing our employment agreement? You work for me through the end of the year."

"Doing what?" I gasp.

He lifts the shirt over my head and drops it on the floor next to my feet. I've never felt so exposed as in that moment, wearing nothing in broad daylight, facing a wall of windows that open to an endless Argentinean horizon.

"Officially? Blogging about the production cycle, showing off the samples, taking meetings with retailers."

His mouth runs down my neck and I gasp as his fingers brush my nipple. "Of course, there's nothing, contractually speaking, to also keep us from having a bit of fun."

As he presses me up against the wall he says, "We're nowhere near being done."

I realize I'm not in control of this situation quite the way I thought.

We're going to back to New York.

And I'm getting too comfortable letting Gareth make decisions for me. There's an antifeminist complacency to it that I don't like, or am not supposed to like. But I find myself along for the ride anyway.

He tells me I'm not going back to the Refinery. For the next month or so I'll be taking up residence in his penthouse. In an odd, 1950s sitcom kind of way, this makes perfect sense. We'll be like a fake couple coming home from our fake honeymoon.

I'm worried. But I can't stop myself from grinning when I think about getting back to New York.

This time, Gareth hooks us up with a private jet. The pro of this arrangement is that the flight crew, who know Gareth, have prepared all his favorite things to eat and drink.

The con side is that I know this lifestyle won't last for me. The private plane ride is like enjoying a delicious meal with the knowledge that you'll never have it again.

Plus, I've been washing and wearing the same outfits for

three weeks and it's starting to get gross and terribly monotonous for someone who loves clothes. "Can I have your address?" I ask.

Gareth is in the process of donning his weird eye mask. "Why?"

"I'm going to see if my grandma can ship me some clothes."

He removes the mask as his eyebrows creep up his forehead and he leans in toward me. "I'll let you in on a little secret here, Cookie. I own a warehouse full of clothing. I'll have Darcy send some stuff over to the penthouse."

"But—" I'm about to tell him that I've spent an amount of time bordering on obsessive making my own stuff and I want to wear it.

He yawns. "You work for the company now. It makes sense you'd wear the label," he says before he puts the mask back on and falls asleep.

I shudder at the thought of becoming another one of his black-tee-and-jeans-clad cronies. On the other hand, he's offering me a free designer wardrobe and, as someone who loves clothes, I feel ridiculous objecting.

We arrive back in New York on the first day of October. Gareth says October is the best month in the city. "The weather is nice. Summer crowds are gone. Holiday tourists haven't shown up yet. It's perfect."

Gareth lives in the West Village, a quirky, bohemian neighborhood that people like William Faulkner and Isadora Duncan once called home, in a renovated World War II–era building. To call the place a hipster pad would be a laughable understatement. There are electric-car charging stations everywhere in the parking garage, an indoor lap pool and a doorman who spends his days greeting the florists dropping off Raf Simons arrangements in square vases.

His entire apartment is decorated like one of his runway shows. All white and stainless steel. What he has in the way of furniture is all in cascading shades of beige. It's a strangely impersonal choice from a designer whose claim to fame is dressing people in candy colors and oddball prints.

I call Grandma first of all.

"Of course, you know, this is gettin' more and more worrisome, girl."

"I'm fine, Grandma. I just didn't realize I'd have to stay in New York. I guess I should have read the documents more carefully."

"I'll second that," she says with a snort.

"But it's fine. I'm fine."

"You're just livin' with a man you ain't married to in New York City."

I want to laugh at the way she spits out the words *New York City.* Like I've purchased a summer home in Sodom and Gomorrah. "We're not living together. I'm just staying here...because, well...my internship..."

"I see."

There's a pause and she adds, "Your teacher's been callin' here. Sayin' something about your scholarship. Cookie. I'm not gonna find out you're losin' your scholarship over some man, am I?"

"No. Of course not. This internship is a great opportunity. I'll be back in January. I have until March to finish my makeup work. It's fine, Grandma." I take a deep breath. It has to be fine. I'm living my dream.

"Fine," she repeats. "You know your momma—"

"I'm not her." *I'm not her,* I repeat in my head as I hang up the phone. I'm focused on my career. Not my love life.

One good thing about my new situation is that Piper is in the city. While Gareth's busy doing a million things, I have a daily lunch date with my Aussie BFF.

We've been doing this for a couple of weeks but today, she's brought her new boyfriend, Brian. Or rather, "Brian Howowitz, Columbia pre-med." This is how he introduces himself.

I hate him instantly.

He's already pulled us away from the pub Piper suggested. She'd been texting me since yesterday about the greasy bar food, and I'd been fasting all day in favor of the pulled-pork nachos Piper told me would knock me off my barstool.

Piper's wearing a boring, basic pair of jeans and a boring Columbia tee. "All the kids from school hang out at 1020. Especially on the weekend. There's always a bunch of people playing darts in—"

First interruption: "That's the problem. It's noisy. I can't get through a sandwich without running into someone who wants to copy my notes. Let's hit Toast." Brian straightens his blue shirt. He already dresses like a doctor. He probably has two outfits. A chambray collared shirt with khakis and a gray, pinstriped suit.

We make the half-mile trek up Amsterdam. Piper smiles at me. "Don't worry, Cookie. Toast is excellent too. They have this mac and cheese that—"

Brian snorts. Interruption two: “No, no. It’s all about the burgers. The English burger and truffle fries. That’s what it’s all about.”

Toast isn’t bad. In fact, it has a patio that faces Broadway. We get a seat next to the patio’s red wood fence and, as cars honk and people speed by, I feel important. I’m lunching at a sidewalk café on Broadway—*the* Broadway.

“How is school?” I ask Piper.

“Mayfair is a total bastard. Last week, he announced we’ll be in these study groups and naturally I’m stuck with these tossers—”

Brian opens his mouth again, even though it has a massive bite of hamburger stuffed inside. A piece of bacon hits his chin as he speaks. Interruption three: “I told you. You need to go to Mayfair’s office hours. Tell him the situation is unworkable and you need to be reassigned.”

Not only am I sure Piper knows how to handle her classes, someone needs to stop this asshole who won’t let her complete a thought. I say, “But the professor might not like having someone argue with him about—”

Interruption four: “If she can’t argue with Mayfair, how’s she going to make arguments in court? You need to be more assertive, Piper.”

Piper is one of the most assertive people I know. If she gets any more assertive, she’ll have to become an MMA fighter or something. I give Brian the side-eye.

I turn his constant disruptions into my own drinking game, taking a sip of tea every time he interrupts someone. By the time I’m halfway done with my mac and cheese, I’m pretty much about to pee my pants.

And he sticks me with the check.

"I'm mean, you're with Gareth Miller, right?" he says as he passes me the leather folio containing the bill.

After lunch, Brian walks to the corner searching for a place to hail a cab.

"Let's just take the bus," Piper calls up to him, but he ignores her. She turns to me. "Doesn't he have a sexy, sexy ass?" she asks.

We both watch Brian for a second. I can't deny he probably is pretty hot underneath that boring preppy shirt. But… I snort. "Uh, yeah. Too bad he *is* an ass."

Piper whirls around and her dark, sleek ponytail whacks her in the face. "What?"

Foot-in-mouth much? "Uh, did I say that out loud? That was my inside voice." I'm hoping she'll let this slide as a bit of girl humor.

"Your inside voice thinks my boyfriend is an asshole?" She's got her hands on her hips, and the breeze created by the heavy traffic pushes her T-shirt against her curvy frame.

"Well…"

"Yeah?"

"Come on. He hasn't let either of us finish a sentence in almost two hours. You…you think…you don't have to…" I'm about to say *settle. You don't have to settle.* I see Brian. Handsome, WASPy doctor. With the slamming of a taxi door, it hits me. He's not a *settle*. He's a status symbol. A guy for the girl who, society says, is never supposed to get *the guy*. We've always assumed the thin girl would get the prince, and now Piper has done it. But fairy tales never told us much about the prince's personality or informed us how he treats the princess as they ride off together in the pumpkin coach.

Piper watches Brian and scowls. But I'm an idiot and I keep talking.

I'm almost pleading with her. "I mean, don't you think he's a little…uh…controlling?"

"Controlling?" Piper's raised her voice to be high and shrill over all the noise. "You think *Brian's* controlling?" She's glaring at me. We're having a fight. We've never fought since that first day at Fairy Falls. "Have you looked in the mirror lately?"

"What do you mean?"

Brian is coming back toward us and in a few seconds he'll be within earshot.

Piper steps closer to me. "I mean, your boyfriend tells you where to go, what to do and even what to wear. And you're calling Brian controlling?"

Brian hears that last line and scowls at me.

As if to prove Piper's point, Gareth's hired Town Car pulls up to the curb. I catch my reflection in the dark glass of the passenger window.

I shiver as my mother's face stares back at me.

FAT: Days 31–32 of NutriNation

I've eaten the same thing every day for three weeks.

For breakfast, I make an egg sandwich and a banana smoothie. At lunch, I eat a bento box of cubed cheese, almonds and fresh fruit. Dinner is a Lean Cuisine frozen meal and steamed veggies. Every day. For three weeks.

I keep myself busy making a matching gray jacket for Tommy, creating a full suit. It's not easy. Grandma has to get involved with the shoulder divots and fitting the waist. She's got this pamphlet called *Sewing for Boys and Men*, that cost a dollar back whenever mismatched plaid suits were in style. But the thing knows what it's talking about and Tommy's suit ends up totally *GQ*.

It's after school on Tuesday and Tommy's at my house trying it on. He'll look great for his parents' party this weekend.

And for the dance.

In the halls at school, they've started to hang up posters for the winter formal. Tommy and I always go to the dances together, usually because he's got this lame idea that later on we'll positively remember these moments of forced socialization. Most of the time, I give him a ton of crap.

Not this time.

This is my chance. The only thing I've been thinking about since the meteor shower.

The dance has this kooky James Bond theme. I think it's stupid, but it could be worse. They could have gone for *High School Musical* Holiday or something. Plus, the '60s were good for women's fashion in a number of ways. I've been making a killer outfit. I'm down a size since I started NutriNation, and I plan to dress to impress.

I have this idea that the metal accents on my dress will sparkle just right on the dance floor. Like falling stars. And Tommy will see me. Really see me. Then we can be more than best friends and go to the prom and live happily ever after in a Barbie Dreamhouse that has a design studio for me and a terrace for Tommy's telescope.

I'm seriously thinking this can happen.

"You wearing this to the dance?" I ask Tommy.

"The dance?" he echoes.

"You know, 00-Snow?" When he continues to stare at me like I'm a martian, I add, "The winter formal. Should I get the tickets? Or do you want to?"

"I got tickets last week," he says.

"Oh. Great." I smile at him. "You've got the suit. I'm almost done with my dress. And it's fabulous."

Tommy's running his hands over the gray wool of the jacket and turning red in the face.

"You mind if I pay you for my ticket on Friday? That's when I get my check from Donutville."

"No," he says. "I don't mind. I mean, you don't have to pay me."

"Of course I do," I say. But my mind is doing cartwheels. *Omigod. Omigod.* He's asking me on a real date. Sparkle. Sparkle. Barbie Dreamhouse. Genetically perfect, postcareer children with dimples.

"No, I mean, I thought that… I didn't think… You always say…"

"Stop doing that to the wool or it'll become felted or something," I say with a frown as he's still rubbing his coat. The sparkles are fading. "What's wrong?"

"You hate dances. I assumed you'd be happy to get out of this one. I didn't think you wanted to go. I should have said something."

"But you just said you already got the tickets." The sparkles are completely gone. A bulldozer is knocking down the Barbie Dreamhouse. I realize what's happening. The expression on his face says everything. "You're going with her."

"You hate dances, Cookie."

"I don't hate them. They're okay."

"When we went to homecoming, you said that the school should use the dance to recruit volunteers for a eugenics program. You said you wished the DJ would get dragged off by a sun bear. You said you needed to get home to sanitize your toothbrush."

"Well…" Things have changed. I know what I want now.

"Kennes loves dances."

"Of course she does."

He slides the jacket off his shoulders. He's gotten hot and sweaty. "What's that supposed to mean?"

I reach out and take it from him and put it on a hanger. "That she's a superficial narcissist who is probably always on the lookout for opportunities to show off and make herself feel superior to other people."

Grandma comes out of her room. It's almost time for *Wheel of Fortune*. "Cookie, that ain't too nice," she says, setting her lips in a white line. Grandma is many things, but she is never rude.

"No, it's not," Tommy agrees.

Tommy and Grandma watch *Wheel of Fortune* together. It's kind of their thing. The value of a friend who has a thing with my grandma isn't lost on me.

On TV, Pat Sajak says, "And the category is Phrase."

"Friends with benefits," Tommy calls out.

Very funny, universe.

Grandma marks a point for him on her score pad. They tally it up. It's 246 to 232. Tommy's gaining on Grandma.

After he leaves, Grandma shuts off the TV and turns to me. I don't want to hear what she has to say. Grandma really gets me, without us having to talk a lot, without having to put a bunch of awkward stuff in words. Mostly that's a good thing, but sometimes…

"At church today, Father Tim told me your daddy's been trying to get ahold of you on that fancy machine of yours. Sending you that E stuff."

"Email."

"Yes. That. E-*mail.* E-*banks.* E-this. E-that. Honestly, is it too much trouble to send a real letter these days? People are so busy but…"

I tune out the rest of her lecture on the good ole days and am staring out into space when she pats my arm.

"Tommy likes that girl," she says.

"I know."

"That don't mean he'll be with her forever. That don't mean someday he won't be with you. You all are seventeen, for crying out loud."

"I know."

She gets up from the couch and lumbers into the kitchen. Pots and pans clank as she starts dinner. "Well, if you *know*," she calls from the other room. "Then what the *H E* double hockey sticks are you doin', Cookie? 'Cuz surely you must *know* that if you keep after that girl, you ain't gonna have a boyfriend nor a *friend*. Mark my words. This too shall pass. Wait it out with a smile on your face. He'll come around."

Her head of gray curly hair pops in from the kitchen. "You want some dinner?"

I shake my head. "I'm doing Lean Cuisine."

She nods and ducks back into the kitchen. "Take the high road, Cookie.

"And use that doodad to E-whatever your father," she adds.

"Hmm," I say, noncommittally.

"Heartbreak is a funny thing, Cookie. It does things to people," Grandma says. "Your daddy, he's doing the best that he can."

"So am I."

I go back to my room and open up my laptop. Sure enough, I see another message from Dad with the subject line Greetings from Gwabe. The messages he sends always read like personalized versions of his fund-raising newsletters, not letters that a father should send his only daughter. I move it into my "From Dad" folder without reading it. If Dad wants to talk to me, he knows where to find me.

But I do give what Grandma said about Tommy some real thought.

Her advice rattles around in my brain as I work at the *SoScottsdale* office the next afternoon. The phone in the bull pen rings. The caller ID displays *Ms. Butterfield.* Brittany makes a noise that's part disgusted snort and part cough. I pick up the receiver.

"Uh, hello?" I say. Kennes sits maybe ten feet from us and my left ear can hear her talking from her office while her snotty voice comes through the telephone into my right ear.

"Good afternoon, Cookie. Could you please come into my office for a brief meeting?" This is what she says. Like a child impersonating her father.

There's a collective eye roll among the interns as I make my way across the room. Somehow the blog that has, in the past, been unable to work a bagel bucket into its budget can now afford a garish redecoration of Kennes's office.

Pink-and-black damask is everywhere. There's damask wallpaper and a desk mat and a pencil cup *and* a bulletin board. Yes, there is a pink-and-black damask bulletin board on a pink-and-black damask wall. It creates this weird optical illusion that probably gives you a seizure if you stare too long.

I'm surprised to find Marlene's already in there, sitting across from Kennes in one of the room's two visitor chairs. She's nodding and laughing and examining a small statue of the Eiffel Tower. It's one of many that clutter Kennes's desk.

"Because I love fashion, you know," she tells Marlene. They both laugh.

I want to say, *What the hell does collecting tacky razzmatazz trinkets that would bring a smile to the face of Dolores Umbridge have to do with fashion? I'm* the one who loves fashion. I have my own collection of designer paper dolls organized by decade and a set full of fangirlish scrapbooks devoted to all my favorite designers.

Take the high road, Cookie.

I say nothing and shuffle around with a bland expression on my face. Marlene waves to the chair next to her and motions for me to sit.

Kennes takes in my dazed look. "Because *Paris* is the fashion capital of the world," she says, like she's explaining a basic fact of reality to a five-year-old.

"New York," I mumble under my breath.

"What?" Kennes demands.

Marlene turns my way. She's still smiling, but her eyes are crinkling up in worry.

"Um...I think Paris *was* the fashion capital of the world for most of the twentieth century. Now I think it's New York."

Marlene cocks her head good-naturedly and Kennes doesn't comment. I could quit there. But because I have a chronic case of foot-in-mouth disease or because I'm pathologically incapable of taking the high road, I add, "I guess I need to get a bunch of Statue of Liberty knickknacks to prove I love fashion too."

Kennes's face shifts into a dark mask. Before she can speak, Marlene says, "Well, we were just having a discussion about new features we could add to the blog. We've got some good ideas and want to have you involved."

Kennes is glaring at me. I'm pretty sure the only thing she wants me to get involved in is a Cosa Nostra–style hit. Also, what is with her hair? It's smooth and clipped like there's a servant running around Butterfield manor whose only job is to keep the princess from the horror of split ends.

"We have a great idea for a holiday feature designed to target younger readers. We'll follow Kennes through the process of preparing for a winter formal. Dress selection, hair and makeup..." Marlene is waving her hand as she lists all the fabulous things the daughter of Jameson Butterfield will be doing as she goes to the dance with my...my friend.

It's my turn to glare as Kennes adds, "I'll be partnering with a local designer for my dress for the dance." Oh. Of course she will.

"And best of all, you get to write it," Marlene says, her voice getting loud and full of incredible enthusiasm.

Oh. Of course I do.

I'm choking on the idea of blogging about my archrival's dream date and almost miss it when Marlene throws me a bone. "The presentation is on Friday, December 12. Do you think you can be ready?"

Marlene and Kennes are staring at me again. "What?" I say.

"Can you be ready with an idea to pitch to Jameson Butterfield? He'll be accepting proposals at the meeting and there are some big promotional opportunities, big marketing bucks, up for grabs. We've always talked about you having your own feature," Marlene says.

We *have* always talked about it, but in the *someday when I win the lottery* kind of way. Sort of like, someday after the blog can afford two-ply toilet paper, we'll also sink some money into promoting a new feature. For it to work, a new feature needs artwork, advertising and, ideally, a launch party.

"So?" Marlene prompts.

I can't imagine what on earth I'd propose to Jameson Butterfield, but Kennes smirks at me from over Marlene's shoulder. "Yeah," I say. "I'll be ready." There's no way I'm backing down from her silent challenge.

"Great." Clad in yet another fabulous outfit, Marlene rises and leaves Kennes's gaudy office. Her little black dress has to be Lanvin, has to be silk and has to cost at least $3,500. She must have really cashed in on the blog sale.

But Marlene is right. This is a huge opportunity. The comeback kind. The kind that could resuscitate my dream of a Parsons scholarship. If I could earn the backing of someone like Jameson Butterfield, well, that's the kind of thing that people tend to notice.

With our boss out the door, Kennes says, "Hey, Cookie, my dad and I are pretty close. If you need any tips on what he likes, let me know." She's doing a decent impression of a thoughtful person and I can see Marlene nodding at me as she walks to her own office. She's grinning like someone who's just set up her two favorite people on a blind date.

I'm leaving too. Kennes follows me, standing in the doorway, talking loud so that Brittany and Shelby, who watch us from the bull pen, will be certain to hear. "Oh. Cookie. One thing. The local designer I mentioned, well, it's *you*. I can't wait to see what you come up with. I'll email you my measurements and my thoughts on the look."

She gives me a white, bright, razzle-dazzle smile. "I'd love to tell my father what a good job you did on this project."

The undertone is clear. No dress. No feature.

I'll be playing the part of fairy godmother to one vicious Cinderella.

SKINNY: Days 780–781 of NutriNation

"I'm not ignoring you. I'm cramming," Piper says.

I've been calling her and leaving messages for days. This is the first time she's picked up the phone.

"Brian is great and I was a jerk. I am a jerk. Can we just have lunch or something?" I ask.

She gives me a do-over. We meet at 1020 and I finally get my pulled-pork nachos. They make the words I have to say almost worth it. "Brian is really great. I don't know what's wrong with me." What's wrong is that Brian is a total douche. But I remember the advice Grandma gave me two years ago. Take the high road. This too shall pass. What if I had listened? Things might have turned out differently.

I can be different now. I can pretend to like Brian. "I mean, pre-med? That's impressive and tough, right?"

Piper relaxes on her barstool. There's a crack as someone in the back starts a game of pool. "He wasn't having the best day when you met him," she says. "But after you left…it wound up being positive. We talked, and he's been different. I think he's trying to manage his stress better."

"Well, don't worry, I'll be on my good behavior next time."

She pushes her thick hair back. "Living in New York is a big adjustment."

These are the lies that we agree to accept to preserve our friendship. Brian is not a know-it-all, controlling asshole and my attitude problems are due to the fact that New York has more big buildings than Phoenix.

I point at Piper's jeans and say, "My question is, what are you wearing?"

She laughs. I'm still jealous of her teeth. "I only have a limited number of Cookie Vonn originals. You need to hurry up and finish those plus-size clothes you're working on with Gareth Miller, so I'll have something new to wear."

"I'll see what I can do."

After lunch, the Town Car drops me in front of Gareth's redbrick building. I'm getting too used to special treatment, to the way the doorman says, "Good afternoon, Miss Vonn," to the fact that all my expenses get charged to Gareth and I never hear about them again. A bit of my independence slips away each time I swipe Gareth's Amex.

I enter the apartment and forget about all of that as I hear the shower running. We've had tons of sex since that first time in Argentina, and yet there's something about the idea of Gareth and skin and hot water and steam that makes me shiver.

Creeping into the bedroom, I toss my black leather jacket on the bed, on top of Gareth's camel hair coat, and follow the sound of the water. Visions of stripping and joining him in the shower do a hostile takeover of my brain. The old me wouldn't have had the confidence to pull that kind of thing off and, honestly, I'm not sure if the new me does either.

I'm headed that way when I spot something on the stainless-steel console table outside the bathroom door. A familiar set of eyes peers at me from a photo tucked underneath a stack of paperwork.

My mother.

Hot and flushing for a new reason, I rifle through the papers. I can't believe it.

With the stack of papers in hand, I throw open the bathroom door. "You've been seeing my mom? Behind my back?"

Gareth's wet head sticks out of the white, marble shower and the dickhead has the nerve to look startled. His perfectly plucked eyebrows arch up his forehead. "What? What are you talking about?"

Now I'm thinking maybe I'll jump in the shower and drown him, and I know I need to get out of that room. I stomp into the bedroom, glance at a Louis Vuitton case Gareth gave me, but instead start stuffing my clothes into the canvas tote bag I designed.

Gareth comes in with a fluffy white towel tied around his waist, water rolling down his legs onto the beige carpet. He takes in what I'm doing and says, "What is happening here?"

"We had a deal."

"*Had* a deal?" he repeats. "We have a deal." He bites his lower lip and quietly adds, "And a relationship."

It's his first verbal acknowledgment that I'm more to him

than an intern he's screwing, but I ignore this. I ignore the warmth that's returning to my body at the sight of him pacing around as I pack. Filled with hot jealousy, I toss the papers at him and say again, "You've been seeing my mom," in a flat voice.

Gareth grunts. "I'm not *seeing* her, Cookie. I spoke to her for about two minutes. She needs a job. Needs money. I thought I'd help her out. Have her do a show. Maybe Fall/Winter."

"That's just great, Gareth. You're a real fucking Robin Hood."

"What exactly is the problem here?" he asks. He steps in front of me, stopping me from making it to the closet. "And what the hell are you doing?"

"I'm leaving."

"Cookie, for God's sake. I didn't do your mother in the men's room or something. I gave her a job. For you. I thought you would..." He trails off. Like he expected me to greet him at the door wrapped in Saran wrap.

O Gareth, my savior.

"We agreed this wouldn't happen."

He shakes his head. "We agreed your mother wouldn't be involved in our capsule collection. I assumed it was because you didn't want people crying nepotism."

"It's not."

"She said she was going to lose her damn apartment." He's almost pleading with me. He makes a grab for the tote bag, but I swing it out of his reach.

"She should lose it, Gareth," I say. He takes a step back. I'm being really loud. The bedroom windows shake and vibrate. I force myself to lower my voice. "When I was eight,

I broke my arm. I fell off the monkey bars. They took me to the hospital and...well...my teacher stayed as long as she could. They kept trying to call my mom. She never came. She'd run off that day with Chad Tate. Just took off. I don't even know what would have happened if I'd gone home that day after school. That's why I..." I suck in a deep breath and fight back the tears. "That's when I had to go live with Grandma."

Gareth tries to give me a hug but I push him back. "She hurts people. Destroys everything around her. And there's always someone running behind with a broom and dustpan. Sweeping everything under the rug. Making sure she never has to see the broken pieces. I'm tired of this world that says it's okay for beautiful people to be careless and cruel."

"Cookie, I'm sorry. I thought I was helping you." He waves his hands in frustration and stands in front of me.

"When I want your help, I'll ask for it." I try to move around him.

"Will you?" he asks. He reaches out, first grabbing me by the shoulders and then grasping my chin lightly in one hand. I'm forced to stare into his perfect brown eyes where gold flakes pulse and glow. "You give me a deer-in-headlights look every time I so much as buy you a sandwich. I have to read your blog to find out that you want to go to Parsons. Why don't you ask me for help with that?"

"Because you love it when people use you to advance their careers?" I'm trying to stay hostile, trying to pump up the anger draining out of me.

And now I'm staring at his abs. He smirks at me. "Is that what's happening, Cookie Vonn? You're using me?"

"Of course not," I snap. Flexed arm muscles. Patches of dark hair on his chest. Full lips that turn up at the ends.

He brings his hands to rest on my hips, feeling for the edges of my T-shirt.

I put my hands over his to stop them from moving upward. "Gareth. Would you like it if I contacted *your* mother without discussing it with you?"

"No," he answers. "I guess I wouldn't." Through the windows behind him, lights come on in the brownstones across the street. "But that situation is complicated."

"So is mine."

"Point taken. I just want you to be happy. I want to take care of you." It's a surprisingly frank statement.

Imitating his gesture, I put my hand on his chin and tilt his face down toward mine. "It's her or me, Gareth."

He doesn't hesitate for even a second. "You."

I love him. In that moment. It's real. He's real.

Dropping my canvas bag on the floor, I pull his towel off.

He snaps off the light and whispers in my ear, "It's you, Cookie. Only you."

The next morning, Gareth tries to take the contract, but I keep it. We agree that he'll officially handle things with his manager, but that I'll tell my mom.

I spend the morning writing a series of truly crappy articles for my blog. They're not good enough to post on a sanitation department website, and I drag them into the trash.

Around noon, I call for the car service. My mom doesn't tend to get mobilized until hours that end in p.m. While I don't feel like I have to rush, I want this to be done. I want to close the file and get on with my life.

It says everything about our relationship that I don't even know where my mom lives. I have to get her address off the contract.

She's got a place on Charles Street, a short and squat glass tower with its back to the Hudson River. It's about ten minutes from Gareth's place and if everything is really all about location, then the Charles, surrounded by boutiques like Diane von Fürstenberg and Stella McCartney, is perfect for a shameless supermodel.

There are only two apartments on Mom's floor, so the place isn't hard to find. I spend a few minutes knocking on the door. No sound coming from inside has to mean Chad Tate isn't there. That guy can't go five minutes without ESPN blaring at full volume.

I turn to leave, both relieved and disappointed, and see Mom getting off the elevator. She joins me at the door to her apartment, overloaded with bags from Saks. Typical she'd plead poverty to Gareth even as she's out charging up a storm.

And yes, she's beautiful. She walks the hall like it's a runway in her model's uniform of skinny jeans and a fitted T-shirt that's probably made from cashmere. Her hair is dyed the same shade of blond as mine. This is me in a time-machine mirror.

"Cookie? What are you doing…here?" she asks.

Here. Because I've barely spoken to my mom in the last few years. Because me visiting her at home is freakier than the passing of the Hale-Bopp Comet.

"Gareth told me you approached him behind my back about doing his next show. I'm here to let you know he decided to go in a different direction." I rip the unsigned contract in half, drop the pieces in one of her tote bags.

I turn around and walk back toward the elevator.

Mom leaves her bags next to the apartment door and trails after me. It occurs to me, for the first time, that we're the exact same height. In our heels, we're both close to six feet tall.

"He already agreed. My agent said—"

Without facing her, I shake my head. "I made it clear that he could choose to be in business with you or in a relationship with me. He chose me." I'm pressing the down button over and over as the sound of her heels echoes down the hallway.

"You're going to have to go back and tell him—"

"I won't. Stay out of my life. Stay away from me."

"This isn't about you, Cookie."

I whirl around to face her. "No. See, you're wrong. The only reason Gareth was going to give you the job was as a favor to me. He doesn't need you. He doesn't want you. He was doing it for me. So for the first time in the history of our existence, it *is* finally about me."

Mom runs back to the door, rummages around in one of the bags for something and hustles back. It's a baby blanket. A $500 blanket from Saks probably knitted from yarn they took from Himalayan sheep and dyed with caviar. "I'm pregnant."

"Congratulations." I'm wondering where the fucking elevator is. I swear. *Where the fuck does that thing go? To the moon and back?* "Do me a favor. Don't invite me to the baby shower. Not everyone thinks the second coming of *Rosemary's Baby* is something to celebrate."

The tears start falling from Mom's blue eyes. "I'm begging you. This is my last chance to work before I'm showing. After that, I'll be lucky if I can book another big campaign for a year. No one else will pay what Gareth is offering. I'm your mother and—"

The elevator doors finally swing open and I get inside. "*Now* you're my mother? You weren't my mother when I broke my arm. You weren't my mother when you ran off with Chad Tate. You weren't my mother every time I've ever needed food or clothes or shelter or money for college. I could be dead for all you care. But now that *you* want something from *me*, we're one big happy fucking family?"

She sees the tears won't work and they're gone. Replaced by cold anger. She extends her arm to keep the elevator doors from closing. "Oh sure. I'm the worst mother in the world. Of course, you never mention your father. Where the hell is he?"

"Curing malaria in Ghana."

"He's hiding from his fucking responsibilities. I was twenty and pregnant and he wanted to run all over the world being Jack fucking Shephard. But you love him and you hate me. Fine. Cookie. Fine. But please, you have to help me—"

She's wrong. I don't think dear old Dad is any better, but he does have an excuse for his shithead behavior that's easier for me to swallow. "You know, asking me to have sympathy for you is like the lion eating the zebra and asking for its pity."

The door tries to close again and Mom stands in front of it. "You think I haven't been where you are? Stood in your shoes? Been the nineteen-year-old that men like Gareth Miller would pay anything to fuck?"

I push the first-floor button hard, over and over. "He's not paying to fuck me. We're working together on a collection. Don't assume for a second that you and I are alike in any way. I'm taking care of myself. I've been taking care of myself for years."

"Cookie, please—"

I push the buttons in the elevator a few more times in futility. "Why did you name me Cookie?"

A blank expression settles across Mom's face. "You've heard that story a million times. The nurse—"

"I've heard it," I interrupt. "Be honest with me. For once. One time. Here in this hallway it's only you and me. It was a punishment. Like a curse or something. The first time you saw me. You couldn't stand me and you wanted everyone to know it."

Mom puts one hand on her cashmere-covered hip and her baby blue eyes narrow. "You have no idea what it's like to be me."

There's a creaking sound.

A little old man who looks strangely like Noam Chomsky comes out of the other apartment on Mom's floor and hobbles into the elevator. She has no choice but to move her arm and let me go. I tap my foot the entire way down. I can't breathe. The whole building feels like it's infected with pepper-sprayed air.

On the first floor, I hold the elevator door open and wait for the old man to exit.

"Ah, you're such a good girl. Have a nice day."

This is what he says to me.

Another reminder of the superficial nature of the world.

I glance down at my Gareth Miller black dress with its white Peter Pan collar.

I look like a good girl. But I don't feel like one.

FAT: Day 48 of NutriNation

"I need you to do something for me, okay?" Tommy says.

I'm trying to concentrate on what he's saying, but he has a sandwich. A real one. With white bread and gooey peanut butter dripping out the sides. Not made with sandwich thins and some freaky peanut powder they sell at the health food store.

Grape jelly.

"Can you do it?" he asks.

"What?"

He rolls his eyes at me from his seat at the picnic table. The weather is nice, so we've taken seats outside the Mountain Vista cafeteria. Kennes is across the courtyard. She's mastered the Scottsdale uniform of jeans with rhinestones on the ass and a nearly see-through T-shirt.

I glance down at my tie-dyed T-shirt covered with a swirl of ironic, yawning cats. Kennes and I aren't even living in the same fashion universe.

Once word got out Kennes was a billionaire's daughter,

she had no shortage of attention-seeking sycophants jockeying for her friendship and shored herself up with a snobby mixture of cheerleaders and jocks. There'd been a couple of days when I felt sure she planned to transfer her affections for Tommy to some loser on the lacrosse team, but that didn't pan out. She wanted him because she knew I did.

Kennes crosses the yard to toss her trash and gives Tommy a flirtatious wave. I lean into his field of view as he grins back at her.

"Do what?" I repeat.

He returns to the moment. "Oh. Meet me after school. I have to go over to Toys"R"Us and return some of my Lego sets. But I've been…well…I've taken a lot of stuff back recently and they keep giving me crap. So I need you to return the stuff."

"We'll have to do it fast," I say. "My shift starts at five."

"We'll be in and out."

"Is everything okay?" I ask. He's watching Kennes as she walks off, and I can't tell if it's because he's hot for her and wants to make out behind the portables or if he's worried about something.

He nods, smiles and chews his sandwich.

After lunch, I have to dress for PE. I'm one of the few seniors taking it. You need one semester to graduate, and I should have gotten it out of the way freshman year like almost everybody else.

The only thing that sucks worse than PE is PE on Friday when you're stuck watching the seconds to the weekend tick by as you try to square dance or play volleyball. I reach into my locker for my gym shorts and drop them immediately.

They smell. I mean really smell and I realize that I meant to take them home the day before and wash them. Luckily, I keep an old pair of sweats for an emergency.

It's one of the few times of the year that the temperature isn't a thousand degrees outside, so this is when they make us run. It's only a mile, but in the past, I would have ditched. Or I would have been in the locker room trying to find a way to fake spraining my ankle.

Now I'm kind of okay with the running. I've been doing five miles on a regular basis with my NutriNation group. But today, Houston, we have a problem. My sweats are falling off.

I have to use one hand to hold on to the waistband as I walk-run around Mountain Vista's orange track. I'm still one of the first to finish, even with my weird sideways shuffle.

"Well, Miss Vonn, I nominate you for most improved PE student of the decade," Coach O'Grady says as I pass her. She's the opposite of the butch female coach stereotype. She looks like she might have been Susan Lucci in a past life. She checks her stopwatch and makes a note on her clipboard. "You're just under ten minutes. At the start of the semester, you were over twenty."

"Uh...thanks," I say. It's sort of a backhanded compliment.

"You've dropped a lot of weight. You look great."

I'm down fifty pounds and I should be thrilled, but it's super awkward to have people call attention to me. It's like people think they're saying something that should make me feel really great. Instead, it's a reminder that they didn't like the way I looked before. That I'm fat and everybody has been judging me all along.

"Keep it up, Miss Vonn."

"Uh, sure," I say.

I pick up the pace of my walk both to get away from O'Grady and to have more time to change. I'm almost outside the track fence when I hear her call, "You'll need to bring in some pants that fit, though, Miss Vonn."

Behind me, a couple of girls snicker. I don't look back.

After school, I follow Tommy's truck to Superstition Springs Mall, where there's a Toys"R"Us on the south side. He pulls Lego Mindstorm sets out of the cab of the truck for what seems to be forever. I know he's king of the nerds and captain of the school's FIRST Lego League team, but this is excessive even for him.

"Jeez, did you and your team of dorks hijack the Polar Express or something?"

"No," he says. "Of course not. Why do you ask?"

I roll my eyes. "Why do I ask if you've become a train bandit and joined the Conrail Boyz? It's a joke, Tommy."

"Oh. Okay."

He frowns and is way off his A-game as we load the Mindstorms into a shopping cart and I push it into the store.

Tommy grabs a second cart and says, "All you have to do is take the returns over to Customer Service. Tell them you need store credit. I'll meet you right back here."

"Okay."

As I approach the customer service counter, I can see the bleached-blonde girl behind the counter is thinking the same thing as me. *What the hell?*

"I need to return these." I hand her the receipt I got from Tommy. The total on the receipt is more than $6,000. These fucking Mindstorm sets are $100 each. Tommy's parents do okay, but they're not Jay-Z and Beyoncé. My stomach starts to churn out extra acid. It hits me that I should have asked a few follow-up questions.

But I'm committed now, and Blondie reaches into a drawer and pulls out a form. "What's the reason for the return?"

"Uh..." I realize I don't know the answer. Tommy didn't tell me why he needed to exchange all this stuff.

The clerk reaches into the cart and pulls one of the sets out. "I guess they're damaged?" she supplies.

I look down and see that she's right. Each box is partially torn or smashed on one side. "Uh. Yeah," I say.

"I need your driver's license."

I hand it to her and she starts scanning the Mindstorms. She makes it through the first couple and then the computer beeps. She scowls at the screen and presses a few keys. And then a few more. Then she's typing like she's decided to do a complete rewrite of *Hamlet* while I wait. She picks up the phone. "I need assistance at Customer Service. Code three."

Code three doesn't sound positive.

The speed of my pulse picks up but I tell myself that, with all this stuff, she probably needs a manager's signature or something. I turn toward the store window and wave my hand to get Tommy's attention. He's standing next to his car watching me with a puzzled frown. A few feet from me, there's a loud scene developing as a mom wrestles a Sponge-Bob doll from a wailing toddler.

"I need you to come with me."

I jump as I find a large, balding man in a tan blazer standing right next to my left elbow. Blondie is passing him my driver's license.

"What?" Out of the corner of my eye, I see Tommy closing the distance to the store.

"You need to come with me, uh, Miss Vonn." He reads my name off my ID.

"Wait. Wait," I say. "I'm not going anywhere with you. I don't even know you." I take a step back toward the exit door. It's about five feet behind me and stuck in an open position. I consider making a break for it.

He reaches out and grabs my elbow. It doesn't hurt, but I won't be going anywhere either. "Darren Smith. Store security. You need to come with me."

Before Tommy can make it inside, Darren Smith guides me to a gray door in the rear of the store, up a flight of stairs and into a small office, also gray. A large whiteboard with two columns, one labeled "Police Report Number" and the other "Status," hangs behind a clean metal desk.

He closes the door, drops me into the chair in front of the desk, and takes the seat behind. With the two of us in the cramped, claustrophobic space, I'm flushing and breathing hard.

"I suppose you know you're in a lot of trouble." Darren Smith opens the top drawer of the desk and produces a notepad and a pen.

The pen clicks.

"If you'd like to give a statement, we might be able to avoid making this a police matter."

"What? I don't understand…what?" I stammer in shock.

Smith grunts. "Young lady, you wheeled a cart full of

more than $5,000 in stolen Lego sets into the store. That's not the kind of thing where the cops show up and give you a desk appearance ticket. You get arrested. For grand theft."

"I had a receipt for that stuff. That blonde girl took it from me…and I…I don't know…and um…" I'm trying to make some kind of sense of what's happening. Tommy's behavior. The bizarre amount of merchandise he had.

"Obviously, we're interested in the identities of the shoplifters."

"Shoplifters? I had a receipt…"

He drops his pen and pulls the black desk phone close to him. "So we're doing this the hard way, I guess. Okay. Well, here's the part where I tell you that we've been working in conjunction with the Maricopa County Sheriff's Office on an operation designed to put a stop to this little return-fraud racket of yours."

"Return fraud? Um…"

"We added individual serial numbers to the items in our Mindstorm inventory and sprayed them with code-laced liquid. We can prove the sets you tried to return were stolen from various stores in the valley, and we have your friends on CCTV, so cut the crap, young lady."

He's staring at me with an expression that combines anger with impatience with disbelief. He shakes his head. "Either you are a better actress than Meryl Streep, or you're a complete moron."

This comment fires up my engine. "Or I have no idea what you're talking about."

Darren Smith smirks. "Sure. I suppose you just found all that stuff sitting in the parking lot."

"I had a receipt."

The smirk fades. "Look, I might be able to buy that someone put you up to this. But I would need you to tell me who."

Tommy.

I can't rat him out. "I don't know what you're talking about."

"I'm talking about return fraud. Typically, someone goes into a store and steals an item for the purpose of taking it back and receiving a 'refund.'" Smith makes air quotes when he says the word *refund*.

Tommy.

The guy who spent three weekends helping reroof Grandma's house is involved in a shoplifting ring.

"In this case, your pals come into the store and steal Lego. Since they often have to damage the boxes in the process of removing the security sensors, they come back and buy a set like the one they have stolen."

Tommy.

The guy who'd driven me to Donutville on five seconds notice when my car broke down.

"They bring the stolen, damaged Mindstorms back to the store—using the receipts for the ones they purchased—and trade them in for sets in good condition. Then they sell both sets on eBay, pocketing the profit from the theft. Return fraud, Miss Vonn."

Tommy.

The guy who'd loaned me $600 without blinking when the airline said I was too fat to fly.

"So why don't you tell me who put you up to this?"

I shake my head.

There's nothing quite so disgraceful as being hauled out of a toy store in handcuffs while a bunch of five-year-olds gawk at you. You become the instant example of their parents' cautionary tales. *See, you better not stuff that Pokémon figure in your pocket, Billy, or you'll end up like that girl.*

Tommy's at the front having an argument with the blonde lady at the return desk. I only catch the last part as he says, "I *have* to see my friend."

I see the wide brown eyes of the boy who brought me dinner at Fairy Falls and told me stories of the stars, and I can't let him get in trouble. I'm not even sure that whatever's inside of him is tough enough to handle trouble. "Tommy. Go home."

His voice shakes. "C-C-Cookie. I'm sorry. I didn't know… I'll tell them—"

"You can't tell them what you don't know. Go home."

Mr. Darren Smith watches with interest. Maybe he's got a shoplifting quota and one more arrest equals a bonus. He's disappointed as Tommy walks back to his car. I am too. But I know it's better this way.

Smith calls the cops. We wait for them outside the front of the store.

It's actually the Mesa police who come to arrest me, although there's some talk of jurisdiction issues as they try to figure out exactly which Toys"R"Us stores the stolen Lego belong to.

They've got me in yet another small, gray room and they're discussing if, when and how to book me.

Then the cops call Grandma. Grandma calls Mom.

Mom sends Chad Tate.

Instant fraternity.

Chad Tate. The Chad Tate of the New York Giants. Yeah, the quarterback. The one who made that pass that one time. The one who scored that touchdown. The one with the $65,000 Super Bowl Ring.

Somehow in the span of about five minutes Chad Tate convinces the police I'm a mindless schoolgirl who could be talked into anything at any time by anybody. He signs autographs, poses for pictures and tells the story of that one time he threw the football.

I'd almost rather be in juvie than have Chad Tate's sophomoric antics be my Get Out of Jail Free Card. But Grandma's there too. And the look on her face.

I don't say anything.

They charge me with a misdemeanor and I get to go home.

Yep. I'd prefer jail to having Grandma look at me like that.

"Let's go, girl," she says.

We're in the parking lot and Grandma decides to wait on the bench out front for Chad Tate to bring the car around. I'm about to wait with her when Chad Tate says, "Come on, Cookie. We need to have a little talk."

"You in town for a game?" I ask as we walk through the parking lot.

He nods. He's got a completely sucky personality, but there's no getting around the fact that he's gorgeous. He's tall, has an almost comically chiseled jaw and spends eight hours a day lifting weights. After he retired from playing, the Giants gave their star player some kind of coaching job.

From what I can tell, it consists of pacing up and down the sidelines during games.

"Yep. Giants versus the Cards. Sunday at the University of Phoenix Stadium."

He opens the passenger door of his white, rented Mercedes. "And it's lucky for you that I happen to be in town. Otherwise you'd still be back there with the cops trying to figure out how many different cities they could have you arrested in."

I probably should be relieved. I probably should be grateful. But I'm not. "Yeah. Well, thanks. I'll consider this my Christmas gift for the past ten years."

Chad Tate gives me an appealing grin. "Funny." He pushes the start button of the car but doesn't drive. "I think we need to get a couple of things straight right now."

I roll my eyes at him. "Please don't tell me you plan to give me some lame 'I'm your stepfather' authority figure lecture. That really seems like a waste of time."

He ignores my comment. "First, you look good, Cookie."

Great. Another gross "compliment."

Plus, it's totally out of character, because Chad Tate's never had one nice thing to say about me in his life. He squeezes my arm in a super creepy fashion.

He's still smiling as if he expects the Channel 3 News Crew to show up any minute. "Second, whether you like it or not, I just saved your butt, and now you *owe* me." Chad Tate backs out of the parking space, stops the car in front of the station and waits for Grandma. "Sooner or later, I'm gonna want something from you. And you're gonna give it to me."

My face turns red in embarrassment and shame and anger. I'm pissed at Tommy for getting me into this mess. For putting me in this position with Chad fucking Tate. I'm mad as hell at Mom for being married to such an ass.

Chad Tate winks at me as I move to clear the front seat for Grandma. No one says anything else as we drive to the yellow house.

Tommy's outside sitting on the curb.

Grandma passes him without saying a word. She glares at him and yet again, I know she understands what's happening without me having to tell her.

I stop in front of him. He's been crying.

Chad Tate stares at the two of us for a second and pulls away.

"I'm sorry, Cookie. I'm sorry."

"You have been saying that a lot lately."

He gets up and grabs my hand. "I know. I'm sorry. I would have stayed. But you told me…you told me to go. I will… I can go back to the cops and…"

I stamp my foot on the sidewalk. "You're not going anywhere. There's no sense in both of us getting arrested. But what the hell is wrong with you? You're part of a shoplifting ring? Why? You have money. Your parents have money, and you've saved almost every dollar you've ever made from your lawn-mower business."

He bursts into tears.

This startles me, and I forget how mad I am.

Dropping my hand, he covers his face and sobs. "Yes. No. I don't know. I'm sorry."

I sigh. "Come on."

I yank on his shirt and pull him through the carport, into the backyard and past my old tetherball pole. Roscoe barks a couple times as we go by. I keep walking, through the oleander bushes blooming with pink flowers and into the alley.

"Okay. Talk," I say.

"I...I started out selling my extra Mindstorms on eBay. I had a few that were damaged. I decided to try to exchange them at the store so I could sell them. It seemed harmless. Then I met these people and they said that..."

"They had extra sets too?" I guess.

He nods. "I didn't realize they were stolen. The store didn't tell me that last time. They said I was bringing too much stuff back... I figured that...well, it's obvious in retrospect that they..."

I grunt in frustration. "What are you doing with all the money?"

The wind picks up, scattering pink flower petals across the alley. Tommy turns away from me.

"Tommy. What are you doing with the money?"

"Kennes. She comes from a really wealthy background and she's used to..." He trails off and stares into space.

"Are you fucking kidding me? That girl isn't good for you." It's taking all my self-control not to jump into my car, hunt Kennes down and beat the snot out of her.

"I know."

"You can't steal to buy shit for Kennes."

"I *know.*"

He's now pacing around the alley. He grabs me by the shoulders, and all of a sudden his lips are on mine. He's kissing me. His lips are firm and soft, his breath warm. The very tip of his tongue moves against my upper lip. My first real kiss. I've been dreaming of this. With Tommy. *My Tommy.* A shot of adrenaline explodes inside my veins and my heart soars. I've been waiting for this for so long.

It's too much. It's not enough.

He releases me and I stumble back. A cold settles over me.

We're silent for a few seconds. It's awkward.

I shake off the numbness. "You have to tell her, Tommy."

"I will." His voice is sincere, and he leans over to kiss me lightly on the cheek.

Somehow, this feels off too.

"Thank you, Cookie. Thank you for today."

I nod but then tense up again. The sun is setting behind the alley. I'm missing my shift at Donutville. "Shit. Shit. Shit. What time is it?"

Tommy smiles. "I called Steve. He's covering for you."

I relax. Sort of. I feel like I've done a hundred loop-the-loops on a roller coaster.

A dull confusion sets in as I wonder what this means for the future.

Tommy pats my back like things are going to be okay.

I hope they'll be okay.

SKINNY: Days 816–822 of NutriNation

Winter in New York.

In all of my fantasies about Parsons, I always had a bolt of fabric in one hand and a pair of shears in the other. I pictured myself in the classrooms shown on the school brochure. I never got around to thinking that going to Parsons would mean living in New York. I never imagined that reality.

I never imagined winter in New York.

I go with Piper to the lighting ceremony for the Christmas tree at Rockefeller Center. Thank God Brian's out of town so we don't get stuck with him, but he did tell us "…exactly what you need to do to see the tree. It's a mess down there if you don't know what you're doing."

I hate to admit it, but his advice turns out to be spot-on. He told us to check into the Jewel Hotel and head up to the Terrace Club. "Miller can afford it," he explained, "and his name will get you the best room and table."

They seat us at a table for two right up against the glass that surrounds the terrace. On the center of our white table, a small, golden candle glows. From where we are, on the balcony sipping Diet Cokes, we can sort of see the Rockettes and hear a Christian singer belt out "All I Want for Christmas." A huge crowd gathers below and every once in a while I spot a glow stick or light-up hat.

It's exciting to have an excuse to wear cute hats and gloves and the expensive green plaid wool coat Gareth gave me. When the lights on the tree pop on, there's the sound of "Oh!" from the crowd below. Something special has happened. I wonder if it's possible to capture the twinkle of the red, green and blue lights, the magic of the sparking crystal star and the collective dreams of the crowd into a garment. I snap a few pictures and make a mental note to blog about this idea.

Piper grins at me from across the table.

We watch the tree for a while. Her smile fades and she says, "Tommy called."

"He called you?" I haven't spoken to Tommy since his graduation party. Part of me wants to keep it that way. The other part doesn't want him talking to Piper and not me. The childish part, I guess.

"He knows about Gareth."

"So?"

"He doesn't like it."

I push my empty glass toward the edge of the table, hoping for a refill. "Good."

Piper's mouth hangs open for a split second, as if she intends to challenge me. Instead she asks, "What's Gareth up to tonight?"

"Some kind of a meeting."

The waiter takes the hint and pours more Diet Coke from a glass pitcher for me. We've got one of the better tables on the terrace, one right in front of the Christmas tree. Two tables over, some guy who looks like a banker and his Russian mail-order bride keep checking us out.

They must be wondering who we are, because as our waiter heads over there to take their order, I hear him whisper, "Gareth Miller's girlfriend."

"The fashion designer?" asks Mr. Banker.

"She's *young*," Mail-Order Bride replies, which is pretty rich since she can't be a day over twenty-five and her date could easily order off the seniors' menu.

"And…blonde," adds Mr. Banker.

As I turn to glare at Mail-Order Bride, Piper asks, "So are you?"

My head snaps back around to our table. "What?"

"Gareth Miller's girlfriend?"

I snort. "I don't know. I mean, I am so blonde."

Piper laughs. Even her laugh has an Australian accent. "And young."

The truth is, I don't know what, if anything, Gareth and I are to each other. My work for G Studios will be over in three weeks. All Gareth's planning seems to stop at Christmas. He hasn't mentioned any timeline beyond. And neither have I.

"I hope it snows before I go back. I want to see it snow in New York."

Piper becomes serious. "It probably will. But sometimes there's no snow until January. You could stay here, you know. For the snow. And…Parsons is here. Maybe this is your chance. What if you gave up too quickly before?" I don't answer, so she says, "And, I'm here, so there's the BFF factor."

I smile at her. "That's a big check mark in the pro column, for sure. But I didn't even apply to Parsons for the spring. And where would I live?"

"You got into Parsons before," Piper points out. "I'm sure you're an even better prospect now that you've worked with Gareth Miller. And if anyone could work out the details, it's him. Why don't you just ask him?"

I roll my eyes. "You mean sort of like, 'Hey, can you pull some strings at Parsons and also can I live here while I go to school?'"

"You don't have to live there. You have the NutriMin Water money. You could stay with me until you find someplace."

"In the dorms at Columbia?"

She shrugs. "My roommate goes home to South Dakota for semester breaks."

"I'll think about it."

Piper tosses her dark hair over her shoulder. Below us, crowds from Rockefeller spill into the streets. "You're afraid to ask him?"

"I'm not afraid," I say quickly. "I just don't want to…" I don't finish my thought.

But Piper does. "Be like your mom? Shagging a guy to advance your career? You're not like that, Cookie."

I suck down the last bit of my second Diet Coke and can sense the waiter becoming annoyed as he moves to refill it again. "I know," I say. "But in relationships, if things become unequal, that can lead to manipulation or hurt feelings or—"

"Not in relationships in general," Piper interrupts. "You're talking about your mum and Chad Tate. She's using him for status and fame. He's using her for money. They're both constantly giving each other shit because each of them thinks that the other one is getting the better deal. My parents have been married thirty years, and they're not totting up a scorecard of the favors they owe each other."

I sign. "It's not only that. Here. I feel the rhythm of my life is off. I guess."

She almost chokes on the last bite of her steak. "'The rhythm of your life'? You do realize that sounds like a bad song title from an iTunes new-age playlist?"

I nod and take one last look at the giant Christmas tree off in the distance.

We leave the Terrace Club. Piper decides to stay in the room rather than go back to the dorm, where her roommate "won't stop clicking her damn pen while she studies."

"Hey. Your parents… Are they happy?" I ask.

"Yeah. As much as anybody ever is."

She walks me to the curb where Gareth's car is waiting. She's dressed in a sparkly black miniskirt and a light blue sweater with a Pac-Man ghost on it. I'm glad to see she only wears her Reagan-era Republican uniform of slacks and polo shirts when Brian is present.

But what if she marries the guy? Will sassy, surfer girl Piper become a generic doctor's wife with two bland children and a schedule packed full of golfing and hospital fundraising dinners?

Do the people we love change us?

"Think about what I said," she tells me as she gives me a hug.

"I'll call you when I get home."

We exchange a look. I've just called Gareth's penthouse my home. An uneasy feeling settles inside me. I think I've answered my own question.

The next morning, Gareth sleeps in, but I'm up on the treadmill at seven as usual.

He walks by his home gym on the way to the kitchen. "You ever think about taking a day off once in a while? Someday I'd like to wake up in my bed and find you're still in it next to me," he calls.

I want to laugh at his sort of ridiculous appearance, but laughing takes air and I need my air for running. Gareth is dressed in what could only be described as a smoking jacket, the kind Hugh Hefner used to wear at the Playboy mansion in the '60s.

He lounges in the doorway of the exercise room as the treadmill's timer beeps.

I've done my time. I slow the machine to a cool-down pace and answer him. "I have to do my sixty minutes on the treadmill each day. That's the plan."

"I see," he says in his familiar drawl. "You think you'll blow up like a puffer fish the instant you decide to get an extra fifteen minutes of shut-eye?"

Spoken like someone who has never struggled with weight issues.

Climbing off the treadmill, I say, "Routine is important."

He's about to say something else—and judging from the

smirk, it's another wiseass remark—when I blurt out, "Am I your girlfriend?"

This wipes the lighthearted look off his face. "Are labels important?"

I answer a question with a question. "You're saying there's something wrong with wanting to know where we stand?"

"I suppose not." He runs a hand over the dark stubble on his cheeks. "But where we stand is that I suck at romance and you're an inexperienced nineteen-year-old."

That hurts. It hurts that he can *hurt* me. I try to keep my expression neutral. "I'm going to take a shower. I've got a meeting with Darcy at ten."

Gareth sighs and grabs my hand. "But, Cookie, that doesn't mean we shouldn't give this thing our best shot. Because you're the first person in a long time that I've wanted to give a label to."

It's not exactly a Shakespearean declaration of love, but it's something. I grin at him and kiss him gently on the cheek. He tugs me into the kitchen and opens one of the white drawers, full of neatly stacked mail. "I was saving this for later, but under the circumstances..."

He places an envelope with a travel agency logo on the front in my hands. Inside, there's a copy of a plane ticket. "Omigod. You got Grandma to come to New York? For Christmas?" I'm grinning from ear to ear.

"Well, it *is* the most wonderful time of the year," he says. "And my dad's coming too. So you'll get to spend the holidays with all the Miller men."

I giggle. And cover my mouth to stop myself from giggling, because who really wants to squeal like a little girl in front of the most famous name in fashion? "How did you get her to agree to come? She's always saying she thinks New York City is America's Sodom and Gomorrah."

Gareth is smiling too. He puts his arm around me. "I told her you were homesick. And I get the idea that she doesn't like me so much. When I called, I tried to make myself seem especially weird. I mean, I went for it. Tried to channel my inner Andy Warhol. I think she felt she needed to get out here."

"I'm not homesick," I say with a rueful smile.

"I had to say something."

We spend the next week getting ready for the holidays. In yet another surprise, Gareth Miller loves Christmas. Really *loves* it. He plays *Miracle on 34th Street* and *White Christmas* until I think I'll be sick if I have to listen to Bing Crosby sing "Snow" one more time.

He forks over a huge pile of cash to have a fourteen-foot grand fir hauled up to the penthouse and invites about twenty people from G Studios over for a massive tree-trimming party. Piper and Brian come too. After a couple of Brandy Alexanders, Brian isn't so insufferable. The two of them sing Christmas karaoke and take turns decorating each other with bits of tinsel.

Darcy helps Gareth load up the tree with Mosaic Murano glass ornaments. I'm glad she's doing this. With their delicate, hand-blown glass in swirls of red, gold and green, the fragile orbs look like they cost a fortune, and Gareth's got an elaborate story for each one. I really wouldn't want to be the one who drops the glass orb handmade by Mister Geppetto and blessed by the turquoise fairy.

I make my way into the kitchen to restock the food. As I load up stacks of prosciutto-wrapped pears and chocolate peanut butter pretzel bites left by the caterer onto the white serving plates, Nathan meets me in the kitchen.

Gareth's business manager no longer watches me like he expects me to make off with the estate's silver. He stuffs a pear in his mouth and gestures with his elbow. "He's happy, you know. The happiest I've seen him in a long time." I stand next to Nathan and we both watch Gareth climb a ladder to reach the high branches.

No man ought to look so sexy while perched on a ladder.

The doorbell rings. I wonder who else Gareth could have invited.

"Cookie, get the door, will you?" he calls.

I swing open the stainless-steel door and gape at the man on the other side.

There, in a crisp navy suit and clutching a tasteful bottle of white wine, stands Fred LaChapelle.

FAT: Days 98–104 of NutriNation

Here's what I know.

There are two kinds of people in this world. The Abraham Lincolns think mercy bears rich fruit. They send up the white flag during unwinnable struggles and comfort their enemies after the battle.

But there's another kind of person. The kind for whom surrender is never an option. We can't retreat. And there's never enough sacrifice or revenge to satisfy us.

December is shaping up to be the shittiest month of all time.

Not only will I be celebrating the thirtieth straight day of having Lean Cuisine Thai-Style Chicken Spring Rolls for lunch, I'm also staring in the face of hell weekend. The Friday night I make my presentation to Jameson Butterfield and the following evening when Tommy escorts Butterfield's daughter to the holiday dance.

Yes. Tommy's still going to the dance. *I asked her and it wouldn't be right not to go*, he says. *I'll tell her I can't see her any-*

more right after the dance, he says. He doesn't bother to clarify whether he likes her or me, and I'm too afraid of the answer to ask.

I guess there's some kind of possibility that things could work out right. Lightning could strike and leave me with a killer idea to present to Butterfield in addition to burning off my eyebrows. Tommy's going to kick Kennes to the curb. These things could happen.

In theory.

It's Saturday, one week before the dance. I'm sitting in my usual chair at the NutriNation meeting, sandwiched in between Rickelle and Kimberly. Amanda has written *Keep Going* on a whiteboard at the front of the room.

"What are some reasons we might want to quit our weight loss plan?" Amanda asks.

Because we'd rather go back to our old lives of occasionally feeling full after a meal and watching TV instead of running our asses off? Because maybe the world should judge us by our character and not the size of our bodies?

I mention that I've been eating the same thing for lunch for almost a month.

"Okay. Monotony. That's a reason," she agrees.

This leads to a long discussion about changing up my diet. Could I eat an apple instead of an orange? Could I pack a sandwich instead of a Lean Cuisine? What about string cheese for protein? Have I considered low-cal English muffins?

After the meeting breaks, Rickelle taps me on the arm. "You want some advice?" she asks.

"Sure."

"Variety isn't for everyone. Some people need to have a plan and stay with it. If I were you, I'd stick with those spring rolls. Even if you have to choke them down."

She tightens the laces on her running shoes and gets up to leave. I know she's right. Because there are two kinds of people in the world.

Back at home, I stare at Kennes's dress, which I have been hand-beading in every spare second I've got. I can't remember a time when I didn't love to sew, didn't love to make clothes. But I hate this dress. I hate working on it. I hate the idea of it.

The reason the dress even exists at all is because of Grandma. Because Grandma keeps coming by and giving me this look that says, *Take the high road, Cookie.* She keeps reminding me of all the times Tommy's saved my butt. Also because Grandma gave me the silk and beads to make the thing with.

Two weeks ago, Kennes hit my desk and dropped a stack of pictures of French couture gowns that probably cost $20,000 each and had teams of seamstresses working around the clock to perfect them. Since then, she's been ordering me around like I'm a combination of the mice from the *Cinderella* cartoon and the Keebler Elves. She wanted the most expensive materials, and when I asked where I was supposed to get the stuff from, she said, "I'm sure you'll figure that out."

Lucky for her, Grandma coughed up the crepe de chine.

The dress design is the kind of thing that I've never been able to wear. With its Madame Grès–style, side-pleated panels, it's a dress I'd see on the rack and understand was only for the super thin. The kind of people who have bodies that fabric hangs from with ease and who never worry about their cleavage popping out of their bodices.

There are two kinds of people in this world. The Kennes Butterfields and Me.

But what if there were only one kind of person? What if the world gave everyone the same opportunity to look and feel beautiful?

Suddenly, I have an idea, and a plan to present it to Butterfield.

Things will work out.

Again, in theory.

I get the Clothing teacher, Mrs. Vargas, to count my presentation for *SoScottsdale* as an assignment so I can work on it at school. It winds up being fun. There's a girl in class who's really good with graphic design who helps me with a logo. Another girl, Jennifer, shows me how to do a passable job in PowerPoint. By the end of the week, the presentation is pretty good. I'm ready.

After school on Friday, I drive over to the *SoScottsdale* office. My phone buzzes constantly with text messages from Kennes.

Bring my dress.

Did you make a matching clutch?

What's the Wi-Fi password?

Stop for crackers.

It's this last thing that makes me late.

I hit the Safeway. There's nine million kinds of crackers and I choose Cheez-It crackers and saltines. That's what passes for fine dining in my house.

When I show up, Kennes says, "You're late," and takes the bag of crackers from me. We go into the kitchen, where she opens the bag and scowls. "For future reference, when someone asks you to bring crackers to a party, they generally mean Carr's Table Water Crackers."

She pours the Cheez-Its into a crystal bowl, and I will admit, they do look sort of silly displayed that way. She leaves me standing there alone.

From the conference room, I hear a male voice say, "Interesting snack selection, Kennes. Very bourgeois."

"I asked one of the interns to pick up the snacks. You know what they say. Good help is so hard to find," Kennes says.

There's light laughter, and I recognize Marlene's voice.

Kennes, Marlene and Jameson Butterfield are all in the conference room, laughing at the crackers I had to buy with my Donutville tips.

It's too much.

Kennes pokes her head back into the kitchen. "We're ready for you, Cookie."

I run my thumb over the flash drive Jennifer gave to me.

I'm cold and calm and ready to make my last stand.

"I don't have anything ready," I say.

Her mask of mean condescension vanishes. She's scared and nervous. "What? What are you talking about?"

"Well, like you said. Good help is so hard to find."

Kennes follows me to my desk. We pass the conference room, where Marlene's pleasant smile disappears as I pass by and don't enter. A handsome man in a gray Caraceni suit rises from his seat and leans into the doorway. I assume this is Butterfield and he's taking an interest in the situation with his daughter.

Out of the corner of my eye, I see Brittany and Shelby with their mouths hanging open as I stuff the few personal items I keep in my desk into my bag.

"Cookie Vonn! Cookie Vonn," Kennes sputters, "if you walk out that door, you're fired. I hope you know that. Fired."

"You can't fire me. I quit. Please consider this my resignation. Effective immediately. I'd rather have a job cleaning truck-stop restrooms after the chili cook-off than spend one more minute in the same office with you."

Kennes continues to tail me into the parking lot. And Butterfield follows her. I'm a little worried at first. It's one thing to go up against a know-nothing, snobby brat, but I don't want to fight a tech tycoon. I don't have a plan if he decides to intervene.

But he doesn't. He lights a cigarette and steps into the shadows of one of the strip mall's pillars, watching the scene unfold like he's discovered some bizarre foreign film that he can't understand but can't look away from.

I'm several paces ahead of Kennes. She catches up as I unlock the car door and shouts, "Fine. Just give me the dress and go."

Despite the fact that I know she can see the garment bag hanging in the back of my Corolla, I say, "There is no dress."

"What the hell are you talking about?" Her eyes have widened to a bizarre degree.

I open my car door and toss my bag on the passenger seat. "There. Is. No. Dress. For. You." A sound that's part snort and part laugh escapes my lips. I'm on the verge of completely cracking up. Kennes looks like something from a cartoon. I half expect steam to blow out of her ears.

"It's right there! We had a deal. You agreed to make it. Give it to me, or our next conversation will be with my father's attorney."

As I land on the seat and stick the keys in the ignition, I call back, "I'd relish that meeting, Kennes. Because this is America, not North Korea. We have labor laws here. A state and federal minimum wage. I'd love to watch you say, for the record, that you ordered an unpaid intern to slave away as a seamstress at night using materials you refused to pay for. Tell me when that meeting is so I can be there. I'll clear my fucking calendar for that one, for sure."

"The term *sore loser* doesn't *even* describe what's happening here. I've got Tommy and *SoScottsdale*. I'm the one in the spotlight, and you can't stand it," she says.

The little snothead is standing behind my car. Like she can fix everything if she keeps me from leaving.

I get out and stalk toward her, and she flinches. There's one wild moment where I think I might actually grab her by the hair and body-slam her onto the asphalt. But I don't. I stop a few feet from her.

"You don't have *anything* I want. You took the best guy on the planet, who lived to study stars and had something to contribute to the world, and infected him with your vapid disease. And now he's out stealing to pay for your caviar cocktails and *Carr's Water Table Crackers.* You took this blog and made it worse. You take good people like Brittany and Shelby and make them wish they hadn't gotten out of bed in the morning. You ruin everything you touch. Everything is shit the instant you show up."

In my periphery, I see Jameson Butterfield, puffing on his cigarette. He approaches my beat-up car, eyeing it like an exhibit in an oddball museum. His suit is cut exactly right. His pocket square is neatly folded. His shoes perfectly shined. I'm scared for the first time. This is a guy that worries the FBI.

Butterfield doesn't reach out to comfort his daughter and instead says, "You should consider what you're about to do here, Miss Vonn. You've clearly got talent and I've got the resources to make sure your abilities are seen by the right people."

This is the moment Kennes picks to burst into tears. She gives me this look. Like a wounded animal. It's galling, really. She set out to ruin my life, and now I'm supposed to commiserate with her? But she does get her ass back onto the sidewalk.

Her father takes one last puff of his cigarette, hands me his business card and follows Kennes back to the office.

I get into the car and pull onto Hayden Road. In the rearview mirror, I see the two of them standing in front of the office window. Butterfield doesn't look at his daughter, who stands there with mascara running down her face.

He watches me as I drive away.

For a sliver of a second, I feel bad for Kennes. Like I ought to introduce her jackass dad to my mom. I crumple up Butterfield's business card and toss it out the window.

For an instant, I wonder if I've gone too far.

And I feel like shit for littering.

But those feelings don't last.

Tommy shows up at Grandma's an hour later.

Grandma is asleep, but I'm at the kitchen table. I'm sort of expecting him. It seems kind of clear to me where things are headed.

He takes a seat in one of the vinyl-covered chairs and stares at the old gas stove instead of me. "You told her I'm stealing so I can take her on dates?"

Kennes Butterfield is ruining my life, and this is what's concerning him. His reputation. That she might think less of him.

"You *are* stealing to take her on dates."

He grunts in frustration. "It wasn't your place to tell her that."

I shake my head at him. "No. Apparently, it's my place to get arrested for the theft and cover for you. I have my court appearance next week. *That's* my place."

Oh yeah. I need to add Court Date to my to-do list for Hell Month.

"I already told you, I'm sorry."

The table shakes as I pound my fist on it. He looks me in the face for the first time. "I don't want you to be sorry. I want you to be the way you used to be."

"I'm sorry," he repeats.

He turns away again. "I need you to give me the dress, Cookie."

I can't even believe what I'm hearing.

"Please?"

"No," I say in a cold, dark tone.

"You already did what you set out to do. You made her look stupid in front of Marlene. You humiliated her in front of her father. Give her the dress. It's the least you can do," he says.

"The least I can do? Why? Because life's been so tough on her that now she's entitled to order me around like I'm her slave and make me produce her clothing on my own time with my own money? What's her problem, Tommy? Maybe the nanny didn't wipe her ass with organic alcohol-free wipes fast enough? Or her *Citizen Kane* daddy gave her a black pony when she wanted a white one?"

He puts his hands up defensively. "She's just like you, Cookie. She's a nice person trying to do her best—"

My blood pressure is reaching levels that are probably considered medically unsafe. "Kennes Butterfield is a bitch who takes everything that's been handed to her on a silver platter and uses it as an excuse to take advantage of people and shit on everyone else's feelings. If you think I'm like her, get the hell out and don't come back."

"Cookie." He's pleading with me. "Calm down. Please. Just give me the dress."

"You want the goddamn dress?"

Without waiting for an answer, I stomp into my room and return with the garment bag. I *hate* this dress. I hate the design. I hated the process of making it. I know I shouldn't ruin Grandma's silk but...

Tommy reaches out to take the garment bag from me but

I walk past him. I approach the coffeepot that waits on the kitchen counter, full of the cold remains from Grandma's breakfast. Tommy's mouth falls open in horror as I unzip the garment bag and pour the liquid inside.

It's silent in the kitchen except for the tapping sound of cold coffee as it drips down the dress and pools up inside the plastic bag.

Grandma's door swings open and she enters the kitchen with her hair set tight in pink foam curlers. I doubt anyone would be able to sleep through my loudmouth ranting. She sees everything. Tommy. Me. The coffeepot. The dress.

Tommy leaves through the side door. His truck starts a few seconds later.

Grandma's mouth is pressed into a thin, white line. "Was that really necessary?"

Yes. Yes, it was.

"You've got mail," she says, pointing to a stack of papers on one end of the table. I can tell that her arthritis is bothering her as she hobbles over to the coffeepot, taking pains to avoid putting weight on her right foot.

Great. Now I've ousted my arthritic grandma from her bed.

"Could be good news," she says. She puts on a new pot of coffee. As the machine starts to gurgle, I pick up the mail.

On top there is a large envelope from Parsons.

The letter reads, "Congratulations! On behalf of the Admissions Committee, you have been offered a place at Parsons The New School for Design." There's a bunch more paperwork in the envelope. Grandma grins at me while I leaf through it.

Page two tells the whole story. It's labeled "Financial Aid Award Notification." Underneath the header, "Expected Financial Aid," there's a big fat zero.

Grandma's still smiling. But it's over.

My dream of going to Parsons is dead.

~~soScottsdale New Feature Proposal~~

Cookie's Manifesto

Dior once said, "No one person can change fashion—a big fashion change imposes itself." Until recently, I thought he was wrong. I thought that anyone could change fashion the instant they wanted to pull something different from the closet.

But I've realized Dior is right. Fashion changes when ideas change, and right now the world is ready for a big change.

It's time to give everyone the same opportunity to look and feel beautiful. It's time to embrace fashion and beauty ideals that are accessible to all.

~~My new feature~~ The new world order isn't about skinny jeans or halter tops or feeling bad because you're not a fourteen-year-old Eastern European model. But it's not about shaming people who can eat boxes full of Twinkies and still stay a size two either.

We need fashion and style for all girls everywhere. We need fabulous fashion finds from size two to thirty-two. We want a place for style that will put a smile on your face.

It's time for fashion that makes people feel happy.

SKINNY: The odyssey of Day 822 continued

"I'm a big fan of your blog."

This is what Fred LaChapelle says to me.

There's this whole awkward interlude where I stand at the door and stare at him. I try to take the bottle of wine and almost drop it. Three times. Nathan comes to rescue me. LaChapelle finally gets inside the penthouse and somehow the wine ends up in the kitchen.

Gareth comes down off the ladder, takes one look at my face and shows me some pity. He ushers LaChapelle into the living room, makes sure he gets something to eat and drink and starts a conversation about holiday decor.

When I've had time to adjust to the fact that the guy I've been hoping to meet for years is sitting next to me at a party, Gareth steers the conversation back to me. "I mentioned to Fred I'd like to keep you in New York."

Fred.

Gareth's on a first-name basis with someone I should be calling Dean LaChapelle.

I think about all the questions I've dreamed of asking. *What's it like to mentor the top names in fashion? How does it feel to be in charge of the world's most influential design school?* But nothing comes out and instead I'm a spectator, sitting there like a well-behaved child who is quiet while the adults are talking.

"Yes," LaChapelle says. He's got his crimson, striped tie in a Van Wijk knot, which I've never seen in person because you pretty much have to be a wizard to do it. He leans in toward me, as if we're now very good friends. "Gareth mentioned you had an interest in Parsons and asked, in light of your studies at Arizona State and your successful blog, if I might be able to pull a few strings to enable you to bypass the usual application process. But as you were accepted last year, that doesn't appear to be necessary."

There's a pause and Gareth is frowning in a way that suggests we'll be discussing this topic later on.

"May I ask why you didn't attend?"

Everything about LaChapelle is proper and polished and friendly. Behind him, Gareth is the opposite, all raw animalism with the glow of the Christmas lights reflecting in his dark eyes like lightning over the Whitefish Mountains.

They're waiting for an answer, and there doesn't seem to be any advantage in skirting around the real issue.

"Um. I couldn't afford it. My mom wouldn't pay, and I didn't qualify for any financial aid because of her income. I got a scholarship from ASU." My face is turning red but Gareth relaxes back into his seat.

"Ah, an easy problem to resolve now, I would assume," LaChapelle says with a nod to Gareth.

"Indeed," Gareth answers.

"Well, we'd be delighted to have you, Cookie," LaChapelle says, although he's still turned toward Gareth when he makes this remark. "Just delighted. I really do enjoy your blog. And as I was saying last week, the industry needs more of that perspective. How I would relish a return to a time of more generally accessible trends." He turns back to me. "Of course, I'd arrange for you to get transfer credit for classes you've taken thus far and you'd be able to graduate on schedule, I should think."

LaChapelle pats my arm. "We need you, Cookie."

Gareth nods again. "Send me the paperwork," he says.

"Of course. I'll need it back ASAP. The semester starts in four weeks."

Just like that, it's done. In a single conversation, Gareth Miller accomplishes what I'd failed to do myself in three years.

I can go to Parsons.

The dream I'd let go of more than a year ago could now come true. My brain struggles with this reality. It's as if I've bumped into a dead relative in the supermarket. Or found the set of keys I'd lost years ago and have long since replaced. Fate's offering me a do-over. Or Gareth is offering me an opportunity I couldn't get on my own.

"Cookie. It's snowing."

It's Piper's voice, coming from over by one of the floor-to-ceiling windows that line the back of Gareth's living room. She and Brian are watching the weather with their arms wrapped around each other.

Being from Phoenix, I have limited experience with snow.

Somehow, though, this snowfall is different than what I expected. It's coming down in round orbs, creating a pattern of different-sized white polka dots wherever the street and building lights shine into the city night. Clouds hover above the tall, tall buildings, and the snow has an impossibly long way to fall before it can build up on the rooftops and sidewalks.

This must be some kind of a sign.

A sign of what?

I could stay in New York. But if I did, would I become one more white dot, falling in silence into a city waiting for me to blend into its walkways?

FAT: Days 111–114 of NutriNation

I spend the next week avoiding Tommy at school and ignoring the calls I receive from Marlene. I've permanently taken up a seat in the back of History class and will myself to focus on taking notes instead of staring at the back of Kennes's head and trying to find a way to hex her *Harry Potter*–style.

From Twitter, everyone on the planet is aware that Kennes spent last Saturday enduring the horror of shopping for "an off-the-rack dress at the last possible minute," but that she triumphed and had a delightful evening of dancing at 00-Snow. Judging from the fact that I pass Tommy and Kennes sitting together, holding hands, as I carry my lunch to the Clothing room, the *I can't see you anymore* conversation never happened.

I can't figure out what I'm supposed to make of that kiss behind the oleander bushes, and I try not to think about it. The truth is, in that moment, either Tommy was being a jerk to Kennes or he was being one to me. I don't have the emotional bandwidth to try to analyze the latter scenario.

Mrs. Vargas reminds me that I can't dodge Marlene forever. "You're getting school credit for your work at *SoScottsdale*," she says.

But I can't go back. No retreat. No surrender. "What if I make my own blog? Using the idea I worked on in class?"

Mrs. Vargas is cool and we agree that she'll be my faculty supervisor. I'll have to put in the same number of hours as I did at *SoScottsdale*, and be able to prove it by keeping a log of my time. "You do need to advise your current employer of the change," she adds. "I don't want to get another phone call from Marlene Campbell."

Marlene always breezes out of the office around three, so I wait until after school and well past four to call in hopes of being able to leave a message. Sure, quitting by voice mail is tacky, and yeah, it's what you do when you're chickenshit. But this plan eases the weird fluttering in my stomach. And anyway, I'm pretty sure I've already burned the *SoScottsdale* bridge, so what the hell?

Because this is my life and not some alternate reality where things work out as planned, Marlene picks up the phone on the second ring.

"Hey, Marlene. It's Cookie. Mrs. Vargas asked me to call and make sure it's clear that I won't be continuing my internship."

"Hang on, Cookie," she answers. She puts down the receiver and I can hear her close the door to her office. "Okay," she says. "Look, I know that thing with Kennes—"

I interrupt her. I want off this call and I don't want to rehash last Friday. "Marlene, I get it. You have to do what's best for your family. And in this situation that means helping Kennes and not helping me."

"No, it doesn't mean that." Marlene surprises me with the force of her statement. She's being loud. I have to hold the phone a few inches from my face. "This thing with Kennes, you're letting it get the best of you. You're so hurt and bitter because you think life is unfair—"

"It is unfair!"

"—that you can't be objective. You can't see that Kennes is all opportunity and no talent. But you're all talent and sooner or later opportunity will catch up and *you* will know what to do with it. She won't. You'll have to work hard—"

"She doesn't have to work at all."

"—but you can make it. You can get where you want to go. Whatever her advantages are, she doesn't have that shot. Not really, anyway. She's only ever going to be Jameson Butterfield's daughter."

"I won't feel sorry for her." I can't keep the bitterness from my voice.

"I'm not asking you to."

"I can't come back to the blog."

There's a pause. "I know. But, Cookie, my door is always open. I'm rooting for you. We all are. You're stubborn. But if you take one piece of advice, take this. Forget about Kennes Butterfield and focus on yourself. You're going to be fine."

I hang up the phone. I'm done at *SoScottsdale*.

I fight the impulse to wallow. There's no real point in thinking about how I didn't get a send-off from the office or how a couple years of really hard work feels like a massive waste of time. I've got shit to do.

Now I get to start my own blog. Yay.

Who's got two thumbs and can barely operate her iPhone?

This girl.

The one fringe benefit to high school, where people are sharply divided into cliques based on interests and appearances, is that it's easy to figure out where to turn for expertise. It's lunchtime on Friday, and I'm about to journey into the land of *The Big Bang Theory*.

The computer lab is in the main Mountain Vista building on the side farthest from the football field. Black posterboard covers the windows, creating permanent night in a classroom that could best be described as a computer junkyard. There are beige towers and monitors and green components lying all over the place. I have to be careful where I place each one of my knockoff Céline wedges.

I'm searching for Carson Graham. He's one of the few geeks who's ever made an attempt to cross over. Everyone knows he auditioned for the fall play and asked a drama nerd to the dance.

He's in the back corner, staring deep into his computer screen, and doesn't notice me when I approach. I clear my throat. That doesn't help.

Before I can say anything, he says, "Where's Rich? We need a shaman to do a solo wipe recovery." There's the faint sound of someone else talking and then, "Getting pizza? What the fuck? The whole point was to do this battle during lunch to level up the guild for later."

Carson's talking into a small headset mic and listening to headphones. I walk around him to see a game of *World of Warcraft* loaded on his screen. My first impulse is to think, *how typical.* But then, I'm in the Clothing room sewing during most lunches, so I guess I'm not really any better than he is.

"Yeah?" he says. He's looking at me and, I think, speaking to me.

"I need to talk to you about a project."

"I can't."

"You can't talk to me?"

"I can't come over to your house and fix your dad's wireless printer or figure out why your modem keeps going down or tell you why your iPad, iPhone, i-whatever won't sync to the cloud." Streaks of Carson's greasy brown hair cover his forehead. He's so white that he'd probably catch on fire if he went out into the sun. But otherwise, he's not bad looking.

"That's not why I'm here. I have a deal to offer."

"A deal?" he repeats.

"Yeah, I need to—"

"Hang on. I'm about to be killed."

A second later, he removes the headset and I have his undivided attention. "I want to know if you'd like to swap services."

He eyes me with skepticism. "What exactly are your services?"

I try to smile but it feels unnatural. "You do computers. I do clothes."

"You think I want clothes?" he asks.

"You're saying you're deliberately going through your high school years in a uniform of stained *Grand Theft Auto* T-shirts and khakis?"

"Well..." He glances down at his own shirt.

"When you asked Hayley to the winter dance, don't you wish the answer had been yes?" I ask.

He shifts around in his office chair and in the monitor's light, I can see his face turning red. "So you're offering me the plot of the movie *She's All That*?"

"I have to set up a blog and I don't think it's going to come as a big shock to you that I need help. I'm offering you clothes in exchange. Three full outfits. Whether or not you want to dance around in a teen movie montage is up to you," I say.

"That thing with Hayley. Five years from now, I'll have a seven-figure income and a house in Palo Alto. She'll be on a barstool next to me begging for my phone number. Look at Zuckerberg." Carson's gaze returns to his screen and he makes a few taps on the keyboard.

"Look at Steve Jobs," I counter. "If you believe that Ashton Kutcher movie, he always got girls. And he wore nice clothes."

"Steve Jobs?" Carson repeats.

He sighs and types for a couple more minutes. "I want five."

"Five?"

"Five outfits."

"Deal."

It quickly becomes clear that I've gotten the short end of the stick. In about ten seconds, Carson sets me up with a website address and a site using WordPress. Half an hour later, he's dressed the site up with the logos my Clothing class made and given me a crash course in how to blog.

But a deal is a deal, so after my homework is done and the

doughnuts have been made on Saturday morning, I spend the rest of the weekend sewing. Thanks to Grandma, three of her bingo buddies from church and *Sewing for Boys and Men*, we finish a collection that would be right at home on the rack at Banana Republic. Carson is a fashion noob, so I stick to a simple color palette. Basic blues and grays, khakis and a bit of black. I try to add a few techie touches here and there, like using a Space Invaders printed fabric to line the collar of a polo shirt and the waistband of the pants.

I drop them off at Carson's house late on Sunday night. The Grahams must be the perfect postmodern family, with a place in posh Las Sendas and a giant Christmas tree in the window. He tries on a pair of navy slacks and a plaid button-up shirt. They fit great and the sky blue is especially good for his pale complexion. I'm getting pretty good at menswear.

"This isn't too bad," Carson says. "I was sort of worried you'd try to dress me up like a boy-band singer or something."

As I leave he smiles and says, "Hey. Let me know if you have any trouble with the blog."

Perfect. Fashion changes lives, and I've got tech support.

The next day I'm off to city court.

The hearing goes better than expected. Grandma's there and the judge seems to buy the idea that I'm a good kid caught in a bad situation. I get sentenced to twenty hours of community service. Grandma signs me up for work at St. Vincent de Paul, a food bank and homeless shelter. I'll be making sandwiches on some days and going to grocery stores asking for donations on others.

I volunteer for a shift on Monday after school at the Bashas'

Grocery near Mountain Vista. We work in teams of two, and it's easy. We have a table inside the store, which we stock with generic peanut butter, jelly and bread. When people come by, we ask them to take some to the register, pay for it, and bring it back to us for the shelter.

Julie from church is my partner. She goes to Mesa High and is volunteering to look good on her college application. She assumes I'm in it for the same reason, and I don't correct her. We're doing pretty good and have managed to convince shoppers to pay for most of the peanut butter we'd stacked on our table.

"One of us needs to go back to the stockroom and get more peanut butter," I tell Julie. We've been trained to go to the back of the store, ring a buzzer and wait for a store employee to give us more boxes of food.

"I'll go," she says. She grabs the cart and heads toward the rear of the store.

While Julie's gone, Tommy shows up. Inwardly, I groan. Also, I sort of want to punch him.

He's got a third chair he must've lugged out of the store office. I don't move over to make room for him. "You don't need to be here," I say coldly.

He stares at the ground. "They're always looking for volunteers." Tommy's not wearing his usual T-shirt and cargo pants. He's got an expensive polo shirt with an enormous logo on the pocket area and a pair of designer jeans.

Volunteer some other time, I'm about to say.

Tommy speaks first. "Cookie. Come on. I'm—"

"Sorry?" I finish. "I'm sick of hearing that."

"I wasn't going to say that," he says, raising his head. "I

was going to say that people can disagree. Okay. So you don't like Kennes, so…"

I never get to hear the rest of Tommy's speech or point out that he kissed me and then blew me off to take Kennes to the dance. A woman with a tween daughter approaches our table and adds several jars of peanut butter and loaves of bread to our stash. "Say hi to Father Tim, okay?" she says as she and her daughter leave the store.

I hear a familiar voice.

"Hey! Tommy!"

It's Kennes.

Oh. Perfect.

Tommy's face turns red but the situation has left him with no option other than to join Kennes where she's standing in line at the Starbucks inside the grocery store. The barista calls, "Iced skinny vanilla latte," and Kennes picks up the cup.

Julie's making her way back to our table pushing a cart loaded with boxes of peanut butter. She and I are about the same size, which is to say that she's another person society would classify as fat.

As Julie passes, Kennes says loudly, "Yeah, if they need food for the homeless shelter, that girl ought to skip lunch a couple days a week. They could probably feed half the city with the leftovers."

Julie's face turns red and she pushes the cart faster. Maybe we can combine our powers and disable Kennes with our death glare.

Tommy joins Kennes near a display of coffee mugs and, a second later, is smiling and nodding along with her. Then he's walking with her, and they're holding each other's tanned hands and bouncing with light steps like a Ralph Lauren ad set in motion.

The Lean Cuisine spring rolls I ate for lunch creep their way up my throat. I'm doing volunteer work to pay for Tommy's fancy Ken-doll outfit. I wonder what the hell has happened to my best friend. I wonder if there's still time to rat him out. I wonder what the punishment is for face-punching.

Kennes puts her arm around Tommy's waist as they pass me at the table. "What do you think, hon? You think if we donate a few jars of peanut butter at least one will make it to the shelter?"

Hon.

What the hell?

"I'll walk you to the door." Tommy maintains a bland face and an even tone.

"Yeah. Good call. I don't think they'd make it either." Kennes laughs again.

Tommy comes back as I sit there with my blood boiling and my face frozen in shock and rage. He faces me straight on. For a second, he isn't laughing or smiling, and he's that same real guy from the first night in Wyoming. For a second, I can see the old Tommy in his slouch and seriousness.

Julie's back, and her eyes are watering like she's about to cry. I silently pray that she doesn't. Not that there's anything wrong with releasing your emotions or anything. But girls like Kennes thrive on their ability to make people feel like dirt. Crying gives them their power.

Julie's barely holding it together.

"Don't let her get to you. She's just really..." I trail off.

"Having a hard time," Tommy says in a quiet voice. "Her parents' divorce. It's been really rough on her. She doesn't mean to…" He trails off. Like even he can't figure out what Kennes doesn't mean to do.

"*I* was going to say horrible," I say through clenched teeth.

Julie laughs but asks, "Mind if I cut out early?"

I shake my head, and she takes a few steps toward the door.

"Julie. Hey," I call. "What happened here today…don't think about it. It's what's inside us that counts."

She glances at Tommy. "We may be the only ones who think that."

"No, no, you're not," Tommy sputters. But the damage is done. Julie eyes him skeptically and then disappears through the store's sliding doors.

"Twenty bucks says she's in tears by the time she hits the parking lot," I say.

Tommy squirms in his seat. "Cookie—"

"Don't. Just don't."

He sits there with me for the rest of my shift, a tense silence between us.

Afterward, I drive the bags full of supplies over to St. Vincent de Paul. Father Tim is there, and he helps me unload the Corolla. As we stock the kitchen cabinets with bread, I say, "Can I ask you something?"

"Shoot."

"You think Jesus was serious about all that turn-the-other-cheek stuff?"

He brushes the dust off his black shirt and leans against the counter. His gray hair is a total mess. "Do I think he was serious? Oh no. See, Jesus said, 'When someone strikes you on your right cheek, turn the other one to him, as well,' and Matthew forgot to write down, 'Just kidding.'"

Yep. Note to self: Father Tim doesn't like to talk.

He surprises me when he continues, "But that quote is taken out of context all of the time. People think it means Christ intended for everyone to make doormats of themselves and allow others to mistreat them. But it's really a warning against retaliation, especially when reacting in anger. The Old Testament permitted a certain amount of vengeance. An eye for an eye. Jesus is saying that's no longer possible."

I frown in confusion. "So what does that mean? In terms of behavior. If someone hurts you, what do you do?"

He snorts. "Has someone hurt you? Out of professional obligation, I'm required to ask and also to hint with subtlety that you've missed Mass a few times lately."

"This is hypothetical," I say, rolling my eyes at the Mass comment.

He resumes stacking jars of grape jelly in one of the cabinets. "Well, hypothetically, it's more about what you can't do. You can't get revenge. You have to try to love your enemy."

"What if it's your friend that hurts you?"

Father Tim turns back to me with his piercing blue eyes, and I get the sense he knows what I'm talking about. "You should forgive your friend. But also realize that when we offer forgiveness, we don't need to keep putting ourselves in a position to get hurt. Just because you love someone doesn't necessarily mean being around that person is good for you."

We finish our work in silence.

"Good work," he says when we're done.

I turn to say goodbye to Father Tim.

"Cookie, your father doesn't know about any of this stuff, does he?" Father Tim sighs. "He's asking about you *again*. I'm a simple man. Once in a while, I'd like to get a mission report that doesn't end with Martin asking me to track down his kid. Is there some particular reason you can't manage to squeeze in a couple emails between your toy heists and doughnut frosting?"

"Ha ha."

Father Tim frowns. "That's a real question."

My shoulders tense up. "I told you, he knows where I am."

He doesn't press any further, and says, "Hypothetically speaking, Catholics aren't supposed to miss Mass. I'm sure I'll see you Sunday."

I smile at him. A fake sort of smile.

As I drive to Grandma's yellow house, I think about the situation I'm in.

Tommy sends me a couple of text messages. Call me when you're ready to talk. We'll always be best friends. I delete them so that I'm not tempted to answer.

Grandma says, "This too shall pass."

Maybe the time will come when I forgive Tommy. Maybe the time will come when I will have Grandma's faith that everything works out in the end.

Right now, I can take only one part of Father Tim's advice.

Tommy isn't good for me.

That night, I make the first entry on my new blog. It's my mission statement.

Roundish <New Post>

Title: Welcome to Roundish

Creator: Cookie Vonn [administrator]

There's a certain very famous designer who's been quoted as saying, "No one wants to see roundish women." For this guy, fashion is a world of dreams and illusions where only certain people are welcome.

Of course, it's true that fashion mocks and humiliates fat people relentlessly. But the real deal is that we've all been Roundish at one time or another. We've all been made to think we're less than we ought to be. We've all faced superficial shaming about our sizes, shapes, skin tones, hair or age and have been led to believe that our value is based only on what we see in the mirror.

Yet this designer is totally wrong about fashion. He's completely missed the point. It's not an illusion or a dream. It's a tool that should help people feel good about themselves and achieve their dreams.

The Roundish are the thinkers, dreamers, doers and believers. Your heart, your spirit, your hopes—these are the things that matter.

This blog is for the Roundish in all of us, full of fabulous fashion finds from sizes two to thirty-two designed to empower you to be the best version of yourself.

SKINNY: Days 824–847 of NutriNation

"Going to JFK is a nightmare, Cookie."

Gareth hires cars and drivers to pick up my grandma and his father from the airport. I imagine a grim man with a mortician's face holding a sign that reads "Edna Phillips," and leading Grandma to a creepy car that resembles a hearse.

Grandma and John Miller arrive at the penthouse within minutes of each other. Mr. Miller is what you'd expect. His skin has the leathery, saddlebag texture of a man who has spent most of his life in the Montana sunshine. He wears Wranglers and a threadbare plaid Pendleton button-up shirt he must have purchased sometime during the Carter administration.

Gareth makes drinks and Grandma mentions the "fancy" driver several times, which I suppose is her way of voicing her dissatisfaction at the impersonal pickup. Her answer to Mr. Miller's cliché Western wear is an olive green polyester pantsuit that I'm sure she'd describe as her "traveling clothes."

Gareth has two drinks, one in each hand, and he gives one to Grandma.

"And this is?" she asks.

"Eggnog," Gareth answers. "With Rémy Martin Cognac."

"I don't indulge, sonny," Grandma says with a deep frown.

Without missing a beat, he takes the foaming glass from her and replaces it with the one from his other hand. "Shirley Temple," he says. He gives the spiked eggnog to his father.

Mr. Miller and Grandma treat each other with suspicion. Their attempts at making conversation are loaded with suggestions. That Gareth is a cradle robber intent on subverting my education. That I'm a teenage gold digger trying to leverage my sex appeal into a ten-figure fortune.

Round 1

Grandma: "Well, Gareth. Do you do a lot of entertaining up here? I expect that all the white surfaces make cleaning up after *affairs* a snap."

Mr. Miller: "My son's success has made him very popular, and I'm not just talking about with the ladies."

Round 2

Mr. Miller: "Cookie, how're you enjoyin' New York? Is my boy showing you the finer aspects of the city?"

Grandma: "We sure are grateful for your son's hospitality. I hope this little internship will be beneficial when she comes back home to finish her schooling."

Round 3

Mr. Miller: "I understand that your mother is a fashion model? I guess you sort of hit the jackpot in the looks department, eh?"

Grandma: "Her father is a doctor. And Cookie was a straight-A student in school. I'd say she's pretty lucky in the brains department, as well."

They keep going but I get stuck.

My dad. I haven't thought about him in ages. Every once in a while he goes into Kumasi or Sunyani, where they have internet access, and posts stuff on Facebook. He's given up on emailing me except on my birthday or major holidays.

Mr. Miller's voice breaks through my thoughts. He poses a direct question. "So, Cookie. What's your ambition?"

"To make clothes that anyone can feel good wearing." I blurt this out and as I do, I realize that it's true. My personal manifesto. Real and from my heart.

This shuts both of them up for a minute. I guess the fact that I have an ambition or haven't lost my ambition is enough to calm them down.

Then Grandma says, "These big ole buildings make me nervous. But I suppose we can hide under all this stainless steel if there's a fire or somethin'."

Mr. Miller laughs. This forms some kind of truce between them. It suggests that there's some kind of a way for Gareth and me to merge our lives together.

I help Gareth finish making dinner and when we come back out, Grandma is "indulging" in fine brandy and swapping old ranch stories with John Miller.

"My daddy kept a few cows," Grandma says with a small hiccup. "And good thing too. My girl, Leslie, almost died as a baby. Spit up every kind of milk and formula I tried to give her. She was so weak. It was just pitiful. My daddy said the girl needed milk from a Jersey cow. He brought it down from Buckeye in a little glass bottle."

"Rich in butterfat. Good choice for a finicky baby," Mr. Miller agrees.

"You keep Jersey cows?"

Mr. Miller shook his head. "I've got Simmental. Imported them in the '70s. From Switzerland. I was one of the first American ranchers to do it."

"From Switzerland?" Grandma repeated in an impressed tone.

Gareth and I exchange a look. I guess Swiss Miss cows provide a common link.

This chatter carries us through dinner. It's sort of funny to watch Mr. Miller poke with skepticism at his butternut squash ravioli. "This is some fancy eating, son," he says. "But when will you be serving the main course?"

"Funny, Dad. As per your cardiologist, this is the main course." Gareth gives me an appealing wink.

"That quack. I keep telling him. I raise beef. I eat beef."

During the next couple of weeks, Gareth pulls out all the stops. It's fun to watch him have so much fun. I'm not sure whether he's trying to impress his father or Grandma, but he succeeds on both counts. He buys killer seats to the Radio City Music Hall *Christmas Spectacular* and *The Nutcracker.* He takes us on a tour of the city and somehow gets Big Top Toys to open early so Grandma and Mr. Miller can dance on the store's famous, giant piano.

Their favorite part winds up being the Holiday Train Show at the New York Botanical Garden, where they spend hours watching a model train roll over a miniature Brooklyn Bridge. "It looks so lifelike," Grandma says over and over.

Christmas day is very Norman Rockwell meets IKEA. Gareth's got all the traditional trappings of the holidays crammed into his sparse and trendy, white apartment. He hangs rich green holly all over, ties red bows on all the door handles and even sprinkles silver tinsel liberally around his living room.

Gareth's appearance contrasts sharply with his father's. He is clad in a thick and luxurious black turtleneck sweater and his usual worn designer jeans while his dad wears an old chambray shirt, Wranglers and a bolo tie.

I'm stunned by all the effort and thoughtfulness Gareth puts into personally shopping for and wrapping presents. He bought me almost everything I've even mentioned since I got to New York. I feel like I'm unwrapping for an eternity, ending with a huge collection of vintage fashion books, hard-to-find patterns, cool sketching pencils and pads and a million pairs of sunglasses.

I got him a few things. Mr. Miller has a rancher buddy in town who makes frequent trips to Cuba and hooked me up with expensive cigars and bottles of rum. I ordered a custom-made wallet from a shop in London, which they produced at the speed of sound the instant they found out it was for Gareth.

But still, the gifts are unbalanced in a way that makes me a bit uncomfortable. "You got me too much stuff," I say.

"Never," he says with a wide smile.

Grandma and Mr. Miller are in the kitchen, cooking an

old-fashioned prime rib roast dinner. Gareth says, "I have something else for you. For later."

I assume he means lingerie or something. But that night, after my grandma and his father are snoring in their beds and I'm snuggled under his massive white comforter, he hands me a glossy white envelope.

Inside, I find two pieces of paper. The first is a G Studios accounting statement of the preorders from our capsule collection. It's all been presold and will launch as an exclusive in ten key stores across the country.

The second piece of paper is a tear sheet. A page from the February issue of *Par Donna* magazine. It's a review. Gareth taps his finger on a prominent block quote.

"Gareth Miller's capsule collection, a collaboration with fresh-faced, girl-power blogger Cookie Vonn, delivers big on its promise to offer wonderful whimsy and fabulous flair to the plus-size woman. Following the snoozer that was Fall/Winter, GM is back with game-changing looks that are gorgeous and, dare we say, even fun. Get in line now, for these pieces are sure to sell out fast."

Celine Stanford. She just mentioned me in print.

"It worked?" I stare at Gareth.

He laughs. "You're on the map, Cookie Vonn."

I grin back at him.

He ruffles my hair and heads for the bathroom. The water runs as he brushes his teeth. "Oh. LaChapelle called. He needs that paperwork by next week. I had Reese fill most of it out. But you need to add your Social Security number. And sign it."

"Okay." I'm glad he's in the bathroom and not sitting next

to me as my insides become mushy with indecision. I turn off the lamp on my side of the bed.

Gareth returns a few minutes later and wraps his arm around me. "Merry Christmas, Cookie."

"Merry Christmas," I say.

Then, "Gareth, what's the best thing about Parsons?"

He yawns. "The best thing? About Parsons? It *is* the best."

That's not much of an answer for someone whose career was launched by the school. A few minutes later, when he's asleep, my mind won't shut down. I've always had to do everything myself, but now things are happening with a momentum I didn't create. My life has taken on a life of its own.

Piper and Grandma are here in the city. My temporary life intersecting with my permanent one.

I can't sleep, and I curl up with my laptop in a white armchair near the window. It's snowing again and occasionally I catch a glimpse of flakes falling past a lit window in the building across from Gareth's.

In my blog email box, I find a familiar name. I open a message from Dr. Moreno.

Dear Cookie:

I've been emailing you at your university account and am concerned you haven't received my messages. I notice you have not completed your spring registration and haven't contacted me about finishing your work from last semester. As I'm sure you know, you will forfeit your Regents Scholarship if you don't register for the spring semester.

There it is. The thing that Grandma warned me about. And let's face it, the thing that has been nagging at me since Fred LaChapelle turned up at the door. In going to Parsons, I'd be giving up my ability to pay for my own education. I'd be at the mercy of Gareth or LaChapelle. I'd be right back in that airport, hoping for a seat on the plane.

I'll be in NYC next week and would like to meet with you to discuss these topics. Can you get back to me with a day and time that works for you?

Dr. Lydia Moreno
Fashion & Costume Design Chair
Honors Faculty
Arizona State University

I'm going to Parsons. I'm living in the city of my dreams with the man of my dreams going to the school of my dreams.

No. I'm staying at ASU. I imagine the campus. Outside the art building, there are rows and rows of succulent plants. The smooth scallops of green and purple echeveria. The spiky stalks of agave. I love to sit back there on the concrete as it cools in the evening, dreaming of collars that jut up like the mountains behind campus, skirts that twist into cactus forms.

I haven't seen anything like that in the city.

I haven't seen Gareth design even one thing since we've been in New York.

I'm ignoring Dr. Moreno. No. I'm emailing her. It's curiosity that gets the better of me. Makes me want to find out why my teacher would go to all the trouble of seeking me out while on vacation. I email her a date and time for the following week.

They say curiosity killed the cat.

They also say cats have nine lives.

I hope this last part is true. In fact, I'm counting on it.

Mr. Miller takes Grandma to JFK a few days later. Before she leaves, we're alone in the building lobby for a couple of minutes.

"Your fella ain't too bad," she says, squeezing me into a hug. "But it don't change things none. Finish your schoolin'. Invest your time in things that will last."

Yet again I chicken out and don't tell Grandma what's going on.

"I'll be expectin' you back at home shortly," she says.

I nod and smile and watch as she walks through the glass door.

Dr. Moreno and I meet on Wednesday. She picks the place, a dive in Spanish Harlem called Cuchifritos. Even before I get my butt off the Town Car seat, I can smell the sizzling pork. There's a service counter that faces the street and it's loaded with food deep-fried beyond recognition. They say you can eat anything on the NutriNation plan, but I suspect *they've* never seen the frituras at Cuchifritos.

I barely recognize my teacher. Every time I've ever seen her in class, her dark hair has been tied back in a neat bun and she's been wearing some variation of a Diane von Fürstenberg wrap dress. Today, she's got spiral curls that explode in every direction. She's dressed in a pair of 1980s vintage Guess jeans and a worn-out Echo & the Bunnymen concert tee.

The conversation doesn't go the way I expect it to.

I'm expecting some rah-rah ASU is the best school ever speech. Or possibly a request to meet Gareth Miller and get free samples.

Dr. Moreno's taken a small table for two right up front, just a few feet from the register. The cash drawer slams closed. People call out their orders. I get a plate of something that I know I won't take a bite of. The fried and refried thing is probably more addictive than meth and won't fit in my food journal.

I have to lean way in to hear Dr. Moreno over the restaurant noise. I think I've misheard when she says, "Did he tell you about this place?"

My face must be blank because she shakes her curls and continues.

"Gary. He used to come down here all the time. In the early days. Back when Mr. High and Mighty wasn't scared to leave Manhattan. He would even take the bus. He *loved* the alcapurria." She points at something that looks like a cross between a corndog and a burrito on her plate.

"Gary?" I repeat. "Who's Gary?"

For a minute, I'm worried she emailed the wrong person. That she has me confused with another student.

She almost chokes on a bite of breading as she barks out a laugh. "Miller. Gareth *John* Miller. GM. Today's top name in fashion."

"You know Gareth?" I ask. My insides spin in confusion.

The skin around her brown eyes crinkles as she laughs

again. If I had to guess, I'd say she's around the same age as Gareth. And I know she went to—

"Parsons." She nods as if reading my thoughts. "He graduated a year faster than me, though. And…he didn't mention me? Yeah, well, shacking up with some Puerto Rican broad living in Spanish Harlem probably doesn't make his bio these days."

The way she says all of this. It's not bitter. It's more wistful. Like she pities Gareth. Or remembers him from better, bygone days.

She drops her fork and watches me. "You've changed a lot since the first time we met. No longer that scared high school student, huh? And you look a lot like your mother."

If I weren't so flustered, I'd probably be enraged. But I kind of sputter. "Dr. Moreno…I…uh…I'm not…"

"I keep telling you, it's Lydia. And I know. You're not your mother. Believe me. I get it. For the past three years, I've been paying seventy-five bucks a week to some Freud wannabe in Scottsdale trying to avoid a future where I shrink six inches and spend my evenings cursing out all my relatives in Spanish."

I frown at her. "Well, *Lydia*, I don't understand—"

"What we're doing here?" she interrupts with a wide grin. It fades into a Mona Lisa smile as she adds, "Sorry. I have this annoying habit of finishing people's sentences. My grandmother was a bruja fortune teller."

"Yeah…okay…" I'm back to stammering and staring.

Finished with her food, Dr. Moreno pushes her plate away. "I know Gary—sorry Gareth—is encouraging you to stay here in New York. I need you to understand that this would *not* be the right move."

"How do you know—"

I haven't spent much time with Lydia Moreno outside of class. She must have taken interpersonal communication classes with Piper's boyfriend, Brian. Neither he nor Lydia can allow other people to speak in complete phrases.

"LaChapelle called," Dr. Moreno says. "Asked about you. Sort of wanted a reference. I told him you were the brightest up-and-coming designer I'd ever seen. Told GM's people the same thing when they called a couple months ago."

This rings a bell. I remember that it was Dr. Moreno who sent Darcy pictures of my work.

I'm a jumbled mess of emotions. Upset that Dr. Moreno understands Gareth way better than I do. Angry at being caught off guard by this whole conversation. And afraid. That Gareth's had a lot of other women. The kind of women who don't struggle to come up with coherent sentences.

Dr. Moreno waves to someone behind the counter and a few seconds later a plate of food lands at her elbow. She cuts into yet another deep-fried dish, releasing the fragrance of banana and nutmeg.

I've never been more jealous of absolutely anyone in my life. Dr. Moreno is sitting there in a pair of thrift store jeans and a twenty-year-old T-shirt, chomping down on this thing that oozes oil and spice and probably has a zillion calories. I'm in a $2,000 GM floral print shift dress and suede ankle books, and there's no comparison. Lydia Moreno is not only the kind of woman I want to be, she's the kind of woman who makes me want to make clothes. Worry begins to gnaw at me, because I suspect that someone like Dr. Moreno would never find a happy ending with someone like Gareth.

She smiles. "Gary doesn't know how to teach you what you need to learn. He needs you. Not the other way around."

My anger starts winning the emotional battle. "He's considered one of the best American fashion designers of all time. Parsons is the best school."

"Oh, you and your Parsons." There's a pause. Dr. Moreno appears to be thinking carefully about what she says next. "When you think of great fashion, do you imagine the collection Gary put together last season? When you think of the life you want, do you picture yourself living in that residential version of the Apple Store my friend Gary calls an apartment?"

"All designers make a bad collection at some point," I say coldly.

She sighs. "I know you want to be like Gareth Miller. So did I. But what you want, what I wanted, was to be him like he *used to be*. Back when he was just some kid from Montana who made clothes that were fun to wear. He isn't that person anymore, Cookie. He's changed. Gotten cynical. He can only teach you how to become what he is *right now*. And you don't want to be that."

"You don't know what I want to be."

Dr. Moreno smiles again. "All I'm saying is, think about it. You and Gareth are alike in many ways. He took the path you're considering. See where it got him and ask yourself if that's where you want to be."

I open my mouth to protest. Tell her I'm a New York

City kind of girl. That Gareth isn't swimming in a river of complacency.

In other words, say a bunch of lies.

Dr. Moreno taps my arm, breaking me from my zoned-out trance. "The struggle makes us, Cookie. Getting off the bus with ten bucks in his pocket, eating his dinner in dives like this," she says with a wave, "that's what made Gary."

My stomach drops even further because I don't even know *Gary*.

She's finished with her banana dessert and pushes herself up from the table. "I'm putting you on the spring schedule and adding a pre-semester meeting to your calendar. I hope you show up. I'm expecting you to show up."

"Why are you doing this?" I ask.

"I need you as much as he does, Cookie. Gareth is a designer in search of a muse. I'm a teacher who wants good students. You're my best student by a long shot. Oh, and hey, don't forget, at the end of the year, I get to send a student to work with Stella Jupiter for the summer. It should be you."

Stella Jupiter. The queen of designer cashmere. Oh. Fuck. I had forgotten.

Dr. Moreno is almost to the door when she turns back. For an instant, a motherly expression crosses her face. "Listen. I know this kind of stuff is hard to hear, and the heart wants what it wants. All I ask is that you do some serious thinking about what's right for *you*. Think about where you want to be in life and how you plan to get there."

I want to pick something up and throw it at Dr. Moreno. But she blends into a crowd on the sidewalk before I can get my hands on anything. My body pulses with a desperate energy I can't get rid of.

As I wait on the curb for Gareth's driver, I try to hate Lydia Moreno. Except she hasn't really done anything except be blunt about a bunch of stuff I ought to already know. She's a personification of an unknown part of Gareth's past. A part I'd brushed aside since the day his lawyer had me sign more paperwork than you do when you buy a car. She told me she wanted to help me. My heart screamed to forget all about this lunch from hell. My brain believed her.

On the way back to the apartment, I think about my blog. I'm supposed to be writing articles about how, thanks to NutriMin Water, all my dreams are finally coming true.

But I can barely figure out what my dreams even are.

Distracted, I almost miss the hulking figure milling around in front of Gareth's apartment building until he calls my name.

The opposite of my dream.

My nightmare.

Chad. Fucking. Tate.

FAT: Days 119–122 of NutriNation

A lot of people don't buy into all that astrology stuff.

I'm a Capricorn. I guess we're supposed to be all about hard work. A lone goat climbing to the top of Success Mountain.

A glance at my homework planner makes me question that idea. I owe Mr. Smith a paper on the presidents. I need to work on my blog for Mrs. Vargas. We actually got homework last week in PE—keeping an exercise log. I already have to do this for NutriNation, but I'm still pissed Coach didn't get the memo that Phys Ed teachers aren't supposed to assign homework.

And my Donutville shift starts in fifteen minutes.

I'm not sure I believe that your birthday can determine your entire personality, but there's no denying that I'll be turning eighteen on Tuesday. This is the birthday that's supposed to mean you're an adult. You can get your own Mastercard. And vote. And get tattoos. You can make permanent choices and your decisions won't be corrected by some authority figure. Like writing your name on your underwear in black Sharpie. After Tuesday, some things won't come out in the wash.

I dig around through a pile of messy clothes on my floor until I find my cleanest brown work apron. It's a lot easier to tie the apron strings around my waist than it used to be. This is one for NutriNation and Amanda Harvey's list of non-scale victories.

Keys in hand, I head for the door, silently praying the old Corolla will make it downtown and that I'll get enough in tips during my shift to refill the gas tank.

I pass Grandma on the way out.

"I got everything all set," she says.

"What?" I ask. I kind of think maybe she's referring to her hair, which is wrapped up in more foam curlers than I can count.

"For Tuesday. Your party. They're lettin' us use Father McKay Hall."

"Oh. Okay." I'm not sure if I missed the discussion where we agreed to have a party at the church. I sort of hate my birthday. And birthday parties. They feel like nothing more than a reminder of everything that's missing in my life.

Grandma thinks these kinds of things are unskippable rites of passage. She's watching me and clearly expects a better response.

"Oh. Cool. Thanks. Thanks for setting that up."

She smiles at me. "Don't work too hard, girl."

At Donutville, I frost extra fast, making trays and trays of chocolate and sprinkle-covered pastries. Out front, there are a few regulars at the kidney-shaped counter who don't mind if I set up my homework. I refill coffee cups and Google for examples of presidents behaving badly. Mr. Smith's in love with the idea that all leaders abuse their power, and I'm sure this tactic is the clearest path to an A on the essay.

I make a few bucks, get some gas. Monday comes whether I like it or not.

Then my birthday.

I wake up feeling, looking, acting exactly the same as on any other day. Except now everything that happens is going on my permanent record.

Grandma's put together a nice party. It's sort of old-fashioned, with a punch bowl, pink streamers and a sheet cake. But nice. A bunch of people from church come, but so do all the girls from my Clothing class. And Shelby and Brittany from *SoScottsdale*. There's a video from Piper, and they play it on a screen. She's there in front of the Sydney Opera House, yelling "Happy birthday."

Steve from Donutville shows up with another birthday cake formed from pink, powdered doughnuts. He's a man of limited interests, I guess. But it's the thought that counts.

Grandma even made me a dress. In yet another quasi-hilarious, eye-roll-inducing bit of irony, it's made from the scraps of crepe de chine left over from the holiday dance debacle. She's made a simpler version of the dress I designed for Kennes, one without the bulky hip panels.

I'm having fun. But here's what's missing.

Tommy.

The dress. The party. It all underscores the fact that my best friend is missing this big milestone in my life. I wonder if he remembers it's my birthday.

He does.

Tommy shows up looking more like himself than he has in ages, wearing a Carl Sagan Is My Homeboy T-shirt and clutching a black-striped gift bag.

I'm cutting my cake into tiny bites, trying to make the small slice into an epic eating experience, when I see him come in.

We stare at each other from across the church hall.

Awkward.

"I guess you're eighteen and I can't make you go over and say anything," Grandma says. "But you should. Friendship's important. If you can save it, you should."

I stay glued to my chair. Grandma sighs and points at a portrait of Father McKay hanging on a far wall. He was a priest, although I'm not sure when or where or why he has a hall with his picture in it. "Cookie, the church says we reach an age of accountability, where your parents or your grandparents aren't responsible for you anymore. These choices are yours. And the consequences are too," Grandma says.

The snarky part of me wants to tell Grandma that she hasn't been to catechism in a while. That the church now says the age of accountability is seven years old. This is when you need to start worrying about going to hell in a handbasket. But she's gone to a lot of trouble to throw me a party, and she's probably right. I won't get too many more chances to bury the hatchet with Tommy, and I'm the one who won't have a BFF.

As I walk over to him, a mixture of relief and apprehension crosses his face. "Nice shirt," I say.

"Nice dress," he answers with a small smile.

I start to read a million things into that remark. Like

maybe it's a slam for the whole thing with Kennes's dress. My face is getting red.

"Yeah…my Grandma made it. I didn't ask her to…and…"

He shoves the gift bag at me. "This is for you," he says, sounding as nervous as I do. "But don't worry. I bought it with money I got from my lawn-mowing business…and not from…well…you know."

I peek in the bag to find a new copy of the Fashionary sketchbook inside, which is awesome since every page of my old one is completely full.

"Hey, thanks," I say.

We stare at each other for another minute.

"The other day in the grocery store…the whole thing with… I just want things to be the way they were before," he blurts out.

"For things to be the way they were, we have to be who we were," I say.

"We haven't changed. Things haven't changed."

It's a lie. We both know it. Everything is changing. Who we are. What we want. What we expect from life and from each other. It's all in flux. Shifting.

I want to ask about Kennes. If he's still going out with her. Or if he cares about the way she treats people like Kleenex. Grandma shoots me a look of warning. *This too shall pass.* If I want to rebuild my friendship with Tommy, its new foundation might be shaky, less solid than before. But what's the alternative?

Tommy joins me at a table where Shelby and Brittany are replaying Piper's video, grinning at the sights of the port and trying to copy Piper's accent. "You're one yee-ah older," Brittany is saying as we sit.

It's fun. Easy. The way it used to be.

"You look good," Tommy says, before he leaves. "I guess NutriNation really works."

"Yeah. I guess." For a split second, I think it's still possible that my original plan might work. That I could have it all. That I could get skinny and get the guy of my dreams. Except the guy of my dreams doesn't fat-shame people in the grocery store, doesn't run some kind of retail return racket and definitely doesn't hang off Kennes Butterfield's arm.

The original plan isn't proceeding like I hoped.

Grandma and I and a few ladies from the church clean up the hall. I drive us back to the yellow house and I'm that good kind of tired, the kind where you've spent your energy doing things you enjoyed.

After my shower, I smell the coffee brewing. Grandma's getting her decaf on. Like I expect, I find her at the kitchen table with a crossword puzzle and a hot cup. She motions for me to take the chair opposite her and pushes a stack of papers in front of me.

It's the stack from Parsons.

"You've got a deadline coming up," she says.

Stay calm. Look happy.

I slap a bland expression on my face. "Oh, I got a better offer. The Regents Scholarship. To ASU. Full ride."

Grandma blinks at me.

"New program? Girl, you been talkin' about Parsons since you had fewer candles on your birthday cake than fingers on your hand. What do you mean *a better offer*?"

I get up. I can feel the tears coming and I don't want Grandma to see them.

She follows behind me as I make my way down the hallway. And then I'm guilty and sad. Grandma's been working on my party all day and she's hobbling slow as she tails after me, saying, "I'm not through talkin' to you, girl."

"I'm really tired, Grandma," I say in a choked voice. "Thanks for the party. It was—"

"Spill the beans," she orders. She grabs the wall for support and I have to say something. I can't make Grandma mill around in the hall all night.

"I didn't get any financial aid from Parsons. I can't pay for it."

The tears come.

"I'm calling Martin."

"No. Don't call Dad." I wipe my eyes. "He's busy."

"Busy doing what?" Grandma spits.

"Curing disease in Africa."

"Charity begins at home, Cookie. He has a responsibility to you. You've been goin' on and on about Parsons and Claire McCardell since you could talk. Your daddy is a doctor capable of earnin' a living and sendin' you there."

"Why don't you call Mom? She's capable. She's got millions." I feel bad taking this approach. I know Grandma's got all kinds of guilty feelings about my mom.

There's a pause and Grandma shrinks down even smaller, older and sadder somehow. "Believe me, if I thought it would work, I would. I've had to reconcile myself to the fact that my daughter will never own up to her responsibilities. Your daddy, on the other hand, he might—"

I'm sort of grateful for the anger that floods me. It helps me steady my voice. "I don't know why you're pretending he's any better than she is. He ran away too. Ran away to Africa. To get away from having to deal with me."

"Cookie, that's not true. He's just...he's just..." Grandma trails off, trying to put her finger on what my dad *just* is. It's the first time we've ever said any of this stuff out loud. Acting like my dad is some big hero is a fiction we've both always felt more comfortable with. And from Grandma's perspective, I get it. It's hard to tell a kid that neither of her parents gives a damn about her.

"All the other doctors come home. For Christmas. Or important birthdays. Or the summer," I tell her in a low voice. "He stays in Africa. He'll never own up to his responsibilities either. And I won't beg him to." I can't ask him for help. What would I do when he said no?

Grandma puts her hand on the wall to brace herself. "You don't understand. You were a little girl and you couldn't understand what happened. Leslie is selfish. But Martin loved her. She broke his heart and I don't think he ever recovered."

"It doesn't matter." In a calmer, more pleasant voice, I go on. "Please. Don't call Dad. ASU will be great. I can stay here. I won't have to go to New York."

This has an impact. Grandma hates New York. "Well. Still..." She trails off.

I've won.

The preservation of the status quo is my reward.

So I'm eighteen.

Everything's supposed to be different.
But all I want is for everything to stay the same.
All alone in my room, I make an entry in my blog.

Roundish <New Post>

Title: Forever Fashion Finds

Creator: Cookie Vonn [administrator]

When people talk about fashion, they're often thinking about change. Magazines show what's coming next season. Stores show off the new stuff you can buy. There are makeovers and makeunders and total transformations. It's true that fashion lets us continually reinvent ourselves; it gives us all that superpower. But there's something to be said for the things that last. Wardrobe staples like jeans and turtlenecks and cardigans. That T-shirt that fits perfectly, that's worn in all the right places. The favorite pair of shoes that make you feel confident. Let's celebrate the new and remember the old. Let's make fashion forever.

SKINNY: Days 847–848 get even weirder

Chad Tate.

I'd never given much thought to what Chad Tate might be doing when not making my life miserable. I sort of imagined he went into cryosleep or something. That the Giants or Mom pulled his brain-dead body from the vault whenever the script required him to make an appearance.

But here he is. Right at home in the hustle of New York. In his city clothes, black slacks and a tailored wool coat, which make him look refined and polished.

"Cookie."

There it is. The toothy grin. The fake affable charm.

"What are you doing here?" I'm standing in this weird spot in front of Gareth's building, between the car and the door with the tips of my heels touching the edge of the doormat. The doorman is trying to figure out whether or not to open the door. The Town Car driver is still there, eyeing Tate, seeming to wonder if I plan to beat a retreat into the sedan.

"Cashing in my chips," he tells me.

I wave to the driver and, after giving me a small nod, he gets behind the wheel and steers the car off into midday traffic. "What are you talking about?"

"Is *he* home? The doorman says he's not usually home this time of day."

Chad Tate is watching me. Looking at me in a way that makes my skin crawl. That makes me want to take a very long shower.

"I haven't been home all day. I don't know if Gareth is upstairs. If that's who you're talking about. And I don't have anything to say to you." I take a step closer to the building and the doorman pushes the door open a crack.

Chad Tate grabs my arm. Hard. I don't know what to do. I could get the doorman. But I don't want some big melodramatic scene with my lame-ass stepfather. I don't want that crap to be a part of the little world I share with Gareth.

"Five minutes, Cookie. In private."

He tries to steer me toward the door but I know I don't want to be alone with him in Gareth's apartment. He's got his hand way too low on my back.

"There's a coffee shop next door," I tell him.

"There's an empty penthouse straight ahead." He wags his dark eyes suggestively and this gives me the resolve I need.

I shake free of him. "Coffee or nothing."

We take a table near the window of the shop. Ever the chauvinist, he orders me some kind of drink overloaded with whipped cream and caramel sauce that I stab with a stir stick. I don't bother correcting him. I want to get out of here as fast as possible.

"If this is about that thing with Mom—" I'm pretty sure he's come to beg for Mom's job. Chad Tate never likes to go without a meal ticket.

He shrugs out of his ashen gray coat and it falls over the edge of the wooden chair. "She kicked me out," he says. "This is about me. I need money."

"What? I don't have—"

He interrupts me again. "You have a boyfriend worth $100 million. From what I hear, you shake your ass in his general direction and you get what you want."

I hate that there's a kernel of truth in this. I spend my nights wrapped in Gareth's beige Sferra Milos $600 sheets and my days with his platinum Amex tucked in my purse. My face heats up and I ball my hands into fists. "What you hear? From who?"

He ignores this. "I've got an opportunity to put a new bar in Vegas. Right on the strip. I'm looking for investors."

Something about this makes no sense. Even for Chad Tate. "Wait. Aren't you going to have a baby?"

He snorts. "Is that your way of saying nobody's given you the birds and the bees lecture yet, Cookie? Because it's the female of the species who—"

"Go to hell. You know what I mean. Isn't my mom pregnant with your kid?"

He covers his hand with mine. I jerk it away and put it under the table in my lap.

Chad Tate laughs. A false, harsh, imitation of a laugh. "I told Leslie a million times. I don't want kids, and I certainly don't want a bunch of lectures on how I need to step up to the plate from some dead-broke, over-the-hill supermodel. I told her to get rid of it. She wouldn't, and that's her problem."

Emotions are hitting me in waves, building into a tsunami of confusion.

I'm vindicated. My mom's being forced to reap what's she's sown, finally having to deal with the asshole mess that is Chad Tate. She appears to be reaching the limit of what she can con from people by batting her eyes at them.

I'm mad. The nerve of Chad Tate. Taking all Mom's money and then complaining that he's not being supported in the manner to which he's become accustomed.

There's this other part of me that's worried and fearful and sad. The part that doesn't hate my mom quite as much as I wish I could. The part of me that remembers Lydia Moreno's face.

Chad Tate licks his lower lip. I'm fresh meat.

Situations like this have been one of the hardest things about losing weight. My body changed, and suddenly I became a player in this game where people are trying to get sex or approval or whatever from each other. It's one more reminder that losing weight hasn't worked out exactly like I thought it would.

"What about your job?" I ask.

He laughs again. "You're not a sports fan."

No. I'm not.

And Chad Tate's jaw is tightening, his eyes narrowing in a way that says he's losing patience. His good-guy smile is gone. "I haven't been with the Giants in over a year. There was a regime change. New coach didn't think I was worth having on the payroll. He said he'd prefer to, ah, invest in other areas."

Yeah, I can see that.

"Hey. Cookie. Do I need to remind you that you're sitting in that chair right now and not wearing pink underwear and eating veggie burgers at the Maricopa County Jail because I came through for you?"

"You ruined my life, and you want a medal pinned on your chest for telling your stupid football stories to a bunch of guys clueless enough to be impressed by them?" I sneer.

He leans forward and his coal-black sweater is pulled taut over his chest, still defined from all those hours at the gym. "Look, I was one of the best quarterbacks in the NFL. Ever. And I ruined your life? I was up front with your mom from the beginning. I can see why you needed me to be the big bad wolf when you were eight years old. But you're all grown up now." He stops for a second to look me over. "You gotta know that your mom didn't need much prompting from me to walk out on her responsibilities. You really think *I'm* the reason she didn't want to be a suburban housewife in Mesa, Arizona, kid?"

He's challenging the fiction I've always accepted. That Mom and Dad were happy until Chad Tate arrived.

The whipped cream has sunk into the diabetic nightmare of a drink in front of me, creating milky white swirls that rotate and churn. "I have to go."

I stand up and Chad Tate rises, as well. "We're not finished."

"Yes, we are."

Chad Tate has this look. Some weird mixture of fear and

regret and remorse. "Cookie, I came through for you when you needed it. Now it's your turn."

"Believe it or not, I can't make Gareth give you a bunch of money."

I get up from the table and he blocks my path.

He's getting older. The hair on his temples has gone gray. "I'm going to Vegas for a couple of weeks to get the details buttoned down. When I get back, there'll be an investors meeting. Make sure Calvin Klein Ken Doll is there. That's all you have to do."

I want to throw up and I'm relieved I didn't drink that sickly sweet coffee. "Fine. I'll try. But I'll eat my boots if you get Gareth to invest in one of your money-pit man caves."

Chad Tate sinks back into his chair and smiles. "You might want to start stockpiling ketchup to help you choke down all that leather."

I walk back to Gareth's building. I have to pass by the coffee shop window where Chad Tate remains at the table. He's resting his hand on his chin, staring off into space, like a male model in a fragrance ad.

I head straight to the penthouse. It's late in the day when I finally arrive, wound up like a toy top waiting to be released into wobbles and spins. Gareth takes one look at me and says, "Rough day, huh?"

"Yeah. I guess. I just saw Chad Tate outside."

Gareth doesn't know what to make of this revelation.

"My stepfather."

He steers me into an oversize white armchair and rubs my shoulders. "Tell Uncle Gary all about it."

Gary. It's the use of this little nickname that triggers the memory of my lunch with Dr. Moreno. That was a few hours ago, but the memory has already faded into a sepia-toned type of flashback.

“Do you *love* alcapurria?” I ask him.

“Cookie, I’m pretty sure you have a heart attack at forty if you eat too many of those damn things. Why do you—”

I interrupt him. “Do you know Lydia Moreno?”

He freezes for a second. “What does that have to do with your stepfather?”

“Nothing. Lydia…Dr. Moreno is my faculty advisor at ASU. She’s in town and she wanted to meet with me today. She said she knew you. Quite well.” I try to keep my voice neutral but it sounds like the beginning of a jealous girlfriend routine, even to me.

“We used to see each other. Back during my Parsons days.”

He doesn’t say anything for a minute and neither do I.

“Is she giving you a hard time?” he asks. He reaches into his pocket for his phone. “I’ll call her and tell her to—”

I put my hand on his arm to stop him. “No. No. Don’t do that. I just think…shouldn’t we be doing something? Designing something?”

Gareth rolls his eyes, sinks into a chair opposite me and checks his phone. “The design phase of the project is over. We’ve moved on to the production and marketing phases now.”

“Yeah. I get that,” I say in voice that is high-pitched and weirdly desperate. “But shouldn’t we always be making things? Always designing something?”

“Always designing something?” he echoes.

"I mean, when are you sketching?"

He lets his phone fall into his lap and regards me, chewing the inside of his cheek. "I have people doing that."

"People? Designers besides you?"

His gaze drifts to the cold glass window panes.

Seeing Chad Tate and Dr. Moreno on the same day was like being visited by the ghosts of Christmas Past and Christmas Future. I'm so uncertain about what I used to be and what I want to be in the future.

"Gareth, if I stay here in New York, what's going to happen?"

"Happen? *If* you stay in New York?" he repeats.

"To us. In our relationship. Will this be my apartment?"

Gareth's face pales. "You want me to give you an apartment?" His tone is icy.

"No. It's just… I want to know I have somewhere to live… I think that's a normal concern…" I stammer. His black eyes intimidate me.

He nods a couple of times, his face tense with anger. "Oh, okay. So here we go. You saw Lydia this morning and she told you a bunch of shit about me. How I can't fucking make clothes anymore on account of the fact that I don't want to chase cows round Lonesome Dove Ranch. How I'm an asshole who fucks everybody over. Well, let me tell you, Cookie, my relationship with Lydia didn't work out. And that says as much about her as it does about me."

I want to figure out a way to get out of this emotional shithole I'm digging for myself. "I'm sorry. I'm really sorry. I—"

Whatever storm is inside of him passes quickly and he gets

up and kneels beside me. "No. It's my fault. I shouldn't get so upset. There's something about you that I can't quite... You make me feel something when, for the longest time, I thought I couldn't feel anything at all. Cookie, I'll take care of you. I promise," he says, squeezing my hand. "We can talk about this later. But right now, you need to get ready."

The tension drains out of my shoulders. "For what?"

He smiles at me in a way that's a bit subdued and reaches behind the chair for a small gift bag. "Tell me why I have to find out from Facebook that it's your birthday."

Oh. Yeah. I'm twenty today.

I check my own phone for the first time in hours. There are a bunch of texts from Piper. Several messages from Grandma and a ton of "Happy Birthday" notifications from social media.

"I forgot," I tell Gareth.

"We need to celebrate the arrival of Cookie Vonn in style," Gareth says, standing and giving my back a final pat.

"Arrival? I didn't land on the planet's surface in a UFO."

Gareth smiles at me, waiting for me to open the gift. There's a long, velvet jewelry case inside. A single strand of Mikimoto pearls, graduated as they approach the clasp.

"Beautiful." It's a wardrobe staple. The classic kind of thing that passes from mothers to daughters.

"Yes. You are."

I get ready and do my best to forget about the day.

Gareth somehow gets all twelve seats in the tiny, but trendy Chang's Noodle Bar. We eat gourmet ramen with Piper and Brian and a bunch of people from G Studios. Nobody asks me for ID as I'm served glass after glass of expensive, warm sake.

I can't remember much of what happens after that. I end up snuggled against Gareth's chest, dreaming of fabric that spools endlessly off a massive loom.

It's mostly dark when Gareth wakes me by poking me in the rib cage a few times. "Come on. You said you want to work. So let's go."

He nudges me a few more times so I know he's not being ridiculous. I throw on leggings and a sweater and meet him in the kitchen. He's in there in a normal pair of jeans, a Toad the Wet Sprocket T-shirt and is carrying a backpack.

I can't even believe Gareth John Miller *owns* a backpack.

He slides into a leather jacket as he says, "Let's go."

We take the subway. "I didn't realize you knew where the station was," I say.

Reaching into the backpack, he hands me a thermos of coffee. "Keep your strength up, funny girl."

I assume we're going to the Brooklyn Bridge since we get off at that stop. But instead we walk to where the Williamsburg Bridge extends over the East River. Its steel trusswork glows gold as the sun rises.

Gareth finds a grassy area and produces a thin blanket from the backpack. He spreads it on the ground and hands me a sketchbook as we sit. "Okay," he says. "Describe the bridge in three words."

"Um. Silver. Straight. Long."

Gareth snorts. "Very creative."

"It's six in the morning!"

He nods. "Okay. Now there's a woman coming across

the bridge. Sketch something for her to wear that could be described with those three words."

I start making scratches with the pencil he's given me, but he stops me immediately. "First rule of design, Cookie. Always ask who the woman is."

With a smile, I ask, "So who's the woman?"

"Let's say midthirties. Professional. She's got money for the clothes we want to sell. But she's got kids at home. Likes to look good. Comfort is key."

I pick up the pencil again. This time Gareth says, "Second rule. Ask where the woman is going. Is she headed to Pilates? To a cocktail party? A funeral?"

"We're making funeral wear now?" I roll my eyes even though he's right.

"Nah. Let's say our gal is having breakfast with her boss."

I snort. "Very funny."

This time I do get to sketch. Gareth is drawing something too, but it looks more like a take on the lattice pattern of the bridge. He leans over my sketchbook. "That's good. But you have to think about proportion. Especially if you want to do plus-size."

I'm taking stabs at a pantsuit that would be made from a gold and silver ombré fabric, the colors reflected across the metallic surfaces of the bridge. "This is your process?"

"Sometimes." He kisses my forehead.

We've been at this for about an hour when my phone rings. Gareth passes me the beeping and buzzing rectangle.

One more surprise.

A gravelly voice travels through the speaker. "Cookie? I need to talk to you."

It's Dad.

He's calling from a Phoenix number.

For the first time in ten years, Dr. Martin Vonn has returned from Africa.

FAT: Days 265–266 of NutriNation

Graduation Day.

It's a hip-hop song. A rite of passage.

Another occasion celebrated with food.

Of course there's cake. Usually with a cheap, plastic version of a mortarboard cap plopped in a pile of buttercream icing. Somehow every party involves cake and me saying, "Just a tiny, tiny slice, okay?" Somehow, I always end up with a ten-thousand-calorie serving that weighs down the thin paper plate it's being served on.

This is yet another one of the ironies of being fat.

People assume you love food. And they really want to help you out with that.

In the windup to graduation, I'm actually feeling good. I'm down seventy-five pounds and I celebrate by treating myself to a Banana Republic T-shirt.

My blog is doing better than I thought it would. Carson helped me set it up so that promos of my articles get posted to Twitter and Instagram. He told me I have to go on a couple times a day and tag people with a lot of followers. I'm following his instructions and it's working. So far this month, *Roundish* has gotten twenty-five hundred page views.

Tommy and I are okay. We hang out. We avoid any mention of Kennes. It's like his life has two separate realities. The one where he's a Monopoly-loving astro-doofus, and the other one where he's a reanimated Dream Date Doll.

Kennes is now one of the most popular girls in school.

Yeah.

Sometimes I think high school needs a new vocabulary. One that explains how a girl nobody can stand to be around can be defined as popular. But she is. The kids who probably wouldn't bother tossing her a life preserver if she fell off the back of a boat flock to her parties and jockey for a seat next to her at lunch.

She's also the head of the student committee managing the graduation ceremony.

Kennes Butterfield is the head of the committee handing out and collecting the cap-and-gown order forms.

She personally delivers the forms to the vendor.

This fact is important.

The other fact that's important is that Grandma is running seriously low on cash. She doesn't get her Social Security check until the twenty-fifth of the month, hasn't had much sewing work since she finished all of the prom dresses, and I suspect that whatever extra money she's got is going toward my graduation party.

At Donutville, Steve decides to "accidentally drop" a large bag of decaf coffee so Grandma doesn't go bonkers without her usual daily pot. I can tell Mr. Kraken doesn't buy it, but

Steve is the best baker he's got and the only one willing to work holidays. Kraken doesn't say anything as I lug the big bag to my car.

The graduation ceremony is on Saturday. If it doesn't rain, it'll be held on the football field. It seems weird to worry about the weather in Phoenix because it's sunny here, like, 364 days of the year. But my iPhone says 70 percent chance of scattered showers for Saturday.

On Friday, I head to the office where the caps and gowns we've preordered are being distributed. And this happens.

Me: "This gown is the wrong size."

Cheerleader and Friend of Kennes: (fiddles with gown order form) "It's what you ordered."

Me: "No, it isn't."

Cheerbot2000: "The gown matches the form."

Me: (checks form, finds it's not in my handwriting) "That's not mine. Why would I order a medium?"

Cheerbot2000: (grins) "Maybe you got a little too optimistic about your diet?"

Me: (growls, bares teeth) "I need a gown that fits."

Cheerbot2000: (huffs, rolls eyes three times) "We have extras in each size. But you'll have to pay for it. That'll be $54.20."

Me: (clenches teeth) "Fine. Refund me for the one that's too small."

(Several more minutes of arguing)

Enter Mrs. Vargas.

I like Mrs. Vargas. But still she says: "I'm really sorry, Cookie. You have to keep the robe you ordered. Sales are final to the school. If you need another one, you have to pay the additional fee."

(Several more minutes of smug looks from Cheerbot2000)

I should have seen it coming.

I should have realized Kennes wouldn't let me walk away from that fucked-up scene outside *SoScottsdale* unscathed. That she wouldn't let me keep my portion of the proceeds from the war between us.

It doesn't seem to matter to anyone that the handwriting on the yellow carbon copy doesn't match mine or that most of the info, like phone number and address, is missing. I own that medium gown. No amount of debating will change things.

I don't have $54.20 for another set and I don't have anywhere I can go to get it. I won't ask Tommy. Somehow, asking him for money feels like it would turn me into Kennes. I spend the next twenty minutes roaming the hot Mountain Vista campus looking for her. But the lawns and hallways are empty. The year is coming to a close and people are moving on.

At home, I unwrap the gown and measure it. I can fit my arms into the sleeves, but when I do they look like sausages hanging off my body. I might be able to cut the sleeves on the underside and add a couple inches of elastic.

The gown itself is the bigger problem. It needs at least eight inches of additional fabric to be able to zip up. Even more than that to drape properly.

I'm screwed.

There's not too much I could do to fix the gown even if I wanted to. I could maybe rip out the side seams and add fabric. But what kind would I add? Where would I get it? And there's no telling that I'd be able to get the thing back together again. The $50 gown is made of disgustingly cheap acetate. Designed for single use. Not for tailoring.

Kennes Butterfield screwed me.

I take to the internet and Google my problem. It turns out I'm not alone, which is sort of reassuring. But no one has successfully resolved the problem either. The best advice is to wear something of a similar color and leave the robe open in the front.

Great. I'll just start searching for everything shiny and royal blue that I own.

I have to do something, so I cut the sleeves and add strips of elastic every few inches. It takes hours. The acetate bunches and gets stuck under the presser foot a billion times. But I do it. The sleeves fit, and as long as I don't lift my arms over my head like the girls in the deodorant commercials, no one will ever know.

That leaves the gown.

I have a plan, and I stay up all night.

Around two in the morning light rain drizzles. It stops, but the morning sky is overcast, the kind of thing most people would describe as gloomy. But it's special. Rain. Water. Weather. It means change and birth and rebirth.

The next afternoon I show up to the graduation ceremony. My history teacher, Mr. Smith, has been given the thankless job of organizing us into our rows. Like usual, I'm sandwiched in between Luke Vaughn and Chris Vonne in the line waiting to be seated. We've had four years of this and I know we'll be happy not to see each other again after today.

And this happens.

Mr. Smith: "Cookie, I'll need to ask you to zip up that gown."

Me: (telling myself to keep a calm, even tone) "I can't. It doesn't fit."

I've got the full attention of Vaughn and Vonne and a few other kids.

Mr. Smith: "Um. Well. The dress code says…"

Me: (feeling bad that Mr. Smith is in this position—he's a nice guy; but no retreat, no surrender) "Kennes Butterfield deliberately changed my robe order form, forcing me to buy one that clearly wouldn't fit. I didn't have the money for a second one."

Mr. Smith: "That's a serious accusation."

Me: (face turning red) "It's the only explanation that makes any sense. I would never have ordered this robe. I've been making my own clothes since I was ten. I wouldn't mess up my size."

Mr. Smith: (face also turning red and lips pressing into an embarrassed white line) "You're a good student, Cookie. But you can't walk if you don't conform to the graduation dress code."

Me: (keep calm, keep calm) "Through no fault of my own, I have a gown that doesn't fit. If you want to tell me I can't walk, that I'm too fat to walk, then okay. Just let me get my phone out so I can get video of it for Twitter."

Mr. Smith: (face now angry red) "You're not too fat. You're out of dress code. If I make an exception for you, I'd have to make one for everyone."

Me: (iPhone in hand) "You should make an exception.

For me. And everyone in the same situation as me. I'm tired of being part of a world that tells me I have to be a victim of people like Kennes Butterfield. And I'm tired of people saying they won't help when they see something wrong. You've known me for four years. Have I ever lied? Have I ever accused anyone of anything? I'm telling you. Kennes changed my form so I'd either have to look or feel fat. If you don't let me walk, you're doing the same thing."

Mr. Smith looks at me. Really sees *me*.

I get the whole thing out. The entire speech exactly as I practiced it in front of the mirror. There's a bunch of people crowded around me. Whispers are traveling up the line. Up to the front where they will surely reach the *B*s.

It gets back to the *W*s even faster.

Tommy Weston is about fifteen people behind me. Staring with his mouth open. Like I've just punched him in the face and left his jaw inoperable. He steps out of his place in line and moves toward the front, where I'm sure Kennes is waiting.

I didn't plan for this.

For collateral damage.

A bunch of things hit me fast. Why Grandma says to take the high road. What Father Tim meant that afternoon when he said you can't seek vengeance.

But it's too late. My plan is in motion.

Mr. Smith is back with a bunch of teachers and someone I think might be the vice principal. They're murmuring and whispering and huddling.

They have a decision.

I can walk.

The world will see the T-shirt I spent all night screen-printing by hand. The one that reads, We Are All Roundish.com.

Mr. Smith straightens out our line formations and when "Pomp and Circumstance" plays, we take to the football field. The ceremony itself is unbelievably boring. Tommy's seat, which is at the end of my row, sits empty for the whole thing.

Some mean old lady lectures about consumerism and youth culture and how everyone who graduates today needs to avoid gobbling up the world's resources the way our parents and their parents have. Some nice old lady talks about how promising the future is. Some kid I've never seen before says YOLO over and over. By the end of his speech, I sort of hope the Hindus are right and that *you only live once* is a bunch of crap. I sort of hope we live a thousand lifetimes and that guy keeps coming back as a blob fish.

When blob fish is done, we wait. Because my last name is Vonn, I'm waiting awhile. There are awkward pauses when they read Kennes's and Tommy's names.

As it turns out, we're waiting for nothing. Well, for an empty vinyl diploma holder, anyway. I smile and get a picture of myself holding a note that reads, "Your diploma will be mailed to you over the summer."

Awesome.

But as I pass by the rows of other students who already have their empty holders, I see quite a few phones out. I see my blog loaded up on several screens. My plan is working. In the way that I intended. And a couple ways I didn't.

I later find out, I got more than six hundred hits during

the ceremony itself, and a bunch more later on. Here's what people see:

Roundish <New Post>
Title: Independence Day
Creator: Cookie Vonn [administrator]

Today, we graduate. We're independent of our school. Less accountable to our families. Everyone wants to talk about the future. Everyone wants to leave their failures behind and take their successes with them. Are you weird or wired? Fat or skinny? Gay or straight? Jock, emo, wannabe, loser, skater, punk, stoner, geek, loner, nerd? We need to leave those labels behind. They're in the past. Like those old spelling bee ribbons you won't be hanging in your dorm room. But let's also leave behind the desire to be labelers. Let's have more important things to do than sit around and judge each other. Happy Graduation! Here's to us and whoever we want to become.

The ceremony ends, and the clouds that have patiently waited all day release their water onto the dry grass of the field. People root through their bags for umbrellas. AV guys run around covering and packing equipment.

I want to stand there forever. To roll into the gutter with the rainwater.

But in a way, we're all like planets in a solar system. We've got certain trajectories. An emotional gravity that can't be resisted.

Grandma's throwing me a party right after the ceremony.

At the church. Father Tim gives a sort of weird lecture on how the cap-and-gown outfit was inspired by Catholic clergy. There's something about an increase in vocations to the church. I'm not sure what the point is. I'm not cut out to be a nun.

Tommy doesn't show up to my party.

Shit.

We're cleaning up and Grandma says, "Mrs. Weston called. Wanted to make sure you're still headed over there tonight."

"Tommy didn't come *here*," I say, desperate for any reason not to have to show my face over *there*.

"And I suppose you didn't have nothin' to do with the fact that they called his name and no one showed to take his damn diploma?"

I don't answer and devote all my focus into wiping a school cafeteria–style table.

Grandma stuffs the remains of the cake into a white garbage bag. "You're lettin' that girl get the better of you, Cookie. It's gonna cost you your friendship."

I frown. "He's not the same as he was."

She pats me on the back. "Maybe you're becomin' something else too. Either way, you said you was gonna be at that party. You're gonna be at that party."

The last-ditch effort of a coward. "He said he was going to be *here*."

"Cookie..." Grandma's tone carries a warning. There's no more arguing. I'm going to the Westons' house.

I drive over in my old Corolla and park between two nicer sedans. Tommy's house is one of the smaller ones in

Las Sendas, the fancy community on the north side of town, but it's still nice. It's got the usual suburban trappings. The marble countertops. The hardwood floors.

Tommy's mom lets me in and I stand in the foyer making small talk with her for a few minutes, my sweaty hand wrapped around the string of a gift bag containing an antique brass gyroscope. Mrs. Weston takes the gift bag and disappears into the kitchen.

The party is out by the pool, which glows with blue lights and clear, floating beach balls. I see Tommy standing on one side of his backyard, talking to Kennes. They see me. She squints and turns away, and Tommy stays focused on her.

There's a DJ who's probably friends with Tommy's dad. The guy is playing the kind of stuff you hear at weddings. Sister Sledge. Kool & the Gang.

Mrs. Weston breezes by and hands me a drink. "Tommy's party punch."

My gaze drifts over the custom cup that has *Tommy* written on it in gold glitter letters and a striped paper straw sticking out.

She's watching Tommy with a soft, unfocused smile. "He's probably getting too old for the glitter." Her face sharpens as she turns back to me. "But you know I love my Pinterest boards."

Yeah, I've seen Mrs. Weston's massive online collection of craft ideas.

There's a break in the music, and Mrs. Weston shoos me toward the DJ booth. "We were hoping you could say a few words."

I make a big show of picking at a hangnail. "Oh. Um. Me?" I stammer. "I think Tommy might rather have Kennes..."

Mrs. Weston takes me by the elbow. "You've known him longest, Cookie."

And then I'm standing next to the weird DJ with a bunch of kids from school surrounding me, a cheap microphone in my hand. Kennes glares at me.

Take the high road.

If there was ever a moment to heed Grandma's advice, this is it.

Think about it. Think about Tommy.

"Oh. Hi..." There's feedback from the mic. A few people groan. I keep going. "I met Tommy at camp. I...uh... wish I had a bunch of hilarious camp stories to share, but the truth is, Tommy's never done anything even remotely embarrassing."

No. He let me take the hit at Toys"R"Us. He let me staff the PB&J table.

"Tommy's been the best friend, the best student and the best son. Even though we're going on to different things, I know we'll always be there for each other. And no one's future is brighter than Tommy's. He's always loved the stars, but really, he's the one who's out of this world."

It's horrible and corny.

There's a quiet "Aww" from the small crowd. Tommy's parents beam at me. I guess this means I have, in fact, taken the high road. Grandma failed to mention that doing this would be as unsatisfying as doing the wrong thing.

I hold the mic out to the gray-haired DJ and head through

the sliding glass doors. I'm almost to my car when Tommy catches up with me.

"Thank you for that," he says. He steps in front of me, leaning against the Corolla door. I think he wants to say something, but he's focused on the asphalt sparkling under the yellow streetlights. "The speech," he mumbles into his collar. "It was nice."

"I have to go."

Tommy puts his hand on my arm. "Cookie. Did you have to start that shit with Kennes at the ceremony today?"

I grab his chin and force him to look at me. "You know she did it. You know she screwed up my gown order, don't you? And you don't care. We're supposed to be friends. Best friends."

"Jesus, Cookie. Why does everything have to be such a fucking cartoon with you? You're the sheep dog. That makes Kennes the wolf. And the world's full of fucking anvils dropping from the sky and birthday cakes with dynamite inside."

He shirks out of my hold, but his face is only inches from mine. Orange Tics Tacs. That's what I smell as he keeps going. "I told her that thing with the gown totally sucks and she really is sorry. But you've dished out as much crap as you've taken here. Your take-this-job-and-shove-it routine caused Kennes plenty of trouble. At the office Brittany and Shelby made you their personal Norma Rae complete with a shrine of coffee mugs and Post-it pads next to the copy machine. I don't know if she was deliberately out to ruin your graduation day. But you ruined hers. And mine."

My defiance surges up. "It was your choice to go. It was

your choice to stand by her even though you knew she did something totally shitty to me."

His eyes plead with me. "What kind of choice did I really have? I've got two friends trying to rip each other apart."

Kennes means as much to him as I do, and that really, really hurts. "Whatever. I have to go," I say again, motioning for him to move away from my car.

He shakes his sandy hair. "This is it? You'd rather end our friendship than try to get along with Kennes? You won't even try? Try for me?"

No.

No, I won't.

No retreat. No surrender.

He shoves his hands into the pockets of the suit I made for him. The memory of hemming those wool pants belongs to another life. Or to another person. I want to be anywhere else but here. And I'm not going to cry.

"I'm not going to move until you answer me," he says.

I guess I could try to yank him off the door. For a second, I have a vision of me lifting him over my head like a misshapen barbell and tossing him into his neighbor's gravel yard. But that seems like it might be going too far, even for me. So I answer. "People like me can't *get along* with people like her."

I won't cry.

"Cut the crap," he says. He knows I haven't made every fat-shaming, mean girl in school my nemesis. He knows there's more to this than Kennes making me feel like a fat girl on a plane.

I glare at him. This is why it's easier to fight your enemies than your friends. Friends know your weaknesses, your vulnerabilities. They know when you're not being real. And honestly, what do I have to lose? Our friendship is gone or about to go into long-term hibernation.

I decide to go for it. "I thought…I thought…things would be different. I thought, if I lost weight, you would see that… I…I liked you. Liked everything about you. The way you always forget to tuck your shirt in on one side. The cowlick that makes your hair stick up when it gets too long. Your weird Lego robots. That you actually think 'Backpack' is a good song. The way you always buy Boardwalk even though I never land on it. I—"

"You liked me? *Liked* me?" Tommy's voice is laced with thick, hard sarcasm. I can't remember him speaking to me like this before. "You think I would only have liked you back if you were stick skinny? You think I'm like that? Or maybe you're only saying this now because I'm finally with somebody."

I'm grateful for the hot anger bubbling up in my blood. "What the hell are you talking about?"

He grabs me, placing one hand on each of my shoulders, and jerks me back and forth a couple of times. "I did *everything.* I took you to every school dance. Spent hours and hours watching TV with your grandma. I was *there* for you. I waited. And waited. And you…you…all you could do was be mad as hell at the world. And now…now you want to tell me that you liked me? Past tense? You *liked* me? Well, you never did one fucking thing to show it."

I take deep breaths to keep myself calm. This would be that moment in romantic comedies when the hero says, *Wait here*, goes back into the party to break up with his horrible girlfriend and comes back to kiss the girl-next-door. But this is real life, my life, and this won't end like an old episode of *Friends*.

We stare at each other like opponents on opposite sides of a chessboard. It's suddenly so, so obvious that Grandma was right about everything. I started this bullshit war with Kennes, and I'm its real casualty. But it's too late.

"And for the record," Tommy says in the same harsh voice, "I liked you exactly as you were. As you are. Everything about you."

I have to do something or in seconds I'll be bawling my face off. I push myself up on my tiptoes and press my lips against his. At first, he's motionless, frozen with closed lips. My face flushes and I sink back down.

His eyes dart back and forth as my heels hit the pavement.

I expect him to move out of the way and go back inside.

But he grabs me, swirls me around so that my back is against the car door and wraps his arms around me in a way that would have been impossible a year ago. This is the romantic scene I've been taught to expect. This is what the Hollywood ending looks like.

An electric energy jolts through me. His tongue is in my mouth, at first, swishing awkwardly, then moving with purpose along my lower lip.

He's into it.

And then.

"We can't." He steps back.

A coolness fills the space between us.

"You know, you could have said something too." I unlock the car. I won't cry.

"Yeah. Well. Maybe we'll…um…see each other on campus." He turns to go.

"Yeah," I whisper as his curly blond head vanishes through his front door.

I *won't* cry.

They show you pictures of the heart in Biology class. A powerful mass of muscle, pumping lifeblood, in and out, all day, day after day. The human heart never rests, never takes a day off. And yet, in that instant, my heart has no volume or shape or substance. It's like a glass ornament that has fallen from the Christmas tree. It's been reduced to shiny, scattered pieces you could brush away with your shoe.

I drive to the yellow house and I'm beginning to think there's no upside to this whole becoming-an-adult thing.

At home, Grandma's waiting at the kitchen table. She pours me my own cup of decaf, pushes a regular-size envelope across the worn wood surface and gets up. She's making a plate of food for Roscoe, the giant Labrador barking in the backyard.

It's a strange thing. But the fact that time is passing, that things are becoming different, hits me full on. Especially about Grandma. There's no one else who serves their dog sandwiches on a porcelain plate. Who covers their windows with aluminum foil. Who still plays with paper dolls. The lines on her face have grown thick and deep. Time is running out. She won't be at the table forever.

She turns from the stove, where she's flipping a grilled cheese with a spatula. "Open it," she says with a wave at the envelope. "You're a good girl, Cookie. You deserve something nice. To spend a nice summer with your friend."

I open the envelope and immediately understand why we've been so broke.

It's a plane ticket. To Sydney.

Australia.

I burst into tears.

SKINNY: Days 848–855 of NutriNation

"Dad? Where are you calling from?" I wish Gareth would have brought more coffee to this little picnic of ours. Or maybe eight or ten shots of espresso. More caffeine would definitely improve my ability to handle this situation.

"I'm at Edna's," he says.

I shove the phone hard against my face. "At Grandma's? You're back from Africa? What's wrong?"

Pause.

"Didn't your mother call you?" he asks.

"Mom?" I snort. "Are you serious? I haven't gotten so much as a Christmas card from Mom in two years."

Pause.

"Chad Tate is dead."

Pause.

"So?" I ask in a heated tone. My blood pressure is rising. The situation dawns on me. Something's happened to Chad Tate, and Mom went running to Dad. Like she wants to press rewind on the men in her life.

Pause.

"So?" my dad repeats in that stern tone he used when I was five and wouldn't eat my broccoli. "So there's going to be a service next Thursday. I'll email you your plane ticket and then we can figure out—"

"That won't be necessary."

Pause.

"Well, I guess if you'd prefer to make your own reservations, then—"

"I'm not coming."

"Cookie. Your mother's quite upset, she needs us to—"

"She needs a lot of things, Dad. If you want to help her, good luck with that." I press the red end-call button on my phone. Let him spend some time wishing I would call for a change.

It feels strangely empowering.

I get up and pace around the park, kicking at the corners of our picnic blanket, muttering, "The nerve of him. The nerve of him," over and over.

I'm not even sure which *him* I mean.

There's Chad Tate, who's managed to die on a schedule that both deprives me of reaching the high point of my life and looking down on him *and* puts pressure on me to feel pity for my mother.

There's my dad, who didn't step foot on this continent for my sixteenth birthday or my high school graduation, but returned the instant Mom called him.

There's God. Everything is really his fault anyway. He could have given me Mike and Carol Brady as parents, but instead I got the disappearing doctor and the supermodel who shows up just long enough to make me feel like shit.

Screw them.

Screw.

Them.

Gareth leads me back to the train. I pay very little attention to how we get home. I keep thinking *screw them, screw them* over and over. We arrive at the penthouse, where Gareth spends half an hour rubbing his chin and trying to get a coherent set of facts from me. Right then, there is no fashion impresario. Only a good guy from Montana. When he understands what's going on, he puts his arm around me and guides me to the sofa. He turns on the TV. ESPN is covering Chad Tate's death.

The New York Giants' publicist deserves an Academy Award.

She gets on TV and acts shocked. "We're deeply saddened at the loss of one of the NFL's all-time greats." She manages to say this with a doleful expression.

I guess after he corralled me into having coffee with him, Chad Tate did end up in Vegas, where he got bombed and wandered into traffic. Trolls on the internet have a field day. "Ex–NY Giant Chad Tate stumbles out of nightclub and tackles minivan," one blogger posts. "NFL Hall of Famer Chad Tate learns bar is out of Pabst Blue Ribbon and rushes Las Vegas Boulevard," writes another.

They show the poor lady who hit him. She's got tears squirting out her eyes, and she wrings her hands and keeps saying, "I couldn't stop in time."

I want to tell her it's not her fault. That Chad Tate is, or was, a useless asshat. That when you spend half your time drunk off your ass, accidents are bound to happen.

They put Mom on TV. She's in a tasteful, black Calvin Klein sheath dress and a strand of pearls. She cries and whines, but her emotions don't impact her waterproof mascara and airbrush foundation.

"You sure about this?" Gareth asks. "About not going to the funeral? You know, Chad Tate's not gonna die twice."

"Yeah," I agree. "Once'll have to be enough."

There's just one problem.

God gave me one person on whom I can't wish a plague of locusts.

Grandma.

She calls about nine New York time. "I expect you know why I'm callin'."

I do.

"Girl, I suppose there ain't no love lost between you and your momma and, yes, you're entitled to be disappointed at the hand you've been dealt. But there are times in life when we have a duty to do right, to stand with family even if we don't wanna, even if they haven't stood by us. You need to be at the service on Thursday. Not for Martin or your momma or even me. You need to be there for yourself. Because you're a person who'll rise to the occasion and do the right thing."

I'm not sure Grandma is right on that one.

Still, I decide to go to the service.

For all the wrong reasons.

I tell myself, and Gareth, that I have to go for Grandma. He arranges for his plane to take us to Phoenix. I'm surprised at the automatic nature of his behavior. I'm going home. And he's going with me. If the idea of meeting my father bothers him, it doesn't show.

Early Thursday morning, Gareth has them fly us to the Mesa Gateway airport, which is a few miles south of Grandma's house. Off the plane, the air is warm and familiar. Technically, the air is what we would consider freezing in Phoenix—around fifty degrees. But I've spent the last month in snowy New York, and shedding my thick Gareth Miller overcoat makes me feel like a snake leaving behind an old skin.

Chad Tate wasn't Catholic, so they can't have his funeral at the church. I doubt he had much faith in anything. Possibly money. Or football.

They set things up at Morton's Mortuary, sort of the Walmart of funeral homes. It's on one end of Main Street nestled between a hair salon and the music store. The front is covered in an artificial kind of vine that might have been sculpted by gardeners who were fired from Disneyland's Haunted Mansion. I tell the limo driver to drop us off in the back. Back there, I see one guy unloading a hearse and another offloading a truck full of tubas. Gareth squints and adjusts his jacket. He's not used to the rear entrance.

Morton's has packages ranging from the "Take Those Ashes and Get Out of Here" variety to the pomp and circumstance of Princess Diana's procession to Althorp. Chad Tate's funeral is more like the first option. It takes place in one of the small rooms, and Gareth and I are two of a dozen or so people scattered among padded beige chairs. Everything in the whole place is the color of partially digested butterscotch candies. I steer us to a seat in the back.

I recognize most of the people in the room. There's

Grandma up by Mom in the front row. Mom's sobbing into an expensive handkerchief while Grandma pats her back. Dad's on Mom's other side, facing front and staring straight ahead.

The only thing I can think is this:

What the hell happened to all Dad's hair?

It used to be black and thick and mowed by clippers in a perfect line right above his collar. But now? Well, now I can see his scalp through a round patch on the back of his head, and the gray hairs, growing like stiff weeds, are choking out the black ones.

Shit. Dad is old.

Cue terrible organ music, and a man comes to stand at a podium. He's tall and gaunt and grim and looks like, well, an undertaker. I wonder if the appearance is a job requirement. Or if being the steward of death would transform anyone into the austere figure at the front of the room.

"We are gathered in this place of mourning in loving memory of..."

The man has to check the sheet lying on the podium before going on.

"Chad Wesley Tate, who merged with the infinite on..."

I elbow Gareth. "Chad Tate merged with oncoming traffic."

He bites his lower lip and fights off a laugh.

I get an irritated look from my dad.

Gareth has never seemed more out of place to me. He's there in a cheap seat. He can't even pronounce Mesa correctly. He says the town's name with a posh affect. Mess-uh. That's where he is with his perfectly tailored bespoke suit, his gelled-up hair, his trendy day-old stubble. He's a Twitter meme waiting to happen. An online "Caption This" contest in the making.

"Life is too short. It can end at any time."

It's then that I see Tommy.

I hadn't noticed him before, but there he is in the second row with his parents. It figures they'd show up here. They'd never miss an opportunity to be seen doing their duty, and Mrs. Weston works in sports PR and knew Chad.

Tommy's glaring. Not at me. At Gareth.

He's trimmed his hair short and is wearing the gray suit I made for him.

Back when we were still friends.

"You're gonna get us both in trouble," Gareth whispers into my ear.

"While heartache is as much a part of life as happiness, while for every laugh we shed a tear, today we can take comfort in our memories of..."

Mr. Undertaker has to check his paperwork again. How hard is it to remember Chad Tate's name?

"...Chad. We can recall those moments we treasured. Remember his love, his compassion and his strength..."

Dad puts his arm around Mom and pats her shoulder.

And that's it. Anger explodes inside me and overtakes my brain.

They can somehow pull it together to be there for each other. But never for me. I stumble out of the tiny room in what could best be described as a blind rage.

I hear the door snap shut with a quiet click and find Gareth is standing next to me.

"Ah, poor Chad Tate," he says.

I shrug. "I have to use the bathroom."

Inside the bathroom, there are plaques and framed quotes that say things like, "Your life is a blessing. Your memory is a treasure," and, "Those we love live forever in our hearts." I sit in the stall for a little while thinking that maybe if I stay on the toilet, my obligation to be at this funeral will pass.

The bathroom door slams. I'm sure, without peeking out of my stall, that it's Grandma.

I come out and start to say something, but she puts her hand in the air. "Comin' late. Leavin' early. You might think you're sendin' a message to your momma just now. But *I* raised you. What you're doin' is reflectin' on me, girl. And I brought you up better than this."

My shame fills up the tiny bathroom. "I'm sorry, Grandma. I'm sorry. But he deserved—"

Grandma gets mad. Madder than I've seen her in years. She braces herself on the bathroom counter, rolling her arthritic ankle.

Man. I'm really a shit sometimes.

"Good Lord," she says. "People don't get what they deserve. In life or death. You of all people ought to know that. And there ain't nobody, in as far as I know, that's gone and made you judge and jury of the human race. A life's been lost. You didn't like the man. Well, I didn't much care for him neither. We still gotta be decent, Cookie. That ain't optional."

I nod and mumble, "Sorry," again.

When we return to the hall, Tommy's left the service too.

I'm stunned by the sight of him talking to Gareth. "I know who you are," Tommy says. "I've heard all about *you*."

Gareth stuffs his hands in his pockets. "Wish I could say the same, friend. I'm sorry to report that I don't have the slightest damn idea who you are."

"I'm her best friend," Tommy says.

Stepping closer to Tommy, Gareth hunches his shoulders forward. "*Her?* Are you referring to Cookie now?"

"You're no good for her," Tommy says.

"Well, now, you've got a bit of a pocket advantage here, son. See, 'cause Cookie's never said word one about you."

This is true. I've been trying to forget Tommy and run away from what happened.

I'm not sure what really gets to Tommy. The fact that I don't talk about him, or Gareth's casual dismissal. He puts his hands on the lapels of Gareth's black jacket and shoves hard. Gareth tumbles back into the chair, whacking his head on the wall behind him, leaving a depression in the textured cream stucco.

There's a brawl.

I can barely make sense of what's happening and can't bring myself to intervene.

Tommy and Gareth travel down the hallway toward Morton's lobby, taking swings, knocking each other into the walls. Glass breaks, and there's a scraping noise as the pictures hanging on the stucco swing from side to side.

Growing up on a working ranch has left Gareth better prepared for situations such as these. He gets Tommy pinned to the ground. I'm trying to pull him off and am saying,

"Gareth! Gareth. Come on," when there's another figure in the foyer.

"What the hell is going on here?"

It's my dad.

Here's the thing about doctors. They like to complain about how there's no money in medicine anymore. How the good old days of guaranteed six-figure incomes and Friday golf games are gone. But being a doctor is one of the few remaining professions that still confers instant authority. Like army generals, they get to write orders that *have* to be followed. And believe me, they know it. In almost any situation, a doctor can and will assume the leadership position.

That's what happens here. My dad uses the booming voice he's developed barking out instructions to nurses and orderlies. "Stop this behavior at once."

Gareth releases Tommy. There are sheepish looks and red faces.

Dad ignores Tommy. And me.

He's dressed in a brand-new Men's Warehouse dark gray suit with too-long pants pooling around his ankles. He rounds on Gareth. "Care to explain what's going on, sir?"

I step in front of Gareth. "Why don't you ask me, Dad?" I say.

Dad turns to face me. He's looking at me like he never has before. In a strangled voice, he says, "Cookie. Hello. You are...you look...lovely. Just like your mother."

FAT: Days 294–312 of NutriNation

I don't make my goal.

I'm at my usual Saturday NutriNation meeting, staring at the three numbers written on my tracking form. Two. Two. Five. I weigh 225 pounds.

My goal was to be in the one hundreds by the time I left for Australia.

Our leader, Amanda, smiles and shakes her head. "That was never a very realistic goal, Cookie. You've done it exactly right, around two pounds a week. People who drop weight faster don't usually keep it off. Don't let this get you down. We have something special planned today."

Dave, Kimberly and Rickelle come in carrying flowers and balloons, and there's an unfamiliar face in the meeting room. Turns out, she's from NutriNation corporate and we're celebrating.

I'm down one hundred pounds.

One hundred and five to be exact.

Rickelle gets up and stands next to Amanda. "Everyone knows I love to run."

There's laughter from the group.

"And I *love* running metaphors. So here it goes. Losing weight isn't a sprint or even a 5K, it's a marathon and for most of us it'll never end. It's a journey that requires us to change, sometimes to change our most ingrained behavior. That's why I'm so proud of Cookie. I've seen her go from barely being able to walk a mile to running five miles a day. Sure, we're celebrating her hundred-pound loss. But really, we're celebrating what she's gained. Healthiness. Perspective. Confidence. We love you, Cookie."

I hug Rickelle as my eyes tear up and everyone claps.

I get a big, blue ribbon pinned to my chest and my group makes me feel like going to Sydney at 225 isn't such a big deal.

Amanda gives a lecture called "The Vacation Equation." "A lot of people gain weight during vacations. But it's basically an equation. Determine what kind of results you want and create the plan that will equal the results."

I take notes and it all sounds good.

And this is how I end up in the international terminal of Sky Harbor Airport with a suitcase that weighs eighty-five pounds.

The thing is stuffed full of all the food I usually eat but am terrified I won't find in Sydney. I've got three boxes of Clif Bars and my diet must-have—NutriMin Water Zero. I should have realized there would be a problem when I arrived at the check-in kiosk out of breath from having tugged the thing from the airport curb to the counter.

"You're overweight," the lady behind the counter says. At least that's what I think she says, anyway.

"What?" I must say this in a manner that's a bit too aggressive because the woman takes a step back and her eyes bug out.

"Your bag," she explains. "Seventy-five pounds is the limit."

"Oh...what...what do...do I do?" I'm still trying fill my lungs with air.

"Pay the $50 excessive baggage fee or take some stuff out. Lose ten pounds."

Easier said than done.

Well, I'm broke. And even if I weren't, I'm not sure I'd pay the fee anyway. Fifty bucks could keep me in sewing fabric for a month.

I unzip the suitcase as it sits on the stainless-steel scale.

And this is how I end up standing at the airline counter with my mouth open, watching bottles and bottles of Nutri-Min bounce and roll all over the terminal floor.

"Well, that does it," says airline lady. "Seventy pounds. I can check this now."

I rezip the bag as she wraps a tag around the handle. She waves at the floor littered with the gemstone-colored water bottles. "You'll have to pick those up."

"Yeah."

And this is how I end up crawling on my hands and knees, rounding up jugs of Berry Berry Blast, The Grape Escape and Orange You Glad We're Sugar-Free, and stuffing them into my tote bag.

The whole thing has the crazed tenor of a feral cat rooting

through the trash of a five-star restaurant. And I'm thinking about this. And asking myself why. Over and over. Why do these things always happen to me?

I fail to notice that I'm creeping too close to a pair of legs clad in tight-fitting olive chinos. A deep male voice says, "I guess you really like your NutriMin Water?"

I tilt my head up.

Fat girl meet health nut.

Everything about this guy screams that he spends half his time running in a loop around his posh NYC condo building and the other half in the organic supermarket picking through stalks of non-GMO rhubarb.

"Oh…sorry… I'm sorry," I stutter. He kneels down, picks up the last water bottle and then extends a hand to help me to my feet.

"You know, we sell this stuff everywhere," he says, inspecting the Perfect Peach. "You don't have to carry this much around with you." He's smiling, giving me an endearing smirk.

I'm close to his face now. I think he might be wearing makeup. His dark hair is graying at the temples. He's probably in his fifties but could pass for thirty. At a distance.

The idea of male makeup gets all my attention and I don't catch the "we" in his first sentence. I'm brushing the airport grime off and turning every shade of red and continuing with my stammering. "Oh…um…I read on the internet… that they don't have NutriMin Water in Australia…and that's where I'm going…and I can't stay on my diet without this stuff… I mean maybe I could… I haven't tried…and they said at the meeting…" I trail into an incoherent mumble and reach out for my water.

"Can't stay on your diet? Without NutriMin Water?" he repeats. I look around and notice that we're right in front of the airline's first-class counter and that a smiley version of the lady who helped me is tagging a stack of Louis Vuitton luggage. The guy's a rich and important health nut.

This unnerves me even more. "Yeah. I'm doing this weight loss thing and I have a NutriMin Water with every meal. At least it's something that tastes good, you know?"

"How much weight have you lost?" He's still got my Perfect Peach.

"What? Oh. Um. A hundred pounds—105 actually."

"Wow!"

My flush deepens. "I still have a long way to go, but…"

He grins at me. "But a hundred pounds is incredible."

"Yeah. I guess, yeah." I'm wondering if I should yank the bottle from his hands.

"I'd like to hear more about your story," he says.

"Uh, well…" I mumble. Announcements are being read over the loudspeaker. I need to get to my gate. The NutriMin's pink liquid catches the sunlight streaming in through the airport windows. "It's on my blog. *Roundish.* I talk about NutriMin all the time. I've even made outfits to match my water."

"Roundish?"

"You know, I'm taking the term back," I say. "Roundish women rule the world."

"Ah, sure. That's great." He extends his hand for me to shake. "I'm John Potanin."

He says his name like he's used to introducing himself to

people who already know who he is. If I had any brains at all, I would be trying to figure out how to surreptitiously Google this guy. Instead, I'm whipping my head around like a dog distracted by a squirrel.

John Potanin shakes the container of rose liquid. "They won't let you through security with this stuff. But don't worry. We just signed a distribution deal in Oz. By the time you get there, it should be hitting store shelves in Woolies and Coles."

"Oh. Uh. Cool. Thanks."

He hands me the bottle. "I hope we see each other again."

It's a sort of weird, semiflirtatious remark. But he's Mr. Physical Fitness and I'm Miss Fat Girl on a Plane. I blink a few times, take my water and go.

While I sit in the waiting area, I look him up. I find out that John Michael Potanin is a businessman who started NutriMin Water from the spare room of his apartment in Queens and is now on the verge of selling it to a soft drink company for $3 billion.

Of course, he winds up being right. I have to leave all my NutriMin Water at the security counter, and they do have an endcap full of the stuff at the Woolworths around the corner from Piper's house.

On the plane, I have a couple of non-scale victories. The guy sitting next to me doesn't roll his eyes when he sees me or make that "I always get stuck next to a fat person" face. I'm able to use the regular seat belt without the extender.

On another note, I had no idea that it's winter in July in Sydney. This is what happens when you pay almost no attention in Geography and aren't really familiar with the whole southern hemisphere thing. The day I arrive, it's rainy, and a gray fog rolls in from the beach, making the big city buildings look blurry and mysterious. Note to self: always check the destination weather before packing.

I imagined my two weeks in Australia would be one big Outback Steakhouse commercial where we would spend the whole time swimming in the ocean and holding skewers of shrimp over an open fire.

Instead, I have to borrow a series of light sweaters from Piper.

Her family has a cute creamish-white house in Maroubra, a suburb of Sydney. Piper's room is upstairs and overlooks a smallish tiled patio. She stands in front of her closet and tosses out a couple of cardigans on hangers.

"I'm not sure if these will fit you," she says, passing me a lime-green sweater.

I'm sitting on her bed. "It's fine." Anything is better than freezing my butt off.

"You've lost a lot more weight than me," she says with a frown.

I shrug and repeat something Amanda Harvey told me. "It happens differently for everyone. You have to go at your own pace."

Piper sits down next to me. "The plan doesn't seem to be working for me anymore. The doctor thinks it might be my thyroid. I'm having tests next week."

"Yeah," I agree. I've heard this in my NutriNation meetings too. Health issues can have a massive effect on weight loss and weight gain.

"Truthfully," she whispers, "I think the plan sort of sucks."

I think of the mountain of diet spring rolls I've eaten. "Yeah," I say. I want to agree with her but my dream is still to rule the world of fashion. And fashion hates fat.

I stand up and move around Piper's room, over to her bulletin board that's on a wall opposite the bed. I find a couple of pics of me. There's also a letter of acceptance to Columbia University in New York. Piper's always gotten top grades, so there's also a scholarship notice.

I turn around and frown at her. "You didn't even tell me you got your letter."

"Yeah. Yeah," she mumbles. "I'm not sure I'm going."

"What?" I ask. Like me, Piper's always wanted to study in New York.

"I…I thought…I would have lost more weight…and…"

"Piper! Seriously? You can't be—"

She stands up too. "Let's talk about it later, okay? My dad said he'll give us a ride to the beach." She leaves the room, giving me no choice but to follow her downstairs.

The trip is fabulous and we do everything. Sort of like that montage at the beginning of *Grease*.

We hike and camp and run around Coogee Beach. Piper surfs like every day. She loans me one of her extra wetsuits, and I make a few attempts at standing up on the board. Epic, epic wipeouts ensue.

We tour the Royal Botanic Garden. Unlike the Desert Botanical Garden in Phoenix, the Sydney garden has plants that don't look like they're from the Coyote and Roadrunner cartoons. There are bromeliads with pineapples and fire-colored flowers shooting from low, leafy plants. Evergold sedges spill over rocks and into the pathways.

So the legal drinking age in Australia is eighteen.

Yep. Piper can sip her Foster's anytime she wants, but back stateside, I'll be waiting three more years to legally have a waiter hand me a Corona Light.

My last night in Sydney she takes me to a pub called The Anchor on the south side of Bondi Beach and rolls her eyes at me as I say, "We're going to *a bar*," over and over. Her friend from school, Mia, shows up to drive us. To me, the girl's a dead ringer for *Dance Academy* mean girl, Abigail Armstrong.

"You'll like her, I promise," Piper says. "I swear. She's really been there for me, you know?"

I *don't* know. Mia looks like the kind of girl who'd steal your kidney for a pair of Louboutins, but I go along with it anyway.

Mia's short, bronze sequined skirt sways as we walk past a sign that reads, Tacocat Spelled Backward Is Still Tacocat.

It's taco Tuesday.

It's tacos versus beer in a battle for my calorie budget.

This is actually a lucky break. I hail from the land of the taco, where anytime, day or night, there's somebody in a food truck rolling a Monterrey street taco, or griddling up Sonoran-style tortillas. And Australians make sucky tacos.

Beer it is.

Piper hooks it up because I have no idea how to order a beer. There are about a hundred million different kinds served in a billion kind of glasses. The waiter brings me a bottle and then I'm looking all around waiting for the cops to bust in and rip it from my underage palm.

Mean Mia pats her glossy, black hair and says, "Hey, Piper,

what's up with your mate? She's got a few roos loose in the top paddock."

I laugh right then. Piper later explains that Mia's calling me an idiot.

After two beers, I'm buzzed and have a full bladder. Because girls can't go to the bathroom by themselves, Piper takes me to the ladies, leaving Mean Mia alone at the table. She's making doe eyes at every guy who passes by.

We walk back to the table to find Mia in huddled conversation with a really hot guy. The convo is a game changer.

"Your friend. Will you just give her my number?" This is what Hot Guy is saying as we approach the table.

"She's American, dumbass. By this time tomorrow, she'll be on her way back to the land of Cokes in cups the size of buckets and no gun control."

Oh, screw you, Mean Mia. But if Hot Guy's interested, I'm willing to overlook Mia's snark. An Aussie summer romance would be the perfect way to bounce back from that shit storm with Tommy.

"No. I'm taking about the redhead."

Piper. He means Piper.

I laugh and cry and cheer all in that one moment. The guy's line, well, I picture the animatronic figures from the Pirates of the Caribbean ride at Disneyland who used to shout, "We want the redhead." He's not talking about me, so there's one more guy I won't be getting. But Piper's face. All of a sudden soft and rounded with a rose flush glowing under her rows of freckles.

It's the best thing ever.

Until.

"Her? You realize she's my designated ugly fat friend, right? At least if we were talking about the Yank, I *might* be able to understand. Her mom's a supermodel. If the girl drops another fifty pounds, she'll be Leslie Vonn Tate's doppelganger. But Piper? Sweetie, that's ordering a hamburger when you can grill up a steak for the same price." Mia points to her body like a model on a game show showing off the suitcase of money.

Piper and Hot Guy are wearing identical expressions, mixtures of confusion and horror. They've both been forced into a place where the rules of civilization no longer exist and they don't know what to do about it.

"Hey!" I shout out. I'm developing a very ranty rant and my hands are balling up into fists. Hot Guy vanishes, retreating to his own table, as I start my incoherent rambling. "You…who are you…what the hell…"

I can't decide what would work better. Using Mia's face as a punch pillow or organizing my words into real thoughts designed to show her what a horrible bitch she is.

"Cookie. Cookie. Don't." Piper turns and retreats into the bathroom.

I follow her. By the time I get in there, she's already in one of the stalls.

I assume we're doing that thing.

That thing where there's one girl crying in a smelly bathroom stall and another one pacing the pee-stained floor, trying to coax her friend out.

"Piper, come on. She's just an insecure bitch." A bitch that, luckily, has the sense not to follow us into the bathroom.

"I thought she was my friend," Piper says in a tight voice.

"Well, she's not," I snap.

There's a pause. "She always stuck up for me. Anytime people would call me fatass. I just don't… I don't get…"

I lean against the bathroom wall.

And I think about Tommy.

About what people expect from each other. About the roles we cast each other in. I'd cast Tommy as teen heartthrob in my makeover *Cinderella* story, and he'd rejected the part. What if Mia was doing the same thing? Piper was supposed to be her DUFF. But Mia's obviously figured out that cool, confident Piper will give her a run for her money.

"Okay. Well. Maybe she is your friend, Piper. Maybe she really cares about you. She just cares about herself more." I approach the stall door and peer in through the slit. I see a sliver of Piper, fully dressed, sitting on the toilet. "Come on. Please. Stop crying and come out of there."

"I'm not crying," she says.

The stench in the bathroom is really getting to me. I remember reading once that women's restrooms have way more germs than men's. The Anchor's ladies' room is definitely validating that idea.

The grimy blue stall door creaks open. Piper pokes her head out.

She's right. She *hasn't* been crying. Rage fills her every feature. "I'm only staying in here until I'm absolutely sure I won't go out there and murder Mia," she says, through clenched teeth.

This is going different than I thought. "Oh. Oh-kay," I say.

She paces in front of the bathroom mirror, a blur of red

hair. Finally, she stops and turns to face me. "That's it. That. Is. Absolutely. Fucking. It. From now on, I'm doing what *I* want to do. I'm going to find that guy and get his number. I'm going to Columbia and then law school. And I don't give a single, solitary fuck what anyone has to say about it."

Piper whirls around and leaves the bathroom. I have to almost run to catch up with her. Back in the restaurant, Mia is gone. She's left us at the taco joint without a way to get home. But Piper does find Hot Guy and does get his number.

We're forced to call an Uber, and it costs us every cent we've got to get back to Piper's house but it's so worth it.

As we walk up her driveway, Piper grins at me. "I have become a Giver of Zero Fucks," she announces.

I grin back.

I envy Piper.

I can't figure out why I can't seem to be more like her.

Later that night, I work on my blog.

Roundish <New Post>
Title: Round Oz
Creator: Cookie Vonn [administrator]

I've spent the last two weeks in Oz. I've put together a list of fabulous fashion from the land down under. But before I get to that, I've got a question. Is life one big role-playing game? Lately, I've been thinking about social roles, about what people expect of me, what I expect of them and what I expect of myself. It's like we're all in a giant RPG, making a series of moves designed to make ourselves look and feel like a friend, a boyfriend, a son, a daughter, etc. But do we always get to decide what roles we tackle? Or if we want to play the game at all?

When I get back to Phoenix, there's a package in my room. It's a case of NutriMin Water. There's a note from John Potanin attached to a bottle of Perfect Peach. "Love your blog and think it could be the sponsorship opportunity we're looking for. Contact Lucy for details."

SKINNY: Day 855...a wake

They've put Chad Tate in what's called a sports-themed urn. A glass case tops the pine box. There's a signed football on display.

The earthly remains of Chad Tate will forever rest under a patch of leather autographed by...Chad Tate.

Fitting, I guess, for a guy who loved himself best.

Even though the douchelord had no children he ever cared to acknowledge, Mom's had a brass engraved plaque attached to the urn that reads, "Beloved husband and father and football star."

Okay, okay. I know. Grandma just chewed me out for being a douchelady. I'm going to make an effort to have compassion for Chad Tate. I'll try. I promise.

Mom's clutching the small wooden box as she enters the church hall where Grandma's holding the wake. She plunks it down on one of the cheap cafeteria-type tables and starts to work the room.

Dad sent Tommy home, but Gareth is milling around behind me. Mom's talking to him, or more accurately at him.

Out of the corner of my eye, I can see him backing his way behind the cake table, toward where Grandma is talking to Father Tim.

Mom's sobbing and batting her eyelashes at Gareth while striking a modelish pose. It's this cringe-worthy combination of mourning and flirting. I think I'll call it mirting. Or flourning. Either one would work.

"Oh, Gareth. Chad would have been so honored you came..." she says.

I shake my head and roll my eyes. I'm working on having sympathy for Chad Tate. Mom on the other hand...

"Cookie. I need to speak to you."

It's Dad. It's been so long since he's been around that I jump at the sound of his voice. It's only vaguely familiar. I doubt I could pick him out of a voice lineup.

I nod in his general direction but keep staring at the bizarre case on the table. Chad Tate. The box is death. The end.

Grandma's right. It is sad. It is a loss.

"Outside," Dad says, pulling me from my thoughts.

He motions for me to follow him into the courtyard, where he sits on a marble bench underneath a statue of the Virgin Mary. He pats the spot next to him.

I stand.

"I'm very disappointed in you."

I glare at him. "Right back atcha."

I'm going back into the hall to get Gareth and get the hell out of there. Dad steps in front of me and puts his hand on the door to stop me from going in.

"What exactly is that supposed to mean?"

I try to duck around him and open the door anyway, a maneuver that doesn't work and only serves to increase the rage on his face.

"I'm asking you a question. I expect an answer."

There he is. Dr. Martin fucking Vonn. With his medical degree. His ramrod posture. His skin tanned deeply from the African sun. His look of smug superiority. Like everything he's ever thought to do is right, and anyone who's ever doubted him is wrong.

"I've told myself..." I start to say. I have to stop because I'm on the verge of tears. And I won't cry for Dr. Vonn.

Taking a deep breath, I try again. "I've told myself so many times that you couldn't be there for me because you were busy savings lives. I've told myself that you couldn't come home because other people needed you more than I do. But that's a lie. You could have come back anytime. And now you have. For *Chad Tate*."

"I didn't know you needed me. You certainly never said anything, nor have you made the slightest effort to communicate with me in years. And I came back for your mother." His face flushes red and he clarifies himself. "To assist your mother."

The tears come. "You *needed* me to tell you a girl likes to see her father once in a while? You *needed* me to tell you that it was important for you to be there for my birthdays and graduation?"

Dad loosens his hold on the door and shuffles back toward the wall. "I haven't been a very good father. I know that. But now, your mother—"

I take a deep breath and force myself to stop crying.

"Grandma thinks that Mom and Chad Tate are the reason we don't have any kind of life as a family. That their relationship is why you've been hiding in the bushes in the fucking Serengeti for the past decade. I think you're a selfish coward who's too much of a chickenshit to come home and try to be a father. Either way, though, you're a fool if you're willing to chase after Mom now and mop up her crocodile tears."

Dad purses his lips in a thin, white line. "I won't be spoken to in this manner by my own daughter."

I yank the hall door open and Dad's arm recoils to his body. "Then go back to Ghana and you won't have to talk to me at all."

Back in Father McKay Hall, Mom's nowhere to be found. But Chad Tate's still sitting there.

Yeah. I'm beginning to think that Father Tim is right. Missing Mass is taking its toll on me.

I help Grandma stash what's left of the cheese and crackers and Tang in the church refrigerator. We can't find Mom.

So Chad Tate comes home with us.

It's Gareth who gets the job of toting the urn into the yellow house. Grandma's hands are full of houseplants from her church friends that she's taken from the funeral, and I can tell she doesn't trust me not to dump the ashes all over the grass.

Grandma finds a "temporary" home for "good ole Chad" on the entertainment center between the TV and the unused goldfish bowl where Mr. Fins swam until his sad disappearance down the bathroom sink.

Gareth asks if I want to spend the night in town. "I could get us a room at the Fairmont," he says.

"I want to get out of here."

When Gareth's already in the limo, I say goodbye to Grandma. "And I expect I'll be seeing you soon," she says.

I nod and think about Dr. Moreno. Lydia. I've got my academic advising appointment with her. I wonder if I should cancel it. Or go. Or say something to Grandma.

Or do something besides board a private jet in the middle of the night.

Like a coward.

Like my father.

Gareth tugs on his weirdo eye mask and is snoring a few seconds after takeoff.

I watch the lights of Phoenix become smaller and smaller until they're specks. Until they're gone.

Blue-black vapor surrounds us, and for the first time I understand Dr. Martin Vonn. For the first time, I can admit that I am my father's daughter.

I dig my laptop out of the bag I tossed on the seat next to me, open it and log in to the plane's Wi-Fi. As I suspected, there's already a message from Dad.

For the first time in years, I open it and read it.

FAT: Days 326–353 of NutriNation

Ultrasharp Bordeaux shears.

Retail price: $79.

You know you're some kind of nerd when you spend your first adult paycheck on a new pair of scissors.

But the right kind of shears glide through fabric the way a boat does along the water, creating shapes that billow like waves.

Thanks to my status as an official employee of the NutriMin Corporation, a couple of things happen. I'm able to afford my supplies for the fall semester at ASU without rooting through the couch cushions. I invest in high-quality pattern rulers, bobbins and tons of muslin.

And I can leave my job at Donutville. In fact, Lucy, my contact at NutriMin Water, pretty much tells me I have to quit. "You're going places, Cookie. Places other than behind the pastry counter."

At first I'm excited, but on my last day of work, there's Steve's face.

He's got that "you're like a daughter to me, don't leave" kind of face and has made me a goodbye cake (yes, again with the cake) that is a tower of glazed doughnuts.

"You're not too bad," Steve tells me.

"Neither are you," I say. We're both sort of staring at our feet. "I'll try to come by. To harass you. To make sure you keep things regulation size."

"Yeah. Okay. I'll say hi. If I see you." He's turned his attention back to the industrial mixer, where some kind of blueberry mixture that looks like it's been made from the blood of sacrificed Smurfs is churning around.

I grab the paycheck attached to my last time card and start for the car. But I turn back, drop the tower cake on the steel frosting counter and give Steve a hug. He smells like clove cigarettes, and I notice all the tangles in his gray ponytail.

He must not get many hugs because he shuffles around for a few seconds before giving me a few awkward pats on the back. It's the kind of hug kids give to each other at the end of camp. *See you next summer. Don't change.*

But he grins. "Someday I'll say I knew you when."

"Yeah," I say with a laugh. "Remember me. I may be here next week applying for my old job."

He's serious again. "You won't be back."

This is true. I'm leaving Donutville behind.

August 18 arrives.

The first day of school. Of college.

I am a college student.

The thought almost makes me giggle.

I try to manage it like any other day. I pack a lunch of apple wedges, cheese cubes and Diet Coke, and I've sewn a midi skirt from fabric I shibori-dyed with indigo powder Grandma brought back from Israel.

Also thanks to NutriMin, I'm able to afford a parking pass in a lot that isn't on the dark side of the moon. Even though it's hot, the walk isn't as unbearable as it might be. Oddly though, the campus is under siege by insects. Every few minutes, my phone buzzes with bee warnings. Bees swarm the Language and Lit Building. Then the Memorial Union. Then they chase the coffee drinkers off the patio in front of Hayden Library.

The art building is wonderful. It has a cool, gray, concrete exterior, and inside there are students carrying oversize sketchpads and pieces of canvas. It smells of chalk and turpentine and wax.

I can already tell I'm going to love my first class. I can tell from the textbook alone—*5000 Years of Textiles.* Sure, the book set me back around a hundred bucks, and sure, the idea of fashion spanning all of memorable time might be overwhelming. But it's amazing too how clothes have made men and women special through the ages.

There's a whiteboard at the front of the room. Written in red marker I see Dr. Moreno's name.

I'm picking at a hangnail and doodling on the cover of my notebook when Kennes Butterfield walks in.

Of course she'd be in this class.

She's hell-bent on getting everything I want.

For someone supposed to be into fashion, Kennes is clad in almost nothing. Her microscopic shorts barely exist, and she's wearing a tank top with straps the width of strands of linguine. I find myself rubbing my sweaty palms up and down my skirt.

Kennes slides into the chair in front of me. We glance at each other for a moment before she starts a conversation with the guy in the desk next to me who desperately needs a haircut. Soon, they're in a braggish, semiobnoxious chat.

I hear the smack of flip-flops against the soles of feet, growing louder as it comes closer to our room. By the end of the fall, I'm conditioned to respond to that sound. Like one of Pavlov's dogs. It signals that Dr. Moreno is near. She breezes through the door and takes her place up at the front and begins writing on the whiteboard. She's got her hair in the same tight bun as the day I met her last year, the same makeup-free tanned face and another wrap dress, today made from a blue floral print.

Meanwhile, in front of me, Kennes is going full steam ahead. "So there we are in Paris and I happened to be chatting with a woman who's an editor at French *Vogue*. So she tells us about this fabric market at Saint-Pierre. So we go over there and—"

"So. So. So," I mutter. "That's your favorite word. At least when it isn't spelled S-E-W."

Kennes turns around. "What's wrong with you, Cankles?"

Her insult attracts a confused look from the guy next to me. I'm not as cankle-ish as I used to be. He's regarding Kennes in a new way, like she's not as nice as he thought.

Dr. Moreno also turns around. "Is there a problem, girls?"

"No," Kennes says quickly.

"Cookie?" Dr. Moreno asks.

I want to say yes. Yes. That Kennes Butterfield is to fashion what McDonald's is to fine dining. Or what Vanilla Ice is to rap music.

Kennes tenses up and has a worried frown on her face.

The truth is, I'm tired of fighting with Kennes. And Dr. Moreno is someone I really respect. I don't want to be the girl who starts shit on the first day of school.

"No, Dr. Moreno."

Kennes relaxes back into her chair and class begins.

College classes all seem to start the same way. There's the syllabus. A big, long-winded speech about how and when to contact the teacher. How the grades will be figured out… I'm falling forward onto my elbows. My eyelids are heavy.

And then.

"Your first assignment will be making your own textile from a nontraditional material." Dr. Moreno has her back to me and is pulling down a projection screen.

She's got my full attention for the rest of the hour as she shows us clothing made of paper and used grocery store bags and waxy banana plant leaves. "In this class, we take nothing for granted. Beginning with Adam and the fig leaf, human beings had to be creative, had to look to their surroundings for their fashions. You can make your textile out of anything. But it must be from something you collect or find on campus."

I'm kind of bummed when the people around me start packing up their bags as the class is scheduled to end. "Oh, one more thing," Dr. Moreno calls out. "Make each assignment count. I'll be selecting a few students for special opportunities throughout the year, and Juniors in the program will be competing for an internship with Stella Jupiter."

An internship with Stella Jupiter. The idea is downright dangerous. I can imagine myself stuffing my bra with skeins of her epically rad cashmere and trying to smuggle them out of the designer's iconic LA studio.

Kennes is packing up her stuff too. "I hope you know, I'm going to get the internship," she whispers.

The mental images of luxe sweaters emblazoned with hooting owls and beavers reading books vanish.

Keep cool. Keep cool.

Keep it casual. I shrug. "I guess that's possible. Your daddy could always buy Stella Jupiter. Or this university."

Kennes's face contorts in a rage. "You are such a—"

"Any questions?" Dr. Moreno interrupts as she drops the red marker on the rack at the bottom of the whiteboard.

I shake my head and leave the classroom.

Outside, I see Tommy's sandy brown, curly mop through a slit created by a row of untrimmed hedges.

Walking forward to peek through the gap, I watch him, and for a second he's exactly the same as he used to be. He's sitting on a bench, bent over his backpack, chewing his lower lip and scratching on a notepad with a worn-down pencil.

For a moment I experience our friendship in a series of flashes. That first starry night at Fairy Falls. The view of the universe through Tommy's telescope. It's like nothing has really changed. The world has remained fixed and constant.

Some things never change.

And then I see her.

Kennes.

Of course he'd be waiting for her.

She has everything I want.

Tommy doesn't look up from his books as she wraps her arms around his shoulders, but a smile creeps up at the corners of his lips. She scoots onto the bench next to him and pushes an iced coffee up to his elbow.

Kennes looks my way.

Her sticky, red-coated lips press into a smug line.

It's the same expression she wore that first day on the plane. It's the kind of face you make when you know you can take whatever you want.

They're together.

And I'm alone.

Some things do change.

Kennes has become Tommy's sun.

I'm icy Pluto, drifting at the edges of outer space.

No longer a planet. No longer anything.

I jam my sketchbook shut into my backpack and leave the art building behind, passing by the same things that, just half an hour earlier, were full of inspiration but now drip with drabness. Aging olive trees instead of lively greenery, oppressive heat instead of optimistic sunshine.

Food vendors line Hayden Mall. By the time I arrive at the social sciences building where my schedule says that Anthropology 101 is being held, I'm clutching a chocolate chip cookie, a bag of Cool Ranch Doritos, two Smucker's Uncrustables Sandwiches and a Drumstick ice-cream cone.

A breakfast, lunch and dinner of champions.

The food accountant who's had a small office in my head since the day I joined NutriNation is busy crunching numbers.

The oversize cookie alone means an hour on the treadmill.

The peanut-dipped drumstick is five hundred ab crunches.

The social sciences building is a low, squat, redbrick building with a cool, shaded atrium in the center. There's a small fountain near a cement staircase and I take a seat on a bench near it. Against the soundtrack of trickling water, I rip into the plastic covering the ice-cream cone.

I'm just a few seconds from feeling better. From feeling full.

Kennes may have Tommy but *I* have chocolate candy coating.

That's fair, right?

Except it isn't.

I think of all the mornings I've gotten up before dark to run, of every carrot stick I've eaten, of every time I choked down a Caesar salad without dressing. This whole thing started because...well, because I thought that when I was thin I'd have it all. I'm a size twelve and people are no longer staring at me like they're waiting for me to order a five-pound hot dog. But I'm still alone in the dark with my pals Mr. Corn and Mr. Chip.

Don't cry.

Don't do it.

The sticky white ice cream starts to run down my fingers. If I'm going to eat the thing, now's the time.

Now.

Right now.

Except I just sit there and stare at it. Until the people passing by start to stare at *me*. Until I'm holding most of the ice cream in the palm of my hand.

For the first time, I realize that eating all this stuff is a form of self-defeat, a way of giving myself an excuse not to go for the things I want. As much as I hate Kennes, it's getting harder and harder to hold her responsible for everything that's wrong in my life. She's not in the courtyard with me right now.

I take the ice cream in my hand and throw it in a trash can a few feet from the fountain. After washing my hands in the bathroom on the other side of the atrium, I take my seat on the bench.

It's lunchtime and I *am* hungry. I open one of the PB&Js and the chocolate chip cookie, putting the rest of the food in my bag to give to Grandma later. Because it's what I want to eat. Because it's possible to have lunch and not have an emotional meltdown. Because a sandwich is only a sandwich and not a symbol of self-sabotage. And because this is what I think Lydia Moreno or Piper would do.

The fountain in front of me is a pyramid of river rocks with water spouting from a hole in the top rock. Someone's put a sculpture of an odd ceramic head on one of the lower stones and a stream flows around its neck. It's like a super weird, contemporary art piece. The kind of thing some snotty hipster would be pacing around and telling everyone how it's a metaphor for the overconsumption of society or something.

I open my sketchbook and work on the assignment for class, using the fountain for inspiration.

I'm there.

Doing what I want to do.

This moment.

It's going down as a non-scale victory, for sure.

SKINNY: Days 856–863 of NutriNation

Back in New York, white winter continues.

"You must be excited," Gareth comments as the private plane touches down on the tarmac.

"Um. What?" My thoughts are a tangled ball of yarn. Chad Tate in a wooden box. My father's wooden expression. The fight at the funeral. Gareth and I don't discuss these things. They're part of a future that probably won't exist. Working out the details doesn't matter.

"The press junkets. The microshow," Gareth explains with a casual wave of his hand. The microshow. This is what his people are calling the presentation of our plus-size collection. Old habits die hard and I'm pretty sure that Gareth is making "big clothes, small show" jokes behind my back. Well, whatever it is, it's happening in a week.

"Darcy's got a great model call set up for tomorrow. She thinks you'll get some strong material."

I nod. This was one of the facets of the project that excited me from the very beginning. We'll be calling top plus-size models. I get to help choose who walks, the music we use and what the set looks like. I've managed to convince Gareth to use a series of images shot at his ranch in Argentina instead of his usual white walls.

I smile at Gareth and try to act excited about what's coming. But he's become strangely detached from our show. I can't help but feel like my life has gone off the rails somehow, like I'm further away than ever from those images of Claire McCardell and her girls from the pages of old *Time* magazines.

Gareth slides into the back of the Town Car and immediately begins to review spreadsheets on his iPad. He isn't bothered about his bags. Someone will pick them up. Someone will take him home. I wonder if the Gary who rode the bus into Spanish Harlem for cheap burritos and fabric inspiration is in there somewhere. Or if Lydia Moreno is right. That now there's only Gareth Miller. A man who makes things to be worn and sold and thrown away in an endless cycle that exists without love or passion or bliss.

Darcy's staged the event at the Morgan Library, an old building in Murray Hill that used to be a place for old-timey robber baron banker, Pierpont Morgan, to store all his books. "We're going for something, you know, kind of different," Darcy says.

Gareth will host a presentation in the library's auditorium. I'll wave and smile and blog. Afterward, there will be a Q&A with top fashion journalists in "Mr. Morgan's Library," the ultraopulent reading room.

The week is supposed to be exciting. This is, after all, my first real show. The first one that isn't taking place in my living room with Grandma and her church friends as the audience.

But there are a couple weird things going on.

My phone buzzes with a new email from my dad. I don't answer. He's tried to contact me several times since Chad Tate's funeral. I can sort of tell he's hoping I'll apologize for what I said.

Don't hold your breath, Dad.

Nobody's seen Mom since the wake at the church. I guess because he's determined to be the biggest idiot on the planet, Dad's on a mission to find her. He hires a private investigator to help and sends me status updates in his emails. Dad actually seems surprised when the PI reports that Mom made it safe and sound back to New York, taking up at the Carlyle. She's probably hoping to run into Woody Allen.

Setting off for NYC tomorrow. I'll find your mother. Don't worry.

I'm not worried. Mom's great at only one thing. Taking care of Mom.

The other thing is that there's something going on at G Studios.

Darcy makes a big show of getting my opinion on major issues. We listen to a ton of fusion music and spend a whole day selecting shoes to match the collection. I blog about the model fittings and keep tweeting how excited I am about the show. But when I'm walking through the studio, certain doors get closed and people cover certain things on their desks as I pass. I try to tell myself this is business as usual. I mean, it's probably normal not to show all the private details of a multi-million-dollar corporation to a twenty-year-old blogger, right?

As I'm staring out into space, Darcy pushes two credit-card-sized pieces of plastic into my hand.

"Uh. What's this?"

She smoothes down her dark purple hair and rolls her eyes. She must have already told me what these things are. "Tickets."

When I stare blankly, she snorts and goes on. "To the show. I thought you might want to invite your friend. That Australian girl. What's her name?"

Piper.

Maybe I should invite her.

For some reason, I don't.

Friday.

The day of the show arrives fast. Gareth's people keep us on a tight schedule. They send him to the library early for a few meetings. I'm supposed to make a series of posts on my blog and host a Twitter chat with Lucy from NutriMin Water. Darcy's got me scheduled to arrive at the venue a few minutes before the show starts.

There's my first clue, Sherlock.

I've also got a huge block of time designated for me to "get ready" at Gareth's apartment. GM sends a hairstylist, a makeup artist and wardrobe stylist as well as a massive rack of clothes from Gareth's Fall collection. For most of the day, I'm basically living through a reality TV makeover segment. All that's missing is some montage music, like "Eye of the Tiger" or "Walking on Sunshine."

It's around four in the afternoon by the time I take the car over to the Morgan Library. Darcy meets me at the entrance.

She leads me into "Mr. Morgan's study." In our short, GM black dresses, we both contrast sharply with the plush Victorian-style furnishings of the red room. After sitting on the velvet sofa for a few minutes, I pace the room and wait for Gareth. I try to imagine life as Pierpont Morgan, whom the museum describes as a banker of vast wealth who divided his time between hunting down rare books and having dinner with Thomas Edison. I notice that someone has left a half-crumpled brochure on one of the low bookcases.

There's a picture of a blond-haired, size-two model on the front with the caption, *Poción de Amor.* Love potion in Spanish.

It's my mom. On the cover. Wearing a slightly sexier version of one of the skirt-and-blouse designs Gareth and I patterned together.

I quickly flip through the booklet. It's all the same. Standard-size versions of the clothes I helped design with the words *Also available in plus-size* in tiny letters underneath. There's a huge picture of Gareth in the inside jacket, but my name isn't mentioned once.

To see our work that way—the indigos and umbers of our nights in Salta, the verdant greens and dusty browns of the days at Camino a Seclantas—is worse than a slap in the face or a punch in the gut. It's like someone reaching into my chest and digging their fingernails right into my heart.

Suddenly, the brochure is made of needles. I drop it and turn on Darcy. "This isn't a presentation of the plus-size capsule collection, is it?"

She fidgets with her purple hair and tucks a loose strand behind her ear. "We're doing everything we talked about, Cookie. All the models you chose are walking. The music. The backgrounds."

And suddenly everything makes sense. "My mom's doing the show."

Darcy doesn't answer.

I leave Mr. Morgan's study. Everything in the room is red, but even in the white halls, everything I see is *still* red. Darcy's heels click on the tile floor as she runs behind me. I've got almost a foot on her, and her tiny little legs are in overdrive.

"Cookie. For God's sake," she huffs from behind me. "Try to see it from our perspective. We already sold through the plus-size merch you guys created."

"When you say 'we,' are you referring to yourself and the guy that's supposed to be *my* boyfriend?" I call back.

"The editors…the buyers…they were in love with the stuff. It only made sense to launch it in all sizes, to do a fuller collection." We're nearing the museum entrance, where crowds of people are clustered together, waiting for the doors to the auditorium to open.

"Cookie. *Cookie*," Darcy is whispering frantically and puffing, out of breath. "Please. Stop for one minute. One minute."

I whirl around to face her. She jumps back, taken a bit off guard by the intensity I can feel radiating from my body. "This collection was supposed to be about *something.* About showing people who usually get treated like crap by the world of fashion that they really do matter. Instead, it's…

it's…" It's people like my mother getting everything they want at other people's expense.

I'll say one thing for Darcy, she keeps her cool. Her face stays neutral. Even as I'm towering over her, she puts her hands on her hips and delivers this speech.

"It's not about you. Or even Gareth, for that matter. We're taking a financial bloodbath on that last collection. We need a hit. Or we'd be talking layoffs. Store closures. This sets us up nicely for Resort and Spring."

"And my mother?" I ask.

Darcy's hands fall slack by her side. "Nathan said it was too late to cancel the contract. We would've had to pay her anyway. Might as well use her. And after Tate's death…the PR value…"

I can't figure out if I want to laugh or cry or throw up. My brain is so busy processing emotions, I probably have sparks coming out my ears. "Use her? You used *me*. I am *such* an idiot."

As I resume walking, she calls out, "No. No, you're not."

We both know that I am and so I don't stop. "I hope you got what you needed," I say to no one in particular. Darcy doesn't follow me any farther.

I run through the bright and airy court in the center of the library, passing Gareth, who's deep in conversation with *Par Donna* editor Celine Stanford. I move through the glass doors facing Madison Avenue.

There's a beautiful, dark-haired girl crouching down near the entrance, crying into her hands. I almost trip over her as I leave the library building.

"Sorry. I'm sorry," the girl says, trying to stifle another sob.

The voice is familiar. Way too familiar.

Of course it's Kennes.

"What are you doing here?" I'm pretty sure God has sent Kennes as one final *fuck you*. She's probably about to hand me a wedding invitation and tell me that she and Tommy will be getting hitched on Richard Branson's private island and riding off in his personal submarine.

I can't take it. Not today.

Kennes looks up at me for a second in her normal, snotty way, but that expression fades immediately, replaced by a mouth that sags downward and squinty eyes with tears rolling out of them. With her perfectly shaped bob hairdo and glossy nails, she looks like a super sad little doll.

I don't know why, but she gives me a real answer.

"Um…*SoScottsdale*. I'm supposed to… Marlene told me to come here and ask you for tickets to the show… I was too embarrassed… I tried…I tried to sneak in… I'm such a total screwup." She breaks into another round of sobs.

I'm startled, shaken for a minute from my own self-pity and I find myself saying, "No. No, you're not."

Kennes rubs her eyes, trying to stop the waterworks. "You're a terrible liar. You know, nobody…nobody expects me to do anything. I'm supposed to be polished up like a trophy, trying to figure out how to marry a Mellon or Rothschild. Even my own father…he wishes *you* were his daughter."

"I seriously doubt that," I say with an indignant grunt.

"'There's a girl who knows what she's doing,'" Kennes says in an imitation of Jameson Butterfield's baritone voice. "That's what he said. He thought you were right. To stand up to me. That day at the office. You're a lot like him. When he was young."

"Well, if it's any consolation, I have no idea what the fuck I'm doing. And I'm sure your dad loves you, Kennes." It's weird to be in this position. To be offering aid to the enemy. But I do. Because I've never seen anyone quite so lost and pathetic.

She stops crying. "You and I both know there's a difference between liking someone and loving them."

Yes.

Yes, we do.

I reach into my GM by Gareth Miller handbag and fish out the two plastic tickets from Darcy. "Here."

She stares at them and doesn't reach out.

"They're tickets. To the show. At least you can cover it for *SoScottsdale*." She still doesn't take them, so I roll my eyes. "Or don't. I won't force you to take them."

I'm about to tuck the tickets back in my bag when she takes them.

"No. I do. I want them." There's a pause. "Thanks."

Kennes rises from where she's kneeling on the concrete steps. "Why are you helping me?"

I shrug. I'm not sure I even understand myself. Maybe because I don't want to be trapped in one, big, never-ending cycle of *what goes around, comes around*. Maybe because, at some point, I have to get out of the revenge business. "You seem like you need it."

I'm about to turn toward Madison Avenue when she says, "About what I said. What I did. I'm sorry. I was mean. I was…going through something and…"

"It's okay, Kennes. It's going to be okay."

This is what I tell myself. *It will be okay.*

"Cookie, about the internship at Stella Jupiter. I'm sure you'll get it."

I think for a second. "May the best designer win, Kennes. And if that's you, I'm okay with it." As the words come out, I hope they'll be true.

She smiles and moves through the library door. Behind me, I hear it close with a quiet click. It opens as I'm walking away, and Gareth calls, "Cookie!" He catches up with me a few paces later.

"Cookie." He grabs me by my shoulders. There's a strange mixture of anger and fear on his face. But it's not the right kind of fear. He's not afraid of me leaving. He's afraid of being exposed as a fraud. Or being alone. "It's business. That's all. It doesn't mean anything. It has nothing to do with you and me. I need you. Come on. Stay."

I shake free of him and resume walking.

"Where the hell are you going? The show starts in five minutes."

I stop and turn around. I feel certain that this is the last time I'll be seeing his perfect, chiseled features, his dark moody eyes, his thin lips, somewhere other than in the pages of a magazine.

"Home," I say.

I'm going home.

FAT: Day 737 of NutriNation

Certain things are strangely hollow.

Like cheap chocolate Easter bunnies.

Like achieving a goal that doesn't seem to get you any closer to what you really, truly want.

I lost 199 pounds. I made my goal weight. I like my classes at ASU. I have a job that pays good money. Grandma's arthritis isn't bothering her right now. Even old Roscoe doesn't bark as much at night as he used to.

NutriMin Water hooked me up with a massive opportunity. A personal interview with my fashion idol, Gareth Miller. I leave for NYC in the morning. They're flying me first class.

What the fuck is my problem?

It's Friday.

My last meeting as a paying NutriNation customer.

Rickelle, Kimberly and Dave have more balloons. I get a certificate and a special card that lets me come to any NutriNation meeting for free for all the rest of eternity. There's more hugging and crying. There's talk of more running and walking and food journaling.

I miss those nights in Tommy's backyard. In late November. When the air is cool but not cold. When the winter grass is full in. Telescopes. Star wheels.

The night sky. It never looks the same. It never really changes.

It's over.

And it's only just begun.

SKINNY: Day 866 of NutriNation

"Bless me, Father, for I have sinned. My last confession was… well, it was never I guess… I mean I had to confess as part of confirmation…but I don't think I had anything specific to say at that point and…"

I hear a deep grunt through the screen that divides the confessional booth. Then the door to the booth swings open and I'm face-to-face with Father Tim.

"Cookie, what the hell is the problem now?" he asks. He motions for me to sit alongside him in one of the pews. It's a Monday morning and the chapel is empty except for the two of us.

I've been home for two days. Gareth hasn't called. Or texted. Or emailed.

I know I shouldn't be surprised. But I am.

The horrible irony of the situation isn't lost on me. The fact that everything my mother said to me that day on the elevator was true. I allowed myself to be used. I couldn't even say if Gareth had any real feelings for me. I would have done anything to avoid being like my mom. But here I am. Like my mom.

My meeting with Dr. Moreno, the one she scheduled with me that day at Cuchifritos, is on Wednesday. I've got two days to figure out if I really can go home again.

"I'm…I'm mad," I spurt at Father Tim as I slide in on the bench. It's only anger that gets me out of bed these days. If I stay mad, I can stop crying.

He bites his lip, fighting off a smile, and leans forward, facing the stained-glass mural at the front of the church. "At?" he prompts.

"God."

Father Tim rests his hands in a prayer formation on the pew in front of him. "I see. Because things aren't fair. Because life should be one run-on episode of *Leave It to Beaver.* Because experiences should be strung up like beads on a necklace, neat and orderly, each event preparing you for the next."

I face the stained glass too. Red and orange light is streaming into the chapel. "You're too cynical. If God is so powerful, why can't he make things fair?"

He doesn't say anything. Then he turns to me. "The world isn't perfect. But things might be a little more fair than you believe. All that stuff you think you want or need, how much of it do you really need *God* to deliver? And how much could you do yourself if you really tried?"

We sit in silence for a few minutes. "Aren't you going to forgive me? Or give me penance or something?"

Father Tim rolls his eyes. "I'm going to advise you." He

gets up and makes his way across the pew, straightening out the hymnals as he passes.

"And here's my advice, Cookie. Go back to school. Stop worrying so much. You're young. Not every problem has to be solved right this minute."

The tears squirt from the corners of my eyes. I hurry to blot them with the edge of my long-sleeve, black GM tee. "Look at me!" I blurt out. "I look exactly the right way. I'm a size six, sometimes even a four. I have the right hair. The shoes. This outfit is probably worth $5000."

"Then you should sell it and put the money in the collection plate next Sunday," Father Tim says. He replaces the hymnals on the holder in front of him and returns to his seat beside me on the bench.

I half laugh and half sob and keep going. "I did everything I was supposed to do. Things are supposed to be perfect."

He pats me on the back for one short, awkward second. But he smiles. It's a real smile. Not the fake one he uses when he invites everyone to the church picnic. "Cookie. You were never *supposed* to be anything. You're supposed to live your life the way you want to live it. Nothing is ever perfect, but what makes people happy is that they make choices they feel good about. Sure, you lost weight. That's fine, I guess. But the real weight that you carried around, that you're still carrying around, is the attitude that what is on the outside means more than what is on the inside. Lose that and you'll be happy. I promise. You have it in you to accomplish great things."

Father Tim gets up again and moves toward the altar while

I stay seated, staring at the golden light streaming into the chapel through the stained glass.

He turns back. "Yes. You'll do big things. And when you do, don't forget that the Lord says to tithe 10 percent."

Back at home, I think about Father Tim's advice. I box up my GM wardrobe and put it in the trunk of my Corolla to take to St. Vincent de Paul's.

Grandma finds this amazing pineapple-print, mint-green knit fabric and I spend the rest of my day making myself a new dress, adapting a design from one of my old Claire McCardell patterns.

I'll be wearing Cookie Vonn originals from now on.

When I've cut the last thread, I take to my blog.

Roundish <New Post>
Title: Why Fashion Is Power
Creator: Cookie Vonn [administrator]

Okay, here's the real deal about how money gets made in fashion. Most fashion brands—the Pradas, Ralph Laurens and D&Gs of this world—make less than 25 percent of their money from actually selling clothes. So where does the rest come from?

Generally, from accessories (bags, shoes, jewelry, etc.) and licensed goods (fashion brands slap their logos on everything from bedsheets to vodka). And designers have a special place in their hearts for things like fragrances and eyewear. A handful of companies manufacture the vast majority of perfumes and sunglasses. The designer shows up with a few notes about what he or she thinks their brand looks or smells like. The company's experts go to work and—*bam!*—store shelves get stocked and designers get royalty checks.

But who is buying all of this stuff? Because unless the size-two women of the world are taking daily baths in Marc Jacobs Daisy Dream and wearing four expensive watches on each arm, someone else must be joining them at the sales counters.

Here's the dirty little secret of fashion: most designers hate fat people but love fat wallets.

It's plus-size women who are buying the lion's share of these handbags and home goods.

And we need to stop doing it.

STOP. Right. Now. Quit. Cold turkey.

Yes, I know it's hard. A lot of designers make *nothing* over a size fourteen and make their best pieces only up to a size eight. If you're bigger than that, the only way to have any kind of fashion brand experience is through accessories and other goods. You can't dress like the cool kids, but they might let you sit at their lunch table if you have the right bag or shoes.

There's a perfume I love love love. I won't mention its name, because the blog doesn't make enough money to pay a lawyer. But it's musky and floral and fashion magic. My grandma got a small bottle for me once for my birthday. I picked up that iconic glass square and imagined myself in the party, the glamor, the conversation of fashion.

I love this perfume.

And I will never ever buy it.

The company that makes this fragrance doesn't want to

see plus-size people, and they certainly don't want to dress them. Their message is very clear. *Hey, fatties, come pay for your eau de toilette and then go spray it on yourself in a closet.*

I see a lot of girls getting upset about this kind of stuff on social media. There's anger, there's talk about body positivity, and that's okay.

But, ladies, we don't just need to get mad. We need to get results.

We need to flex our economic muscle. We need to stop paying the people who mock us and shame us and refuse to make products for us. We've given these designers money, fame and power, and they are using these things to abuse us. We need to stop buying the message they're selling.

Now I'd like to talk to my other niblets for a minute, my readers who are NOT plus-size. If you frequent my blog, then you know I'm about great fashion for *every* body and I *always* have fashion finds for sizes two to thirty-two. I love you girls, and I do not want to take away your nice things. Yes, these great designers make clothes for you and, yes, you do look mighty fine all gussied up in your fancy pants. But your plus-size friends need your help.

We need you to stop supporting these designers too. We need to be united in our opposition to mean-spirited shaming, to a culture that values physical beauty over human potential and to designers who profit from women even as they demean them. Look around. At your friends, your mother, sisters, daughters, nieces. Chances are pretty good that at least one of them would be called plus-size. Do you want that person to disappear? Would you tell that person you didn't want to see them?

But—reality check—if we say goodbye to some of the fashions we've loved, that leaves the age-old question. *What will we wear?*

We do have some friends and allies in the fight. I've got you covered with a list of designers who take an inclusive approach to fashion. And they've got some amazeballs sunnies, fragrances and shoes.

We're at war. Fashion is your superpower. Your wallet is your weapon. Let's go.

Day 1 of the rest of my life

Grandma wakes me up early on Wednesday morning. I can tell she's glad to have me home. She also wants me to feed the dog.

I realize a few things.

One, I want my friend Tommy back.

Two, I'm not giving up on my dream of being the next great sportswear designer.

Three, I want a bagel for breakfast.

I hit the Starbucks and have the mocha that I want with the whole milk that I want. And I get the bagel that I want.

It's not because I feel bad or sad or angry. Gareth Miller's not driving me into a pint of ice cream. It's because I'm hungry for a bagel and I have one. I'm ready for the little food accountant who's been keeping an office inside my brain to take a permanent vacation. It's time to say goodbye to NutriNation forever.

This is the fourth thing that I realize.

My weight will no longer control me.

I'm going to be who I want to be and do what I want to do and eat what I want to eat. And I am going to get where I want to go.

I leave the old me there in the coffee shop. The me who thought being happy meant looking perfect. I don't know if she'll stay there forever, but I kind of hope she will. Today, I am light. Free. Floating into the future.

I call Piper on the way to school and we discuss the situation.

"I'll miss you," she tells me. "But I'm proud of you. You've finally done it, as I knew you would. You have become a Giver of Zero Fucks. Welcome to the best club on earth, my friend."

This makes me grin as I park my car.

"And don't worry," Piper goes on. "We'll unplug even more people when I'm able to prove that yo-yo dieting shortens your lifespan more than fat does."

I hang up the phone. If anyone will be able to do this, it will be Piper.

I make my way across campus to meet Lydia Moreno. Her new office is in the art building, and it's pretty fabulous. She has some of the same fashion paper dolls as I do, and she's hung them up strategically around the room. We have our meeting. It's not too bad. I'll be busy for a while doing makeup work, but I sew fast and can catch up.

She offers to help me with my makeup work and gives me my own worktable on one side of her office. I'm unpacking my shears and scraps of fabric when Tommy's head pops in the doorway.

Dr. Moreno, or Lydia, as she keeps reminding me, glances

between the two of us and says, "I think I'll hit the vending machine. Want a Coke?"

"Sure," I say with a smile.

Tommy still looks like a walking Ralph Lauren ad in his navy polo shirt and khaki cargo pants. "I saw you come in here. I thought I'd say hi. We haven't seen each other since…"

My smile spreads into a rueful grin. "That thing at Chad Tate's funeral? Yeah. Sorry about that."

Tommy presses his lips into a frown. "It's not *your* fault." There's a pause. "Are you still with him?"

"No. Are you still with her?"

His face flushes red. "Kennes said she saw you in New York. That you were really nice to her. I thought maybe things had changed. That you might want to…"

I put down the cheap green tackle box. "I really want things to go back to the way they were. But I'm not sure they can. The world doesn't need more people to make excuses for the bad behavior of all the beautiful people. To dry the crocodile tears that roll down their symmetrical faces. It needs a line in the sand. Something that says there's a dignity to being human that all people deserve. Right now, I'm on one side of that line and you chose to be on the other side with Kennes."

"I'm not sure if you've looked in the mirror lately, but you have way more in common with the beautiful people than I do."

I shake my head and resume unbundling my fabric swatches. "I will always be that same fat girl on the plane. The one who knows what it's like to have people refuse to look you in the face. Knows what it's like to face a world that wants to sideline you because you don't look the right way. Well, I'm taking a stand. I think there's something beautiful about everything, and I'm going to discover what it is."

Tommy shuffles over to stand right in front of me. "You're wrong. We're on the same side of the line, Cookie."

I look up into his brown eyes, which are watching me with a kind of fear. The right kind. It's a fear of hurting me. Of making me unhappy. "You once told me that my world was like a cartoon, full of black and white. Good and bad. Well, your world is like the solar system, and you think people can orbit around you without ever touching each other. But it doesn't work like that. Kennes has done things that have impacted me, like…like…" I trail off, struggling to finish the analogy.

"Like the Tunguska event?" he supplies. "You know, the meteor that…" He trails off at the sight of my blank expression.

"Yeah. I guess," I say with a laugh. "I can try to play nice, but for this to work, you have to respect me *and* her."

He leans across the cutting table. "Yeah. I see that now." He adds, "You're not all that different, you know. You and Kennes."

I smile at him. It's not the massive insult it once was, but Tommy's wrong. Seeing Kennes outside the Morgan Library, huddled down like a lost puppy…I knew that look. I used to be that person. Desperate and unsure. Tommy needs to save somebody. The old Cookie Vonn, the one I left at the coffee shop, she needed to be rescued. The new one wants to save herself.

This is how I know I'll be okay with being just friends.

Tommy shoves his hands in his pockets. "Want to grab a coffee sometime?"

"Sure."

He goes back the way he came. As his footsteps disappear down the hall, Dr. Moreno peeks back around the corner. "How's the next great American designer? Ready to get started on those makeup assignments?"

I grin at her. I'm already unpacking my notions from my green case. "Yep."

Cool light comes through the narrow window near the ceiling of Dr. Moreno's office. Soon it will be twilight and everything will be bathed in blue.

"I'm ready."

★★★★★

ACKNOWLEDGMENTS

Since writing Trixie Belden fan fiction during fifth-grade recess, becoming a published author has been my dream. A dream that would have never come true without the help and support of all these fantastic people:

My rock-star literary agent, Katheen Rushall of the Andrea Brown Literary Agency. I can't thank you enough for your support and encouragement and for always believing that Cookie's story would find the perfect home.

My incredible editor, Natashya Wilson. I am so grateful for your time and help in making this book as good as it could possibly be. Working with you has made me a better and more thoughtful writer.

The whole team at Harlequin TEEN, including Evan Brown, Linette Kim, Shara Alexander, Gigi Lau, Laci Ann, Margaret Marbury and Gabrielle Vicedomini. Extra-special thanks to Bryn Collier for being an early advocate of my story, to Lauren Smulski for all your support (and not being annoyed every time I ask for books), to Laura Gianino for believing in this book and Krista Mitchell for all your encouragement on social media.

The HarperCollins Children's Sales Team. A huge part of the dream for writers is seeing their books on store shelves and you make that happen. Thank you for all you do to connect writers with readers.

My daughter, Evelyn. Thank you for your love, patience and for always being my instant teen focus group. Whenever I feel down about the world, I remember that someday you and your generation will be running it. Nothing fills me with optimism more than that idea.

My mom, May Porter. Luckily, my real mom is nothing like Cookie's. Thank you for always being there for me. I couldn't have done this without you!

My friends and family. Massive thanks to Cassidy Pavelich, JoAnn Fuller, Amie Allor, Debbie Pirone, Shanna Weissman and Rita Sivigny for not laughing when I said I was working on my novel and for always enthusiastically supporting this book.

Riki Cleveland, my BFF and BBFF—best book friend forever. Thanks for all our Sunday writing sessions, for being my very first reader and, above all, for your friendship.

The Kick-AZ girls, Tawney Bland, Lisa Arneth and Amy Trueblood. I still miss our old critique group and was so fortunate to find you all when I did.

The AZ YA/MG writer community. Thank you all, especially Dusti Bowling, Stephanie Elliot, Kristen Hunt and Lorri Phillips for sharing your books, coffee, advice and camaraderie.

Kate Brauning, Sarah Hollowell and Abigail Johnson.

Thank you for reading early versions of this book and providing invaluable feedback. Any mistakes are my own.

Kaitlyn Sage Patterson, an incredible author and person. I'm inspired by your work and am thankful we are friends.

Patricia Nelson. I'm so grateful for your early support.

The online writing community. Thanks especially to my Pitch Wars 2014 buds for being the best community ever, to the Electric Eighteens for sharing our debut experience and to Class of 2K18 for friendship and fearless fiction.

My amazing husband, Jim deVos. Thank you for your unconditional love and support and always believing in me and my dream. Taking that seat next to you in Junior English was the best decision I've ever made.

Finally, to you, the reader. Thank you. I can't tell you what it means to me that I was able to share this story with you.